WISE CHILDREN

WISE CHILDREN

—————

ANGELA CARTER

Chatto & Windus
LONDON

Published in 1991 by
Chatto & Windus Ltd
20 Vauxhall Bridge Road
London SW1V 2SA

A CIP catalogue record for this book is available from the
British Library.

ISBN 0 7011 3354 6

Extracts from 'It's Only a Paper Moon' by Arlen/Harburg/Rose,
'My Heart Belongs to Daddy' by Cole Porter and 'The Way You Look Tonight'
by Kern/Fields, copyright © Warner Chappell Music Ltd,
are reproduced by permission of Warner Chappell Ltd, and Polygram Music.
The lines from 'I Can't Give You Anything But Love' by Jimmy McHugh and
Dorothy Fields, copyright © 1928 Mills Music Inc, USA, are reproduced by
permission of Lawrence Wright Music Co. Ltd, London WC2H 0EA.

Photoset by Rowland Phototypesetting Ltd
Bury St Edmunds, Suffolk

Printed and bound in Great Britain by
Mackays of Chatham, PLC, Chatham, Kent

Brush up your Shakespeare.

COLE PORTER

It's a wise child that knows its own father.

OLD SAW

How many times Shakespeare draws fathers and daughters, never mothers and daughters.

ELLEN TERRY

One

WHY is London like Budapest?
A. Because it is two cities divided by a river.

Good morning! Let me introduce myself. My name is Dora Chance. Welcome to the wrong side of the tracks.

Put it another way. If you're from the States, think of Manhattan. Then think of Brooklyn. See what I mean? Or, for a Parisian, it might be a question of *rive gauche, rive droite*. With London, it's the North and South divide. Me and Nora, that's my sister, we've always lived on the left-hand side, the side the tourist rarely sees, the *bastard* side of Old Father Thames.

Once upon a time, you could make a crude distinction, thus: the rich lived amidst pleasant verdure in the North speedily whisked to exclusive shopping by abundant public transport while the poor eked out miserable existences in the South in circumstances of urban deprivation condemned to wait for hours at windswept bus-stops while sounds of marital violence, breaking glass and drunken song echoed around and it was cold and dark and smelled of fish and chips. But you can't trust things to stay the same. There's been a diaspora of the affluent, they jumped into their diesel Saabs and dispersed throughout the city. You'd never believe the price of a house round here, these days. And what does the robin do then, poor thing?

Bugger the robin! What would have become of *us*, if Grandma hadn't left us this house? 49 Bard Road, Brixton, London, South West Two. Bless this house. If it wasn't for this house, Nora and I would be on the streets by now, hauling our worldlies up and down in plastic bags, sucking on the bottle for comfort like babes unweaned, bursting into songs of joy when finally admitted to the night shelter and therefore chucked out again immediately

I

for disturbing the peace, to gasp and freeze and finally snuff it disregarded on the street and blow away like rags. That's a thought for a girl's seventy-fifth birthday, what?

Yes! Seventy-five. Happy birthday to me. Born in this house, indeed, this very attic, just seventy-five years ago, today. I made my bow five minutes ahead of Nora who is, at this very moment, downstairs, getting breakfast. My dearest sister. Happy birthday to us.

This is *my* room. We don't share. We've always respected one another's privacy. Identical, well and good; Siamese, no. Everything slightly soiled, I'm sorry to say. Can't be doing with wash, wash, wash, polish, polish, polish, these days, when time is so precious, but take a good look at the signed photos stuck in the dressing-table mirror – Ivor; Noel; Fred and Adèle; Jack; Ginger; Fred and Ginger; Anna, Jessie, Sonnie, Binnie. All friends and colleagues, once upon a time. See the newest one, a tall girl, slender, black curls, enormous eyes, no drawers, 'your very own Tiffany' and lots of XXXXXs. Isn't she lovely? Our beloved godchild. We tried to put her off show business but she wasn't having any. 'What's good enough for you two is good enough for me.' 'Show business', right enough; a prettier girl than little Tiff you never saw but she's showed her all.

What did we do? Got it in one. We used to be song and dance girls. We can still lift a leg higher than your average dog, if called for.

Hello, hello . . . here comes one of the pussy cats, out of the wardrobe, stretching and yawning. She can smell the bacon. There's another, white, with marmalade patches, sleeping on my pillow. Dozens more roam freely. The house smells of cat, a bit, but more of geriatric chorine – cold cream, face powder, dress preservers, old fags, stale tea.

'Come and have a cuddle, Pussy.'

You've got to have something to cuddle. Does Pussy want its breakfast, then? Give us a minute, Puss, let's have a look out of the window.

Cold, bright, windy, spring weather, just like the day that we were born, when the Zeppelins were falling. Lovely blue sky, a birthday present in itself. I knew a boy, once, with eyes that colour, years ago. Bare as a rose, not a hair on him; he was too young for body hair. And sky-blue eyes.

You can see for miles, out of this window. You can see right across the river. There's Westminster Abbey, see? Flying the St George's cross, today. St Paul's, the single breast. Big Ben, winking its golden eye. Not much else familiar, these days. This is about the time that comes in every century when they reach out for all that they can grab of dear old London, and pull it down. Then they build it up again, like London Bridge in the nursery rhyme, goodbye, hello, but it's never the same. Even the railway stations, changed out of recognition, turned into souks. Waterloo. Victoria. Nowhere you can get a decent cup of tea, all they give you is Harvey Wallbangers, filthy cappuccino. Stocking shops and knicker outlets everywhere you look. I said to Nora: 'Remember *Brief Encounter*, how I cried buckets? Nowhere for them to meet on a station, nowadays, except in a bloody knicker shop. Their hands would have to shyly touch under cover of a pair of Union Jack boxer shorts.'

'Come off it, you sentimental sod,' said Nora. 'The only brief encounter *you* had during the war was a fling with a Yank behind the public convenience on Liverpool Street Station.'

'I was only doing my bit for the war effort,' I replied sedately, but she wasn't listening, she started to giggle.

''ere, Dor', smashing name for a lingerie shop – Brief Encounter.' She doubled up.

Sometimes I think, if I look hard enough, I can see back into the past. There goes the wind, again. Crash. Over goes the dustbin, all the trash spills out . . . empty cat-food cans, cornflakes packets, laddered tights, tea leaves . . . I am at present working on my memoirs and researching family history – see the word processor, the filing cabinet, the card indexes, right hand, left hand, right side, left side, all the dirt on everybody. What a wind! Whooping and banging all along the street, the kind of wind that blows everything topsy-turvy.

Seventy-five, today, and a topsy-turvy day of wind and sunshine. The kind of wind that gets into the blood and drives you wild. Wild!

And I give a little shiver because suddenly I know, I know it in my ancient water, that something will happen today. Something exciting. Something nice, something nasty, I don't give a monkey's. Just as long as something happens to remind us we're still in the land of the living.

We boast the only castrato grandfather clock in London.

The plaque on the dial of our grandfather in the front hall says it was made in Inverness in 1846 and, as far as I know, it is a unique example of an authentic Highland-style grandfather clock and as such was exhibited at the Great Exhibition of 1851. Its Highlandness consists of a full set of antlers, eight points, on top of it. Sometimes we use the antlers as a hat rack, if either of us happens to go out wearing a hat, which doesn't happen often, but now and then, when it rains. This clock has got a lot of sentimental value for Nora and me. It came to us from our father. His only gift and even then it came by accident. Great, tall, butch, horny mahogany thing, but it gives out the hours in a funny little falsetto ping and always the wrong hour, always out by one. We never got round to fixing it. To tell the truth, it makes us laugh, always has. It was all right until Grandma fixed it. All she did was tap it and the weights dropped off. She always had that effect on gentlemen.

But, as I passed by our grandfather clock this windy birthday morning, cats scampering in front of me maddened by the smell of bacon, it struck. And struck. And struck. And this time got it right, straight on the nosey – eight o'clock!

'Nor'! Nor'! Something's up! Grandad in the hall got the right time, for once!'

'Something else is up, too,' Nora says in a gratified voice and slings me a thick, white envelope with a crest on the back. 'Our invites have arrived at last.'

She starts to pour out tea, while Wheelchair fizzes and stutters when I pull out that stiff, white card we thought would never come.

The Misses Dora and Leonora Chance
are invited
to a celebration to mark the one hundredth birthday
of
Sir Melchior Hazard
'One Man in his Time Plays Many Parts.'

4

Wheelchair fizzed, sputtered and boiled right over; she screeched fit to bust but Nora consoled her:

'Hold hard, ducky, we're never going to leave you behind! Yes, Cinders, you *shall* go to the ball, even if you aren't mentioned by name on the invite. Let's have *all* the skeletons out of the closet, today, of all days! God knows, we deserve a spot of bubbly after all these years.'

I squinted at the RSVP, to that posh house in Regent's Park and Lady Hazard, the third and present spouse. Whereas our poor old Wheelchair, here, was his first, which accounts for her spleen, as ex, at failing to feature personally on the invitation. And the Misses Leonora and Dora, that is, yours truly, are, of course, Sir Melchior Hazard's daughters, though not, ahem, by any of his wives. We are his *natural* daughters, as they say, as if only unmarried couples do it the way that nature intended. His never-by-him officially recognised daughters, with whom, by a bizarre coincidence, he shares a birthday.

'They've not given us much time to reply,' I complained. 'It's only tonight, isn't it?'

'Something makes you think they don't want us to go?' Nora's lost a couple of back molars, you can't help but notice when she laughs. I've kept all mine. Otherwise, like as two peas, as ever was. Years ago, the only way you could tell us apart was by our perfume. She used Shalimar, me, Mitsouko.

All the same, identical we may be, but symmetrical — never. For the body itself isn't symmetrical. One of your feet is bound to be bigger than the other, one ear will leak more wax. Nora is fluxy; me, constipated. She was always free with her money, squandered it on the fellers, poor thing, whereas I tried to put a bit by. Her menstrual flow was copious to a fault; mine, meagre. She said: 'Yes!' to life and I said, 'Maybe . . .' But we're both in the same boat, now. Stuck with each other. Two batty old hags, buy us a drink and we'll sing you a song. Even manage a knees-up, on occasion, such as New Year's Eve or a publican's grandbaby.

What a joy it is to dance and sing!

We're stuck in the period at which we peaked, of course. All women do. We'd feel mutilated if you made us wipe off our Joan

5

Crawford mouths and we always do our hair up in great big Victory rolls when we go out. We've still got lots of it, thank God, iron grey though it may be and tucked away in scarves, turban-style, this very moment, to hide the curlers. We always make an effort. We paint an inch thick. We put on our faces before we come down to breakfast, the Max Factor Pan-Stik, the false eyelashes with the three coats of mascara, everything. We used to polish our eyelids with Vaseline, when we were girls, but we gave up on that during the war and now use just a simple mushroom shadow for day plus a hint of tobacco brown, to deepen the tone, and a charcoal eyeliner. Our fingernails match our toenails match our lipstick match our rouge. Revlon, Fire and Ice. The habit of applying warpaint outlasts the battle; haven't had a man for yonks but still we slap it on. Nobody could say the Chance girls were going gently into that good night.

We'd got our best kimonos on, because it was our birthday. Real silk, mine mauve with a plum-blossom design on the back, Nora's crimson with a chrysanthemum. Our beloved Uncle Perry, that is, the late, and by his nieces grievously lamented, Peregrine Hazard, sent us back our kimonos from Nagasaki, years ago, before Pearl Harbor, when he was on one of his trips. Underneath, camiknickers with a French lace trim, lilac satin for me, crushed rose crepe for her. Tasty, eh? 'Course, we were wearing camiknickers before they *came back*.

Our hipbones stick out more than they used to; we look quite gaunt in our undies, these days, but she's the only one who sees me in the altogether, and me her, and we pass muster with our clothes on. Our cheekbones stick out more than they used to, too, but they're the very best cheekbones, I'd have you know — these cheekbones are descended from some of the most profitable calcium deposits in the world. Like all those who spend much time before the public eye, our father has always been dependent on his bone structure. God bless the Hazard calcium; it's kept osteoporosis at bay. Long and lean we always were and long and lean we are now, thank God. Some superannuated hoofers put on the avoirdupois like nobody's business.

'What shall we wear tonight?' asked Nora, stubbing her fag

out in her saucer, pouring herself another cup. She's a regular teapot. Wheelchair moaned a little.

'Don't fret, dear,' Nora soothed. 'You can wear your Normal Hartnell and the pearls, all right? We'll do you up something lovely.'

That calmed it down, poor old stick. Known to us as Wheelchair, known to the world, once upon a time, as Lady Atalanta Hazard. A Lady in her own right, she'd have you know, a perfect lady, unlike our father's next two wives. She married Melchior Hazard when he was just a matinée idol, and divorced him long before that knighthood they gave him for 'services to the theatre'. Née Lady Atalanta Lynde, 'the most beautiful woman of her time', born with a silver spoon, etc. etc. etc. but now an antique divorcee in reduced circumstances, to whit, the basement front of 49 Bard Road.

All in good time I shall reveal to you how it has come to pass that we inherited, in her dotage and, come to that, in ours, the first wife of our illegitimate father. Suffice to say that nobody else would have her. Least of all her own two daughters. Bloody cows. 'The lovely Hazard girls', they used to call them. Huh. Lovely is as lovely does; if they looked like what they behave like, they'd frighten little children.

We've been storing Wheelchair in the basement for well-nigh thirty years. We've got quite attached to her. Earlier on, Nora used to take her out shopping, give her some fresh air and that, until she nearly starts a riot, she says to the bloke at the salad stall: 'Have you got anything in the shape of a cucumber, my good fellow?' After that, we had to keep her home for her own sake.

Sometimes she goes on a bit, on and on, on and on and bloody on, in fact, worrying away at how Melchior took the best years of her life then deserted her for a Hollywood harlot – his Number Two bride – and how the 'lovely Hazard girls' did her out of all her money and how she fell downstairs and can never walk again and on and on and on and *on* until you want to throw a blanket over her, like you do to shut up a parrot. But there's not a scrap of harm in her and, besides, we owe her one from way back.

I had a go at the teapot, too, but too late, got half a cup of sodden leaves, went out to the scullery to put the kettle on, again. Here we sit, in our negligées, in the breakfast room in the leather armchairs by the Readicole electric fire. Sometimes we sit there all day, drink tea, chew the fat. Wheelchair plays solitaire, does tapestry. The cats come and go.

At six we switch to gin.

Sometimes when we've had our supper we plug Wheelchair into the TV – she loves the commercials, she watches out for the ones with Melchior in them, then she heckles the screen – we go and don some bits and bobs of former finery such as, for example, those matching silver-fox trench coats Howard Hughes gave us, and we sally forth to the local, where we are occasionally invited to perform one of the numbers that brought us fame, once upon a time. And sometimes we perform uninvited.

'Anything else in the mail?'

Nora shoved across the bundle. The electricity bill, again; Neighbourhood Watch, again; next door complaining about the cats, again; some kid in New Jersey wanting to interview us for his Ph.D., Film Studies, bloody *Midsummer Night's Dream*, again. At our age, you feel you've seen it all before. I note that little Tiff, our darling love, our chick, our cherished one, our goddaughter, is too preoccupied with her Big Affair at present to drop us birthday greetings. Youth, youth.

Then the doorbell rang and made me jump. The gas man? Never the gas man, he never leans on the bell with all his weight like that, he just gives a reticent little tinkle ever since he got Nora in her altogether except for her nail polish, she'd jumped straight out of the bath, she'd thought he was a telegram. No. This was a fierce, long ring. Then another. And another. We started up, we stiffened. Then he on the doorstep hammers with his fists and shouts:

'Aunties!'

Our father's youngest son, young Tristram Hazard. Why does he call us 'aunties' when we are, in fact, his half-sisters, even if on the wrong side of the blanket? You will find out in due course. And has he come to wish us 'Happy birthday'? If so, why the panic? He shouted so, I was all of a flutter. I fumbled with the lock, the bolts, the chain – like Fort Knox, round here. You can't be too careful, these days. We had a mass breakout from Brixton Nick last year, they came over the garden wall like formation dancers.

Young Tristram fell into my arms as if legless when I got the door open. Unshaven, mad-eyed and all his red hair was coming out of his funny little pigtail and blowing about in the wind that was blowing all the garbage in at the front gate. He looked deranged. And he'd put on a lot of weight since I last saw him, too. He hung on to me, panting for breath.

'Tiffany . . .' (pant, heave, pant) ' . . . is Tiffany here?'

'Do pull yourself together, Tristram, you've made a big, wet patch on my silk,' I said sharply.

'Didn't you catch last night's programme?'

'You wouldn't catch me dead watching your poxy programme.'

But Wheelchair catches it from time to time, cackling away in her genteel fashion, rejoicing even in her approaching senility at how low the house of Hazard has sunk in this its last generation – or, as she sometimes wittily puts it, cackling harder than ever, 'the final degeneration of the House of Hazard'. And we did watch the first five minutes, once, we felt we ought to take in our little Tiff's television debut.

Tiffany is the 'hostess', whatever that means. She smiles a lot, she shows her tits. What a waste. She'd have made a lovely dancer, if only she'd stuck with it. We watched her first five minutes. Five minutes was enough, I can tell you; then we adjourned to the boozer, muttering. His programme goes out live. That's its speciality.

'They'd get better ratings if he was dead,' said Nora. 'The only posthumous presenter on TV. What a coup.'

Tristram wiped his eyes with the back of his hand and then I saw he had been crying.

'Tiffany's missing,' he said.

That took the smile off my face, I can tell you. Nora yelled up from the kitchen. 'What's biting young Lochinvar?' He *was* in a state, blubbering and babbling, Scotch on his breath to knock you over. When we got him settled in an armchair, he thrust a cassette into my hand.

'Have a look,' he says. 'I can't explain. Watch it, see what happened.'

Then he spotted the photo of little Tiff in the silver frame that we keep on the breakfast-room mantelpiece and the waterworks started up again. I felt quite sorry for the poor kid. 'Kid', I say. He's all of thirty-five; he'll be pushing forty in no time. All the same, his stock in trade is boyish charm. God knows what he'll do when he loses that. But we were all a-tremble, all anxiety; what the fuck was going on? So Nora bunged his cassette in the VCR sharpish.

We got the VCR to catch up with those Busby Berkeley musicals they put out Saturday afternoons. We tape them, watch them over and over, freeze-frame our favourite bits. It drives Wheelchair mad. And Fred and Ginger, of course. Good old Fred. Nostalgia, the vice of the aged. We watch so many old movies our memories come in monochrome.

A burst of buzz and static shocked Wheelchair out of the trance she falls into when she's nicely greased with bacon after breakfast. 'What's happening? What's *he* doing here?' She fixed Tristram with a suspicious eye, for he was no kin of hers, while the picture settled down on a flight of neon steps in a burst of canned applause as he came bounding down with his red hair slicked back, his top-of-the-milk-coloured rumpled linen Giorgio Armani whistle and flute, Tristram Hazard, weak but charming, game-show presenter and television personality, last gasp of the imperial Hazard dynasty that bestrode the British theatre like a colossus for a century and a half. Tristram, youngest son of the great Melchior Hazard, 'prince of players'; grandson of those tragic giants of the Victorian stage, Ranulph and Estella 'A star danced' Hazard. Lo, how the mighty have fallen.

'Hi, there! I'm Tristram!'

The camera closes in as he sings out, 'Hi, there, lolly lovers! I'm Tristram Hazard and I've come to bring you . . .' Now he throws back his head, showing off his throat, he's got a real, old-fashioned, full-bodied, Ivory Novello-type throat, he throws

his head back and cries out in the voice of an ecstatic: 'LASHINGS
OF LOLLY! LASHINGS OF LOLLY!'

The show begins.

Freeze-frame.

Let us pause awhile in the unfolding story of Tristram and
Tiffany so that I can fill you in on the background. High time!
you must be saying. Just who is this Melchior Hazard and his
clan, his wives, his children, his hangers-on? It is in order to pro-
vide some of the answers to those questions that I, Dora Chance,
in the course of assembling notes towards my own autobiogra-
phy, have inadvertently become the chronicler of all the Hazards,
although I should think that my career as such will go as publicly
unacknowledged by the rest of the dynasty as my biological
career has done for not only are Nora and I, as I have already
told you, by-blows, but our father was a pillar of the legit. theatre
and we girls are illegitimate in every way – not only born out of
wedlock, but we went on the halls, didn't we!

Romantic illegitimacy, always a seller. It ought to copper-
bottom the sales of my memoirs. But, to tell the truth, there was
sod all romantic about *our* illegitimacy. At best, it was a farce,
at worst, a tragedy, and a chronic inconvenience the rest of the
time. But the urge has come upon me before I drop to seek out
an answer to the question that always teased me, as if the answer
were hidden, somewhere, behind a curtain: whence came we?
Whither goeth we?

I know the answer to the second question, of course. Bound
for oblivion, nor leave a wrack behind. Never spawned, neither
of us, although Nora wanted to, everso, and towards the end of
her menstrual life greeted each flow with tears. Me, no. I was
pleased as Punch each time I saw it and even more so when it
stopped, short, never to go again, like grandfather's clock in the
old song though not at all like *our* grandfather clock, which remains in fine if high-pitched fettle, thank you very much.

But, as to the question of origins and past history, let me
plunge deep into the archaeology of my desk, casting aside the
photo of Ruby Keeler ('To Nora and Dora, four fabulous feet,
from your Ruby').

Here it is. A fraying envelope stuffed with antique picture post-cards. We've put together quite a collection over the years, bought, begged, borrowed, some sepia-toned, some tinted to show off her red, red hair. Our paternal grandmother, the one fixed point in our fathers' genealogy. Indeed, the one fixed point in our entire genealogy; our maternal side founders in a wilderness of unknowability and our other grandmother, Grandma, Grandma Chance, the grandma who fixed the grandfather clock, the grandma whose name we carry, she was no blood relation at all, to make confusion worse confounded. Grandma raised us, not out of duty, or due to history, but because of pure love, it was a genuine family romance, she fell in love with us the moment she clapped her eyes on us.

But we never met our *real* grandmother and only know her as you see her here, captured in the eternal youth of the publicity photo. 'A star danced and she was born,' they said. She was called Estella. Here she is as Juliet, as Portia, as Beatrice. See that 'Come hither!' smile. As Lady Macbeth, she manages to summon up a stern frown, quite the Miss Whiplash, but you can see a wicked little twinkle if you look hard.

She wasn't your Edwardian drayhorse type, she was little and skinny, with enormous eyes. She was a will-o'-the-wisp, all air and fire, and she could break your heart with one single sob but her son, our Uncle Perry, said she used to get the giggles, sometimes, in the middle of some big scene, the casket scene, the sleep-walking scene, she'd double up, everybody else would have to cover for her. Her hair was always coming undone, too, tumbling down her back, spraying out hairpins in all directions, her stockings at half-mast, her petticoat would come adrift in the middle of the street, her drawers start drooping. She was a marvel and she was a mess.

Here she is in drag as, famously, Hamlet. Black tights. Tremendous legs. Wasted on a classical actress. We've got the legs from her. She's emoting with the dagger: 'To be or not to be . . .' The obituary in *The New York Times* – careful with it, the paper's starting to crumble – says how she 'owed much to her New York Horatio, a superbly athletic young American with an exceptional gift of gravitas'.

Watch out for him, he'll pop up again. Cassius Booth. Yes. One of *those* Booths. His parents had a nerve, to call him Cassius.

The obituary hints at our paternal grandmother's enthusiasm for ahem indoor sports in the most tactful way. 'Generous, gallant, reckless; a woman who gave her all to life . . .' But she didn't so much give it away as throw it away, poor thing. She came to a sticky end, all right. This is her as Desdemona, in a white nightie with her spray of willow, just about to go into her number: 'A poor soul sat sighing by a sycamore tree . . .' This one is a real collector's item because —

No. Wait. I'll tell you all about it in my own good time.

Some time in or around the year 1870 (her date of birth, like that of so many actresses, a movable feast) our paternal grandmother was born in a trunk and trod the boards from toddlerhood as fairy, phantom, goblin, eventually, an old stager of eight (give or take a year or two) making her London debut as Mamillius in *The Winter's Tale* at the Theatre Royal, Haymarket, in, it says here, a 'somewhat pedantic' production by the younger Kean (Charles), and a costume copied from a Greek vase, rolling a hoop, a bit of business copied off another Greek vase. Lewis Carroll saw her, sent her an inscribed copy of *Alice*, invited her to tea and got her to slip her frock off after the crumpets, whereupon he snapped her in the altogether but she drew the line at imitating the action depicted upon certain other Greek vases, or so she always maintained. Here's the evidence of the encounter. See? He called it *Sprite*. I bought it at an auction at Christie's. Cost an arm and a leg. Couldn't resist. Not many people can boast a photo of their grandmother posing for kiddiporn. I sold one of poor old Irish's letters to pay for it.

Irish? Who's he?

You'll find out, soon enough. Suffice to say, if it hadn't been for poor old Irish and his philanthropic passion for the education of chorus girls, I'd not be sitting here, now, writing this. He taught me one end of a pen from the other. He gave me the confidence to use a word like 'philanthropic'. In return, I broke his heart. Fair exchange is no robbery.

When she played Mamillius, she doubled up as Columbine in

the Harlequinade. Here's the programme. 'Little Estella.' She could do it all – make you laugh, make you cry, dance for you, sing you a song, but she was a fool for love.

It was a hard life. I will tell you what her life was like: greasepaint, gaslight, horseshit, coal smoke, railways – change at Crewe on Sundays. She was a child star but she grew up. She worked the provincial circuits, Juliet, Rosalind, Viola, Portia, Manchester, Birmingham, Liverpool, Nottingham, a big fish in a small pond; Hermia, Bianca, Iras in London, small fish in a big pond, until, in 1888, back she came to the Haymarket, her big chance, Cordelia to the Lear of Ranulph Hazard.

Ranulph, one of the great, roaring, actor-managers such as they don't make any more. I've read how, during his Macbeth, Queen Victoria gripped the curtains of the royal box until her knuckles whitened. Regicide, no fun for a reigning monarch. On his night, he'd scare you witless in the banquet scene even if his wife, caught by a fit of giggles, had her back to the audience, her shoulders shaking. (Peregrine said she'd told him she thought the Macbeths ought to sack the cook.) Ranulph Hazard's Richard III, 'the very incarnation of human evil,' wrote GBS, not one to go overboard about a ham.

Don't let's sell Ranulph Hazard short. He was *good* on his night, although the punter never knew for sure when that night might be. Because the old man might come reeling on and slur out the words from another play altogether than that billed; or else he might be mopish, hungoverish, out of sorts and you couldn't hear a word beyond the first-row stalls, whatever he might be saying; or then again he might be too sober by half and sunk in some deep vale of despond when he'd just walk through it. There was always that element of chance with Ranulph, he was volatility in person, you'd diagnose a manic depressive, these days, and stick him on lithium.

But, on his night, a marvel.

And Shakespeare was a kind of god for him. It was as good as idolatry. He thought the whole of human life was there.

So it was on one of his marvellous nights, he met a shooting star. What an ecstasy the two of them provoked! Rivers of tears. Tempests of applause. One famous bit of business has got into all the theatre books – when poor old Lear makes it up with his daughter at last, Ranulph always used to put his fingers to his cheek, then look at his fingertips in wonder, touch his mouth then say in a trembly, geriatrically uncertain way: 'Be your tears wet?' That brought out the hankies, all right. They said her smile in answer, 'tremulous, through tears, as April sunshine', almost, but not quite, capped it. So he and Estella fell in love. How could they resist? An old man and a prodigal daughter, the stuff that dreams are made of.

Here's a funny thing. That was just how Tristram's mother, Lady Hazard III, collared Melchior – by playing Cordelia to his Lear.

Old Ranulph was a good thirty years older than Estella, or more, or even much more – *his* date of birth is as variable as hers. All the same, they tied the knot *toot sweet* (as that other grandma, Grandma Chance, used to say) in St Paul's, Covent Garden, the actors' church, with half the profession crossing their fingers for them and the other half staying away on principle due to Ranulph owing them money or having adulterised them. She wore her red hair hanging down her back, a wreath of lilies of the valley, she was nineteen or thereabouts. Lamb to the slaughter, one might have said, seeing his grey hairs, his shaking hand, his dubious finances – he was a drunk, a bankrupt, a gambler, he'd fretted and philandered and beaten and betrayed three wives into early graves, already. But no sacrificial lamb nor shrinking violet she. She was a wild thing, even if she was always true to him in her fashion. I don't have anything of her in me, not at all. I am the sentimental one. But Nora, sometimes.

There's a recording of Ranulph, made on a wax cylinder, I went to that place off Kensington High Street, they played it for me. Crackle, hiss, and then his voice: 'Tomorrow and tomorrow and tomorrow . . .' A shudder ran through me, not because of sentiment, but because of the voice itself. It wasn't what I expected, it was ugly, almost – harsh, grating, the words sounded as if they'd been wrenched out of him. And there I was, in tears, too, like the snufflers in the Haymarket all those years ago, but not just because of what he said and who he was but because of the way he said it, that sounded so alien to me, so strange in my ears, because of his flattened 'a's, and his consonants, that were cut, like glass. Only a hundred years ago ... My own grand-father. Yet it was a voice from before the Flood, from another kind of life entirely, so antique-sounding that it scarcely seems possible his granddaughters now sit in silk camiknickers in the basement of a house in Brixton, drinking tea and watching on television his great-grandson address an invisible audience out of a plastic box, in that between-two-worlds, neither Brit nor Yank, twang of the game-show host:

'Say it again for me! LASHINGS OF LOLLY!'

Lo, how the mighty have fallen. An S-M game show? How low can you get?

So Ranulph and Estella were married and first of all he loved her madly and vice versa and then Barnum, F. T. Barnum, Barnum of Barnum and Bailey, *that* Barnum, struck by her legs in *As You Like It*, made her an offer. *Hamlet* in a tent in Central Park. A tent because, he prophesied, no theatre on Broadway would be big enough to hold the crowds.

She must have eyed her old man sideways, wondering how he took it; he'd been the most melancholy Dane of his generation, hadn't he, but that had been a generation or two before, Hamlet is nothing if not a *juve* role. Ranulph, though, was all agog to give to America the tongue that Shakespeare spake. So they crossed the Atlantic and Ranulph did them proud as Hamlet's father, while suave young Cassius Booth stepped into the lime-light beside her as Hamlet's best friend.

Hamlet under canvas, a smash. It ran and ran and would have run ad infinitum except the twins announced that they were on the way and a female Hamlet is one thing but a pregnant prince is quite another. So twin boys, our fathers, were born in the USA. Melchior and Peregrine. What names, eh? What delusions of grandeur went into the naming of them? If you shorten them to 'Mel' and 'Perry', they've got a democratically twentieth-century and transatlantic ring to them but Old Ranulph, rattling old nineteenth-century romantic that he was, never did that, al-though Estella, with a wink, often.

Note how I call them both 'our fathers', as if we had the two and, in a sense, so we did. Melchior it was who did the biologically necessary, it's true, but Peregrine *passed* as our father – that is, he was the one who publicly acknowledged us when Melchior would not. I should tell you, now, that Melchior's entire family, Wheelchair apart, always maintained this fiction, too, which is why Saskia told Tristram we were his aunts and not his sisters. But Peregrine was so much beloved by us and behaved so much more fatherly to us, not to mention paying most of the bills, that I know I need to claim him as something more than uncle.

Speaking of illegitimacy, there was more than a hint of romantic, nay, melodramatic illegitimacy in the Hazard family long before Nora and myself took out first bows. Because Ranulph Hazard, during all his lengthy marital and extramarital career, had produced no issue, as yet, until his wife's transvestite Hamlet met her Horatio's exceptional gift of gravitas, not to mention his athleticism. Tongues wagged. Did Melchior lend an ear? Who can tell, at this distance in time. All the same, he loved his boys. He cast them as princes in the tower as soon as they could toddle.

One thing you must know about Ranulph. He was half mad and thought he had a Call. Now he saw the entire world as his mission field and out of all of us it has turned out that Gareth Hazard, SJ, has stayed most faithful to the family tradition of proselytising zeal, for now the old man was seized with the most imperative desire, to spread and go on spreading the Word overseas. Willy-nilly, off must go his wife and children, too, to take Shakespeare where Shakespeare had never been before.

In those days, there was so much pink on the map of the world that English was spoken everywhere. No language problem. Off to the ends of the Empire they went, rolling to the rhythms of the sea as they crossed, crisscrossed the oceans. I see it in my mind's eye as if it were a movie – the ocean liner slipping her moorings, gliding away from the quay, the siren blaring, the crowd throwing flowers, the red-haired woman on the deck, smiling, waving, smiling.

Our Uncle Peregrine inherited her scarlet hair. So did our half-sisters, Saskia and Imogen. Tristram, too. Not us, worse luck. The red hair only went to the legit. side. As for me and Nora, first of all, we were mouse. Then we dyed it. When we stopped dyeing (black), we found out that we had, all unbeknownst to ourselves, gone grey.

Our Uncle Peregrine was his mother's boy.

We were hurrying down the street, he told me, on tour in Australia. It was in Sydney, down by the Circular Quay. We were on our way to some ladies' lunch club – she did guest appearances, it helped with the finances, Ranulph was chronically short of a bob. We were late, of course, because she hadn't been able to find a clean frock but after much rummaging came up with one with only a couple of little wine stains and smear of marmalade so she pinned a bunch of frangipani over the worst of it and got her hair up, somehow. Melchior stayed behind with Father, to watch him running through Julius Caesar. We came to an organ-grinder, we stopped to admire the monkey. She gave the organ-grinder sixpence and he played 'Daisy, Daisy'. She took my hand and we danced, right there, on the pavement. Her hairpins scattered everywhere. My celluloid collar burst in two. The monkey clapped its paws together. Everybody stared. 'Come on!' she said to the world in general. 'Join in!' Then everybody started dancing, they all took hold of the hand of the next perfect stranger. 'I'm half crazy, all for the love of you.' She looked upon what she had accomplished and was glad. We missed soup, we missed fish, we arrived at the table at the same time as the chicken. Her hair was down her back, she'd lost her flowers, one slipper with a broken heel, her small son collarless, tieless, and I'd got the monkey on my shoulder – she'd swapped her gold watch for it. She did them Portia's speech, 'The quality of mercy . . .' She made them happy. There was mango ice-cream for dessert, our favourite. We had three bowlfuls each. In Melbourne, they named a sundae after her, 'Ice-cream Estella', mango ice-cream topped with passionfruit purée. If ever we get to Melbourne, together, Floradora, I'll treat you to an 'Ice-cream Estella'.

Always the lucky one, our Peregrine, even in his memories, which were full of laughter and dancing; he always remembered the good times.

Peregrine Hazard, adventurer, magician, seducer, explorer, scriptwriter, rich man, poor man – but never either beggerman

nor thief. At our age, Nora and I have got more friends among
the dead than with the living. We often go visiting in cemeteries
to trim the grass growing over the friends of our youth but we
don't even know where your grave might be, dear Perry, to go
and lay a flower on it. You spent your childhood on the road,
here today, gone tomorrow; you grew up a restless man. You
loved change. And fornication. And trouble. And, funnily
enough, towards the end, you loved butterflies. Peregrine Hazard, lost among the butterflies, lost in the jungle, vanished away
as neatly and completely as if you had become the object of one
of those conjuring tricks you were so fond of.

If an ice-cream sundae was named after Estella in Melbourne,
then an entire dried-out township in New South Wales was renamed Hazard, after she and Runulph put on al fresco *Coriolanus*. A street in Hobart, Tasmania. And they toured India, not
once, but several times – crossing, crisscrossing the subcontinent.
The gleaming rails sliding beneath the churning wheels, the
puffing smokestack, the leaves falling off the calendar and blowing away in the wind ... A maharajah gave the boys a baby
elephant but they couldn't take it with them on the train. He fell
in love with Estella, and promised her her weight in rubies if she
would stay behind and recite him every night Viola's 'willow cabin' speech. What did she do? we asked. She made him happy,
said Peregrine. She had a gift for that. She made him happy, then
she left him. She had a gift for leaving, too.

The red-haired woman, smiling, waving to the disappearing
shore. She left the maharajah; she left innumerable other lights
o' passing love in towns and cities and theatres and railway stations all over the world. But Melchior she did not leave.

A theatre, long since demolished, named the Hazard, in Shang-
hai. Then Hong Kong. Then Singapore. Everything a little
threadbare, now, a little shabby. The ocean, again. North
America, again – Montreal. Toronto. Crossing, crisscrossing the
prairies. Hazard, Alberta, flat as a plateful of snow. Hazard,
North Dakota – no township too small to receive them, nor to
reciprocate the honour by rechristening itself. The touring was
turning into a kind of madness. In Arkansas, the Hazards'
patched and ravaged tent went up in the spaces vacated by the

travelling evangelicals: Ranulph, lean, haggard, bearded, more and more resembled John the Baptist had John the Baptist reached old age.

They arrived at last in the south-west and pitched their tent in arid scrub in a town called Gun Barrel, Texas, renamed Hazard, after the Hazards played *Macbeth* there with a hired band of campesinos as the Scottish army, holding spiked ears of prickly pear above their heads to mimic Birnam wood. Of all these wild, strange and various places, Hazard, Texas, was the one that Perry remembered best; he went back there, later, a grizzled old-timer or two wept in his beer to recall how Estella made him happy, they made her son an honorary sheriff.

Props and costumes were lost or stolen or fell to pieces and then were begged or improvised or patched and darned. Ranulph drank and gambled and declaimed; he was going to pieces, too. He shouted at America but it would no longer listen to him. One night, in a bar at Tucson, Arizona, he gambled away his crown from *Lear* and Estella put together a new one for him out of a bit of cardboard. She dabbed on some gold paint. 'Here you are.'

Why did she stay with him? Perish the thought, perhaps she truly loved him; perhaps all those people she made happy were just so many sideshows. But she'd lost the knack of making Melchior happy.

Then, one day, deep in the Midwest, as they were setting up in a townlet where they had hopes of a decent-sized audience since all there was to do in the evenings, otherwise, was to watch the corn grow, Ranulph received a cable from New York. While the Hazards roamed themselves to rags for the greater glory of Shakespeare, Cassius Booth, Estella's old Horatio, stayed in one place and prospered. Now he was an actor-manager himself, with his very own theatre on the Great White Way. And was he a man to forget old friends? Not he! Estella looked enigmatic and she smiled, said Perry. She was still a girl, remember. No more than thirty. Or, at most, thirty-five. While Old Ranulph was pushing seventy and staked his final gamble on it, on one last triumphant prayer meeting. He'd show 'em all! He'd flare up one last incandescent time on Broadway in a sort of Shakespearian funeral pyre. But the play he picked on was, alas, *Othello*.

Thirty or thirty-five, whatever she was, she doesn't look more than a schoolgirl in the picture on the postcard, in her nightie, with her hair down her book. 'Sing willow, willow, willow.' Cassius Booth played Iago. There is no handkerchief in this story. All the same, her husband killed them both, first her, then him. They'd slipped out together during the first-night party. Old acquaintances. Perhaps, by then, Old Ranulph couldn't tell the difference between Shakespeare and living. Next morning, the notices were magnificent but the murder itself had to wait for the noon editions because the chambermaid didn't find the bodies on the bed in Estella's hotel room until she brought up late breakfast. Three bodies. He shot them both and then he shot himself.

Exeunt omnes. She'd always had a gift for exits.

But life goes on.

The two little boys were stranded in New York, poor tragic waifs, and there they almost expired themselves, or so Perry said, because they were so stuffed with candy, hot dogs and pie à la mode by the lovely ladies with low-slung bosoms and feathered hats who went about their business in the hotel lobby. There was no money left as such, only an actor's inheritance of unpaid bills, paste jewellery, flash attitudes, but the Plaza extended them credit and so they learned to live beyond their means.

Now, although these two were twins, they were *not* alike as two peas. Melchior, at ten, was dark and brooding, registering already the beginnings of the profile which would dominate Shaftesbury Avenue. That profile was to Melchior what Clark Gable's ears were to him. Dark eyes, lashes of the kind they say are 'wasted on a boy' and a physique that turned out to be ready-made for leaping and fencing and climbing up to balconies and all the things a Shakespearian actor needs to do. I know that all these things, not forgetting his 'splendid gift of gravitas', all together point the finger at Cassius Booth as his father, but don't forget that poor old Ranulph had been a matinée idol, too, in his day, even if in his day women wore crinolines, and there remains a gigantic question mark over the question of their paternity, although whoever it was who contributed the actual jissom, no child need ever have been ashamed of either contender and, as for me, the grandchild, I like to think *both* of them had a hand in it, if you follow me.

But Peregrine was a holy terror and couldn't keep a straight face, just like his mother. As young Macduff, he'd entered with a piss-pot on his head and given an audience of sheepshearers outside Perth their best moment of the evening. Melchior never let him on the stage again. Even as little scraps, Melchior was all for art and Peregrine was out for fun. Don't think that, just because they were brothers, they liked one another. Far from it. Chalk and cheese.

They lived on room service and the kindness of strangers until the boat docked from Leith and off it came their comeuppance – Miss Euphemia Hazard, dour as hell, Presbyterian to the backbone, their aunt. Warden of a workhouse near Pitlochry and sworn enemy of the stage and all who trod it, who never shed a tear for brother or for sister-in-law because she thought their violent ends were the Lord's revenge, a kind of wild justice. She grabbed Melchior by the scruff, stuffed him shrieking into a trunk marked 'Not wanted on voyage', and reached out for Peregrine but he gave a shrug and a wriggle and left his old tweed jacket in her hand while he himself was gone, whoosh! out of the window, down the fire escape, a shirtsleeved, carrot-topped ten-year-old hurtling helter-skelter down the pavement, sending a hot-dog stand flying, a bootblack sprawling and . . . he vanished.

Vanished clean away into America and though, later on, he told a wondrous tale of all his doings and hoboings as a boy, as to what *really* befell him, I do not have a notion except that it can have been no cakewalk and, when he first found us, he was as rich as Croesus.

So Peregrine ran for it, lickety-split, hell for leather, but Melchior was trapped.

Now, Melchior had adored his father, worshipped him, even, and took away from the grand catastrophe of his parents' lives only one little souvenir – the pasteboard crown that Ranulph wore for Lear, the one Estella made. God knows how Melchior smuggled this relic past his aunt.

It was in his blood, wasn't it? Every night, during the dour years of rain and porridge, as he lay in his freezing bed under the one plaid rug his aunt permitted him, he'd recite to himself word for word his father's greatest roles. Macbeth. Hamlet. (Although never Othello, of course.) Aunt Effie's Highland clock – you've seen it for yourself, the antlered grandfather now resident at 49 Bard Road – struck twelve, then one, then two. He would so move himself with these solitary renditions he would cry himself to sleep. His aunt forbad Melchior point-blank to so much as think of the stage, although she recognised how he had sufficient talent in that direction – that is, rhetoric, etc. – to urge him to give the ministry a go and, when she became insistent, then he took matters into his own hands.

He wrapped the pasteboard crown up in a change of shirt and underthings, tied all in a handkerchief and said goodbye to Pitlochry for ever. I can see him now, setting out to seek his fortune like Dick Whittington in panto. Miss Effie's clock sang out five times as he shut the workhouse door behind him. It would have been bitter cold, no stars, still pitch-dark. A cart went past with a load of kale; he got a lift a mile or two. The sun would have been coming up, by then. No friends, no kin except a lost brother half a world away whom he'd never got on with. Mad with pride and ambition and nothing in the world except his dark eyes and gift of gravitas and a toy crown with the gold paint peeling off.

And so he finally found his way to London, and, in due course, down on his uppers, nay, down on the uppers of his uppers, he arrived at this very house, which was, in those days, a boarding house that catered for theatricals, though not, I should say, theatricals of the well-heeled variety.

Brixton, before the lights went out over Europe, hub of a wheel of theatres, music halls, Empires, Royalties, what have you. You could tram it all over from Brixton. The streets of tall, narrow houses were stuffed to the brim with stand-up comics; adagio dancers; soubrettes; conjurers; fiddlers; speciality acts with dogs, doves, goats, you name it; dancing dwarves; tenors, sopranos, baritones and basses, both solo artistes and doubled up in any of the permutations of the above as duets, trios etc. And also those who wrung a passion to tatters for a living and therefore considered themselves a cut above.

In those days, our mother emptied the slops, filled the wash-stand jugs, raked out the grates, built up the fires, brought up the cans of hot water, scrubbed the back of the occasional gentleman and herself occasionally –

or perhaps only the one time.

Chance by name, Chance by nature. We were not planned.

Melchior slept here. This attic, the cheapest room in the house, cheaper still because he never paid. I picture him in front of a square of mirror, trying on that shabby crown, emoting, listening to the sycamores at the end of the garden thrashing about in the wind and pretending the sound they made was applause. Desperate, ravenous, on the make, tramping round the agents day after day after day, back to the boiled cabbage at Bard Road and the hard, narrow bed. I wonder if he lent his mouth here, his arsehole there, to see if that would do the trick. I suppose my mother must have felt sorry for him. I can imagine her stripping off in the cold room, turning towards the starving boy. How did she do it? Shyly? Nervously? Lewdly?

Then everything fades to black. I can't bear to think any further. It hurts too much. You always like to think a bit of love, or at least a little pleasure, went into your making but I do not know, I cannot guess, if the dark-eyed stranger who put his hand up the skirt of the penniless orphan was cynical, or tender, or desperate, or carried away by the moment. Had she done it before, did she know what she was doing? Was she scared? Or full of desire? Or half raped? He was good-looking enough, God knows. Women went mad for him. Perhaps she was the first woman who went mad for him. Did she think about him when she made his bed up in the mornings? Had she pressed her cheek against the pillow and wished the pillow were his cheek?

'She was only a slip of a thing but she was bold as brass,' Grandma used to say.

I'd like to think it went like this: She closed the door behind her, locked it. There he was on the bed, brushing up his Shakespeare. He looked up, hastily laying aside his well-thumbed copy of the *Collected Works*. She started pulling off her chemise. 'Now I've got you where I want you!' she said. What else could a gentleman do but succumb?

Nine months later, her heart gave out when we were born. Apart from that, I don't know anything about her. We don't even know what she looked like, there isn't a picture. She was called Kitty, like a little stray cat. Fatherless, motherless. Perhaps Mrs Chance's house was even a haven to her, in spite of the stairs – she must have run up and down the stairs twenty times a day, thirty times a day. And the grates to be leaded, the front steps to be scoured.

Not that Mrs Chance was what the French call *exigeante*. She didn't run the fanciest boarding house in Brixton, it barely managed to cling on to respectability by the skin of its teeth, and you could have said the same of her. There were Boston ferns, in green glazed pots, on stands, and Turkey rugs, but the whole place never looked *plausible*. It looked like the stage set of a theatrical boarding house, as if Grandma had done it up to suit a role she'd chosen on purpose. She was a mystery, was Mrs Chance.

Melchior Hazard slept here, but not for long. His theatre-doorstep vigils, his audition ordeals paid off. He and his cardboard crown were gone by the time our mother missed her first period. She vomited every morning, quietly, so that Mrs Chance would not hear. The war began, that August, but I don't think our mother cared. Mrs Chance never heard the vomiting but she heard the tears.

We came bursting out on a Monday morning, on a day of sunshine and high wind when the Zeppelins were falling. First one wee, bawling girl; then the other, while Mrs Chance did all the necessary. She'd called the doctor but he never got there. Our mother took a look, too weak to hold us, she'd been in labour since the day before yesterday, but Mrs Chance always told us she took a good look and managed a smile.

Why should she have smiled? She was just seventeen years old, no man, no home. There was a war on. All the same, Mrs Chance always told us that she smiled and Mrs Chance was sometimes stingy with the truth but never lied. 'Why shouldn't she smile? She hadn't got a mum or dad. A baby is the next best thing.'

The sky was blue, that morning, said Mrs Chance, and there was a wind that made the washing on the clotheslines dance.

Monday, washday. What a sight! All over Brixton, long black stockings stepping out with gents' longjohns, striped shirts doing the Lambeth Walk with flannel nighties, French knickers doing the cancan with the frilly petticoats, pillowslips, sheets, towels, hankies all a-flutter, like flags and banners, everything in motion. The bombs stopped and the little kids came out to play again. The sun shone, the kids were singing. When Grandma Chance had had a couple, she sometimes sang the song they sang when we were born:

> The moon shines bright on Charlie Chaplin
> And his shoes are crackin'
> For want of blackin'
> And his little baggy trousers they need mendin'
> Before they send him
> To the Dardanelles.

Poor old Charlie, pushing up the daisies, now. Old Charlie. Hung like a horse.

So there was dancing and singing all along Bard Road and Mrs Chance picked us up, one on each arm, and took us to the window so the first thing we saw with our swimming baby eyes was sunshine and dancing. Then a seagull swooped up, past the window, up and away. She told us about the seagull so often that although I cannot really remember it, being just hatched out, all the same, I do believe I saw that seagull fly up into the sky.

There was a little sigh behind us and she was gone.

The doctor got there ten minutes after, he wrote out the death certificate. That was that. So Mrs Chance adopted us but never let us call her 'mother', out of respect for the dead. We always called her 'Grandma', and 'Chance' became our handle.

But I don't think for one moment that 'Chance' was her own name, either. All that I know about her is: she'd arrived at 49 Bard Road on New Year's Day, 1900, with a banker's draft for the first year's rent and the air of a woman making a new start in a new place, a new century and, or so the evidence points, a new name. If she decided to call herself 'Mrs', it was part and parcel of that shaky swipe after respectability I've mentioned, because I never caught one whiff of husband and, to tell the truth, she never lost a rakish air.

She wasn't tall, about five foot two, five two and a half, but solid-built like an armoured car. She always put on so much Rachel powder she puffed out a fine cloud if you patted her. She rouged big, round spots in the middle of her cheeks. She used so much eyeblack that kiddies on Electric Avenue used to give her a chorus of 'Two Lovely Black Eyes' as she passed by. For all the thirty years we knew her, thanks to peroxide, she was canary-coloured blonde. She always pencilled in a big, black beauty spot below the left-hand corner of her mouth.

For outdoors, she wore black and she never went out without one of those square oilcloth carrier bags in which she kept her fat leather purse, a clean handkerchief in an envelope she'd marked in pencil 'clean hankercheif', a couple of safety pins, in case, as she said, her drawers fell down, and often an empty or two on its way back to the off-licence. There'd be a little black toque on her head, with a spotted veil. And I always remember her grey lisle stockings, that she secured below each knee with two lengths of knotted elastic.

Indoors, providing the boarders weren't around, she never wore a stitch, as often as not. She was a convert to naturism. She thought it was good for us kiddies, to get the air and sunlight on our skins, as well, so we saved a lot of wear and tear on clothes and often gambolled naked in the backyard, to the astonishment of the neighbours, who were a proper lot. Brixton's changed, a good deal. These days, you could stage a three-point orgy in the garden and nobody would bat an eye except that bloke with the earring next door might pipe up, 'Got enough condoms?'

She didn't so much talk as elocute. She rhymed 'sky' with 'bay', and made 'mountaynes' out of 'molehills', except sometimes she forgot herself, the air turned blue. We'd been out in the market, once, stocking up on rabbit food – she'd a passion for salads, it went with all that naturism. During her strictest periods, she'd make us a meal of a cabbage, raw in summer, boiled in winter. There we were, picking over the greens, when some prim voice behind us, rudely referring to Grandma, opined: ' . . . no better than she oughter be . . .'

Grandma swung round, dukes up: 'What the fuck d'you mean?'

We never found out who set her up in Bard Road and she never volunteered the information of her own accord. She'd invented herself, she was a one-off and she kept her mystery intact until the end, although she left us everything, we owe her everything and the older we grow, the more like her we become. Triumph of nature over nurture, ducky. Only goes to show.

To this day I swear, sometimes, late at night, I hear a soft thump, thump, her bare feet on the stairs, coming down to make sure the gas is off in the kitchen, the front door is locked, us girls are safe home. And there's a smell of crushed mint that lingers in the breakfast room, sometimes, because her favourite tipple was crème de menthe frappé, with a sprig of mint, in season, but she'd drink whatever she could lay her hands on the rest of the time. And that boiled cabbage of hers. There's an aroma in the area we can't get rid of, no matter what we try. At first we thought it was the drains. We never touch cabbage, ourselves, not now we're grown up. I couldn't look a cabbage in the eye after what Grandma did to them. Boiled them to perdition. The abattoir is kinder to a cow.

She took to children like a duck to water, enough to make you wonder why she'd not had any of her own. I asked her about that, once, years later; she said she'd never, not until she picked us up and cuddled us that very first morning, known what men were *for*. 'I'd often wondered,' she said. 'When I saw you two, the penny dropped.'

You must remember that there was a war on, when we were born. If we made her happy, then we didn't add much to the collective sum of happiness in the whole of South London. First of all, the neighbours' sons went marching off, sent to their deaths, God help them. Then the husbands, the brothers, the cousins, until, in the end, all the men went except the ones with one foot in the grave and those still in the cradle, so there was a female city, red-eyed, dressed in black, outside the door, and Grandma said it then, she said it again in 1939: 'Every twenty years, it's bound to happen. It's to do with generations. The old men get so they can't stand the competition and they kill off all the young men they can lay their hands on. They daren't be seen to do it themselves, that would give the game away, the mothers wouldn't stand for it, so all the men all over the world get together and make a deal: you kill off our boys and we'll kill off yours. So that's that. Soon done. Then the old men can sleep easy in their beds, again.'

When the bombardments began, Grandma would go outside and shake her fist at the old men in the sky. She knew they hated women and children worst of all. She'd come back in and cuddle us. She lullabyed us, she fed us. She was our air-raid shelter; she was our entertainment; she was our breast.

The boarders dwindled off. Too much babyshit in the bathroom. Naked babies crawling in the hall. Nobody made the beds, nobody made the porridge – the help all found good jobs in the armaments factories, didn't they, much to Grandma's disgust. They would depart while she harangued them. What did Grandma do for money? The odd, and I mean 'odd', lady vocalist might rent a room for an hour, to practise her scales, or a not-too-fussy adagio dancer want to put her feet up for twenty minutes, ahem, ahem. Visitors used the front door, up the front steps; we went down the area steps to the door in the basement.

When we were just babbling our first 'g'anma', that clock turned up. The stag-topped grandfather. Shipped to us direct from Pitlochry, from the estate of Miss Euphemia Hazard, deceased, with a note to say that 49 Bard Road was the last known address of her nephew, Melchior, so they sent it here. She left it to him in her will. Everything else went to the poor.

Grandma cursed and swore when she read that. She couldn't bear to think that clock was all we'd get. She moved hell and high water to seek our father out. She left no stone unturned lest, as she told us later, she found him lurking underneath. Then, all of a sudden, it was the Armistice, and there he was, in the West End, playing Romeo, no less! so Grandma put on her toque and went to a matinée. Some acrobatic dancer who'd put up in the first-floor back while she was resting kept an eye on us while Granma was gone, she taught us back-flips, we were having a whale of a time until Grandma came back with a face like the wrath of God. 'You look like you need a cuppa,' said the acrobatic dancer so they adjourned and we went on back-flipping until we fancied a bit of bread and dripping, which is when, tripping into the breakfast room, we overheard our grandma. 'He flatly denies it and there's sod all I can do.' Neither Nora nor I could make head or tail of that, but both of them picked us up and hugged us. 'Poor little things!' And we got double rations, two slices each, and a bit of raspberry jam on it, too.

That acrobatic dancer upped and married a peer, in the end. It's a funny old world.

So life went on, as usual, until, one fine day that self-same year, just a few weeks later, came a knocking at the door.

Knock, knock; who's there? And off I stumped to answer it.

Knock, knock.

The knocker got a shock.

A naked child greeted the stranger. Not a scrap on but for the big, blue bow in my brown hair, and a black eyepatch. There was a big scimitar of silver paper in my hand and another child perched on the stairs, the spitting image, not so much a twin, more of an optical illusion, like as two peas except that *her* ribbon was green and she wore a red flag with the skull and crossbones on it knotted round her shoulders as a cloak. Both of us little girls stared at the newcomer with cold, round eyes: what have we here?

What an unwelcome! Such an unwelcome that he couldn't help but laugh.

Ooh, wasn't he a handsome young man, in those days. If I find myself describing him in the language of the pulp romance, then you must forgive me – there was always that quality about Perry, especially when he was glorious in his twenties, broad of shoulder, heavy of thigh, with his unruly thatch of burnished copper hair, the lavish spattering of freckles across his nose, laughing green eyes flecked with gold. He wore a scratched, weathered flying jacket with the shoulder flash of the US Flying Corps and his left arm was in a sling. It was our Uncle Peregrine from America but we didn't know him from Adam.

When he saw that he was hurting our feelings he smothered his laughter but there was still a delighted little quiver playing around his lips as he dropped down to his knees so that we were all three more equal in height to inspect his new-found nieces more thoroughly. He rummaged in his pocket and produced, not candy, nor pennies, but a pristine white handkerchief which he shook out and displayed to the girls: am I hiding anything?

We shook our heads. No. We could see that, like ourselves, he hid nothing.

He knotted the handkerchief and showed it to us again. A simple knot: nothing but a knot.

We inched closer to him, fascinated.

Ceremoniously he unknotted his handkerchief and, lo and behold! a white dove flew out, flew twice round the hall, then perched on top of the antlers on the grandfather clock, went: 'Voo, croo!' and, to the immense annoyance of our grandma, who just then ascended the basement staircase to find out what was going on, crapped on the carpet. Grandma had got her knickers on, thank God. Then we all went into the kitchen and drank tea and we little lady pirates sat on Peregrine Hazard's knee and ransacked his pockets in search of more doves, finding none, but a Fuller's walnut cake, instead, which Grandma accepted with wary politeness. Fuller's walnut cake has gone the way of all flesh, worse luck, I wouldn't mind a slice of Fuller's walnut cake right now. It turned out we were all very partial to Fuller's walnut cake so we had some slices of that and things eased up a bit, although Peregrine was thoroughly upset and embarrassed by the mission he'd undertaken out of a sense of duty to the brother he'd only just met again.

And not even so much out of a sense of duty to Melchior as to the dead ones, the grandparents.

Now, how had it come to pass that Peregrine Hazard, with a dove in his pocket, popped up in Brixton that glorious afternoon to make us all happy? Remember, you last saw him haring down the Great White Way out of the clutches of his Aunt Effie into –

Into what? That's a poser.

Over the years, Peregrine offered us a Chinese banquet of options as to what happened to him next. He gave us all his histories, we could choose which ones we wanted – but they kept on changing, so. That was the trouble. Did he really meet up with Ambrose Bierce in a flophouse in El Paso and go off with him to

31

fight in Mexico? (In confirmation of this, in *sole* confirmation, I'm bound to say, one personalised dedication in a copy of *The Devil's Dictionary*.) Was it true he'd posed as Ben Traven? I knew for a fact he'd worked in circuses. Unless it was on the halls. Or else he'd perfected his stage magic, his juggling and conjuring tricks, to entertain his fellow prospectors during the long winter evenings in Alaska. Above all, how did he grow so rich?

'That's easy,' he said and his face split in a big grin. 'I struck gold in Alaska.'

But he was a *very* good juggler. You couldn't deny him that. He told me once that W. C. Fields taught him how to juggle, but I'm not sure I believe that.

Grandma was pleased to see that such a handsome young man had got out of the clutches of the old men with only a flesh wound to show for it, i.e. shrapnel in the upper arm; it gave her hope for the continuance of the human race, she said. The more he and Grandma chewed the fat, the more they saw eye to eye until at last, all embarrassment, he told her the reason for his visit . . . it turned out that he'd volunteered to bear Grandma the glad tidings of Melchior's impending marriage.

Yes! Melchior was engaged to be married and wanted to pay us all off in case we made trouble at some future date.

'He's changed his tune,' said Grandma. 'I bearded the bastard in his den after a matinée of *Romeo* the other day; he was at a disadvantage, he'd only got his tights and some mascara on but he still denied paternity.'

'Between you and me,' confided Peregrine, 'I do believe he's afraid you'll show up at the wedding with the girls in tow.'

They roared. We kiddies didn't understand one word, of course, but we looked from one to the other and started laughing because they were laughing. 'Poor little innocents,' said Grandma. The pirates' father was joining high society – a grand wedding in St John's Smith Square, with twelve bridesmaids, and dukes present, and the bride in white by Worth, which is when we first heard the name, Lady Atalanta Lynde.

'The bride is loaded, ladies,' Perry assured us.

'Well,' said Mrs Chance, 'let him unload some of his ill-gotten gains on us.' Seeing Perry's dubious look: 'If you haven't got a ticket, you can't win, me old duck. Remember the Russian proverb: "Hope for the best, expect the worst".'

That was her motto. Ours, too.

But after all that, it was Peregrine himself who did the gentlemanly thing. That is, *his* name was on the cheques that now started to arrive the first of every month at Bard Road. When Grandma quizzed him, he went pink under his freckles and said, Melchior and he decided to give out that it was Peregrine who'd done the dirty deed, if anybody asked, and, begging her pardon, would she ever forgive him? but he'd used her name in vain. That is, Mrs Chance, our adoptive grandma and guardian, had gone down in the account books as our mother to keep the accountants happy. 'They've as good as married us!' she said. She laughed so much she fell off her chair.

But we little girls paid no attention; we crouched over Perry's latest gift, a phonograph, as, with the most exquisite care, Nora set down the needle on the wondrous black Bakelite pancake our Uncle Perry had told us would sing for us, if we wound up the handle. Hiss. Whirr. Then, thin, faint and as astonishing as if it were another of his tricks, out of the big horn came music – a trumpet, a trombone, a banjo, drums. A song, our song, a song that made us a promise our father never kept, though others did: 'I can't give you anything but love, baby.'

At the first bars, we couldn't help it, it was as if a voice told us to do it, we were impelled, we got up and danced. 'Dance,' I say, but we didn't know how – we jumped about in time and clapped our hands. Perry watched us for a bit, smiling, then said: 'Come on, girls, I'll show you the real thing.' He gave the gramophone another wind.

> I can't give you anything but love, baby,
> That's the only thing I've plenty of, baby . . .

Grandma calmed down a bit, he held his hand out. She'd still got the rudiments, stout though she was; the way she danced was the only clue to her past she ever gave. Then we were all dancing, right there, in the breakfast room, and, as for us, we haven't stopped dancing, yet, have we, Nora? We'll go on dancing till we drop.

Dream awhile, scheme awhile . . .

What a joy it is to dance and sing!

Perry gave us a lot more than love, in those days. He added another digit to his monthly cheque to pay for dancing lessons. He was a dutiful father. He doubled as sugar daddy, too. Every other Sunday, he arrived with parcels from Hamleys and Harrods and Selfridges, he'd pull red ribbons out of our ears and flags from his nostrils, he'd sit us on his knee and feed us Fuller's walnut cake and then he'd wind up the gramophone and we'd dance. After that, he and Grandma would have a couple of drinks and a few laughs; they were like conspirators.

But, pilgrim by name, pilgrim by nature, came the day the wanderlust seized him by the throat again. He must be up and off, he must be up and doing. He dropped off a crate of crème de menthe for Grandma, tap shoes for me and Nora. Then he was gone and left no forwarding address although the postcards came every month or so and every Christmas we'd get a hamper full of rotten fruit or a box of straw and shards that had been fine china when he packed it from places we could never find on the map. He never knew what would travel and that wouldn't.

But one last little gift arrived on its own two legs and announced itself, not with a knock on the front door but a humble little scrabble down the area, where the family went. When Grandma went to open up, there she was, a wee scrap of humanity thin as a lathe, busted shoes, no stockings, just a shawl around her shoulders and a man's cap on her head. She'd have been fourteen, then. She thrust forth a scrap of paper and there was our address, in Perry's hand.

'He said you'd give us a job,' she said. 'Help look after the kids, or something. He said you'd give us a roof.'

'I wasn't planning on running a hostel for fallen women,' said Grandma in a huff. It was pissing down with rain, Our Cyn was soaked.

'I haven't fallen yet,' said Our Cyn. 'But I *might*.'

Once she got her feet under the table, she never took them out again. One of the fixtures and fittings. She was a breath of fresh air. If Grandma lingered too long down the local and forgot to grate the evening carrots, Cyn would do us a couple of lamb chops, a bit of liver and bacon. Forbidden fruit! Delish. Her kids were in and out all the time after she married that cabby, the second generation to call our grandma 'Grandma'. It was Cyn's eldest, Mavis, who got off with a GI which resulted in our Brenda, whom we took care of when she had *her* bit of trouble and brought home our precious little Tiffany, the first Black in the family.

'Family,' I say. Grandma invented this family. She put it together out of whatever came to hand — a stray pair of orphaned babes, a ragamuffin in a flat cap. She created it by sheer force of personality. I only wish she'd lived to see our little Tiffany. There is a persistent history of absent fathers in our family, although Tiffany *did* get a daddy of her own, in the end, because Brenda married this ex-boxer, after all that. Light-heavyweight. Strict Baptist. They live round the corner, Acre Lane. Brenda's a pillar of the community, now, you'd never think her first fellow was here today and gone tomorrow.

Tiffany. So pretty! I never saw such a pretty baby. 'Born for the stage,' I said to Nora. We took her on, ballet and tap, from the age of three. We used to run a little school, in those days, the Brixton Academy of Dance. In the ground-floor front. Our Bren would bang away at the piano; she played the harmonium in church, too. We'd roll back the carpet. It's quite a lovely room, the ground-floor front — big, with a bay. We'd done it up in a Thames green Regency-stripe wallpaper. We put in a big mirror. The little girls laboured with sweat moustaches on their upper lips. One, two, three. The cats kept out in the garden, well away. One, two, three. Not good enough for Tiffany, though, not when she got to nine, ten, eleven. She wanted to do disco and funk, that kind of thing. Greek to us, of course. After our time.

She moved out into a flat with some other girls. After that, she blossomed out. She'd still come back to see her old aunties whenever she got a moment, wearing black leather and red eye-shadow and hairpieces down to her bum and God knows what.

Her dad wouldn't let her into the house done up like that, he's a lay preacher, so she'd stop off at our place from the club where she was working, wash off her make-up, slip on flatties and a nice frock she kept in the spare room.

Correction: *one* of the spare rooms. This house is nothing but spare rooms, these days. Wheelchair lives in the front basement, so that she can roll her appliance in and out of the breakfast room and get to the downstairs lavvy on her own. Nor' and I take up an attic apiece. The rest is old clothes, dust, newspapers stacked in piles tied up with string, cuttings, old photographs.

The rest is silence.

So Tiffany dropped in one fine day and who did she find taking tea with her aunties but a handsome young man she'd never seen before and who came as a bit of a shock to Nora and me, too, because he was the first Hazard child who'd ever come to visit us.

And no sooner did poor little Tiff set eyes on him than she fell.

Tristram. His twin brother is called Gareth. Bloody silly Celtic names. The other one, that Gareth, is a Jesuit, he converted in his teens. Then he went off to be a missionary, or so his Old Nanny told us. His Old Nanny drops round from time to time, friend of the family, it's a complicated connection – she used to be Wheelchair's Old Nanny, back in the Dark Ages, before the Flood. Then she was Wheelchair's daughter's Old Nanny. Then Tristram and Gareth's Old Nanny. She is, you might say, the Hazard family's generic Old Nanny. Indestructible old girl. We rely on her for gossip, to tell the truth. Old Nanny told us how Gareth went off to the jungle, it must have been ten years ago. He's probably been barbecued long ago, or had his head shrunk by the Jivaro.

Gareth and Tristram, the priest and the game-show presenter. Not so different, really, I suppose. Both of them in show business. Both, in their different ways, carrying on the great tradition of the Hazard family – the willing suspension of disbelief. Both of them promise you a free gift if you play the game.

Tristram and Gareth, the offspring of our father's third wife. Let me recapitulate. Number One: Lady Atalanta Hazard, née Lynde (a.k.a. 'Wheelchair'). Number Two: Miss Delia Delaney, of Hollywood, USA (a.k.a. Daisy Duck). Number Three: the girl who, once upon a time, played Cordelia to our father's Lear; marrying your Cordelia, evidently something of a Hazard family tradition. She was just twenty-one years old, in those days, and fresh out of RADA, where she had been, oh! the betrayals of youth! Melchior's own daughter, Saskia's, best friend. As for Melchior, he was old enough to draw his pension, already, and freshly knighted, for his 'services to the theatre', so at least he made a lady of her but she and Saskia never spoke again from that day to this, although Old Nanny, she's an indefatigable gossip, told us Saskia turned up at the boys' christening like the wicked fairy in *Sleeping Beauty*, balefully eyeing the plump little bundled twins, perhaps already laying out her wicked plans for the future.

Numero Tre, however, had her own plans for the future. She was a forward-looking woman. She looked ahead and she saw – television! In those days, all everybody else saw was a little grey rectangle the size of a cornflakes packet, with vague forms flickering across it, like Trafalgar Square in a peasouper. Who would have thought that little box of shadows would put us all out of business, singers, dancers, acrobats, Shakespearians, the lot? But Melchior's third wife planned for the late twentieth century. She put the entire family on camera. They prospered.

Or perhaps it was a case of, needs must. Melchior was starting to muff his lines, trip over his sword, muddle up his business so you could hardly tell his Brutus from his Antony; old age was creeping up behind him and now he started to cash in on his own fame. He deeply mined the rich new seam that opened up before him – old buffers in pipe tobacco, vintage port and miniature cigar commercials. You started to associate his face – and though I take the piss out of him from time to time, all the same I have to thank him for bequeathing me the good old Hazard bones that improve like fine wine with age – with the music of Elgar.

His clever young wife gave up her own career to devote herself to her two wonderful sons but she often found time to pop up on the box, too, touting pan-scrubbers, washing-up liquid, toilet paper ... 'The Royal Family of the theatre gives its seal of approval.' Her *pièce de résistance* was a turn in a long yellow frock with a ruff, standing on a rampart, gazing sternly at a half-pound pack on a dish before her: 'To butter or not to butter . . .' My Lady Margarine. She also did celebrity guest appearances and bazaar openings at negotiable fees. She reached middle-age quicker than any woman I ever knew.

Not that I *knew* her, exactly, but we read the papers, we kept in touch. After all, the Hazards belonged to everyone. They were a national treasure.

In the fullness of time, the older stepchildren took to television, too. Saskia, my half-sister and *bête noire*, started that cookery series; now she's the TV chef *par excellence*. Imogen, the other one, developed a unique line as a goldfish. I kid you not. It was a series for the kiddies, set in an aquarium, about this carp called Goldie. It's run for twenty years, now, carp live a long time. Sometimes I don't understand the English.

Apart from catching the odd glimpse if we mistuned the set, we never saw hair nor hide of any of the Hazards, except in the papers. Ever since his doomed production of *A Midsummer Night's Dream*, Melchior's one and only stab at the movies, he steered clear of us because he only had us in the film for mascots and look what a debacle that turned out to be! We've sat at the same table with him only the one time since World War II, and that encounter ended in tears, too. As for My Lady Margarine, she never fancied breaking bread with her husband's by-blows, especially since those by-blows were old enough to be mother to *her*. But we read in the papers how the boys went to Bedales, from whence Tristram was expelled for tippling and fornication, although Gareth, not.

What a rustling of the tabloids when Tristram was expelled! Wheelchair cackled with glee. Little Tris, busted for pot in '68, in a satin vest and velvet knickers. Titian ringlets. He danced naked on the stage in *Hair*. In '76, he crashed his first Lotus Elan whilst under the influence, wearing (ever the snappy dresser) his hair in spikes and tartan bondage trousers. Ooh, he was a naughty boy and how his mother worried. Never off the gossip pages, always in the papers, sex and drugs and rock-and-roll.

Gareth, no.

It must have been My Lady Margarine got Tristram the job on

the telly. She must have been at her wits' end. Unless it was that Saskia, the conniving bitch. The first time he came to see us, a couple of years ago, it was before his first major investment in gents' natty suiting, he was still at the jeans-with-necktie stage, just an assistant producer, and he wanted us, or so he said, for a chat show.

'Gawd,' said Nora. Though it was not yet the time we usually dressed, she'd slipped on a frock because he'd come on business, and had muzzed up her hair a bit. She looked quite debauched. 'We're as old as the hills and still you want us to show a bit of leg!'

'I'm proud of my aunts,' said Tristram. 'When Saskia told me the legendary Chance sisters were my very own aunts, I was over the moon.'

'Aunts', see? That Saskia! We raised our eyebrows at each other but we held our peace. He's got charm, I must say. A slippery kind of charm. I could tell Nora was almost taken with the idea, she was tapping her front teeth with her fingernail in the way she has. We could have done with a bob or two, at that juncture, too. But the very thought of us two aged ladies performing a geriatric Charleston for the delight of the viewers made me nauseous and if Saskia had anything to do with it, I smelled a rat.

Then Tiffany came in. She's got her own key, she can come and go. No knock. The door opened. There she was.

What an entrance! She looked like a proper harlot, poor little thing, in her fishnets and her leather mini. Bren and Leroy always overprotected her. Nothing was too good for her. First kid in the school to have a personal stereo. 'You just wait until she kicks over the traces!' we always said. Only a virgin would have worn a skirt like that. Never a sweeter or more innocent girl than our Tiffany, even though she didn't know enough not to flash her tits all over the papers. 'Six feet two of lithe, coffee-coloured loveliness,' said the caption on page three. She never dared tell her father but he won't have *The Sun* in the house on principle, fortunately. The sweetest girl in London, but naïve.

Tristram knocked over his chair as he got up when she came in. He was all of a dither and no wonder. Wheelchair was widely touted as 'the most beautiful woman in England' in her day but she never held a candle to our Tiffany, she says so herself.

The chat show never came off because he was offered the game show the week after on the other channel, so he took that. And he took Tiffany, too. He took her home to his flat, in a warehouse in Bermondsey, above a wine bar, and he bought her a beaded gown, and there she was, every week, with her five-year-old's smile, offering the entire viewing public a peek down her cleavage while she sang out: 'Yessir! Lashings of Lolly!' with a ringing conviction that could only have been born out of true love.

Because she fell for him, head over heels. Her dad fumed and cursed when she went home to pick up her spare underwear; she came round to our place, she wept. Brenda nipped round on the q.t., gave her a big hug. 'I love him, Mum.' 'Aunty Dora, I love him.' 'I love him, Aunty Nora.'

The three of us looked at each other sadly. We'd well nigh two centuries' experience of love, between us, and the omens were not good. She sat knuckling her eyes, getting mascara everywhere. She'd got it bad and Tristram wasn't worth the paper she wiped her bum with. So we prepared ourselves for heartbreak, but the organ was proving a touch more resilient than we'd feared. No sign of shipwreck, yet.

Mind you, we hardly ever saw her, these days. She'd swanned down in a cab at Christmas with a bottle of gin tied up in red ribbon, printed a lipstick heart on our cheeks, left a big package for her mum and buggered off out again to some soirée or other. She was always good to her mother, mind, though Bren had to keep all the prezzies at our house so Leroy wouldn't lay eyes on the wages of sin. Easter, she brought us some daffs.

But Nora and I know what hoops the kept woman has to jump to work her passage and our little Tiff had looked very haggard and wan last time we saw her and kept excusing herself to go to the bathroom, too.

Press the button for 'Play'.

'Lashings of Lolly!' cried Tristram Hazard, live from London in a special birthday tribute to his famous father. If, God help you, you've seen the rotten show before, you'll know this is the moment when Tristram introduces the lovely Tiffany. She shimmers forward in her beaded gown, smiling like a good child on its birthday, and she adds her sweet little husky voice to his: 'Yessir! Lashings of Lolly!'

But where is the lovely Tiffany tonight? Nowhere to be seen, although Tristram gives an expectant look towards the neon staircase down which she usually descends. No bloody Tiffany, and we're going out live, too!

Still, consummate pro that he is, he doesn't miss a beat.

'And I'd like you to give a very special "Lashings of Lolly" hi, there! to a truly grand old gentleman, to – Mr British Theatre, himself.' His voice dropped a tone; he adopted a plummy smile and made a half-bow, half-curtsey, a sort of unisex obeisance. 'My father . . . Sir Melchior Hazard.'

Radiant, he swung round, open-armed: 'Hi, there, Dad!'

Roars of applause as My Lady Margarine, the face that launched a thousand pot-scourers, assisted the old man to the microphone. We felt the queasiest mixture of emotions – at seeing him in flesh and blood, after so long, in the first place; at seeing him make a fool of himself like this, in the second place; and in the third place, seeing him so silver-haired and shaky, too. But Wheelchair wasn't so complicated. She perked right up, and said:

'Well, well, well! He's awfully well preserved, I must say! He looks quite *pickled*!'

If you haven't seen Tristram's bastard show, it goes like this: there in the studio, which is all done up with neon palm trees for the occasion, there's this big wheel, like a roulette wheel, or a blackjack wheel, only bigger, all over lightbulbs, with a neon arrow in the middle. This is how you play the game: you say a number and Tiffany gives the wheel a twirl. Round and round goes the bloody great wheel, pardon me, vicar, and if it stops when the arrow points to the number you've chosen, they give you half a grand. That's the first round.

Second round: double your money, triple it, quadruple it or lose it altogether, depending upon where the arrow comes to rest. Simplicity itself. It's all about greed. The camera lingers on the faces in the audience, their eyes are popping out, they're drooling and slobbering. Money! Money for nothing! A win on Tristram Hazard's Lashings of Lolly, almost as good as a Civil List pension.

Tristram starts up this slow chant as the wheel goes round; they all begin to clap their hands. 'LASHINGS OF LOLLY!'

Every time I catch a glimpse, I think I've gone mad.

Now Tristram says to his father: 'Are you ready to play Lotsa Birthday Lolly, Dad?'

The old man gives a blink and looks round, as if he's just woken up, doesn't know where he is, startled by the lights. He might be just about to cry. God knows why he's humiliating himself. Is it for his boy's sake, to help out with Tristram's pathetic career? Or just to give his ancient face another airing before the grave? Or . . . is he down on his luck at last, does he need the money?

Funny. I never thought of that.

Our father gathers himself together and gives us, in full measure, that wonderful old smile that goes right to the back row of the gallery, goes down to the depths of the vitals.

Our father smiles and says: 'I'm ready.'

But where is Tiffany, in her purple sequin boob tube?

Tiffany is not.

Remember, all this is going out live, isn't it, so Tris is in a nasty spot. You can see the panic in his eyes.

And then a change comes over the invisible audience, the only evidence of whose existence we've had so far the odd cough and titter, some patters of applause. But now there is an audible shiver. They can see something that we can't, and it bewilders them. An uneasy silence falls. And then is broken.

I never knew our Tiff could sing. Sweet and true. La, la, la. And still you couldn't see her, only hear her song, her wordless song that didn't seem to have an end nor a beginning, that created the silence in which you heard it, so that an awed hush spread like ripples in a pond around that unearthly singing.

Tristram turns his head towards the sound; there is a close-up, in which we see he looks aghast.

Why didn't they kill the transmission then and there? It turns out that one of the cameramen was sweet on Tiffany, thought Tristram, the legover champion of the commercial channels, treated the poor kid like shit. Which Tristram did. But, what have you, he's a feller and I doubt this chivalrous cameraman would have done any better by her, over a period of time. Anyway, this cameraman wouldn't let them pull the plug and he it was who now swung his lens round on to Tiffany herself as she stood at the top of the flight of neon steps.

She was a spectacle to move the hardest heart, I must say. She didn't have her make-up on, she hadn't done her hair and she wore a pair of grey satin French knickers with real lace inserts, purple stilettos and one of those American footballer's shirts with numbers on it – it was purple, too, but with a giant size 69 in red. Tristram put it in her stocking for a joke, last Christmas. Shows what he thought of her, really.

There was a bit of wallflower stuck in her hair, over her ear, and her hands were full of flowers, daffs, bluebells, narcissi, she must have picked them out of the front gardens and the window boxes and the public parks that she'd passed by on her way to the studio during that long walk from Bermondsey.

She wobbled something chronic on those purple shoes, she'd turned the heels right over on the way and now she kicked them off. One, two. She scored a palpable hit with the second one, though I don't think she'd intended to, it got Tristram on the shin. (The real Tristram, sitting here beside his aunties in the flesh, let out a short, sharp cry in unison with himself on the screen, which made the cat on his lap leap up and hump off.)

When Tristram cried out, that attracted her attention and her big, brown eyes fixed on him with some kind of recognition, though only in the vaguest way, as if she were remembering a dream, not a very pleasant dream, but not a nightmare. A sad dream, not a bad dream.

The audience hadn't the faintest what was going on and shuffled and tittered a bit, half trying to convince itself that this distraught girl was just another part of the action and would do something funny, shortly; or else take off her football shirt and give them all a treat. But she just went on singing. La, la, la.

Then, slowly, slowly, keeping her eyes fixed on Tristram – he kept quite still, as if she'd mesmerised him – she started down the staircase.

If Nora and I had a pound for every staircase we'd descended in our lives as showgirls, we'd be rolling in it.

But Tiffany never came down that staircase like a star, poor kid. She wobbled so much on each step I was sure she'd fall and I leaned forward to the screen so that I could reach out and catch her if she tumbled, I was so caught up in it. Nora was crying her eyes out already and even old Wheelchair was sniffing away, reaching up her sleeve for her hankie. But, though my eyes were misting over, too, I saw the hang of our Tiff's shirt, remembered how she'd spent her last visit with us in the toilet, and put two and two together.

'You've put her in the club, Tristram!' I couldn't hold it back, I came right out with it.

Nora turned the tap off sharpish, stopped crying in a flash and pressed the Standby button so the screen froze on our lovely Tiff in mid-teeter.

'What's that? A little baby?'

'I'm not ready to be a father,' said Tristram. 'I can't take the responsibility. I'm not mature enough.'

'No man ever is,' announced Wheelchair, in her grande dame voice.

We all three glowered at him. He cowered.

'Aunties,' he said. 'Forgive me.'

'It's not for us to do the forgiving,' said Nora. 'It's up to that sweet, innocent child and how you make amends to her if she can ever see it in her heart to forgive you. And you'd better make your bloody amends pronto before her father finds out you wouldn't do the right thing or your days of close-ups are numbered. Not to mention your days of breathing. Now let's see what foul thing you did next.'

With that, she smartly pushed the Play button and shut him up.

I can't say if Tiffany *knew* it was Tristram down there at the bottom of the staircase or if she didn't know him at all; whether he seemed familiar from some scarcely remembered time before

her heart broke, or if his face seemed to her a new face that reminded her, just a little bit, of somebody else's face. Somebody
dead and gone. But down the stairs she came towards him, without a smile, flowers in her hair, half-naked on her poor, bare,
shaky feet.

Such pretty feet she always had, long, but perfectly formed,
and pretty little piggies, nicely gradated, not like those long,
root-like toes some people have. Her bare, pretty feet tracked
blood behind her; she'd rubbed her heels raw on her purple stilettos. Fancy walking all the way from Bermondsey in those
heels!

Tristram looked as though he was propping old Melchior up,
now, unless it was Melchior holding up his son; each clutched
the other like drowning men at spars. Tristram's career in pieces!
His old man's birthday tribute ruined! The flower-like child he'd
violated turning up to shame him, mad as a hatter in front of an
audience of millions! Was there no end to his troubles?

She reached up behind her ear, fished out the bit of wallflower
and offered it to Tristram. He, not knowing what to do with it,
sniffed at it. That made her smile. He tried to give it back to her
but she wasn't having any.

'Wallflower,' she said. 'You know what they say about wallflowers – many are called but few are chosen.'

All this while, there's the uneasy shuffling of the studio audience and every now and then some minion would dash across
the set on a frenzied bid to stop the whole business in its tracks.
But on it all went, and on, and on, and on.

'Here,' she says. 'Cop hold.'

Now she thrusts her battered little spring posy at Tristram,
retaining for herself the one daffodil, which she holds to her
mouth as if it were the mouthpiece of one of those sit-up-and-beg
telephones we used to have, years ago. Hello, hello? Then she
holds it to her ear. Nobody at home. And offers that flower to
Tristram, too, with such a sad smile – a smile that changes when
she looks at it again and notes that it is not, in fact, a telephone
at all, to a pale giggle.

'Daffy dill, daffy dilly,' she said. And once more broke into
song, but one with words, this time.

45

Oh, my little sister, Lily, is a whore in Piccadilly,
And my mother is another in the Strand –

I thought: That's it! They'll fade her now, for sure! But still
and still and still they didn't, not even when, now she'd got rid
of her flowers, she cried out suddenly:

'Off with it! You only lent it to me! Nothing was mine, not
ever!'

And stripped off her Number 69 shirt, threw it to the floor and
trampled on it. It was a shock to see her breasts under the cruel
lights – long, heavy breasts, with big dark nipples, real breasts,
not like the ones she'd shown off like borrowed finery to the
glamour lenses. This was flesh, you could see that it would bleed,
you could see how it fed babies.

Then Melchior did something wonderful. Who'd have thought
the old man had it in him? Suddenly, Melchior is in shot, holding
out a blond mink stole which he must have plucked off the very
shoulders of his wife. He put his hand on her bare shoulder and
said, 'Pretty, pretty lady.'

Perhaps it was his tone of voice attracted her attention, that of
a man selling old-fashioned rich black treacle toffee. When she
turned towards him, he draped the stole round her shoulders, he
covered her up.

Then My Lady Margarine stepped in, too. They'd been keeping her on the sidelines, the while, so that she could come in at
the end and take charge of the cheque lest her better half did
something senile with it. She's in good nick, I must say; lots of
exercise does it, and the odd nip and tuck helps. Her cheeks give
the game away; they've got that tight, full, shiny chipmunk look
that spells out: facelift. You can always tell. Nevertheless, good
nick. She was a brunette at her wedding, but had gone blonde
with age, evidently, and now sported a pale gold chignon. She's
crying, too, possibly for the loss of her mink stole but, be fair,
more likely as a tribute to the moment. If My Lady Margarine
gave up the stage for the sake of her family thirty-five years ago,
she must have always regretted it in a tiny corner of her heart for
when Fate offered her another chance out of the blue she grabbed
it with both hands.

'Oh, my dear,' she said to Tiffany. 'We wanted him to marry you so much. I begged him, I implored him.'

That brought Tristram out of his daze with a start, as if this was the first *he'd* heard of it. But Tiffany didn't register, didn't seem to hear. She was still shivering, in spite of the mink, but when she stroked her cheek against the fur, that made her smile, so lovely, so touching, she smiled that good child's birthday smile and it was as if the touch of the fur gave her some of the strength of the animal, she came back together, again. She seemed to grow stronger before our very eyes; she didn't come back to herself, exactly, but to somebody else who was in perfect control. She called out to an unseen presence off the set in a big, ringing voice: 'Hey! Somebody call me a cab, right? A cab! Right away!'

Then she turned towards the camera, as she did every week. The cameraman who was in love with her zoomed in as she tossed one end of the mink stole over her shoulder in a devil-may-care way, as if anything could happen, now, and she gave the viewers the full force of her big smile, the professional one that offered a view of her hundred-octane teeth as far back as the emerging wisdoms. She raised her hand. She waved.

'Goodnight, everybody!' Signing off, as she always did: 'Sleep tight, don't let the bedbugs bite! Goodnight!'

Then, in mid-wave, this new, strong, defiant person with Tiffany's face covered her mouth with her hand as if she were going to be sick, her face crumpled, she bolted off the set in the mink stole and the silk knickers and there they were, the Hazards, all three, left gaping like loons.

Tristram came to himself first, although his hands were still full of flowers. But he remembered the camera was watching him and even managed to scrape up a smile.

'And goodnight, too, from me, Tristram Hazard, and my very special hundredth birthday guest, Sir Melchior Hazard –'

The good old goodbye formula. It reassured the studio audience. One or two of them started to clap, as if by doing that they could change what they had seen into what they ought to have seen.

'– and his Lady –'

More applause.

47

'– my very own extra special Dad and Mum –'

Applause doubled, trebled.

'– and come and watch the lucky people win Lotsa Lolly! again, next week!'

Roars. Applause. Up came the credits over the three of them bravely waving farewells to the invisible punters. Nora rose up with some ceremony and killed the tape. The set crackled. Then there was silence.

'I thought Tiff might be here,' said Tristram after a bit, snuffling and wiping his eyes with the back of his hand. 'We've looked everywhere else.'

'Why didn't you come here first of all, then?'

'God, such a terrible night . . . The police. The casualty wards. We searched the night shelters.'

'Who are this "we"?' enquired Nora sharply.

'Finally, well, I just passed out,' said Tristram. 'I couldn't cope any more. She took me back to her place.'

'Who,' I asked, more sharply still, 'is this "she"?'

As if we didn't know. He was too scared to say out loud or else he wanted to keep it from Wheelchair. Then, again, he'd never shown any consideration for her sensibilities in the past; why did he want to start now? But Nora leaned forward and, with her long, lean fingertips, delicately plucked from his lapel one single hair, as red as his own hair but very, very much longer. She held it high, she let it dangle, proof positive that last night of all nights he'd spent with –

And that is the single, most unmentionable secret in this entire family's bulging closetful of skeletons, that ever since he was little, Tristram and Saskia, although she is his half-sister and old enough to be his mother, in fact, his mother's best friend, once upon a time . . . I thought our Tiff had weaned him off the nipple, but here was the evidence to prove the contrary.

'Like a dog,' said Nora, sneering at the hair, 'returning to its own vomit.'

'Oh, God!' said Tristram. 'Try to be a little understanding. Tiffany had vanished clean away, I was half mad with fear –'

The area door slammed, such a bang the back windows

shuddered. Came heavy footsteps down the passage. We harkened. Brenda always let herself in.

'I suppose,' said Nora with heavy irony, for she knew swift retribution was at hand, 'it never occurred to you to ask at her mother's, did it?'

The kitchen door burst open. You could tell by the look on her face that she had seen his Porsche outside. She'd been a real slip of a thing, when she was a girl, but she'd put on a lot of weight after the kids, now she could give Leroy a pound or two, and strong as a horse, with it. She still had her rollers in, her carpet slippers on, but she was past grief, white with rage.

At least Tristram was spared the task of telling Brenda, the police had done that already. Leroy tried Tristram in his absence and found grounds for a verdict of justifiable homicide. When Bren told him that: 'If her Dad gets his hands on you . . .' she aimed a big whack at him and I thought I'd slip outside and put the kettle on, leave them to get on with it.

All of a sudden, I felt my age. If the youngest goes before you . . .

There's a photo of Evelyn Laye on the wall above the tea caddy. 'To twenty twinkling toes, with loads of love.' I thought of Tiffany, 'this little piggy goes to market'. And her feet, leaving blood behind them as she came down the staircase. She'd have made a cracking dancer, if she'd put her mind to it.

Then my heart felt as if a hand had squeezed it because I'd thought of our darling Tiffany in the past tense, hadn't I?

Little Tiff.

Nora came out into the scullery and slipped her arm through mine. We watched the kettle bounce and hiss on the gas and listened to the sounds of fracas coming from the breakfast room. Smash! There goes a plate. The cats trampled themselves underfoot as they streaked out of the cat door. 'Not good enough, was she!' Muffled cry of pain from Tristram. 'Treat her like dirt, did you! Well, see where it gets you!' Then the telephone rang. I looked at Nora. She shut her eyes. We knew that ring meant bad news.

We took the tea in. Wheelchair was dealing with the telephone because the others hadn't noticed it, in the heat of battle —

Tristram, black eye, bloody nose, ripped jacket, torn shirt and it looked as if she'd tried to throttle him with his necktie but that was the worst of the damage, he was still conscious. The breakfast things had been trashed in the course of the tussle, bacon fat everywhere, but Brenda was spent, her hands hung limp, she was whimpering. 'In her knickers, on the telly, in front of all those people, singing dirty songs. Her dad was watching everything. I can't ever forgive you. Never.' Wheelchair put the telephone down. One look at her face told us the worst.

'That was the police, dear,' she said to Brenda. You've got to hand it to the old girl, she's got the manner pat, cool but not cold, sympathetic without slobbering. 'Do sit down. I'm afraid it's bad news.'

Brenda did not sit down, as if she thought that if she did, she'd never summon the heart to get up again; she hung onto the chair like grim death, making little noises in the back of her throat.

'They found the body of a young girl in the river, this morning.'

There was a whoosh of rubber tyres as Wheelchair made a compassionate swoop upon Brenda, put her arms around as much of her lower torso as she could grapple. Ever the lady social worker.

'Poor darling, prepare yourself. It's something very terrible.'

In the war, in the mornings after air raids, you saw people look like Brenda looked, just then.

'She hasn't got a face left, Brenda. Evidently a police launch, the propellers –'

I remember that thin, high scream from the war, too.

Then she pulled herself together and had a cup of hot, sweet tea, which you give them for shock although she didn't seem to notice drinking it and she and Tristram went off to the morgue in his Porsche. No point in rowing with him, now, was there? All he could say was: 'I'm most frightfully sorry.' He kept saying it over and over again. I'd have clocked him one for that, alone, if I'd been Brenda, but I don't think the poor girl could so much as see him, now, couldn't hear him, could think of nothing but our Tiff in the cold store drowned dead with the baby inside her drowned dead, too.

Wheelchair made her excuses and wheeled off into the basement front and after a while her gramophone started up, she's got her own in there, there'd be bloodshed if we had to share. She'd put on a bit of funeral music, classical stuff, lugubrious, a big, brown, lugubrious voice: 'What is life for me without thee?'

She's overdoing it, a bit. I thought. She didn't know Tiff *that* well. And I wish she could have picked a less affecting song.

What is life for me without thee?
What is left if thou art gone?'

Nora lifted off the lid of the teapot and poured in a tot of rum.

'That'll set us up.'

'D'you think we ought to ring up Saskia and tell her where her boyfriend's gone?'

'We haven't spoken to Saskia for forty years, don't see why we should start now. Let her stew in her own juice. It's all her bloody fault, anyway. If she hadn't got her claws into Tristram . . .'

The singer on Wheelchair's gramophone reprised the query, what would be left; then she sang: 'Eurydice . . .' The saddest sound. 'Eurydice!'

Nora made a dismissing gesture and fell silent. We left the clearing away till after dinner, we put our feet up. Grey skies. Still that big wind, banging away outside. To think, this morning, I thought that wind would blow us an adventure, it wouldn't matter what. Now look what it had blown us! Rain came in gusts over the garden, buffeting the forsythia. Forsythia, the exact colour of peroxide blond. Whenever I see forsythia, I think of Grandma.

'He's left his cassette behind,' said Nora. 'Worth a bit, I should think.'

But she didn't sound too keen. Our blackmailing days are long gone.

'Do you think they'll cancel the party?'

'Oh, no,' said Nora. 'I mean, she wasn't really family, was she? Only in the family way.'

We put more rum in the tea. After all, it *was* our birthday.

'What about us? Are we still going to the party?'

'Life must go on,' said Nora, all of a sudden full of life. 'I wouldn't miss it for a hundred million pounds.'

Two

ONE, two, three, hop! See me dance the polka. Once upon a time, there was an old woman in splitting black satin pounding away at an upright piano in a room over a haberdasher's shop in Clapham High Street and her daughter in a pink tutu and wrinkled tights slapped at your ankles with a cane if you didn't pick up your feet high enough. Once a week, every Saturday morning, Grandma Chance would wash us, brush us and do up our hair in sausage curls. We had long, brown stockings strung up to our liberty bodices by suspenders. Grandma Chance would take firm hold of one hand of each of us, then – ho! for the dancing class; off we'd trot to catch the tram.

We always took the tram from Brixton to Clapham High Street. The stately progress of the tram, occupying by right of bulk and majesty the centre of the road, not veering to the left nor right upon its way but sometimes swaying every now and then with a sickening lurch, like Grandma, coming home from the pub.

One, two, three, hop.

Big mirrors blooming like plums with dust along the walls. I can see us now, in our vests and knickers and our little pink dancing slippers, dipping a curtsey to our reflections. Grandma sat by the door with her bag in her lap, squinting at us between the spots on her veil. She looked grieving, as if she was scared we might sprain ourselves, but this was because she was sucking on a Fox's glacier mint. Everything smelled of sweat and gas fire. The old woman thumped the piano and Miss Worthington in her droopy tutu showed us how to *fouetté*, poor thing, sixty if she was a day.

One, two, three, hop! See us cover the ground.

We did our exercises at the barre. Nora's bum in her navy-blue bloomers jiggled away in front of me like two hard-boiled eggs in a handkerchief. We'd turn around, then she could feast her eyes on mine. Outside, a tram went by with a whirr and a click, knocking out sparks from the overhead cables.

To tell the truth, we lived for that dancing class. We thought that was what the week was for, for Saturday mornings.

Then we were seven.

There was a cake with seven candles in the larder iced up to the eyebrows, its stunning pink and white beauty marred only by one little fingerprint – Nora, unable to resist. It sat in state in the larder, awaiting our return from our birthday treat, our first matinée. Our Cyn waved us off. We had our best coats on, green tweed, quite hairy, with velvet collars so the tweed didn't scratch our necks, and little hats to match. Grandma dressed us like princesses. We always had glacé kid gloves, for best.

Grandma lashed out, she got us seats in the stalls. It was almost too much for me and Nora. We were mute with ecstasy. The plaster cherubs lifting aloft gilt swags and crystal candelabra on the walls; the red plush; the floral and pastel silks of the afternoon frocks of the ladies in the stalls, from whom mingled odours of talc and scent and toilet soap arose; and the wonderful curtain that hung between us and pleasure, the curtain that, in a delicious agony of anticipation, we knew would soon rise and then and then . . . what wonderful secrets would be revealed to us, then?

'You just wait and see,' said Grandma.

The lights went down, the bottom of the curtain glowed. I loved it and have always loved it best of all, the moment when the lights go down, the curtain glows, you know that something wonderful is going to happen. It doesn't matter if what happens next spoils everything; the anticipation itself is always pure.

To travel hopefully is better than to arrive, as Uncle Perry used to say. I always preferred foreplay, too.

Well. Not *always*.

When the lights went down and the curtain glowed that first time of all, Nora and I gave one another a look. Our little hearts went pit-a-pat.

Up went the curtain; there were Fred and Adèle, evicted, out on the street with all their bits and pieces. She set out the chairs, she straightened the sofa, she hung a sign on the lamppost: 'Bless this house'. We thought that we would die of pleasure. We clung on to one another's hands like grim death, we thought we might wake up and find out we had been dreaming. Nora liked Adèle best; she liked it when she dressed up like a Mexican widow and did her Spanish dance, but it was old Fred for me, then and for ever, with his funny little nutcracker face and the Eton crop that looked painted on, it shone, so, and not a hair ever moved. Who'd have thought we'd be on 'Hi, Fred,' 'Hi, girls' terms when we grew up?

God knows what sixth sense made Grandma pick out *Lady Be Good* for our seventh birthday treat. 'I was looking for a nayce musical comedy,' she said, 'but nothing with that Jessie Matthews in it.' She thought Jessie Matthews was common although *I* always found her a perfect lady. But *Lady Be Good* showed us the way. It was the Damascus road for us. We spent hours, at home, afterwards, in the ground-floor front, rolling back the rug, getting the numbers off pat. That finale, she in her Tyrolean costume, him like a sailor doll. We took it in turns to be the lady.

'You've got stars in your eyes, girls,' said Grandma in the interval.

Then tea on a tray arrived, no expense spared. Hotel silver service, cucumber sandwiches. Grandma rolled her veil up over her nose and slipped an iced fancy in between her magenta lips. Even in those days, we always felt defiant of the world when we went out with Grandma, we knew she looked a bit of a funniosity. Just as we were brushing off the crumbs came something of a commotion in the dress circle. Grandma was handing the tray back to the waitress when she froze, the way a dog does when it sees a rabbit. The girl caught hold of the tea-things just in time; Grandma rose up and raised her hand, she pointed.

If you'd drawn a line straight from the end of her finger up into the dress circle, it would have landed on the nose of a man, a very handsome young man, a tall, dark, young man with big, dark eyes, well turned out, red rose in his buttonhole, black hair just a touch long therefore bespeaking an artistic profession. He was escorting a fair-haired lady with a sheep's profile in a chic afternoon frock of lavender wool and they'd evidently freshly arrived, come to kill the hour before cocktails at the smartest show in town, no doubt; they cut a bit of a swathe as they 'excused me's' their way along the row. Glances, stares, even the odd 'ooh' and 'aah'. They were young and glamorous. Everybody there knew who they were but us. The lights were going down, the band was tuning up. Grandma still stood there, quivering.

'That man is . . . your father!'

Her revelation didn't have the force it might have had for us because, at that age, we still weren't sure just what it was that fathers did. Since we didn't know how to put one and one together to make two, we didn't know we were different, either. You'd think, wouldn't you, the neighbours would have nudged and winked a bit but Grandma kept her lip buttoned and maintained the outward appearance of propriety, at least in the hours before opening time, although if the milkman or the postie ever peeked in through the net curtains in the middle of the morning, they might have spotted her doing the dusting in her altogether and *then* there would have been talk.

So when Grandma announced so dramatically, that's your father! we dutifully took a look because she told us to but then the curtain glowed, the overture began.

'I say, do sit down, madame,' said a bloke in the row behind so she subsided mutinously. But it ruined the second half for her. She kept craning round, she was muttering the filthiest things under her breath but we had been transported to a different world, we were oblivious. For us, Fred and Adèle were everything.

There was such a press of people, at the end, and it took so long to get our coats, and we were in such a dream because of the dance and song that we missed them. We got out on to the pavement as our father and his missus sailed off in a cab leaving Grandma waving her umbrella uselessly after them.

'Damn,' said Grandma. 'Damn, damn, damn.'

Her face told you that she meant it.

Now that the spell of the show was broken, we had time to ponder her words.

'Grandma,' said Nora. 'Tell us some more about fathers.'

On top of the tram, on the way home, she told us the lot. She was a naturist, she was a vegetarian, she was a pacifist; when it came to sex education, what do you expect? But we found it hard to believe, neither what she said about the prong and how it could change its shape, etc., but also what she said the prong came in handy for. We thought she made it up to tease us. To think that we girls were in the world because a man we'd never met did *that* to a girl we didn't remember, once upon a time! What we knew for certain was, our grandma loved us and we had the best uncle in the world. Although Our Cyn, the worldly one, thought that Perry was our father.

But something took root in us that afternoon, some kind of curiosity. At first it was a niggling thing. We'd spot his picture in the paper and exclaim. When we went up West to buy new dancing shoes at Freed's, we'd make a detour round Shaftesbury Avenue, to look at the photographs wherever he was playing. Over the years, the curiosity turned into a yearning, a longing. I tucked a postcard of him in ermine as Richard II into a secret place at the back of the drawer where I kept my underwear, and, it was the one thing Nora kept from me, she only told me this afternoon, she did the same with one of him as young Prince Hal on the q.t. You could say, I suppose, that we *had a crush* on Melchior Hazard, like lots of girls. You could say he was our first romance, and bittersweet it turned out to be, in the end.

Anyway, that was the first time we ever saw our father. And the first time we saw Fred Astaire. And the first time we spent a penny – that is, used a public convenience. The one at Piccadilly Circus, with white tiles and a little old lady in a white pinny to take your penny off you and put it in the lock so you wouldn't soil your hands. A child remembers these things. It was a red-letter day all round and its wonders were by no means over. When we got home, the cake had moved out of the larder on to the kitchen table, its candles were blazing and, in our absence, a packing case that took up half the kitchen had arrived. Our Cyn pointed to the label: 'For my two lovely girls.'

'He hasn't forgotten,' she said, pleased for our sakes and also pleased for the sake of fatherhood – that Perry might be errant but did his duty, all the same. Little did she know.

In that packing case there was a toy theatre. It was a lovely one, a marvel, an antique – he'd got hold of it in Venice. In the middle of the gilt proscenium arch there they were, side by side, the comic mask, the tragic mask, one mouth turned up at the ends, the other down, the presiding geniuses – just like life. The *commedia*, that's life, isn't it?

Backdrops of trees and flowers and fountains, a moony night, blue clouds, a carnival, a bedroom, a feast, and little men and women on metal rods, Harlequin, Columbine, Pantaloon, all the old-timers. It was a plaything for princesses and we unpacked it out of its woodshavings with a kind of solemn delight; we hadn't known until that very moment it was exactly what we wanted.

We treasured that toy theatre. We played with it as if we were in church, always on Sunday afternoons, never any other time; we washed our hands, after dinner we put our best frocks on. I cried my eyes out when we were forced to part with it. It went to Sotheby's when Brenda had her bit of trouble. You wouldn't believe what we got for it. It kept young Tiffany in disposables until she learned to piss in a pot.

Grandma lit the candles on our cake.

'Make a wish and blow,' she said. You can guess what wish it was these stagestruck children made.

We closed our eyes and there we were, under the painted moon on the other side of the curtain, where the painted clouds will never move and everything is two-dimensional. Nora looked at me and I at Nora; frills, sequins, fishnet tights, high heels and feathers in our hair. We smiled. We raised our right legs, thus . . . ready for the orchestra.

Let's face the music and –

Of course, we didn't know, then, how the Hazards would always upstage us. Tragedy, eternally more class than comedy. How could mere song-and-dance girls aspire so high? We were destined, from birth, to be the lovely ephemera of the theatre, we'd rise and shine like birthday candles, then blow out. But, that birthday tea-time sixty-eight years ago, we blew out all our birthday candles with one breath and, yes, indeed! life gave us our birthday wish, in due course, because the Lucky Chances faced the music and they danced for well-nigh half a century, although we would always be on the left-hand line, hoofers, thrushes, the light relief, as you might say; bring on the bears!

Or, bares. Our careers went down the toilet along with the profession itself. We ended up showing a leg at the fag end of vaudeville in all those touring revues with titles such as *Nudes, Ahoy! Here Come the Nine O'clock Nudes! Nudes of the World!* and so on, backing up Archie Rice and other comics of that ilk. The showgirls would stand there, topless, living statues, and we would do our number in and out the nipples in our tasselled bras. I saw more nipples in those last five years of touring after World War II than in all my life till then and I was brought up by a naturist, don't you forget.

We had a raddled middle age, all right, but I swear to you we were respectable, in youth. There was nothing so stuffy as the lives of small-time theatricals, in those days, and South London was a ghetto of chorus girls and boys and what not. In the semis, behind the dusty privet hedges, they rested between engagements, sitting on a piece of the leatherette suite in the sitting room where the fumed oak sideboard contained a single bottle of sweet sherry and half a dozen dusty glasses stood on a tarnished silver tray inscribed 'To a great little trouper from the Merry Martins, Frinton-on-Sea, 1919', or something like that, beneath framed photographs of girls with big thighs in tights and men in crepe hair signed with Xs galore and framed colour reproductions on the walls of scenes depicting red-nosed monks eating big meals of venison and boar.

We begged and pleaded until Grandma stood us extra classes and after that we were the teacher's pets, while Grandma and Miss Worthington and her old mother, who played piano, often enjoyed a port and lemon or two under the picture of 'Simon the Cellarer' in the back parlour behind the dance studio, as Miss Worthington chose to call it. Grandma with her little finger hoist aloft, on her best behaviour, all smiles, spitting out her famous vowels like cherrystones; she'd give a big belch in the street, afterwards, glare around, say: 'Who let that out?'

So it went on, year in, year out. The mirror in Miss Worthington's front room showed two times two Chance girls, us and our reflections, doing high kicks like trick photography in flesh and blood. Bang, crash, wallop went Miss W.'s old mum on the piano, and, smack! smack! smack! Miss W.'s cane on our legs but she knew her stuff, I'll give her that. Grandma made pencil marks on the door of the breakfast room at home. Three foot, three and a half foot, four foot, four foot six, five foot, five foot two. Miss Worthington said:

'They're casting.'

'What?'

'Those girls could bring you in a bob or two, Mrs Chance,' said Miss Worthington in her superannuated pink tutu, leaning on her cane, eyeing us in our vests and knickers, five foot two, glossy brown ringlets Grandma did up each night in rags, like as two water drops. Miss Worthington, who used to be a pro herself until her arches fell.

'Only,' she added, because she kept up with the times, 'you'll have to do something about those sausage curls.'

So we were bobbed, sitting in the barber shop, swathed to our necks in hot towels, enduring the dreadful grinding crunch of the scissors, watching the mouse-brown locks fall round us to the ground; we knew that we were shedding our childhoods with those ringlets and we were pleased as punch. When we were cleaning out Grandma's stuff, after she copped it, there was an envelope in her bottom drawer, two curls: 'Dora's', tied with a blue ribbon, 'Nora's', green.

It was a panto, wasn't it? To cut a long story short, we made our first professional appearance on any stage as birds – little brown birds, sparrows, probably, one, two, three, hop, in the forest scene in *Babes in the Wood* at the Shepherd's Bush Empire, Grandma escorting us there and back with a half-bottle of gin in her handbag just in case.

In case of what? In case the pubs run dry, ducky, she said.

Identical birds. They gave us our own speciality number because we were identical. We were the ones who covered up the 'babes' with leaves, what's more. By ourselves, neither of us was nothing much but put us together, people blinked. Which is

Dora? Which is Nora? In those days, we even smelled the same. Phul Nana. We didn't know any better. We used to nick it from Bon Marché.

That first night, of all the first nights of all our years in show business, the dressing room crammed with chorus kiddies, our insides turned to water, our make-up wouldn't stay on, nothing went right. My stocking laddered, her beak came off. All the same, we did our dance, we scattered leaves, we fluttered off, they ate us up. Roars, applause. Come the finale, we pelted the front row with crackers. They went mad. We'd done what we were born to do and, what was more, we'd do it again tomorrow.

Grandma had brought Our Cyn, of course, but, sharing our little triumph, bearing a hatbox-full of Fortnum's chocs and bronzed under his freckles by hotter suns than ours ... our prodigal uncle made his way between the frilly chorus with arms held wide: 'My clever ones!'

Our cup was full to overflowing; he had come home in time to witness our debut.

We loved it all, showing off, fancy dress, Leichner's No. 7. We'd take great gulps of the stale air as soon as we got inside the theatre to set us up for the night. Give me that incomparable old fug of oranges, Jeyes Fluid, humanity, gas ... I'd rather dab it behind my ears than Mitsouko, even. That moment when the band in the pit tuned up ... We were *wet* for it, I tell you! Such a rush of blood to our vitals when we started to dance!

We loved it so much we could scarcely believe it when they gave us our pay packets but Grandma banked the cash, said, the sooner we started earning, the better, although Perry's cheque came regular as clockwork and now he had come home again, his presents fell like rain. But Grandma said, *you never can tell.* Hope for the best, expect the worst, she said.

Impossible to comprehend as it might seem at that time to his bedazzled nieces, our Uncle Perry *did* possess a fault. One single fault. It was his boredom threshold. Our little Tiff at three years old had more capacity for continuous effort than Perry. For him, life had to be a continuous succession of small treats or else he couldn't see the point.

One August bank holiday, we would have just turned thirteen, he roared up in a cab. Big hugs. He pinched our cheeks. 'You look peaky, girlies! Can't have that.' He piled us all in the back of the cab, Nora, me, Grandma, not forgetting Our Cyn ('Oh, Mr Hazard!') along with a ruddy great hamper from Jackson's, Piccadilly. 'Dr Brighton is indicated, my man!' First the cabby gaped; then he beamed. 'You're on, guv'nor.' And off we went.

There was a linen tablecloth to spread out on the beach over the shingle and Perry and the cabby, bosom chums, by now, toddled off arm in arm to pick up some bubbly while we put out the ham and chicken and cut up the loaf and opened the can of foie gras, nothing but the best when Uncle Perry stood the treat. All the punters stared, I can tell you – three skinny girls and a fat lady in a spotted veil, Perry with his shock of bright red hair and his stevedore's shoulders and his big, fat smile, and the cabby in the leather jacket. Grandma filled the glasses, gave her toast: 'Champagne to all here, *real* pain to the other bastards.' Perry picked hard-boiled eggs out of our noses and gave us our coffee piping hot poured from the neb of the cabby's cap.

When we'd all done eating, Perry took hold of the two corners of one end of the cloth and – whoosh! the fine china, the knives and forks (good, heavy silverware, nothing mean), the bones, the crusts, the empties, vanished clean away. He said he'd sent them back to the shop. How did he do it? Search me. Our Uncle Perry knew a trick or two. Bloody marvellous conjurer. Should have set up professionally. Half the beach broke into spontaneous applause and, much encouraged, Perry said: anybody got a saw? If so, he'd saw Grandma in half. Not on your life, she said, God knows what might come out. She'd tucked up her skirts, shown off her big, red bloomers, had her little paddle. She took a crème de menthe frappé, to settle her digestion, she belched, she nodded off. Our Cyn and the cabby were deep in conversation so the rest of us set off for a walk along the pier.

Perry was the size of a polar bear, bless him, in his vanilla tussore suit and the straw boater with the red and black ribbon and white shirt with a red stripe, stiff collar, red tie. He was huge but dapper. The citric brisk smell of his cologne. Later on, during the war, dragging myself up from my slumbers in the blackout,

I got a big whiff of it, Trumper's Essence of Lime. I thought: I must have had it off with Peregrine!!! Dread and delight coursed through my veins; I thought, what have I done ... But when I switched the light on, it turned out to be not Perry at all, but that Free Pole.

Peregrine in his ice-cream suit with a girl on either arm, neither of us anything special on our own – skinny things with mouse-brown bobs – but, put us together, we turned heads. Past the donkey rides and the hokey-pokey man and all the minarets, turrets and trellises of Brighton Pavilion, which always reminds me of our Grandma, somehow, although she tended towards the subfusc, she was like the Brighton Pavilion in blackout. Highly unlikely the Pavilion looked, too, that afternoon. Such a lovely day. The shiny, frilly waves; cackling of the seagulls; laughter of little children; plashing of water. And he'd let us have a glass of bubbly, each, at lunch. Everything conspired to make us happy.

I've been happy before and I've been happy, after, but, swinging along the front at Brighton with Nora and our Uncle Perry, not a care in the world, it was the first time I was old enough and wise enough and knew my way about my own feelings well enough, to put it into words: 'Goodness! I'm happy!' When I think of happiness, I always think of Brighton, and of that August bank holiday when I was thirteen, because we did the heights and depths, that day. How frail a thing your happiness can be! We went from the ridiculous to the sublime, and broke our hearts, as well.

'Why are they called Pierrots?' asked Nora outside the Pier Pavilion.

'Because they do their stuff on piers.'

I love the artificial dark of the matinée, the same, exciting dark you get when you draw the curtains after lunch to go to bed. The sea was swishing back and forth beneath the Pier Pavilion and it was moist and warm, inside, and full of holiday scents of Evening in Paris and Ashes of Violets mixed with dry fish, that is, fried, from outside, and wet fish, that is, dead, from down below, and hot tin, from the roof, and armpits. Nobody there to take a ticket; the first half of the show was nearly over so we sneaked in at the back.

The Pierrots were standing around in their white frills, looking spare, and there was a comic up on stage halfway through his act. He'd got on a pair of plus-fours, huge things, big as a couple of hot-air balloons, in the kind of pink Grandma called 'fraizy crazy' (crushed strawberry, to you; work it out for yourself) – shiny pink satin plus fours tucked into mauve golfing socks with pink clocks plus a pair of pink suede brogues with big, mauve, flapping tongues hanging out. He'd got a golf club in his hand, to go with his outfit, and he made lewd gestures with it; mothers covered their children's eyes.

I'd never heard of him in those days, though he made a big name for himself later on, but when he started out, you'd have thought it was going to be a name you couldn't print in a family newspaper. He called himself . . . he called himself . . . I'll remember it in a minute. He had a catch phrase, 'Nothing queer about our George.' He popped up again in Hollywood, in *The Dream*, with us, what a surprise; he played, of course he would, what else, Bottom.

Gorgeous George. He billed himself as Gorgeous George.

' . . . and this boy's thoughts turned lightly to' – big poke in the air with the golf club – 'so he says to his dad, "I want to get married to the girl next door, Dad."

'"Ho, hum," says his dad. "I've got news for you, son. When I was your age, I used to get me leg over –"'

Roars, shrieks, hoots; but all so much titillation without any substance, I tell you, because he gave them a shocked look, pursed his lips together, shook his golf club in reproof.

'*Filthy* minds, some of you have,' he grieved in parenthesis. Renewed hoots and shrieks.

'What I was about to say before I was so rudely interrupted . . .'

That was his other catch phrase.

' . . . was, I used to get me leg over –'

Mothers covered their children's ears.

'– I used to get me leg over the garden wall –'

He made a fierce lunge in the air with his golf club and looked around, working his eyebrows as if to defy misinterpretation.

'. . . and, cut a long story short, you can't marry the girl next door, son, on account of she's your sister.'

The air turned blue. Mothers forced reluctant children outside, bribing with ice-cream.

'So this boy buys a bike' – he straddled his golf club, mimicked peddling, renewed roaring – 'and peddles off. *Peddles*, I said, Missus; what d'you think I said? He peddles off to Hove.'

Wonderful diction. Grandma herself couldn't have done more with that long 'O'.

'He comes back, he says to his father: "I've met this nayce girl from Hove, Dad." "Hove?" says Dad. "Sorry to say, son, I frequently hove to in Hove when I was your age and –"'

He halted, working his eyebrows, manipulating his golf club. Say no more. They laughed until they cried.

'This poor boy, he buys himself a day return, he goes up to Victoria, he meets a girl under the clock. *Clock*, I said, Missus. But his father says: "We had trains in my young day, son . . ."'

Appreciative gurgles.

'The boy goes into the kitchen for a cup of tea. Big sigh. His mum says: "You've got a face as long as a –"'

Eyebrows. Golf club. Roars.

'What I was going to say, before I was so rudely interrupted, was . . . as long as a fiddle!'

They pounded the floorboards with their feet.

'"Looks like I'll never get married, Mum." "Why's that, son?" He told her all about it, she says: "You just go ahead and marry who you like, son –"'

Split-second timing. That pause. Perfect.

''*e*'s not your father!'

They stamped and pounded so you would have thought the floor was going to give way. Perry gazed on, amazed. 'Well, God bless the bloody British,' he said. 'I never thought they had it in them.'

When the audience quieted down, they put a pink filter on the spot so Gorgeous George flushed all over. He put on a lugubrious look and sucked in his cheeks. It was time for his tenor number. The lady accompanist, one of Mrs Worthington's ilk, gave the piano a good thump. George clasped his hands together on his club, adopted a reverential air, and, would you believe it, there, in his pink suit in the pink spot, on the end of Brighton Pier, on August bank bloody holiday, he gave out with 'Rose of England'.

> Rose of England, breathing England's air,
> Flower of majesty beyond compare . . .

The Pierrots, all turned pink themselves, formed groups reminiscent of posies and nosegays and sank to their knees for the throbbing finale. You couldn't get away with that sort of thing, these days, not unless it was what they call 'camp'. Then George held up his hand to quell the applause and, stepping forward, announced in a voice heavy with emotion:

'Ladies and gentlemen, boys and girls . . . long live the King!'

The lady accompanist struck up 'Land of Hope and Glory' in spite of a couple of bum notes in the bass and George shouldered his golf club as if it were a rifle and commenced to march round and round the stage in military fashion, the mauve tongues of his suede brogues lolling voluptuously half a beat behind him.

Left, right, halt.

He salutes the audience under the spot, which is now bright white again, the limelight falling on his shoulders like dandruff. The lady accompanist simulates a drumroll, to the best of her ability. Off comes his satin cap.

Nora and I looked at one another, puzzled. What on earth was going on?

Another drumroll.

Off comes his rose-pink jacket.

Odder and odder.

And it turned out that George himself, in himself, in his skin, is the prime spectacle on offer, this afternoon.

For George was not a comic at all but an enormous statement.

If I hadn't seen it with my own two eyes, I'd never have believed it. Displayed across his torso there was, if you took the top of his head as the North Pole and the soles of his feet as the South, a complete map of the entire world.

He flexed his muscles and that funny little three-cornered island with appendages on the right bicep sprang out, the Irish

Free State giving a little quiver. The lady accompanist hit the first few notes of 'God Save the King' and half the punters, from sheer force of habit, began to struggle to their feet, scattering shed gloves and chocolate papers, but soon sank down again and let him get on with it when the next thing he did was, take off his plus-fours.

Nora and I were only girls, never seen a man without his trousers on although Grandma had drawn us pictures, and, I must say, we were quite keenly curious so we craned forward eagerly but it turned out he stripped off only to reveal a gee-string of very respectable dimensions, more of a gee-gee string, would have kept a horse decent, and it was made out of the Union Jack. Amply though the garment concealed his privates, now you could see the Cape of Good Hope situated in his navel and observe the Falkland Islands disappear down the crack of his bum when he did his grand patriotic ninety-degree rotation, to the reawakened applause that never quite died down during the entire display but sometimes rose in greater peaks than at other times.

We gazed enraptured on the flexing pecs. 'Rule, Britannia' accompanied his final turn, which revealed how most of his global tattoo was filled in a brilliant pink, although the limelight turned it into morbid, raspberry colour that looked bad for his health.

Then George made a few passes with his golf club, and simulated bayonet practice with it in his patriotic bathers for a bit, with a few more imitation drumrolls and stern cheers from the crowd. And some had tears in their eyes, I swear, and shouted: 'Good old George! Hurrah for George!' But we girls were bemused: what kind of a show was this? Hadn't Grandma told us that wars were a way to get the young men out of the picture, leave all the women for the ugly old codgers who wouldn't have got any, otherwise? So we knew what wars were for and, to tell the truth, from George's joke, it looked as though he thought that that was what fathers always wanted, too.

And as regards the pink bits on his bum and belly, we knew already in our bones that those of us in the left-hand line were left out of the picture; we were the offspring of the bastard king of England, if you like, and we weren't going to inherit any of the gravy, so the hell with it.

After his bayonet practice, Gorgeous George donned his golfing jacket once again, made a reassuringly obscene gesture with that golf club and retired backwards, kissing his hands to the hallooing crowd and murmuring: 'God bless you!' We were all three sweating like pigs, so we beat it, sharpish, before anyone noticed we hadn't paid. The fishermen were out in force on the pier – somebody pulled up a mackerel that shone like a new tin can. Or perhaps it *was* a tin can. I misremember. It was sixty-odd years ago, you know. They used to fancy those patriotic tableaux, in those days. We didn't know what to make of it, really. We were just girls, we'd never seen a man's bare bum before, though one another's, often.

Perry ran a finger round his collar to wipe away the sweat. He looked quite dazed.

'I'll never understand the British,' he opined, and so say all of us, ducky.

'Now,' he said to us girls after having ingested several lungfuls of fresh air, 'you show us what *you* can do, my little chorines.'

Sunshine and glitter off the sea and a little breeze and laughter all around us. People being happy. As I remember it, a band struck up out of nowhere. Lovely little band. Nothing elaborate, just three or four pieces, with a drummer. God knows how they got there, unless they'd come down from London on a cheap day excursion, to busk. Or maybe they were booked into the Grand Hotel or something like that, as cabaret. But I certainly seem to remember four Black gentlemen in suits and straw hats, trumpet, trombone, clarinet, percussion. Or perhaps it was Perry on his harmonica, all the time, who provided the music, so that we could dance for him. We danced the Black Bottom for him; we loved the Black Bottom, he'd given us a record, the one about Ma Rainey's Big Black Bottom. We danced the dance but didn't sing the song, that would have been presumptuous.

Instead, we had a think, we held a consultation, we picked out a song in honor of Gorgeous George's joke, we gave them, 'Is You Is or Is You Ain't My Baby,' and Perry went purple in the face, wanting to laugh and trying to blow at the same time. Then he stowed his harmonica, doffed his boater, took it round the crowd. I can't remember what happened to the band. They faded away. Would you believe it, a quid? In those days, a quid *was* a quid. A quid less a tanner, all in small change. He counted it out and handed it over.

'Buy us a cup of tea, you can afford it,' he said. We went into town to look for a Fuller's Tea Room because he fancied a bit of walnut cake, too, and that is how we came to find ourselves outside the Theatre Royal.

'Shit,' said Perry but he said it in American, like this: 'Shee-it.'

Melchior Hazard and Company
in
Macbeth
His acclaimed production.
'Sheer Genius.'
The Times.

We clustered, we stared, we were overcome, we sought the protection of his bulk, we hid our faces as if shy of the photographs.

'You do know,' Perry told us, 'that you ain't my babies, worse luck. I am not now nor ever have been your father. No. And you *do* know, don't you, that *he* –'

– gesture towards the photographs –

'is.'

We nodded. We knew that Melchior Hazard was our father and now we also knew exactly what it was a father did, and how, and where, and who he'd done it to, and what had happened after that. We knew it all. And here he was, treading the boards like billy-oh, in Shakespeare, and weren't we fresh from singing in the streets? We'd never felt quite so illegitimate in all our lives as we did that day we were thirteen, looking at the glossy photos of Father togged up in a kilt.

And one of my suspenders had come undone, my left stocking at half-mast.

Perry drew out his watch, consulted it.

'Birnan wood,' he said, 'is just now creeping up on Dunsinane.'

I had an inkling of what he might be at and I was frightened. 'Let's get back to Grandma Chance,' I said in a strangled voice.

But, more than anything else in the world, I longed and longed to push through the glass doors and feast my eyes on the sight of my father, my gloriously handsome father, my gifted, sensationally applauded genius of a father, and I knew, without speech, without even so much as glancing at her, that Nora, too, wanted it more than anything. I reached out for Nora's hand. It was hot and sticky, still a child's hand, although I suppose we looked like quite young ladies, already, being tall for our ages and we had on the yellow dresses Perry picked out for us in Paris, from Chanel, and the bows on our heads, more coquette than finishing school, to tell the truth. Nymphettes, I suppose they'd call us now. Jail-bait.

Nora and I clutched each other's hands.

'Grandma will be wondering where we are,' said Nora. 'She'll worry.'

But she never budged and her voice broke on 'worry', she wailed. Perry looked from one to the other of us forlorn little creatures, tears standing in our eyes, love locked out.

'Dammit,' he said. 'Come with me.'

And grabbed our arms and raced us to the stage door, where a bank note changed hands. Whisked up a draughty backstairs, another bank note went to the dresser who let us into our father's empty dressing room, put his finger on his lips to tell us to keep our mouths shut, and left us. Perry parked us on the sofa and we gazed with moonstruck adoration at the very towel our father had dried his hands on, the razor he'd shaved with, the greasepaint he'd put on his beloved face – all these things had far more intimate relations with him than we did and seemed almost holy, in our eyes. His mirror, that had the joy and honour of reflecting him.

I badly wanted to reach out and pinch a stick of his No. 7, to remember him by, but I didn't dare.

There was a photo, head and shoulders, of a sheep in a tiara; we eyed it askance. We knew full well who *she* was; hadn't we seen her on his arm at the first matinée, when we fell in love with him? (Little did we know then that we'd share our twilight years with her, poor old thing.)

But don't think we ransacked the room. Just to sit there and breathe in air he had breathed out was more, much more than we'd ever hoped for. Now we knew for certain that Perry was better than a conjurer, was a genuine magician who could divine our most secret desire of all, the one we'd never confided even to one another because we hadn't needed to, because I knew she knew and she knew *I* knew.

God, we were humble. We'd sneaked off, now and then, now we knew what was what, paid our sixpences, sat in the gods and watched him strut and fret his hour upon the stage, happy with just the sight of him. But as soon as we were in his very dressing room, where we'd never even dared to hope we might one day find ourselves, we grew ambitious. Perhaps, discovering us here so unexpectedly, his lovely girls, lost before birth and now redis-covered on the springtime verge of blossoming (as Irish would have put it), he might let us touch his hand, even allow us to kiss his cheek ... and we might be permitted, just the once, to say the word we'd never used in all our lives: 'Father.'

Father!

The very thought made our skins prickle.

Perry, meanwhile, was gazing absently out of the open window at the roof and chimneys and brick backs; a seagull landed on a chimneystack and mewed. There was a gust of military brass brought on the wind from the seafront bandstand: 'Colonel Bo-gey'. He drummed his fingertips on the window ledge. If I hadn't been so stunned and glorified by the prospect at last of meeting him, I might have noted that, for once, our Perry was suffering second thoughts and, if I'd done that, I might have worried more about our welcome. But I was too overwhelmed to make much of it, at the time. It was warm and close in the dressing room, our armpits moistened. All of a sudden I wanted to pee.

Enormous volumes of applause surged through the old build-ing and, when it faded away, then, more quickly than we thought could have been possible, so that we had no time at all to prepare ourselves, as if he'd flown from the stage to the dressing room on wires, there he was.

He was tall, dark and handsome. God, he was handsome, in those days. And smashing legs, which a man must have for Shakespeare, especially the Scottish play; you need a good calf to get away with a kilt. I do believe we get the legs from him, as well as the cheekbones.

I *did* piss myself when I saw him, in fact, but only a little bit, hardly enough to stain the sofa.

Such eyes! Melchior's eyes, warm and dark and sexy as the inside of a London cab in wartime. His eyes.

But those very eyes, those knicker-shifting, unfasten-your-brassiere-from-the-back-of-the-gallery eyes, were the bitterest disappointment of my life till then. No. Of all my life, before and since. No disappointment ever after measured up to it. Because those eyes of his looked at us but did not *see* us, even as we sat there, glowing because we couldn't help it; our helpless mouths started to smile.

To see him fail to see me wiped that smile right off my face, I can tell you, and off Nora's, too. Our father's eyes skidded right over us, never touched us, didn't make contact. They came to rest on Perry.

'Peregrine!' he cried. His voice still sends a shiver down my spine this day. Up he pops on the telly, tamping down his pipe. 'Rich, dark, fruity . . .' You can say that, again.

He held out his hands in greeting to Perry, to Perry only.

'Peregrine . . . how nice of you to come and visit me.' And then, and only then, we got our little crumb of attention although it shot us down like the same bullet through both hearts.

'And you've brought your lovely daughters, too!'

I have a memory, although I know it cannot be a true one, that Peregrine swept us up into his arms. That when our father denied us, Peregrine spread his arms as wide as wings and gathered up the orphan girls, pressed us so close we crushed against his waist-coat, bruising our cheeks on his braces' buttons. Or perhaps he slipped us one in each pocket of his jacket. Or crushed us far inside his shirt, against his soft, warm belly, to be sustained by the thumping comfort of his heart. And then, hup! he did a back-flip out of the window with us, saving us. But I know I am imagining the back-flip and the flight.

But, truly, what he did was, he held out his arms to us and we scampered to harbour, whimpering.

'It's a wise child that knows its own father,' hissed Peregrine, like the gypsy's warning. 'But wiser yet the father who knows his own child.'

He slammed the door behind us. Us. Unkissed, unwelcome, worse than unacknowledged. Our washers were leaking, I can tell you. How we blubbered. Cried so much we couldn't see where we were going but all at once there we were, back on the beach, transferred from Perry to Ma Chance's voluminous arms and she dried our eyes, sent Our Cyn for a jug of hot tea from a café, so we had some of that, to give us strength, and a cream bun or two that Perry extricated from Grandma's cleavage along with a big puff of talc, to bring back a smile to our lips, which we managed palely, so as not to disappoint him, and we had something to nibble on, to take our minds off, but not much appetite, I can tell you.

It turned out that Our Cyn and the cabby had got along so well together on their day out they'd decided to make a go of it so it was kisses and handshakes all round and Cyn sat in the front with him while Nora and I leaned on Perry's shoulders as we drove back to London through the yellowish, greenish light of a Sussex evening, sweet summer coming in through the windows and the low murmur of the voices of Perry and Grandma talking softly so as not to disturb us as we trembled on the brink of sleep, for it had truly been an exhausting day, but we didn't nod off altogether until Norbury so they had to carry us up to our little beds in the back attic which, at that time, in our white girlhood, we shared.

Cyn and the cabby wanted to go up West, to celebrate, so they dropped Perry off at Eaton Square. Eaton Square? That's what Cyn told us. What could he be doing in Eaton Square, on the spur of the moment, the naughty boy? They left him on the front steps of a most elegant dwelling, he was straightening his tie and dusting off his jacket. He tipped his boater at them as they drove off, flashed them his great, big, cheeky grin.

Love him as I did, I must confess he had a wicked streak.

Although our half-sisters, old Wheelchair's girls, resembled sheep with bright red fleece when grown, they were bald as any other baby when they were born, the dead spit of one another, not far away from Bard Road as the crow flies but the crow is a bit of a prole as far as the bird world goes and most other birds would think those girls were born in a different country, with Sheraton furniture, Persian rugs, constant hot water, and staff, and christened Saskia and Imogen in long lace clothes at St John's Smith Square, shortly thereafter to be photographed with Mamma, the 'loveliest lady in London', by Cecil Beaton, and have their picture published in the *Sketch*, caption: 'Darling buds of May'. For it was in May that they were born, the same day as the first of Our Cyn's five.

We started the very same day those two were born, as it happens. Funny coincidence. I went to have a wee and there was the evidence, all over my underwear. I hotfooted it to Nora and she took a look on her own account. Same thing with her. Grandma got us some cotton wool. Although we are asymmetrical, in many way, we always, funnily enough, came on in unison every time since that first time, barring accidents; came on in unison until we stopped, short, never to go again, the tap turned off just twenty-five years ago.

I always think there was a sort of mean connection between their birth and our puberty. Typical dirty trick that Saskia might pull on us, that we should turn into women just at the very moment when they turn into babies. Always a different generation. That's the rub. We've never been equals. They've always had that final edge on us. So rich. So well-connected. So legitimate.

Sod all that.

So young.

'Darling buds of May.' Grandma Chance did sums upon her fingers and assumed an inscrutable expression but the proud parents looked pleased as punch with the new arrivals although Perry seemed strangely sad, these days, when Saskia and Imogen took the air in a high-wheeled baby carriage pushed by a ribboned nanny while Dora and Nora pounded away on splintering boards the length and breadth. Glasgow Empire. Prince's, Edinburgh. Royalty, Perth. Freeze off a girl's bum, the winters up there. Somebody threw a grouse on stage, once, as a gesture of appreciation. Not even a pair. That was in Aberdeen. Tight as arseholes, in Aberdeen.

We pounded the boards like nobody's business because, by that time, Perry had lost all his moolah in the Wall Street crash, every red cent, and couldn't keep up his contributions any more, so it was just as well we girls could earn our living because after that we had to.

When he came to say goodbye, it was by tram. Lo, how the mighty have fallen. No cab softly ticking away on the kerb, this time. No chocolates from Charbonnel & Walker. And he'd weaned us off Phul Nana ('Phew!') only to find he couldn't afford to give us the French stuff any more. Not that we cared. We only thought how much we'd miss him. We sat on the arms of his chair, one on each side, and watched him eat his buttered crumpets, too down at heart to eat anything ourselves.

He'd work his passage home, he said. Home, to that part of the torso of Gorgeous George that was *not* tinted pink. He'd work his Atlantic passage on the liner doing tricks in the ballroom after dinner.

'What will you do once you get there?' asked Grandma Chance, shoving another pan of crumpets under the grill because he was eating as if he might not eat again until he reached Los Angeles.

'Go into the movies,' said Peregrine.

Dora and Nora. Two girls pounding the boards. At Christmas, we did a panto. One year we did *Jack and the Beanstalk* at Kennington. Would you believe a live theatre in Kennington, once upon a time? Alive and kicking. Beans, in green tights; our speciality number was Mexican jumping beans, in red tights. Two pounds a week each. It went a long way, in those days. Those were the days of pounds, shillings and pence. Two pounds was forty silver shillings; forty shillings was four hundred and eighty of those big, brown, cartwheel pennies that made your hands smell, and every one of those pennies had a hole ready and waiting for it to patch in the threadbare economy of 49 Bard Road. Being at Kennington was a saving on digs. We lived at home, we came home on the night tram, every bone in our body aching in concert and our feet burning, we girls half asleep, half awake, propping against one another, rain slashing the window, soaking our coats as we ran from the stop for home. If we caught cold, disaster! Even identical Mexican jumping beans were expendable so we jumped away with low fevers and septic throats and influenza and the curse, jump, jump, jump, carrying on smiling, smilin' thru', show those teeth, kick those legs, tote that barge, lift that bail.

We could even get home for tea after the matinée, Wednesdays and Saturdays, and that saved the money we'd have spent on a poached egg at a Lyons teashop so we'd put aside those four pennies to save up for silk stockings. Stockings were always a problem. The hours we spent, darning the bloody things.

Then, one afternoon, such a fuss and flutter backstage; what's going on? What a shock we got. A sheep in a couture afternoon frock in a box, with a nanny in ribbons and two little russet ewe lambs. Our humble little company had been honoured by a visit from theatrical royalty.

'I won't go on,' said Nora, always impetuous. She threw her sombrero on the floor and jumped on it. 'What humiliation!'

But the first Lady Hazard was a proper lady, not like the present incumbent, and I didn't think, even then, that she'd set out for Kennington with the gross intention of letting her baby daughters relish the spectacle of her husband's by-blows performing high kicks. I've asked her about it since, of course, and she said that *he* was away on tour, again, and she was banging about all by herself in that great, big house at her wits' end how to pass a wet Saturday afternoon and her Old Nanny, the very same Old Nanny who'd looked after her when *she* was a baby and now was looking after *her* little babies, Old Nanny wanted to take the little girls to the panto in Kennington because her, Old Nanny's, that is, her sister lived round the corner. (And as it turned out that sister was an aunt by marriage of Our Cyn's new husband, so a bond was forged and after Old Nanny's sister moved to Worthing, Old Nanny used to drop in and visit Grandma.) Old Nanny thought she might pop in to see her sister after the panto and the Lady Atalanta, on the spur of the moment, said: 'Hang on, I'll get my hat and come, too.'

The show went on, of course, and so did we. What? Lose a day's pay? Lose the job, too, like as not, and then back to the dreary round of agents' waiting rooms. Anything but that.

She says, as soon as she set eyes on us, she *knew*, and then she checked the programme and was certain, because Perry told her all about us after they got together. She sent us flowers, after, anonymously, but easy to guess where they came from – forget-me-nots. I thought that was quite touching but Nora thought, bad taste. And once she asked us to tea, as well, but Nora said: 'Not on your life.'

Our half-sisters responded to the show in ways already characteristic of their future personalities. Saskia set up a howl like a banshee the moment she saw the beans come on, as if she knew us at first sight and was all agog to steal our thunder, while Imogen fell asleep and left her mouth open through the entire proceedings, in preparation for her career as a fish. But the Lady A. watched us, or so she told me, years on, with tears in her eyes and guilt in her bosom. She may have slipped up the once, but, all the same, she truly loved our father. She *must* have loved him, her with her handle and her bank account and her father in the House of Lords, to marry a man with nothing to offer but the best legs in the British Isles.

She'd had no news from Perry, either.

Then the panto season was over and we were on the road again. Fifteen years old, now. Five foot, six inches. Little brown bobs, though Nora often talked wistfully about going blonde. She felt the future lay with blondes. Should we? Shouldn't we? One thing was certain – she couldn't do it unilaterally. On our own, you wouldn't look at us twice. But, put us together . . .

We were hardened old troupers, by now. We had our printed cards: 'Dora and Leonora, 49 Bard Road, London S.W.2.' You always had to travel on a Sunday, when the trains went slow out of respect for the Sabbath and sometimes stopped dead in the middle of a field as if taken short. We feared not bedbugs, nor cockroaches; fleas could not daunt our spirits. We learned to despise the 'Wood' family, that is, the empty seats. We lived off the Scotch eggs the landladies put out for late supper, after the show. Grandma went spare when she heard about the Scotch eggs.

'It's only sausage meat,' I said. 'They wrap some sausage meat round the hard-boiled egg. You know what they make sausage meat out of, sawdust and the bits of old elastic.' Grandma wasn't having any. 'Cannibals!' she said.

But now we knew the world didn't end when Grandma disapproved. Greatly daring, knowing what she'd say, egged on by the other girls, we finally invested in some little bits of rabbit fur to snuggle into when the wind blew chill. 'Dead bunny,' said Grandma when she saw. As we grew up, cracks appeared between us. She loved us but she often disapproved.

We were just slips of girls but we soon knew our way around. We had our little handbags with the little gilt powder compacts and the puffs; when in doubt, we powdered our noses, to give us time to think up repartee. A rat once ate my powder puff in the dressing room at the Nottingham Theatre Royal. We kept our make-up in the standard two-tier tin – rouge, Leichner, that solid mascara you sliced off into a tiny tin frying pan and melted over a candle. Then you put it on with a matchstick, quick, quick, quick, before it got hard.

Grandma kept the programmes, every show we ever were in, right from that first *Babes in the Wood* up to the ones from ENSA. She made up big scrapbooks. After she went, there they were, stored away in a trunk in the loft – the whole of our lives. We felt bad when we saw those scrapbooks, we remembered how we'd teased her, we'd brought home sausage rolls and crocodile handbags, but she'd kept on snipping out the cuttings, pasting them in. Piles of scrapbooks, the cuttings turned by time to the colour of the freckles on the back of an old lady's hand. Her hand. My hand, as it is now. When you touch the old newsprint, it turns into brown dust, like the dust of bones.

The last scrapbook stops short in 1944, leaving us marooned for ever just turning thirty, on the cusp, caught up in one last pose, would you believe, done up as bulldogs. *Bulldog Breed.* For some bloody silly charity matinée, drumming-up cash to replace lost lovers, lost sons, boys dead on the Burma Road, the irreplaceable. Why did we do it, Nora? 'We had to do something,' she said. 'Anyway, we entertained the troops.'

And so we did.

I can see Grandma now, sitting at the kitchen table, sticking the picture in the book, the tip of her tongue between her teeth, breathing hard, all concentration. She picks up her pen, dips in the ink, writes underneath, in her round, careful hand: 'Duke of York's Theatre, May 20, 1944.'

Then she reached for the stout and found the bottle empty. Oh, Grandma! Talk about the 'fatal glass of beer'! If you'd been able to curb your thirst that night, you'd have lived to see VE-day. She pulled herself up by the back of a chair, humming a tune, humming, maybe: 'There'll be bluebirds over The white cliffs of Dover . . .' or: 'I'll get lit up when the lights go up in London.' She arranged her little toque with the black-dotted veil on top of her head in the fly-blown square of mirror over the sink. She touched up her beauty spot with eyeblack, stowed away the empties in that eternal lino-cloth bag. The siren blared but she wasn't going to let Hitler inconvenience her drinking habits, was she?

She was taken out by a flying bomb on her way to the off-licence.

When we got home after the all-clear, we found the scrapbook where she left it, beside the scissors and the pot of Gloy. And the empty glass, with the lacy remnants of the foam gone hard inside it.

And that was how we lost Grandma.

It was Grandma and Guinness caused us to become brunettes. One night, when we were resting between engagements, we were all sitting round this very kitchen table, our one and only kitchen table, having a few drinks.

'If not blonde,' said Nora, 'why don't we henna it? Copper-nobs. Gingernuts. Let's face it, Dora, we need a little something extra to make us stand out.'

'Not red,' I said, 'because of Saskia and Imogen.'

Grandma took a good look at us, at our big, grey eyes and our good, strong Hazard bones that would come in handy, later on, but weren't much use to fifteen-year-olds because we never had the ingénue look. Hard as nails, they said. That's the Chance girls.

Grandma was partaking of the bottled stout she never knew would later prove her downfall.

'Not red,' said Grandma, eyeing her glass. 'Black.'

The dye came in a bottle labelled 'Spanish Ebony'. The bathroom was as cold as hell. Still is. We stood there, shivering in our camisoles, eyeing the dye as if there were a genie in the bottle and we were scared to let it out. This was a big step for us, remember. We were about to change our entire personality.

'In for a penny, in for a pound,' said Nora, at last, and plunged her head into the washbasin, and I anointed her, poured on the colour, rubbed it in, thick, black stuff, it gave me mourning fingernails for weeks. When she straightened up, big drips ran down her forehead, got in her eyes, stung them, she wept. The splashes got everywhere, the towels looked like bath night at the Minstrel Show and we had to cut ourselves fringes when our hair dried out because of the five o'clock shadow on our foreheads that never washed off. So she was crying off the whole idea before it came to my turn but if one of us dyed, so did the other, no choice, that was that. Then we slipped on our kimonos, cleaned up the bathroom as best we could – but we never got the marks off the towels – put each other's hair in pins to fix the kiss curls and went down to have a cuppa with Grandma looking so downhearted she made us lace it with a spot of the brandy she'd just opened on account of the cold snap.

'Very unseasonal weather for July,' she said, topping up.

But when it dried out and we'd given it a good brush, we didn't know ourselves. Half a yard of black satin that turned into our cheeks like commas. It was the turning point. We called ourselves 'The Lucky Chances' after that. After that, we were a featured turn. After that, we were sixteen and we were legal.

Nora was always free with it and threw her heart away as if it were a used bus ticket. Either she was head over heels in love or else she was broken-hearted. She had it off first with the pantomime goose, when we were Mother Goose's goslings that year in Newcastle upon Tyne. The goose was old enough to be her father and Grandma would have plucked him, stuck an apple up his bum and roasted him if she'd found out and so would the goose's wife, who happened to be principal boy. So finding a place to, as Irish might have put it, consummate their passion (although Irish abhorred a split infinitive) was something of a problem for them because it was before the days we could boast a dressing room to ourselves and his wife was eversuch a hairy woman, always a fresh growth between her eyebrows, under her arms, on her legs, to pluck or shave so she was always holed up in the one she shared with the goose, depilating herself.

The goose had Nora up against the wall in the alley outside the stage door one foggy night, couldn't see your hand in front of your face, happily for them. You don't get fogs like that, these days. It was after the cast Christmas party. I looked round the Green Room but they'd gone.

Don't be sad for her. Don't run away with the idea that it was a squalid, furtive, miserable thing, to make love for the first time on a cold night in a back alley with a married man with strong drink on his breath. He was the one she wanted, warts and all, she *would* have him, by hook or by crook. She had a passion to know about Life, all its dirty corners, and this is how she started, in at the deep end, for better or worse, while I stood shivering on the edge like the poor cat in the adage.

When she saw her man was gone, the plume-hatted goose-wife slapped her thigh. There was a jealous madness in that woman. I took the bull by the horns and started off the masquerade – I answered to the name of Nora and kept out of the same place as myself until Nora came back to the party, ripped stockings, smelling of dead fish, smiling like the cat that got the cream, and pregnant.

But we never found out she was pregnant until she lost it in Nottingham, the Royalty, when she haemorrhaged during a *fouetté*, we were a pair of spinning tops. Nothing like real blood in the middle of the song-and-dance act. It was long past panto-time, the goose gone off to Glasgow to do a *Chu Chin Chow*, he never wrote. Nora cried her eyes out but not because she'd lost the goose. She blazed and then she cooled; she'd always blaze, she'd always cool. No. She wept the loss of the baby.

Oh, my poor Nora! She was a martyr to fertility. After that miscarriage, I took steps, got her to get herself fitted up with the full equipment, but Nora never bothered with the diaphragm, not when she got carried away. A sort of grand carelessness possessed her each time she fell in love. She opened up, she melted down at the first touch, the first kiss; each time she fell in love, she fell in love for the first time, no matter how many times she fell in love and, when she fell in love, a Dutch cap was the last thing on her mind. I was in charge of the chequebook, too. She didn't trust herself with that, either.

After the miscarriage, she went round with a face like a month of Sundays for all of three weeks, then, whoops! head over heels, again, this time with the man who played the drums in the pit band and *he* was old enough to be her grandfather. She was particularly attracted to older men, in those days. Even if her diaphragm always stayed in its little box, the drummer took good care, always pulled out in time, and that went on for half a year, on and off, depending on the touring, although sometimes, when she stripped off, she'd be black and blue. 'Love-taps,' she said. I thought, preserve me from the passion of a percussionist.

The more I saw of love, the less I liked the look of it. I might well have reached the age of consent but that didn't mean I *had* to consent to it, whether I wanted to or not. Until that fateful engagement in Croydon, when I fell. Such was the effect of our new haircuts and our new, bubbling, brunette personalities that we now had second billing and a number in white satin pyjamas sitting side by side on a crescent moon. And, bliss! a dressing room of our very own. Nibbles from London managements. And we always liked Croydon, although it was a dump, just a dormitory town, just outside London, but we could get the late tram home and save on digs. I told you, Brixton used to be everso convenient for public transport.

I felt as if I'd met him somewhere else before, although I never had. I didn't think of love or passion when I thought of him; I only thought about the down on his delicious cheek.

As if it were yesterday. The show was called *Over to You.* Nora was ready for a change. She ditched the aged drummer and took up with a wee scrap of a lad pale as a lily, blond as a chick. He didn't know what hit him. Nora used to give her all. Because we shared the dressing room, I used to have to sit on the stairs outside and listen to them through the wall going at it like hammer and tongs on the horsehair sofa where we were supposed to put our feet up between shows. He muttered broken phrases, sometimes sobbed. Something about him touched my heart. Nora said, he was young enough to be grateful but it wasn't that.

I sat on the stairs outside and listened to them and my mind began to change, until I came to a decision: by hook or by crook, I said to myself, come what may, the day that I am seventeen, I'll do it on that horsehair sofa.

Do *what* on the horsehair sofa?

What do you think?

It was late April but still chilly. Little cold winds whipped round the wings and the bare backstage corners. We turned up our gas fire and plucked our eyebrows. There was a bunch of flowers for our birthday and a cake with candles ready for the party after the show.

'Nora . . .'

'Yes?'

'Give me your fella for a birthday present.'

She put down her tweezers and gave me a look.

'Get your own fella,' she said.

They'd sent us early lilac. The scent of white lilac always brings it back. Seventeen hurts.

'He's the only one I want, Nora.'

I'll only do it once, I said. He's really stuck on you, Nora, he's crazy about you and he's never given me a second look. But won't he be able to tell the difference? I don't know, we won't know until we try; but why should he notice any difference? Same eyes, same mouth, same hair. If it was only the once and if I keep my mouth shut . . . he is as innocent as asparagus, his heart as pure as Epps' cocoa, poor lamb. Why should he guess?

'Nora, I want him so.'

'Oh, *Dora*,' she said, for then she knew that only he would do.

She put on my Mitsouko and I put on her Shalimar. She had a new dress, floral chiffon, peonies, rhodies, dusty pink and misty blue and mauve, long skirts were back, I looked romantic. We took big breaths and blew out the candles on the cake; our wish at seven had come true and ever since I was a true believer in birthday-candle magic so you can guess what it was I wished for at seventeen. I smelled the unfamiliar perfume on my skin and felt voluptuous. As soon as they started to call me Nora, I found that I could kiss the boys and hug the principals with gay abandon because all that came quite naturally to her. To me, no. I was ever the introspective one.

As for Nora/Dora, she kept herself to herself until she'd had a couple and then she forgot to behave herself and carried on in her usual fashion but by the time she started dancing on the table most of the party was plastered so nobody noticed she was behaving out of character and that's how Dora got off with the pianist, to my considerable embarrassment in subsequent months.

There was a scratchy gramophone going full tilt. I laid claim to my birthday present as soon as he came shyly through the door. His face was still shining with cold cream. I took his hand. 'Let's dance,' I said.

'Nothing for me but to love you, just the way you look tonight . . .' sang the voice on the gramophone.

I know I wanted him more than anything, that his sweet face and his silken floss of flaxen hair moved me like nothing else had done in the masculine line before, but, all the same, I scarcely knew what it was I wanted, when all is said and done, in spite of Grandma's comprehensive sex education and all I'd seen during my life in the chorus and, more than all that, I'd seen my sister cry for love, and nearly bleed to death for love, and I'd listened while the one she loved made her shout out loud, when I was full of envy and desire. I thought I knew the lot, didn't I?

And yet I didn't know a thing.

Lilac; and a wind blowing in through the window they'd opened to let the fug out; and the smoke of the candles that I'd just blown out, still lingering in the room, catching at the throat; and the first kiss. I nearly fainted when we kissed, I was scared witless, I thought he'd recognise the ruse at once and suddenly I didn't want to go through with it. I wanted to go home to Grandma, to go back to yesterday's things we'd lost already – back to Mrs Worthington's piano, to our shorn sausage curls, to pick up our discarded liberty bodices and encase ourselves again in them. But he was just my own age, just seventeen, a child, too;

nothing to be afraid of. And for the purpose of the act, I wasn't Dora, any more, was I? Now I was Nora, who was afraid of nothing provided it was a man.

So I kissed him back and we slipped off.

He went to have a wash in the basin, first, while I stripped off and lay on the sofa watching him, the back of his neck bent humbly as he attended to himself. The water purled. Just the lights round the mirror were burning. A cab stopped outside and panted like a dog; there was a chink of coins: 'Ta, guv'nor.' These sounds might have come from another world.

He was too young for body hair. His tender flesh was all rosy in the light behind him. He smiled as he came towards me. It stuck out like a chapel hat peg. What did? What do you think? I couldn't keep my eyes off it. I'd never seen a naked man before although Grandma had drawn us pictures. There was a little clear drop of moisture trembling on the tip, it came to me to lick it off. He gave a gasp. His nipples were quite stiff, too. He was shivering a bit, not that it was cold, we'd left the gas fire on.

He never said: 'Nora, there's something different about you, something more enchanting, tonight.' I never wanted him to, either. I'd have been ashamed. I'll never know if he could tell the difference. If he did, he was too much of a gent to say. Skin like suede. Eyes the blue of the paper bags they used to sell you sugar in, years ago. I never bled or hurt; a decade and a half of *fouettés*, *jetés* and high kicks had done in the membrane without leaving a trace. He used a French letter, don't ever believe them if they tell you it takes away the romance. He sighed, his eyes rolled back so you could see the whites. Eyelashes a foot long.

Some things you can't describe.

Afterwards, I pretended to be asleep, I didn't dare talk. He spread my dressing gown on top of me, to keep the draughts off, and kissed my cheek. After a bit, he got up and put his clothes on, singing softly under his breath snatches of the song we'd danced to. 'That laugh that wrinkles your nose, touches my foolish heart . . .' I watched him secretly between my lashes. He gave me another kiss and a big smile he thought I couldn't see and went to catch the late trolley home to his mum and dad in Camberwell. Off he went, smelling of Shalimar and sex, and I

85

lay on the sofa and breathed in the smells of him and me that were really the smells of him and Nora and I kept a little sentimental tryst with silence and the night and the full moon over Croydon and he never would have done it if he'd known I wasn't Nora. He was the faithful type.

Did we betray the innocence of the boy with our deception? Of course we did. Does it matter? Let the one without sin cast the first stone. He really thought I was the one he loved so he was not deceived. And I got the birthday present that I wanted and then I gave him back to Nora and if Nora's heart had been less easily distracted, they would have gone on together, and on . . . until they stopped.

As it was, they went on together until they stopped, anyway. So that was that.

The lilac started to rot the morning after, went brown at the edges, reeked of bad breath. Irish, who taught me about metaphor, would have made a meal, if you follow me, out of that lilac.

After a decent interval, I got up, too, got dressed, again, dabbed on a bit more scent and went back to the party. By now, most of the guests had faded away, Dora included – she'd roared off in the piano player's little red sports car back to his flat in Chelsea. But that same record was still turning on the gramophone and chorus boys too tired to go home were swaying in each others' arms and there was a lingering sense in the air that something exciting had been happening while I'd been away. Then I saw what that exciting something was; he was fixing himself a Scotch and soda at the drinks tray, the man we'd last seen in a kilt, in the act of repudiating us. But now he was romantically garbed in evening dress, with a black evening cape with a scarlet lining over it. And he was, oh, wonders! smiling! At me!

It transpired the taxi I had heard draw up delivered me – our father.

God knows why Melchior felt the time had come to give us girls a call but I do think the Lady A., who soon emerged out of the shadows in a white Molyneux frock, had a hand in it, which is one of the reasons why we're prepared to put up with the old bag now, in her dotage.

I'll say this for the old man, he always had a sense of style. He took my hand.

'Strange how potent cheap music is.' he said.

The Lady A. smiled kindly on us and went so far as to wind up the gramophone. My heart went pit-a-pat. 'I will feel a glow' ... You'd have thought they only had the one record, the song that might have been written exclusively for that night ... 'just thinking of you, and the way you look tonight.' I'd never so much as shaken his hand before that night of nights. He didn't dance badly, for a Shakespearian. It was all too much for me, suddenly. I couldn't help it, I burst out crying.

'Don't cry, little girl,' my father said. 'Happy birthday. And I've got you a very special birthday present.'

Although he did not live in heaven, our father was in constant communication with the angels. And that is how we came to star, alongside his very self, in that soon-to-be-famous West End revue entitled *What You Will*.

The music stopped, the lights were going out, the boys departing. The party was over. He dropped a kiss on top of my head, a light little kiss, a butterfly kiss, but a kiss, all the same. I thought: I'll never wash my hair again. Then they were gone.

I lashed out, took a cab home, but I was in such a state I stopped it at Leigham Court Road, got out and walked the rest of the way. I needed air. It was getting light by the time I got back to Brixton, the sky was the colour of a gas jet. I had on a new pair of shoes I was very fond of, I thought they were the peak of chic – red morocco. High heels, ankle straps. Cost a fortune. My high heels went clip, clip, clip on the pavement and I never felt more grown-up in all my life ever after than I did that early morning, watching my shadow teeter-totter home in front of me in those sexy shoes. Because, during the night that now was over, I had made love to a boy for the first time; and my father had kissed me, for the first time; I'd heard my name would be up in lights on Shaftesbury Avenue, for the first time, and I was choked up inside with the pleasure and the terror of the world.

Grandma was still up when I got home, sucking at one last

crème de menthe frappé in her kimono. When she saw my face with all the glory in it, she put the kettle on the stove for tea and gave me a hug.

'Whoever he is,' she said, 'he's not worth it.'

Why was Grandma still up?

Why was she dealing the *coup de grâce* to a freshly opened bottle of liqueur?

The answer to these questions sprawled at immense and magnificent ease in Grandma's best armchair, fast asleep and snoring. God, he'd put on weight! Busting out of his waistcoat, and his bookie's suit of ginger plaid, and his fingers a-glitter with big, fat, diamond rings, and his shoes black and white like spotted dogs – correspondent's shoes.

My uncle had come home again.

We dressed up, we made up and then we spent the hour before curtain-up on the West End premiere of *What? You Will?* dashing for the lavatory to throw up. First I thought I'd fallen for it, a bittersweet emotion – I *was* in a state, but my friend, Mr Piano Man, made a speedy diagnosis – nerves, so we all had a brandy and felt better. All London and his dog packed out the house. We'd done a roaring try-out in Manchester, we'd been a smash, but all the same Mr Piano Man now confessed to a touch of nausea himself, because there was more to him than met the eye as one might have guessed by his style, his smart motor, his apartment, etc. etc. He'd done all the music, hadn't he? Every note. It was make or break for him, that night, but after another brandy we started to feel fine.

He went out a piano player and came back a star, *What! You Will?* his first big hit. After that he did a string of musicals, all smashes in their time, every one forgotten now. Not a soul remembers. He always thought of me as 'Dora' and, this was the confusing thing, I *was* 'Dora', but not the Dora he'd fallen for, although he didn't notice any difference, either, and always sent me lilac, lots and lots of lilac, the sentimental thing. I'd got nothing whatever against him; he gave me lovely hot dinners, we had some good times, but when he gave me a kiss for luck that night, I turned the other cheek, I didn't like the way his breath smelled and Nora, ever worldly wise, said: 'That means you're going off him.' I lived in fear he would propose.

'Break a leg,' he said.

He joined up, first thing. Missing in action in 1942. I used to go and see his mother, sometimes, in Golders Green. There was his photo on the piano, and the music for the song I sang, he made a fuss, he got his way – Dora's very own number. 'O Mistress Mine.' You can't say fairer than that. The piano was open, there was the music, nobody to play it. I used to take his mother the occasional black-market egg.

Melchior came in at the last moment and gave us his blessing, with a look that said he knew we knew but he wasn't going to ask for our forgiveness because wasn't he just about to give us our big chance? With the bald wig on, he looked uncannily like; he was personating, who else – the 'Will', in *What! You Will!* in person. Shakespeare.

I must tell you that our father had become a truly great man of the theatre, by this time. Now he was fortyish – although he didn't look it, with all that velvet glamour – and peaking. At the apex. 'Our greatest living Shakespearian.' Luck had a lot to do with it, not to mention the Lady A.'s private fortune financed his Shylock and his Richard III and his Macbeth in Brighton that gave us girls so much grief. (He'd always steered clear of Hamlet, though, and now he was too old; perhaps he was nervous the critics might think he wasn't half the man his mother had been.)

Yet still he yearned for new fields to conquer. Wheelchair swears that ever since she told him how she'd seen his left-hand daughters do the splits, he'd nourished a yen to try out song and dance. I used to think that he and Perry were chalk and cheese – never take them for brothers, let alone twins. But nowadays I'm not so sure. Ambition, the curse and glory of the Hazards, who'll risk everything they've got and a little bit more on a throw of the dice.

For, if Melchior Hazard starred as the eponymous William Shakespeare, then who had written it, conceived it, planned it, put it all together?'

Why, Peregrine Hazard.

So they were a team at last.

What You Will! Dazzling new revue!
They were a team at last and they were a triumph.

We were eighteen years old, hair like patent leather, legs up to
our ears. We sported bellhop costumes for our *Hamlet* skit;
should, we pondered in unison and song, the package be delivered to, I kid you not, '2b or not 2b'. We performed a synco-
pated Highland fling in tasselled sporrans after, as weird sisters,
we burst out of a giant haggis in a number based on the banquet
scene; in abbreviated togas, led the chorus during the 'Roman
Scandals' number; I sang my solo 'O Mistress Mine' in
fifteenth-century drag to a mutely mutinous Nora on a balcony
– she got the last laugh when she poured a bucket of water over
me, and I didn't have much of a voice, anyway, but Mr Piano
Man was besotted; we did a Morris dance with bells upon our
ankles, than sang 'It was a lover and his lass' in harmony and
parts ('Hey nonny bloody no'); and went through a spirited ver-
sion of the Egyptian sand dance on the deck of a large gilded
barge that glided slowly from one side of the stage to the other
in the spectacular conclusion of the first part of the show.

Our frocks were sumptuous. No short-cuts, no half measures
– real silk, real satin, real feathers, sequins by the truckload.
There's a lot of conspicuous consumption in show business. Even
the backdrops were awesome. There was a mural copied from
the British Museum for the *Cleopatra* number, a bit of a John
Martin behind *Macbeth*. The actual finale featured the Lady A.
as Good Queen Bess. She didn't have much to do but stand
around which was just as well because she wasn't the song-and-
dance type but she stood magnificently, in a red wig and a frock
copied off a miniature in the V and A with a farthingale the size
of the Albert Hall and half a ton of imitation pearls round her
neck. Nice touch, her two little girls debuted in doublet and hose
as pages.

Saskia and Imogen would have been, ooh, sixish, sevenish, by
then and, God, we cordially hated one another, especially me and
Saskia. She was only a wee scrap with big eyes and carrot curls
but she'd stick her foot out and trip me up, she snagged my tights
on nails, she was a little terror and if he'd featured her in Alexan-

dria, I'd have dumped her off the barge and let her drown.

Either the markets had recovered, by this time, or a good deal of fiddling went on while Rome was burning because we had charge accounts opened for us at Harrods by gents who kept it from their wives. All day long, vans delivered to Bard Road the proceeds of our shopping – silk underwear, cashmere jumpers, silk stockings in quantity, we couldn't get enough stockings. We never even thought of darning our stockings, now, once we'd holed them, we passed them on to the girls in the chorus and treated ourselves to more.

Grandma ate the contents of the ribboned baskets of exotic fruits delivered daily, but the flowers set the cat among the pigeons.

Grandma read it in a book. I swear, to this day, she only did it to annoy us but, from this book, she took into her head the notion flowers suffered pain. How, when you cut a flower, it emits a fearful scream of anguish – happily, audible only to other flowers, but Grandma claimed her ears were sensitive enough to catch the echo; has a fearful spasm; a crisis, then goes into rigor mortis. After that, she'd cross the road if she saw a florist's shop, so as not to ravage her sensibilities or injure her eardrums. What with dodging butcher's shops, too, and furrier's, going out with Grandma was all ducking and weaving, like a short walk through no-man's-land.

But boys on bikes delivered flowers hourly. Roses, carnations, tuberoses, lilies, orchids, mixed bunches, flowers I'd never known existed, flowers that looked as though they were rotting, flowers that looked rude. Grandma would greet the delivery boy with a long face and moan and keen over our floral tributes.

'Wires through their hearts, poor things . . . criminal!'

She'd take them out to the back yard and stick them in the compost, wailing glumly the while. Then there was the jewellery. Which we concealed from her, in case it entered her unaccountable head to make us give it back. Sometimes we thought, in our youthful, heedless vanity, that the old bag was jealous of us.

Stars on our door, stars in our eyes, stars exploding in the bits of our brains where the common sense should have been.

Our Uncle Peregrine was rich, again, and always laughing. It made a noise in his belly like barrels rolling around a cellar. Melchior went so far as to offer him a walk-on as Falstaff but Perry turned it down. He was happier in the wings. He liked to pull the strings and see the puppets move, he said; you might think, if you heard him say that, he was a cold-hearted bugger but cold-hearted, never! He was the heart and soul of mirth.

He and Grandma would sit hugely wedged in the breakfast-room armchairs, gossiping away for hours, breaking into fruity chuckles, the bottle of crème de menthe, the bucket of ice beside them – nothing but the best for Grandma Chance, these days. When it was growing light, outside, they'd hear our key in the lock, they'd hush up as best they could, one last hiccup of merriment, then the old lady would rise up and put on the kettle. 'Condescended to come home at last, have you, you celestial bodies.' If one of us came home alone, she'd roll her eyes and intone hollowly: 'Ooh la fucking la!' She'd check our handbags to make sure we had our Dutch caps with us. 'Give the girls a break,' said Perry. 'They're only young once. I bet you raised hell yourself, when you were their age.' But references to that forbidden country, her past, were taboo.

Then tenor, Nora's boyfriend, went off somewhere up North, lost touch, and Nora fell, again – blazed, cooled; fell again, blazed, cooled; and again – I lost count of how many times she fell in love, that year. Meanwhile, my friend offered me a fur coat. He liked me very much.

'Not a fur, Mr Piano Man, thank you very much,' I said. 'Whatever would Grandma say?' But he wouldn't take no for an answer and a van delivered a big box next morning. In the box, among the tissue paper, a grey squirrel jacket, fingertip length, frail and lovely, 'like her own virtue', as poor old Irish would have put it a year or so hence in another country, but Irish could never afford to give me furs, he taught me to eschew the double negative, instead.

Once that jacket arrived I hadn't the heart to give it back although Grandma cut up something terrible. I've got it still, it's in the big wardrobe in Grandma's room that we don't use any more, wrapped up in a white sheet, there's a ghost of antique Mitsouko clinging to the hairs, mothballs in one pocket, in the other the dehydrated skeleton of a gardenia left where I stuffed it after a Certain Distinguished Person took it out of his buttonhole and slipped it down my cleavage, such as it was, not that Nora and I were ever over-endowed in the bosom department, but, if I'd had a cleavage, that is what his nose would have come up to, he was only a little chap.

Grandma was apoplectic when I got home. The juxtaposition of flora and fauna on my person was too much for her. 'You wouldn't cut off a baby's head and stick it on your best friend's flayed corpse for decoration, would you?' 'I never met a squirrel socially,' I said. I cheeked her. I brazened it out. Perry guffawed but Grandma blew down her nose, huff huff huff, and when she found out who it was that gave me the gardenia, her fury knew no bounds. She had a real down on the Royal Family.

You know the song about the girl who 'danced with a man who danced with a girl who danced with the Prince of Wales'? I was the original girl. Nora, too. He couldn't tell the difference any more than anybody else could.

He dearly loved to tango. He'd have tangoed all night, if he could. He'd tango on remorselessly for a good half-hour at a time, it was a real test of your stamina. The band had to go on playing as long as he could keep it up, since he was royalty, but a tango normally lasts just the four minutes so it was as much of an ordeal as anything, especially if you'd done two shows and a matinée already. We preferred to do it in the afternoons, at the Ritz, tango teas, after they brought in dancing in the restaurant. I once picked up a flea at the Ritz in the Marie Antoinette Suite but that was later on, during the war, when I was entertaining the Free French.

Now we frequented fashionable nightclubs, smart restaurants and flash hotels. Perry took us all to the Savoy Grill on our birthday, that year, not forgetting Grandma, although she hated going into town, these days, we'd had to push and prod her into her corset and bribe her with gin into the taxi. She'd overdone the rouge, perhaps because she'd overdone the gin, and she looked rakish as hell, sneering at the waiters on two fronts – she despised them for being servile but was the first to take umbrage if they spoke out of turn. And there we were, us girls, done up to the nines, little navy suits, gloves to match, red hats with big brims down over one eye, nice shoes, nice handbags, trying to look as if she didn't belong to us, and Peregrine, at ease, as ever, enjoying every minute, the bastard.

The waiter hovered: 'For the first course may I suggest oysters, caviar, smoked salmon . . .' 'That sounds quayte nayce, thanks very much,' she said so she had all three, washing them festively down with crème de menthe, lifting her pinky like a dog lifts its leg as she raised her glass. 'Bottoms up, ducky!' she said to Peregrine. 'Just say the word, babes!' he replied, clinking. He led her on. We could have dropped through the floor.

She kept her clothes on more and more. I noticed that. She came into the bathroom, once, she never dreamed of knocking, she hadn't got a stitch on. Me neither, I was just drying off after my bath. There we both were, captured in the mirror, me young and slim and trim and tender, she vast, sagging, wrinkled, quivering. I couldn't help but giggle. I shouldn't have. I could have slapped myself, afterwards. But I couldn't take that giggle back.

'That's all very well, Dora,' she said, 'but one fine day, you'll wake up and find you're old and ugly, just like me.'

Then she cackled. I'd never even thought that, years back, she might have been pretty. She cackled and she cackled. All the same, she went to get a dressing gown before she came back to have her wee and there was a coolness between us, after that, lasted for months.

I see it, now, as a defeat that we, her beloved grandchildren, inflicted upon her out of heedlessness and vanity and youth. A nudist might be able to grow old gracefully in the company of other ageing nudists, but she had the misfortune to live with two teenage sexpots, didn't she, who weren't about to honour their Grandma's naturism when it offended their aesthetics and, worse still, might put off any of the young men who came to pick us up and drop us off if they caught sight of it. Nevertheless, we should have spared her feelings more.

All that spring, all that summer, the telephone rang for the Lucky Chances and Grandma took our messages in a wheezing, grumbling, ungracious manner, occasionally announcing our abode as: 'Battersea Dogs' Home'.

She was our grandma and we loved her but, at times, during our year of grace, not much.

I can see, now, that we were à la mode, that year, because we were something piquant, something new; there's a kind of style you can only acquire on the wrong side of the tracks and our grace was a scrawny, alley-cat grace, even if we thought that we were really something. We never saw what other people saw. I would look at Nora, faithful as my looking glass, and see a suave sophisticate with geranium lips and that *faux*-naïve Dutch doll hairdo which had become our trademark. Yet when I flick back through Grandma's scrapbooks, the pictures I see are of a couple of street urchins decked up like Christmas trees in all kinds of risky, frisky, flightly, unbecoming gladrags that they wear as if it were a joke.

We looked as if we had dressed up as grown-ups to go out on the town and, such was the force of our innocence, the champagne they poured out for us would turn to ginger pop the moment it touched our pretty little, silly little lips.

Fate continued to deal kindly with Melchior. Not only had our greatest living Shakespearian triumphed in musical comedy, he was rolling in money. The revue was a licence to print it. He lived in considerable style. Besides the big house in Eaton Square (to which I couldn't help but note we'd never been invited except the once, and then unilaterally by the Lady A., for nursery bloody tea, to which we hadn't gone), there was a major estate in Sussex that had been in the Lady A.'s family since Guillaume Brede de Lynde knocked out some Saxon yokel the year after the Battle of Hastings, and the big house that went with it, plus the Home Farm, assorted hovels for the plebs and a village or two. He'd used his new wealth to do a lot of work on Lynde Court, done it out as befitted the country residence of the Royal Family of the British Theatre – that is, palatially.

But his heredity was too strong for him. He couldn't help it, but that manor house always retained a look of here today, gone tomorrow; he was a player to his marrow so he lived in a permanent stage set. He wanted a house that looked as if each leather armchair in the library had been there at least a half a century, where a misty patina of age softened the reflections in the mirror so they would be kind to the crows'-feet as they gently settled round his eyes, poor old thing, but the Mayfair peeress he'd got in to do it up for him incorporated into the interior just that little bit extra you need for the stage, as if in tribute to his profession. So the aged leather was cracked and fissured a little bit more than was absolutely necessary; the mirrors were distressed so much as to look quite marbled; and the walls turned out the colours of very rare roast beef and gravy, too Garrick Club for words.

'He has given himself,' said Peregrine, looking at the picture papers, 'marginally too august a setting.' Grandma went off in shrieks.

Now I am old, I think I know why Grandma didn't like us at eighteen – we felt no irony; how easily we were impressed!

In this 'marginally too august a setting' Melchior gave the performance of his life as Lord of the Manor, even if the Lady A., though ever at his side, always showed faint sings of embarrassment and little Saskia, plus, when she hadn't nodded off, little Imogen gave spirited impersonations of imps of Satan for, amongst the suits of armour, the dead fish in glass cases, the antique weapons crossed upon the panelling, there was always a place to hide and then jump out of with ear-splitting screeches, something priceless to caress with sticky fingers, a stuffed fox to look for maggots in at dinner-time, and guests, so many guests, to torture at leisure during the extended rural incarceration of the English country-house weekend. Holly in the beds, frogs in the bathtubs. On one memorable occasion, or so I was told, frogspawn in the porridge.

Not that *we* were ever invited down there for the weekend.

So I have to admit, although through gritted teeth, we were thrilled – although we were suspicious – when, that first, triumphant Christmas of the run of *What You Will*, we were bidden, though more in the manner of a royal command than an invitation, to attend the Lynde Court Twelfth Night Costume Ball.

We would drive down, after the show, and join in the fun as if by right and it turned out we didn't even need to worry, 'What to wear?' since we were told to keep on our 'weird sister' sporrans and be prepared to burst out of a bloody great Hogmanay haggis at a given signal clutching lumps of coal and first-foot them with a brisk jig. Melchior's social secretary assured us we would find the stone-flagged floor of the Great Hall admirably suited to this purpose.

'If they want us to sing for our supper,' said Nora, 'they can stuff it.'

'Don't you realise who'll be there?' said my friend, the famous composer, tingling all over. 'Half Hollywood will be there!'

Don't misunderstand me, his breath didn't smell bad; nevertheless, the smell of his breath so repulsed me by now that whenever I paid off an instalment on my squirrel jacket I had to turn my back, to which he, having been to public school, was nothing loath.

Perry laughed and slapped his belly.

'Hurray for Hollywood! Who d'ya think invited these guys? This could be your big break, girls!'

We understood at last that Melchior's party was the cover for a gigantic audition and it behooved us to polish up our tap-shoes until we snugged ourselves in rugs and piled into my soi-disant or now virtually ex-lover's sports car after the show, clutching a greasy paper package of bacon sandwiches we'd picked up from the cabbies' coffee-stall the other side of Battersea Bridge to sustain us en route, because it was a two-hour drive through a raging blizzard and I was starving, again, when we arrived.

The snow had finished falling, there was a muffled hush. Everything gleamed because of the icy moon, up high, and not even later on, in Hollywood, at MGM, whose slogan was, 'More stars than there are in Heaven', never did I see so many. The ancient lawns wore thick pelts of snow, the rose trees loaded with it. A terrace, with statues in capes and hats of snow; a choked fountain. Lynde Court was built in the eclectic style, that is, a little bit of this and that, but all of it ancient, turrets and pediments snow-capped, swagged cornices and fairy-tale lattices caked and frosted. I never saw a house look lovelier. It took my breath away.

All relocated to Memory lane, now, of course, lock, stock and barrel.

To greet us on the steps, a consort of lutes, in costume,

plucking away at some ancient air. Oh, very tasteful, very sweet. Their breath smoked, their noses glowed; the only discordant note, the horn-rimmed spectacles. We'd been to some smart parties since we got the star on our door but never one as smart as this. We clutched hands, we were intimidated, we hung back.

But then we saw our Uncle Perry, who'd gone down earlier with the hosts, bursting genially out of his white tie and tails, blazing away in the middle of the snow like a hot stove, caught in the act of withdrawing a rabbit from a bass viol. And even though the rabbit instantly turned into our little cousin, Saskia, whom he kissed and cuddled with an enthusiasm that filled us with a jealous rage, the sight of him gave us enough heart to jump out of the motor and run towards him.

As soon as she saw us coming, Saskia wriggled out of his arms, pouting, shaking herself like a wet dog, and legged it. Perry was downcast; he could turn her into a rabbit at will but he could never make her love him. He cheered up when he saw us, picked us up one after the other and swung us off our feet up in the air, as he used to do to us when we were Saskia's age but she, evidently, never let him do it to her. I could see her at a distance, glowering malevolently at us.

We made our entrance into the Great Hall in style, on either arm of Perry's. All around there was a rustle and a whisper: 'Here come the Lucky Chances. Of course, they're really Peregrine's daughters, you know.' They all believed it. Only the immediately affected parties knew it wasn't so.

The Lady A., in full Gloriana wig and frock, and Melchior, as – you've guessed! – received their motley guests, all garbed consistently with the Shakespearian motif. A kiss and a handshake, respectively. We were not excluded; we got our kiss and our handshake like everybody else and then we got a glass of bubbly and trooped off into the Great Hall, where my beau, done up in cap and bells, was already installed at a white grand piano tinkling away at a selection of songs from the show while glossy women propped their cleavages on the Bechstein lid.

There was a log fire in a hearth that took up half one wall and a sky like Bristol glass outside the leaded windows and stuffed swan on the buffet, I kid you not. The waiter carved for me, I gagged. Nora, I noticed, was already deep in vivacious conversation with a little, bald, fat man who'd come in boots and riding breeches, I couldn't think as what, who, as he talked, sketched wide circles in the air with his cigar.

'I couldn't fancy swan,' I said to the waiter. 'Too many feathers. Have you got anything else a girl could nibble?'

He raised his face from the carving knife. Those eyes. My heart went pit-a-pat.

'Fancy meeting you,' I said, I stammered, so full of joy I could have wept.

'Times are hard,' he said. 'Too many tenors, not sufficient songs.'

So he was doubling as a waiter. We could not stop looking at each other. Behind my back, my sister's voice was raised in song and, glory be, she'd borrowed mine: 'In delay, there lies no plenty, So come kiss me . . .'

'Nora,' he said to me.

' . . . sweet and twenty.'

We leaned towards each other across the carcase of the violated swan. There was a great press of people. We hid behind the feathers, we kissed, and kissed, and kissed, until by unspoken but mutual consent we ducked under the tablecloth, dropped down on all fours and ran along the whole length of the buffet, under the table. The big, white tablecloth hung down on either side, it was like bolting down a hospital corridor. I put that midnight date with the haggis out of my mind; I'd got other fish to fry. When we came out the other end, Nora was dancing with the bald, fat man; he must have put his cigar down, somewhere, to leave his mouth free so he could nuzzle her neck while the hand that did not stroke her bare back was beating a tattoo on her bum.

My boy and I held hands. We ran up the black oak staircase, everything in monochrome, moonlight, shadow, snow, past carved wreaths of bay and piles of fruit and big-bosomed women with garlands on their heads, until we found what we were looking for, the master bedroom – instantly recognisable by my father's fetish, the cardboard crown once worn by Old Ranulph in *Lear*, under a glass case on the mantelpiece.

There was a log fire glowing away here, too, and the bedcover turned back, and a little draught came down the chimney gently agitating the stumpwork curtains on the fourposter so that Samson and Delilah, Judith and Holofernes, all the needlework men and women moved a little as we lay down as if those old lovers were greeting these ones who now were hastening to renew their acquaintance with one another.

I offed the false eyelashes, snitched a handful of the Lady A.'s cotton wool to wipe off my make-up. Tonight, this night of all nights, I wanted to look like myself, whoever that was.

'I dye my hair,' I said.

'I know,' he said.

To die for love runs in the family. My grandmother did it; so did my mother. And that night was the one time in all my life I thought that such a thing might be worth while. He took his time and I took mine. In the time we'd been apart, a little crown of golden hairs had sprung up around his nipples but not so that you'd notice, unless you were looking hard.

'Nora,' he said, as we lay wet and panting. 'Nora . . . you've changed your perfume.'

I only had to speak, to say: 'Not Nora, my darling, but Dora, who loves you only.' And there would have been one more happy housewife behind some garden fence in Slough or Cheam, and a bellyful of kids. Those words that would have changed everything were on the tip of my tongue, would you believe; but there they stayed, because, at that very moment, my lover crinkled up his nose.

'Can you smell burning?'

I pointed to the cosy logs. He shook his head.

'Not that . . .'

Came a big red scream from down below:

'FIRE!'

After that, pandemonium. Shouting, cries, screams. A crashing of smashing plates from overturned tables; clattering footsteps; and all the lutes went out of tune in unison when dropped in haste. And, yes; now I could hear the roar of the flames.

We were up and running for the door *toot sweet*, I can tell you, but the old oak felt warm and when we got it open a huge hot wind tossed us backwards, we saw the stairwell was alight already. The gargoyles on the beam ends sparked, glowed and blackened; there was a crash below as a ceiling gave way and in the middle of all the rest of the noise I could tell it fell on the grand piano because of one last jangled chord before it expired with a noise like an angel falling off its harp.

A long tongue of flame licked up the stairs, in through the bedroom door; up went the bed curtains behind us – flaming so soon after we got off the mattress that you might have thought the bed caught fire due to what we had got up to on it. I was stuck staring at my little sporran, tossed up and spinning round in the fierce winds that came with the fire, and then the fire snapped it up like a frog snaps a gnat. He gave me a big shove.

'Quick.'

I snapped out of it sharpish and we made it to the window before the tapestries went up, which they did with a whoosh whilst we hand-over-handed it down the ivy, bringing down a deluge of snow with us. Only when we stood once more upon the lawn, chilled to the marrow, singed at the edges, half frozen cod, half barbecued spareribs, did I recall that the fire had got not only my 'weird sister' outfit but also his waiter's monkey suit, so we both were 'naked as nature intended', to quote the title of another of the dubious vehicles of the Chance sisters' declining years. I buried my blushes in his bosom. He stroked my hair. 'Nora,' he said tenderly. 'Nora . . .'

So very tenderly the truth was on the tip of my tongue, again, but then, while Lynde Court blazed and the survivors of the party mopped and mowed upon the terrace, wringing their hands and making noise, and the clanging of the fireman's bell announced the arrival of the engines, even in the midst of all this turmoil I felt the stirring of, ahem, his manhood and couldn't resist. So we bundled off into the shrubbery and did it again on an uncomfortable carpet of twigs and dried earth under the cover of the rhododendrons which our enthusiasm whipped into a storm so they pelted down snow and more snow on us while all around, backwards and forwards, there passed a swift parade of running feet, churning the fall to slush. As far as ambience was concerned, it was from the sublime to the ridiculous, but needs must, it was urgent.

Surprise, surprise, we were quick about it, this time.

And, to my everlasting shame, it was only after he rolled off me and I sat up did I stop to think: 'Oh, my God – *my sister!*'

Believe me, even then, when so much in love, I never, not for one moment, thought, if . . . she's burned to a crisp . . . then . . . he's mine for ever.

Not even for one second.

To tell the truth, I love her best and always have.

It was a proper raree show, out on the Great Lawn. All the former revellers were black with soot and the Lady A., in a scorched wig and a skeleton petticoat of black sticks and smoke, clutched one scrap to her bosom tight enough to choke her, although that scrap, being Imogen, was unconcerned, and slept, while the Lady A. wept and wailed and kept on calling for the other one, who'd made herself scarce, although I, for one, wouldn't have put it past that Saskia to have torched the family seat out of some small pique such as not enough cream on her strawberries or having been sent to bed before the cabaret.

But of Nora I could see no trace and my heart sank.

Nor of Uncle Perry, neither, although, until his plane crashed in Amazonia and, weeks lengthening into months, then years, we were finally forced to acknowledge that he, too, owed a debt to mortality, Nor' and I both privately thought he was indestructible.

Then I spotted Saskia. She, oblivious of her distracted mother, was tucked away under a rosebush, pigging it. She'd dragged out with her the entire carcase of the swan from the Great Hall. Its feathers were so blackened by the soot it looked more like an upstart crow but *that* didn't put the little greedyguts off as she crouched, legs akimbo, disarticulating one by one its limbs and chewing off the meat with every appearance of enjoyment. Of course, later on, she made a career out of piggery. She'd half-inched a bowl of salad, too, but unaccountably left behind the haggis, no doubt upon discovering that it was hollow.

So there was Saskia. But Nora, not.

They say, if you get your leg cut off, you don't notice it, at first, until you try to put your weight on it. Then you fall down. It was like that with me and Nora. The young man was flat on his back under the rhodies, panting heavily, lost to the world, and well might he sing out, 'Oh, Mistress Mine, where are you roving?' when he came to, for I took off in frantic search.

The fire had unleashed a kind of madness. A babble of agitated chorines cross-dressed in ruched knicks and hose had commandeered a crate of bubbly on their way out and now, pop! with a fusillade of small explosions, opened the bottles and hurled the contents into the fire, whinnying helplessly under the strain of their fruitless endeavours, while a row of chorus boys, in jester's garb, lacking champagne, unfastened their flies and added their own liquid contributions to the great arcs of solid water directed by the stout fellows of the East Sussex Fire Brigade into the heart of the blaze, where enormous rainbows formed in the air above the jets.

The tenor and me weren't the only ones who'd succumbed to nature, either. Nothing whets the appetite like a disaster. Out of the corner of my eye, I spotted Coriolanus stoutly buggering Banquo's ghost under the pergola in the snowy rose-garden whilst, beside the snow-caked sundial, a gentleman who'd come as Cleopatra was orally pleasuring another dressed as Toby Belch. Not only that. I spied with my little eye an egg-shaped depression in a snowdrift on the parterre surmounted by the lead soubrette who was grinding away for dear life in the woman-on-top position and it turned out the moaning recipient of her favours was who else but my now definitively ex-lover, his cap was gone, but his bells were all tinkling, and he made her a star in her own right in his next production. Good for her. She said she saw him coming and tripped him up. Irish girl, from Derry. Staunch Republican, in those days. She's a Dame of the British Empire, now.

So there was an orgiastic aspect to this night of disaster and all around the blazing mansion, lit by the red and flickering flames, milled the lamenting revellers in togas, kilts, tights, breeches, hooped skirts, winding sheets, mini-crinolines, like guests at a masquerade who've all gone suddenly to hell. It was a keen and icy night and the stars were sharp as needles.

I ran like one possessed from group to group of thwarted party-goers, searching for my lost limb, the best part of me, whom I'd so thoughtlessly forgotten – forgotten! – in the heat of passion. Then and there, although my nipples were still bruised with kisses, I thought, well, that's it for passion, because, without Nora, life wasn't worth living.

That's sisters for you.

I was crying so much I could hardly see straight so I blundered right into Melchior, still in his hose and doublet, but black with soot all over, and gave myself a big bruise on the hip because he was pushing, pulling, grunting, heaving at a big carved chair with arms that ended up in lions' heads. He'd salvaged it from the blaze, somehow or other, and now he was dragging it into a commanding position in the very middle of the lawn, a place that offered a front-stalls view of the fiery finale of the house he'd planned to be so famous in. 'Give us a hand,' he said.

When we'd got the armchair where he wanted it, down he plumped.

'Champagne!' he called and, marvellous to relate, a waiter popped up like a conjuring trick with a silver ice-bucket on a sterling salver. I wiped off my face with the back of my hand.

'Dora?' he said. 'Or is it Nora? Come and take a glass of wine with the prince in exile, dear child.'

I stepped closer. He cracked me an enchanting smile. Not the sign of a tear. I gaped. Never seen such sang-froid as Melchior's before.

'I must say, you're taking it very well, sir,' I said. (We always called him 'sir' to his face.)

'Can't a man enjoy a glass of wine at his own fireside?'

The waiter poured one for me, so I took it. We clinked.

'You've lost your eyebrows,' he remarked.

'Worse than that,' I said, and sobbed. 'I've lost my sister.'

'I've lost,' he said, 'my crown.'

From the way he said it, I knew the loss of a natural daughter weighed less heavy on his heart than the loss of the old Hazard heirloom I'd just seen in his bedroom. For a weak moment, there, my unreconstructed daughter's heart wished I could have saved it for him but, though my front was toasty warm due to the flames of Lynde Court, my backside was bitter cold and so were my spirits.

'My crown, my foolish crown, my paper crown of a king of shreds and patches,' he lamented. 'The crown my father wore as Lear – to have survived so many deaths, so much heartbreak, so many travels . . . and now, gone up in smoke! Oh, my dear girl, we mummers are such simple folk . . . superstitious as little children. The fire was welcome to take everything, the frills and furbelows, the toys and gewgaws, the oil paintings, the cloisonné, the Elizabethan oak . . . but, oh, my crown! That cardboard crown, with the gold paint peeling off. Do you know, can you guess, my dear, how much it meant to me? More than wealth, or fame, or women, or children . . .'

I'd better believe that, what he said about children. I was amazed to see him so much moved, and on account of what? A flimsy bit of make-believe. A nothing.

'What shall I do without my crown? Othello's occupation gone!'

He began to cry. The tears ran down his sooty cheeks like chalk down a blackboard but, and this was the funny thing, although my own tear ducts remained untickled, my palms itched and prickled like anything and I knew the only way to ease the irritation was to clap them together. Just as I was about to give the old fraud a big hand, couldn't help it, the waiter, who was hovering by, as struck with this performance as I was, caught hold of my arm, spilling my champagne.

'Look!'

A miracle.

Out of the heart of the blaze, through the very portals of flame that now upheld what had been the lintel of the front door of Ye Old Lynde Court, came, vaguely at first and yet his outlines growing every instant more distinct, an enormous figure.

The currents of the heat distorted his shape and size; he looked as big as the burning house, or bigger, and flames lapped and licked around him until it looked as if he were wearing fire. Something was shining; for one dreadful minute, I thought that he was dead and it was his haloed ghost approaching but, as he left the fire behind him, I saw what it was he'd got on his head.

In his arms, a girl.

'Oh!' went I; and, 'Ah!' went Melchior.

Who else could that girl be but Nora? And what else could that shining something be but a battered old crown of gilded cardboard, cocked at a rakish angle, unsinged, unmarked by fire, sootless, as Peregrine was himself and as was Peregrine's burden.

We tried to run to meet them but found we could not, found we bounced back upon an invisible barrier of air so hot it made the hairs upon my forearms sizzle. Peregrine walked firmly towards us, leaving black footprints behind him on the lawn. He walked out of the fire, smiling at Melchior, offering up to Melchior his safe, sleeping child.

That tenor had found something to cover up his nakedness, a cashmere coat, property, it turned out, of the Hollywood producer whose cigar, abandoned on the edge of the dining table while he danced with Nora, had fallen to the floor, there to smoulder away unnoticed on the stone flags until the hem of the white tablecloth began to smoulder, too.

And, after the hem of the white tablecloth had smouldered for a while, an adventurous little blue flame licked up the side of that white linen cloth, to see what was on top of the table and, if that first little flame, satisfied with what it found, fell back, unnoticed, then the second little flame crept up a wee bit further, unnoticed, too.

Why didn't a waiter see and stamp out the conflagration while it was in its infancy?

Because the waiter at whose station the fire had chosen to begin wasn't a *serious* waiter, no pro, just a body hired for the big do, and he, as it happened, quit his post precipitately to slip upstairs with a female guest at the urgent promptings of his –

But we did not know all this until much later.

There they all were, gathering on the lawn behind us, all the guests, every one, in their rags of finery blackened as if plunged into mourning, and the Lady A. and our little cousins, whom even I could pity, now, poor homeless creatures, Saskia still sucking on a charred wing of swan, the arsonist producer, my ex-lover buttoning his fly, all the chorus, every principal, the musicians, the waiters, the cooks, the scullery-maids. Even the firemen abandoned their pumps and came to see.

All watched as Perry brought out my sister safe.

Everything held its breath.

She stirred. Her eyelids shivered.

Before I could move a muscle, my boyfriend, *her* boyfriend, shoved past me and scooped her up right out of Perry's arms; he was laughing and crying all at once, hugging her and showering her face with kisses.

Now she opened her eyes, all right, but she didn't smile to see him, nor did she kiss him back.

'Where's Dora?' she said. Her first words.

'Oh, you brave little girl!' said that innocent young man. 'So you went back to look for Dora! You risked your life!'

Nora looked round a touch wildly, I thought. Then – discretion is the better part – she fainted. Melchior had no eyes for her at all. He was fairly dancing with distress.

'Give me that crown!' he rasped, having suddenly transformed himself into Richard III. 'Give me the crown, you bastard!'

Peregrine threw his brother a marvelling look; then he laughed out loud.

'Now, God, stand up for bastards!' he crowed.

He seemed to grow, to put it out in all directions – bigger, taller, wider. Huge. When he whipped off that crown and shook it like a tambourine, to tease, the famous Hazard crown, shabby as a prop in nursery charades, it was as far out of reach as if Perry had been a grown-up and Melchior a little kid, although Melchior was a tall man, ordinarily.

'If you want it,' said Peregrine, quaking with the joke, 'jump for it!'

But now the focus of attention abruptly shifted to the Hollywood producer, only begetter of this inferno, who had found himself another cigar, although it was tasteless of him in the extreme, I thought, to light up again so soon after his last smoke burned down his host's stately home. Nevertheless, his jaws were clamped around another fat cigar like a babe's around a bottle as he announced through clenched teeth:

'Ladies and gentlemen, out of these ashes . . .'

The whites of their eyes looked huge and livid in their black-ened faces under the moonlight as all turned to look at him.

'... a work of genius will arise!

'There's an up-side to everything, ladies and gentlemen. I'm gonna take all of you fabulously talented people, yes, all of you! to Hollywood, USA. Yessir! Under the direction of this great genius of the English stage –'

But Melchior's mind was only on his heirloom.

'My crown!'

'Jump!' hissed Peregrine and Melchior, disconsolate, essayed a little hop that got him nowhere near.

'– your great genius, Melchior Hazard. Script by that other great genius in the family, my friend ... Peregrine Hazard –'

'– my crown!'

'Jump!'

'– with additional dialogue by William Shakespeare!'

He puffed out a triumphant plume of smoke and the stunned throng managed a baffled patter of applause. Peregrine, evidently caught by surprise, doubled up in a raucous guffaw when he caught those last words, reeling with astonished pleasure.

'My god!' he said. 'A dream come true!'

And then he just lost interest in the crown, he didn't want to tease old Melchior any more. When Melchior wailed: 'My crown!' again, Perry tossed it to him negligently. He didn't care one way or other about the crown. It was a toy, he was playing a game, Melchior was a fool to take the game so seriously, a fool to clasp the thing as if it were alive, and kiss it. A fool. When I saw how, since babyhood, they'd hated one another's guts, it gave me a goose-walking-on-my-grave feeling.

Or perhaps it was just the cold finally getting to me. I was turning blue with it. Perry doffed his tux and covered me up, this soot- and tear-besmirched nude, his niece, as the snow began to drift down again and the company adjourned to make the long drive home.

'Time to go, Dora,' he said, and gave me a cuddle. 'Time to take poor Nora home.'

Nora, apparently insensible in our boyfriend's arms, opened one eye in order to tip me a wink. Perry told him, 'I can give you a lift as far as Clapham Common, you can catch the night tram from there.' So he came a bit of the way with us but Perry wouldn't let him come in and I never saw him again.

Three

E saw it again just the other week, hadn't seen it for years. Haven't been to the pictures for years, in fact, what with one thing and another, not least of which the fact the local fleapit only shows stuff in the original Serbo-Croat with subtitles, a touch tough on yours truly's peepers. My eyes are dim, I cannot see, I have not brought my specs with me; nor do I intend to, ducky. All I have left to sustain me is my vanity. It was showing at three o'clock on a Sunday afternoon, miles away, in Notting Hill. We had to take two buses, change at the Scotch Shop.

God! Times have changed. More people on the screen than in the auditorium, and fleapit's the word, a flea bit me on the inner upper thigh, a particularly sensitive area well-nigh impossible to scratch in public without getting run in. It came on to rain while we were inside and dripped on Nora until we were forced to either raise an umbrella or to move our seats. As we got up, we spotted a bloke in the next row down on his knees at trough in his boyfriend's fly. It was the only thing about the entire expedition that cheered me up, in fact, to think that *somebody* was having a bit of fun in all the damp, draughty emptiness, with the smell of mice, old tobacco, Jeyes Fluid, damp plush, because fun was the last thing *I* was having, sitting there in my used body, watching it when it was new.

Nora nudged me in the ribs one time. 'Gawd!' she said. 'We were a pretty girl!'

Enough to make you weep.

Thin though the audience was, there was a little patter of applause when it was all over, although I nervously suspected irony, and a boy came running down the street, afterwards: 'Can you really be the Chance sisters?' It made our day. We signed his *City Limits*, then he leaned forward and asked us, confidentially, if it was true that *her* real name was Daisy Duck. When he got that close, I could see the little pearly drops of come – is that how you spell it? – on his moustache. They mesmerised me. I said, yes, it *was* true, then – couldn't help it, could have bitten my tongue out, after – I said, had he noticed what a funny shape her mouth was? That it got that way because she'd sucked off every producer in Hollywood, so after he trotted away Nora swore I'd hurt his feelings and *his* mouth looked perfectly normal, to her, but he hadn't seemed at all put out, anyway.

Nora was squinting away at a leaflet she'd picked up on her way out of the cinema. *A Midsummer Night's Dream*, dir. Melchior Hazard, Hollywood, USA. 'Dora,' she said, 'why do they call it a "masterpiece of kitsch"?'

We went to look for somewhere to have a cup of tea, but no more Joe Lyonses, gone the way of all flesh. Do you remember the Lyons teashops? Thick, curly white plaster on the shopfronts, like walking into a wedding cake, and the name in gold: J. Lyons. Poached eggs on toast keeping snug in little tin pigeon holes as you shuffled down the counter. The moist and fruity Bath buns with crumbs of rock candy glistening on the top, and a little pat of butter lined up alongside. The girl would pour hot water, whoosh! in a steaming column into a fat white pot and there you were, your good, hot cup of tea, with the leaves left in the bottom of the cup, afterwards, to tell your fortune with.

I haven't had a cup of tea with leaves in it for years. For decades. I wonder what the fortune-tellers do, these days. Palms?

Fancy getting nostalgic for a Joe Lyons. We only ever used them for a spot of lunch when times were hard, when we were tramping the rounds, agents, stage doors, etc. Then we'd expend a tanner each on something with chips, a banger, some beans.

You only miss an institution like a Joe Lyons teashop when it's gone.

But we couldn't find a place to get a cup of tea at all, nowhere on the Hill, after all that, so we had a gin, instead, to fortify us, in that great, draughty barn of a place down the Portobello.

Outside, it was raining still, and the dark coming on. I sometimes wonder why we go on living.

In those days, four farthings made a penny and Britain was entirely surrounded by water; in these days, there is no such thing as a penny any more and it is as if this foggy old three-cornered island were dangling from a cloud – now we're in the air. You feel that you could pucker up and *blow* away the miles between 49 Bard Road and that apartment in New York where I could be tomorrow morning, if the apartment still existed, if Peregrine still existed, if the past weren't deeper than the sea, more difficult to cross.

The only time I ever flew was in a harness at the end of a steel cable, on the set of *The Dream*, in Hollywood, USA. Hollywood was a long haul from London, in those days; it took weeks, transatlantic, transcontinental. First leg, we went by water, Nor' and I, and so arrived in Manhattan, the gateway to our father's dream, early in the morning and stood at the rail, gawping.

Never seen anything like it. What we'd seen at the pictures had been a pale shadow. All the high towers, in long rows, shifting and parting in front of us as we came into port. Everything seemed to rise up before us out of the sea like a lost city coming up for air. Our hearts began to pound. We thought that anything might happen.

We leaned on the rail and gawped, like mere trippers, although we were smart as paint and I can prove it, I've got the cutting here. There we are, see? On the front page of the *New York Post*, in our best suits – Schiaparelli, I kid you not – charcoal wool, fox wrap collar and cuffs, buttons, typical Schiap touch, in the shape of crochets and quavers, soft little high-crowned hats pulled down over our left eyes. Look hot, stay cool, we'd instructed one another; we'd got the stance to match the suits off pat, you stuck your hipbone forward, let your shoulders droop, put all your weight on the one leg.

Look at the headline: 'New York welcomes Shakespeare treasure.' Sub-head: 'Twins bear precious gift.' See that thing in Nora's arms, that looks like a decapitated doll? You'll never believe it. It was a pot, a sort of jar, about the size of the ones they use for ashes in the crematoria, and it was hollow inside and in the shape of a bust of, that's right, William Shakespeare; our father had had it specially made, in Stoke-on-Trent, and the bald patch lifted off, that was the lid.

And what did this bizarre vessel contain?

Earth.

We travelled with a box of earth, like Dracula, and never let it out of sight. Earth from Stratford-upon-Avon, dug out of the grounds of that big theatre by some reverential sidekick and then entrusted to Nora and myself, a sacred mission, to bear the precious dust to the New World so that Melchior could sprinkle it on the set of *The Dream* on the first day of the shoot.

He and the Lady A. and the twins had all gone ahead long before, of course, to do the 'pre-production'. It took an age to set it up. The bald man – we soon learned to call him Genghis Khan, as everybody else did – had made his announcement on the night of the fire in the heat of the moment and there'd been a long haul after that until 'a wood near Athens' started to go up on the lot near Culver City. But now, oh, thrilling thought! Hollywood was only a three-day train ride away and we trembled on the brink of stardom, or so we might have thought that New York morning. I never saw so many cameras. Snap, snap, flash. We docked. Snap, flash, snap. We even featured in the *Pathé News*. That was when we took the earth through Customs. But we'd had Grandma's motto drummed into us since babyhood: 'Hope for the best, expect the worst.' We were prepared.

Then: 'Girls!'

Perry, the welcome committee, crushed us to his bosom, the old bear hug, blushing and giggling like a little kid.

'Like it?' he asked us, gesturing round the grand horizon as if he'd bought it us for a present. 'Like it?' he said, gesturing around the glove-leather inside of the long, white car that took us home. 'Like it?' he asked us, gesturing around our destination.

It was *outrageous*. Done up like a Spanish chapel in gilded leather panelling with a genuine El Greco nativity under a neon strip that swung back to reveal a wet bar. He popped champagne. Big wrought-iron chairs scattered here and there, enough to give you piles just to look at them. That was the living room.

Then you went up a spiral staircase and, in a room with half the wall a window, where you could see all Central Park and the lacy, steely chorus line of skyscrapers across the other side, there was a round bed a good six feet across with polar bear skins heaped upon it, and a round mirror in the ceiling over it.

'Who's the lucky girl?' I asked him as we peeked, wondering, into her lavish closet. He put his finger on his lips: 'Top secret!' Then the white telephone interrupted us, it rang. Perry picked up the receiver but did not speak; listened, looked grieved; replaced it with a sigh.

'Poor cow,' he said, but did not tell us whom he meant.

A big Persian cat, white to match the telephone, jumped off the bed and came up for a bit of attention, shoving its head against our charcoal skirts, covering us with hairs. Where did Puss do its wee-wee? We were on the fifteenth floor. That was a problem. But a positive *embarras de richesse* as regards toilet facilities for humans – one bathroom for the lady, whoever she might be, done out in pink marble and chrome; one for him, more austere, in black tile, with, smart touch, black towels. Nora put down her glass, stripped off, had a shower. I fancied a lie-down, stretched out on the bearskin rug. Perry took the weight off his feet, too.

'Come on, old man. Tell all.'

You'd never have thought that Perry was past forty. I don't know what infernal deal the Hazard brothers made with time, but he'd not aged so you'd notice. Old Uncle Carrot-Top. His hair was still that bright, offensive, bad-boy red, and still stuck up in spikes. The trowelful of freckles flung over his nose never faded and he was bigger than ever, the size of a warehouse. As for his suit, it was a chocolate brown in colour, with a broad, white stripe; his shoes were dappled white and chocolate. He looked every inch a pimp, but one who'd risen to the top of his profession.

'All this belongs,' he said, 'including me,' he added, 'to . . .'

At that, as if on cue, in she swept; why shouldn't she make an entrance? It was her own house, her very own New York pied-à-terre, after all! She wasn't one whit abashed to find a naked chorine in the shower, nor a clothed one prone upon her mattress dallying, to all appearances, with her inamorato, but cracked us all her famous grin, kicked off her shoes.

'When does the orgy begin?' she enquired.

Delia Delaney. Even the name has a period ring; stars are called Finkelbaum or Hackenbush or Brown, these days. She was a raucous one, née Daisy Duck, on Hester Street, youngest of seven, her father a fish peddler, not a pot to piss in. She was but twenty-five years old that New York morning long ago, just the age of the big sister we never had, and fresh back from her hairdresser, who'd touched up the roots of her pubics, she kept them bleached, then trimmed them into a heart shape. She didn't miss a trick, did Daisy.

From babyhood she sang at weddings, talent shows, Daisy Duck a.k.a. 'Little Dolly Daydream', another period handle. In the movies in New York from 1918, rescued by dogs from burning houses, softening the hearts of crusty misanthropes, etc. In Hollywood from 1921 she dropped the 'Little Dolly'. She became a Mack Sennett bathing belle; then she danced on tables, she rode in rumbleseats, she was 'flaming youth' personified. She was custom-built for the pictures – teeny tiny, one inch less than five foot, and a perfectly enormous head. Her face went right from one side of the screen to the other. Gloria Swanson was like that, as well. Joan Crawford, too. You need the big face, for the close-ups.

Subduing her naturally nasal tones – she hailed from the Bronx – with sound she triumphed, the classic thirties blonde, tough, sweet, lewd, funny, fast, tender. I've got a lot of time for Daisy Duck. She used to lend us all her couture frocks.

She used to punch and pummel old Perry as if he were a giant teddy bear, she fancied older men, her father having been caught in the crossfire in a shoot-out in Fulton Fish Market through no fault of his own in the early days of Prohibition, and her fancy did her no harm at all in Hollywood, I can tell you, where she had, I kid you not, left lipstick on every pair of underpants further up the hierarchy than assistant director on her way to the top.

In she came, in her barathea suit, white, to match the cat that matched the telephone. She thought the world of that cat, it went everywhere with her. After she'd slipped off her mink, we all had some more champagne. Then, brr brr! brr brr! The telephone rang again.

'For you,' said Peregrine. 'I did it, last time.'

She picked up the receiver, put it to her ear – and then she shouted 'DROP DEAD!' down the telephone, you could have heard her clear through to Yonkers. She gave a mighty tug and ripped the cable off the wall, then tossed the entire contraption straight, with a tinkle of broken glass, through the bedroom window, mouthpiece and receiver going up in separate arcs high into the sky to land, who knows where but I trust softly, on the grass in Central Park.

'That's the way to deal with nuisance calls,' she said to Perry.

She'd got real style, she could put on a show. When she was peckish, she'd shout: 'Fishy!' and snap her fingers and up would pop a slavey out of nowhere with a peeled shrimp on a toothpick. She spelled Duck with an umlaut, thus: Dück. No relation to 'Donald Duck and Henry Hen, Were two rather unusual men', said Perry.

Transvestite poultry?

'You'd better believe it,' said Daisy. 'That's Hollywood.'

He loved us both but I was the one he talked to. Just one of those things. I was the one he took out in the white car that last morning in New York. He drew up at the kerb, by a hole in the ground, a construction site.

'That's New York,' he said. 'See it come down, see it go up.'

'What used it to be, Uncle Perry?'

'It was the site . . . the site . . .' He couldn't go on. The tears were running down his cheeks and so I knew he'd brought me on a pilgrimage, the site of the old Plaza, and Desdemona, Desdemona dead.

We left for California on the Twentieth Century Ltd. Now we were part of Daisy's entourage, it was long-stemmed roses all the way. When her white car deposited us all at Grand Central, cops in hats like threepenny bits held back the crowds, who cried and shrieked, thrust flowers at her, papers, pencils: 'Delia! Delia!' and fought and clawed to get at her. She was only a little thing, but she sailed through as to the manner born, smiling, waving, blowing kisses, she couldn't get enough of it, but we were scared stiff, huddling under Perry's greatcoat, hiding from all the hungry eyes and mouths come to gobble you up, like the wolf in *Red Riding Hood*. Daisy was the dish of the day, and we'd have been snapped up, too, like side salads, if we hadn't dashed down the red carpet to the private car sharpish, Daisy's cat racing before us, ears flattened by its own speed.

Even while the train steamed out of the station, the fans still sprinted down the track alongside, 'Delia! Delia!' until forced to fall back as the train plunged into the tunnel, left forlorn, bereft, starving for her.

That was when I got my first taste of fame. It scared me stiff.

Do you want your name card on the door? If you do, you want to party. Daisy always wanted to party. Her berth – well, not really a berth, more of a suite. Done out in white, which was her colour, except her mink, and that was blue. Ubiquitous wet bar; I never met a dry bar. Next door, a three-quarter bed. Lewdly, she opined she'd have to sleep on *top* of Perry, and it was true he took up all of that bed himself – he seemed to grow before our eyes, swell up, expand inside the train that speeded us all across the continent towards our fortunes in a great state of alcoholic euphoria and erotic disturbance, that is to say, of booze and sexy fun.

Needless to say, Nora was soon in love again. There was a young kid on his way to Hollywood to seek his fortune, too, but not in front of the cameras, in front of a hot stove – off to join his uncle in a catering business, or so he said. Very musical kid; never parted with his violin case, came to Daisy's party clutching it, but wouldn't give us a tune, he said a string was broken. He was from what they call Little Italy, below Houston Street, but his father hailed, originally, from Palermo. Eyes drawn in with charcoal, hair like pitch. I'll say this for Nora, she liked a change.

> Tony, Tony, macaroni,
> Show us all your big baloney.

Pardon me, vicar.

Tony was a nice boy but he never moved me. We changed trains at Chicago. Onwards! To the Dearborn Station! To the Super-Chief!

Nora's Tony wasn't, as you might say, in our class, he travelled third, so Nora would tippy-toe down the train and climb up to his upper berth, behind the green baize curtains; they did it for hours in there, she said, like snakes. Once he'd got it in her, they never moved, they let the train do all the work. CHOO-choo-choo-choo, CHOO-choo-choo-choo. The engine would get up steam, the pistons go faster, faster, faster until: WHEEEEEEEEEeeeeeeeeee . . . So Nora never partied, after she met Tony, but I was nothing loath. That white cat sat on the pillow and purred. When I'd a moment, I'd exercise my mind with the problem: where did it do its wee-wee on the Super-Chief?

Daisy put away the gin like nobody's business, pissed as a newt half the time and never wore panties. She said they were bad for the health. Perry had not lost his magic touch and used to saw her in half whenever a few guests gathered together. And amongst those guests was always one man who struck my eye, although he was no chicken, wore glasses, pepper and salt hair. His suit was rumpled, sometimes stained. His tie was loose and sometimes off. If he had a certain air of distinction, down on his luck was written all over him. He always smelled of liquor. Yet of all the gaudy company that partied with Daisy Duck, a.k.a. Delia Delaney, as the Super-Chief rolled down through New Mexico and Arizona, he was the one whom Perry picked out most for conversation, and I would watch them from the corner of my eye even when some assistant producer, or stunt man, or second lead had his leg wedged in my thigh, talk about dancing being sexual intercourse standing upright. I could tell you a tale. But shabby old horn-rims was no dancing man; he'd gulp that Mother's Ruin, gesticulate, pass out, but something drew me.

'Dora, my dear,' said Perry, who hadn't missed my roving eye, 'I want you to meet my dear friend, *mon semblable, mon frère*, my collaborator, just he and I, and William Shakespeare, working on the script. Irish, meet Floradora.'

I had it in my handbag, you never know when you might need

it. Nora was off with her Tony, so I had our room to myself. He wanted to go out into the corridor while I fixed myself up, but I said, 'Don't go; either you can avert your eyes or take a look – I'm not shy.' But *he* was shy, Irish by name, Irish by nature; he looked out of the window at the moon on the mountains while I fixed myself up.

Night, silence, desert, rock, moonlight.

'God, you're lovely,' he said, when he turned to look. I knew he'd say that. They all say that. I'd known in advance I wouldn't be able to return the compliment, alas.

My first old man. No, I do him an injustice. He wasn't really old, not old like I am now; he was only just past forty, neck and neck with my wicked uncle who, at that very moment, was giving Daisy what she always said was the best time she ever had. But Irish had an old soul, you might say. He was a man with a great future behind him, already. He was a burned-out case. I knew I must be very gentle.

See, the row of books. Over there. Take a look at the dedications: 'Light of my life', 'Joy in the morning', 'My last chance'. My half-brother/nephew young Tris, was very impressed with those dedications, he wanted me to do a programme, one time; I said 'No.' No suck old bones. Sometimes a graduate student writes; I burn the letter. Poor old Irish. I gave him all a girl can give – a little pleasure, a little pain, a carillon of laughter, a kerchief full of tears. And, as for him, well, it was he who gave me the ability to compose such a sentence as that last one. Don't knock it. That's lyricism.

You'll find me in his famous *Hollywood* stories. The last flame of a burned-out case, but oh, it had a glorious light! I never rate more than a footnote in the biographies; they get my date of birth wrong, they mix me up with Nora, that sort of thing. And I'm bound to say my best friend wouldn't recognise me in the far-from-loving portrait he'd penned after I'd gone. I'm the treacherous, lecherous chorus girl with her bright red lipstick that *bleeds* over everything, and her bright red fingernails and her scarlet heart, sexy, rapacious, deceitful. Vulgar as hell. The grating Cockney accent. The opportunism. The chronic insensitivity to a poet's heart. And you couldn't trust her behind a closed door, either. Such turned out to be the eternity the poet promised me, the bastard.

But all this disillusion lay before him, and indeed, before me, that night in the Super-Chief with moonlight outside on the bare mountains into which the train began to climb. I straightened up and faced him. He was so shy he hadn't even got his jacket off, although it was quite dark inside and the only sounds the chuff and click and rattle of the train and, drifting on the wind, the laughter out of Daisy's everlasting party. I started to undo his tie. 'Irish' to his friends and of descent, although American to the core. Ross 'Irish' O'Flaherty, a.k.a. the Chekhov of Southern California.

Of course, I remember his name. How could I not? You never forget the difficult customers.

Welcome to the Land of Make-Believe! To where the moon shone on Charlie Chaplin every moonlight night. Welcome to Dreamland.

We'd only ever seen a palm tree before at Bournemouth, it came as a shock. So big, so hairy. And the sunshine. 'Like a benediction,' said Irish. He was so pleased I'd got it up for him that even the weather seemed intentional. But I wouldn't move in with him, not on your life, I'd got too much residual sense for that, although, I must say, I was very struck – struck with his faded but still potent charm; his vulnerability, under his surface assurance; his soft, light baritone with its gracious East Coast modulations; his wasted talent, of which even the morbid scripts he now churned out at so many dollars the yard retained some wizened gleam. And he did wonders for my grammar, not to mention my grasp of metaphor, as witness the style of this memoir. But cohabitation, no. Nora and I put up at the Forest of Arden.

The legendary Forest of Arden, the residential motel of the stars, with its Olde English motif. What could have been more appropriate, in the circumstances? All the little bungalows, half-timbered, thatched – replicas of Anne Hathaway's cottage – each one nestled under clematis, set in wee herbaceous gardens, tended with loving care by Japanese gardeners, and there were

Warwickshire apple trees, imported oaks, you name it. Perry set up there, in a bungalow, too, when he wasn't nine-to-fiving it with Irish at the studio, busy on the script in the office they shared. But Daisy came and went because she'd got her own home, hadn't she? Indeed, she'd got her own thirty-bedroom mansion, besides a tremendous many domestic duties. She was a married woman, after all.

But the Forest of Arden was a lovely, flimsy, fantastic place, where you could live in grand, two-dimensional style among the hissing lawns – those incessant sprinklers! – and there was a pool, shaped like an acorn leaf, of bright turquoise, planted with shocking pink flamingos, everso *As You Like It* even if out of period, and we would lie for hours on canvas loungers, exposing our pale, unaccustomed torsoes to what Irish, in one of his *Hollywood* stories, calls the 'ardent yet somehow insincere sunlight'.

Note it's already ceased to be a blessing.

And how can sunlight be insincere, Irish?

He gave me a pitying look and went on reading *The House of Mirth*. God forgive me, I'd been vulgar again. He'd already noted, with some distress, how vulgar I could be from time to time. All the same, that sunlight's insincerity perplexed me. Did he mean, the sunshine didn't really mean it? And, if so, what did *that* mean? Or, is it that if it saw somebody better than me to shine on, it would switch off me and shine on them, instead? And yet it shone on everyone, whether they had a contract or not. The most democratic thing I'd ever seen, that California sunshine.

And, tell the truth, it changed me. It changed me for good and all. All manner of things conspired to change me, during those months in California, though from what to what I scarcely know, except, if you offered me a tango with the Prince of Wales today, I'd tell you where to stuff it.

Irish was banned from the Forest of Arden because he'd set fire to a thatched roof during the welcome party when he first arrived from New York as fresh talent, years ago, before the hair on his chest turned grey and he started stowing a shaker of martinis in the briefcase he took to the studio every morning. All the same, we'd smuggle him in past the desk clerk whenever we could, trussed up in Perry's cashmere overcoat and a fedora, disguised as a big-name director, and then he'd lay down some speakeasy-style boogie-woogie on Perry's white piano, Irish was a man of parts even if some of them didn't work too well. They'd have a sing-song. 'When Irish Eyes are Smiling', obviously. 'Down by the Sally Gardens.' And that old song about the man who resurrects. They loved that song, they roared out the choruses:

> Whack fol de dah, dance to your partner,
> Welt the flure, yer trotters shake,
> Wasn't it the truth I told you,
> Lots of fun at Finnegan's Wake.

Irish would flop down flat on his back at the last verse and Perry would scatter a few drops of liquor on him.

> Bedad he revives, see how he rises,
> And Timothy rising from the bed

Irish, suiting the action to the words –

> Says, 'Whirl your liquor round like blazes,
> Thùnder and lightning, do ye think I'm dead?'

What larks.

Apart from that, I used to cab it to his place, out in the sticks. You climbed steps to a cabin. There was a little, narrow bed, a chair, a table. All clean and neat, the way men on their own keep things. Clean, neat, a little drear – not a flower in a cup, nor a postcard on the mantel, nothing like that. Only his pencils in a jam jar, a pile of yellow legal pads and a cardboard carton where he stashed his empties. I stretched him out upon that narrow bed and pleasured him, poor old thing, and he was grateful, at the time.

Apart from a few small necessities, his monastically austere cabin was furnished with books. After his day at the studio he'd drive home, unwind over a few drinks, then leaf through his own back numbers – a bestseller at twenty-two years old, a second novel that didn't live up to the promise at twenty-five, a stinker at twenty-eight, and then the one at thirty-two that didn't sell, which is the one they remember him by. That, and the *Hollywood Elegies*, which were yet to come and would be inspired by yours truly – this painted harlot over here, still indecently hale and hearty if by the world forgot on her seventy-fifth birthday while he's dead and gone and immortal.

After he'd thoroughly depressed himself with contemplation of his wasted genius, he'd turn to higher things and finger Shelley, say, until both glass and book slipped from his fingers and he slept.

When did it first enter his head to educate me? Because he didn't have sufficient cash to buy a mink. Therefore he gave me Culture.

I balked at Proust.

His sweet, befuddled head; that faded golden hair; the large, light eyes with the long lashes; the short, straight nose like the nose of Daisy's Persian cat; the soft, weak mouth indicative of that guilty sensuality so characteristic, I've found, of the North American temperament – that is, they like it, all right, but, all the same, they think it's going to give them hairy palms.

Attracted as he was to my conspicuous unrefinement, all the same Irish thought it would only make sleeping with me all right in the end if we could read Henry James, together, afterwards, and I was nothing loath because there'd been precious little time for book-learning in my short life as I'd been earning a living from age twelve and sometimes Irish, when he remembered that, would forgive me everything.

Don't misunderstand me. He was a lovely man in many ways. But he kept on insisting on forgiving me when there was nothing to forgive.

Meanwhile, Nora was eating pasta and making love with the magnificent simplicity I always envied. She was learning how to make cannòli, too, and cannelloni – and she was still all ablaze with love, no sign of cooling, yet, helping out at Tony's uncle's business every spare moment, in fact, apart from whatever else they did together. Sometimes she even sported a domestic air on her return to the Forest of Arden, a smudge of flour on her frock, a trace of tomato paste on her cheek. She was preoccupied with love and so was I, labouring with my lover over his erections, which were difficult to procure and arduous to maintain, not that I ever grumbled, I didn't want to hurt his feelings, and, after all that was done with, we'd send out for a hamburger and attack his well-used library. We did it alphabetically, we started out at A.

He was so smitten by my youth and beauty he started to dry out, poor old thing, so he put away soda, soda, soda by the crateful and belched in an operatic manner, arias of wind. After we'd done a couple of hours on the author of the night, we'd relax with a soda. He'd read me a sonnet: 'Shall I compare thee to a summer's day . . .'

Then up would come the thunder.

The wood near Athens covered an entire stage and was so thickly art-directed it came up all black in the rushes, couldn't see a thing, so they sprayed it in parts with silver paint to lighten it up. The concept of this wood was scaled to the size of fairy folk, so all was twice as large as life. Larger. Daisies big as your head and white as spooks, foxgloves as tall as the tower of Pisa that chimed like bells if shook. Gnarled, fissured tree-trunks; sprays of enormous leaves – oak, ash, thorn, like parasols, or glider planes, or awnings. Bindweed in streamers and conkers, deposited at intervals in heaps on the ground. Yes, conkers. All spikes. And rolling around at random underfoot, or stuck on buds, or hanging in mid-air as if they'd just rolled off a wild rose or out of a cowslip, imitation dewdrops, that is, big *faux* pearls, suspended on threads. And clockwork birds, as well – thrushes, finches, sparrows, larks – that lifted up their wings and lowered their heads and sang out soprano, mezzo, contralto, joining in the fairy songs.

Because no wind blew of its own accord in this wood, they'd got in a wind machine. I'd have let old Irish loose after a 7-Up to do the job myself, but nobody asked for my advice. When the artificial wind stirred the leaves and flowers, they were stiff enough to clank.

What I missed most was illusion. That wood near Athens was too, too solid for me. Peregrine, who specialised in magic tricks, loved it just because it was so concrete. 'You always pull a *live* rabbit out of a hat,' he said. But there wasn't the merest whiff about of the kind of magic that comes when the theatre darkens, the bottom of the curtain glows, the punters settle down, you take a deep breath . . . none of the person-to-person magic we put together with spit and glue and willpower. This wood, this entire dream, in fact, was custom-made and hand-built, it left nothing to the imagination.

> You spotted snakes with double tongue,
> Thorny hedgehogs, be not seen –

And there they were, waiting in cages, snakes and hedge-hogs, not to mention newts, worms, spiders, black beetles and snails, with snake handlers and hedgehog handlers ad lib at hand to keep them happy, waiting for their cue to scatter this way and that across the set as soon as the fairy chorus started up.

It was all too literal for me.

It took me donkey's till I saw the point but saw the point I did, eventually, though not until the other day, when we were watching *The Dream* again in Notting Hill, that time, couple of batty old tarts with their eyes glued on their own ghosts. *Then* I understood the thing I'd never grasped back in those days, when I was young, before I lived in history. When I was young, I'd wanted to be ephemeral, I'd wanted the moment, to live in just the glorious moment, the rush of blood, the applause. Pluck the day. Eat the peach. Tomorrow never comes. But, oh yes, tomorrow *does* come all right, and when it comes it lasts a bloody long time, I can tell you. But if you've put your past on celluloid, it keeps. You've stored it away, like jam, for winter. That kid came up and asked for our autographs. It made our day. I could have wished we'd done more pictures.

Genghis Khan spared no expense. Even the wee folk were real; the studio scoured the country for dwarfs. Soon, true or not, wild tales began to circulate – how one poor chap fell into the toilet and splashed around for half an hour before someone dashed in for a piss and fished him out of the bowl; another one got offered a highchair in the Brown Derby when he went out for a hamburger; and one of the girls in the wardrobe, as she tried on my Peaseblossom costume – pink bra, knicks and fright wig, ever so artistic – told me, giggling and winking, that this one she was measuring up looked to her to be about nine or ten years old, so she did her Mickey Mouse impression to put him at his ease, tempted him with bubble gum, slipped off his jacket for him. Goodness! He was shy. Then his shirt. 'No! No!' he cried in his little piping voice, but she insisted until off came his pants.

'Lo and behold, this is a full-grown, thirty-year-old *man* we have here!'

She was so tickled by the memory she stuck a pin in my left buttock. In my guided tour of the literary alphabet, Irish had just introduced me to the letter B for Burns.

'A man's a man, for a' that,' I suggested and the wardrobe lady blushed and said that some men had more of 'a' that' than others did and, on the whole, the boy-fairies cut something of a swathe among the ladies, except for Puck, who made them run a mile.

Puck looked like a little man but wasn't; he was an aged child. Puck was all fingers, goose you as soon as look at you, unmentionable habits. You might find that Puck in your laundry basket, when you least expected it, curled up inhaling your soiled lingerie. Out at dinner, no matter how chic the venue, if a questing hand reached up from under the tablecloth, you knew it was Puck's night out, too, and he was rummaging round the room at knee level, seeking what he could find. He'd started out years ago as a Hollywood toddler and still ploughed a rich furrow of cute kids, although now well-nigh geriatric, and we were stuck with Puck for box-office reasons, although he drilled holes in the walls of the ladies' toilets and liked to take a peep and I don't know what else. He was the spy on the set, too; would report back to Genghis Khan on the empties in poor Irish's wastepaper basket, the used condoms in the back lot. He had a vile temper, he bit a policeman in the leg, one time, on account of an alleged traffic violation.

Old ladies loved him. He had the most fan mail of any of us, requests for photographs on cards with hearts and flowers on, plus gifts of sailor suits and teddy bears and Kiddicars and offers of adoption because he had the high tenor of an angel. I never heard anything like it. I can hear him now:

'Philomel with melody . . .'

Enough to melt your heart.

Now, if our father was to take the part of Oberon, I'll give you three guesses as to who will play Titania.

Give up?

Why, Daisy Duck, of course.

For was she not the wife of Genghis Khan!?!

And it turns out the whole 'magnificent, foolish, heroically vulgar enterprise' – as Irish called it – was intended just to show her off, to, as they say, 'showcase' her glamour, her talent, her star quality, her – pardon me while I emit a titter – *sheer class.*

Dear old Daisy. She was a trouper and a half all right; she'd got guts, legs, leather lungs, tits out to here, chutzpah, sass, star quality. But class – no.

So it went on. Pre-production they called it. Then the phone rang. The white telephone in Anne Hathaway's Cottage. Nora and I were standing on our heads, at the time; all that pasta was taking its toll on Nora's bum while the sodas up at Irish's place were blowing me up something shocking, so we were doing a few exercises. I picked up the receiver with my foot and toppled over when I heard that voice. It always set me a-flutter. I never got used to it, I never will. If I turn on the telly and get an earful of that magisterial baritone ecstasising over no matter what, from after-dinner mint to toilet roll, I grow alert and wistful as the dog on the record label: His Master's Voice.

Is it as bad as that, Dora?

You've only got the one father.

Melchior's feet were firmly underneath the Hollywood table. He'd rented a lovely hacienda-style home up in the hills, there installed the Lady A., who appeared transfixed in a permanent state of gracious amusement at the antics surrounding her, and, before you could say 'Jack Robinson', he was lording it over what they called 'the English Colony'.

The English Colony was a rum lot. The men all wore monocles, the women all wore tiaras, and they turned up in costume

127

dramas as Gladstone and Disraeli, Queen Victoria and Florence Nightingale, etc. As a group, they kept themselves to themselves, away from the hoi polloi, held tea parties on Saturday afternoons when everybody else was having group sex, played cricket on Sundays, drank pink gin at sundown and talked as if their upper lips wore plaster casts. Old Nanny, the very one whose sister lived in Kennington, small world, wearing a uniform and veil, could occasionally be seen in the Hazards' big yard, supervising a brace of russet-haired moppets in braids and cotton frocks, our bloody cousins, who, it turned out, would tumble through *The Dream* as supernumerary fairies. It was Family Time all round.

But had our father called us up to welcome us to Hollywood? To tell us no dream of his would have been complete without us? Did he, hell. All he wanted was, his little bit of earth.

The Shakespeare casket was the last thing we'd been thinking of in the heady weeks since we lit down in the Forest of Arden. I couldn't think who'd had it last. I wondered if we'd left it on the train? We turned that cottage inside out, went through all our trunks . . . We were in a cold sweat until we stumbled on it at last, by accident, in a little cubbyhole off the master-bedroom, which I think was meant to be a dressing room, or the place where the missus could stow away the master if the master came home plastered. We'd never ventured into this little cranny before, it was quite dark, the curtains always drawn against the sunshine, but *there* was the Shakespeare casket, safe and sound, sitting on the minuscule dresser as if in a little shrine, because somebody had set it up and flanked the pot with candles and lit them. There was a stick of incense on the go too. What a rich sense of ritual, of occasion, in that room. We were astonished.

Who'd gone to all that bother? We found out later it was the Mexican cleaning lady. Catholic. Ever so Catholic. She thought there must be a holy relic in the casket, because it was packed with such care, and she treated it accordingly. We hardly liked to disturb the casket, but we thought we ought to check the earth was still intact so we opened it up. Whew! No wonder she'd lit up incense. She must have thought the relic was starting to rot. As soon as we lifted the lid, a rank aroma wafted from the pot and filled the little improvised chapel with an unmistakable smell.

And that was how we found out where Daisy's Persian cat did wee-wee whilst on the Super-Chief.

We tipped Pussy's night-soil out the window but whatever were we to do now that the sacred earth, thoroughly desecrated, was gone for good? Easy. We filled the casket up again with soil from the Forest of Arden, from the facsimile Elizabethan knot garden itself; we thought that would make it more authentic. So there was the sacred earth, as good as new; and Melchior's plan was, the first day of the shoot, to sprinkle it all over the wood near Athens, as a consecration of the grounds, a dedication of the actors and a photo-opportunity of the first water.

I remember that day, the day *The Dream* began, as if it were yesterday. We all arrived in costume – we were a motley crew and no mistake. None of your soppy fairies with butterfly wings and floral wreaths. No, sir. As Peaseblossom and Mustardseed, our bras and knicks had leaves appliquéed at the stress points, there were little lights in our shaggy wigs, and when we saw how the rest had fared in the wardrobe, we thought we'd got off lightly, I must say, because some had antlers sprouting out of their foreheads and fur patches covering up the rude bits; others were done up as flying beetles, in stiff, shiny bodices split up at the back; and one or two with boughs, not arms, plus a lavish use of leather and feathers all round.

Furthermore, remember that not fairies alone inhabited the wood near Athens. A giant mouse, saddled and bridled, trotted past. A bunny, in a wedding wreath and veil. Some dragonflies, in masks. Several enormous frogs. Dwarfs, giants, children, all mixed up together. Suddenly I had a sinking feeling; I knew it in my bones. This film is going to lose a fortune.

Genghis Khan had dug deep into his pocket for this opening spectacle. There was a hundred-piece orchestra of ancient instruments *in situ*, he'd brought them down from Berkeley and dressed them up in tights and ruffs. One wore a yarmulke. Lutes are a bugger to tune, one reason why they went out, so the wood near Athens twanged and pinged with discords as they tried to get them all in tune.

Puck somersaulted past and goosed me. Irish blew a kiss. Drunk as a skunk and clutching his briefcase to his bosom, soon he would be drunker. He'd fallen off the wagon because I'd missed a date. He didn't own me, you know. He'd got a nerve. I'd only started taking German lessons, hadn't I? One lunchtime when Nora was having a quick linguine and cunnilingus *chez* Tony, I'd taken the book of the day to share with my hot dog in the commissary. This runty little German chap with cropped hair and smelly feet, baggy blue suit, no tie, some kind of script consultant somewhere, he took one look at the title of my book. 'Schopenhauer!' he sneered. His conversation was brusque and surprising. He always looked on the black side. He was a tonic in Hollywood. He kept my feet on the ground.

Irish blew me an ironic kiss. Peregrine had an arm round Irish's shoulders, not only to express affection but to help keep him upright. The Lady A. was there, in a Lanvin frock and pearls, her role in *this* production was only that of the director's wife, but her daughters were there in costume. Melchior had given his little Saskia a cameo. The Indian prince.

> For Oberon is passing fell and wrath
> Because that she as her attendant hath
> A lovely boy, stol'n from an Indian king.

That Indian prince, in gold lamé pyjamas and matching turban with purple feather fastened with an amethyst pin. Pure jailbait. Imogen was just another fairy, with the one line: 'And I.' But the assistant director, the besotted Peregrine, twisted the wardrobe's arm until off came the owl mask and feather camisole of the original design and on went a tiny pink tutu, so Imogen stuck out like a sore thumb.

There was a newsreel team, energising a wisecrack out of Daisy Duck in her fairy queen frock, tulle and spangles, look! no panty-line, while Genghis Khan, in his usual jodhpurs accessorised with whip, straddled a canvas chair and gloated upon the fairyland that he had built. Journalists, photographers, secretaries, sycophants, script girls, continuity girls, and set dressers milled and stirred around him, activity, according to

Irish's acid-tipped pen, irresistibly reminiscent of the movements of maggots upon rotting meat.

But there was one figure in all this mêlée who didn't quite belong, who drew attention to itself by being so inconspicuous, so that it caught my eye – huddled in raincoat, dark glasses, head-scarf, as if wardrobe had equipped her with a 'disguise' outfit from a B-feature. Everywhere that Daisy went, this sad little shadow would go, slipping after her, dissolving into the crowd if ever Daisy looked in her direction. That was odd. What was going on?

Then the ancient musicians gathered themselves together at last at the behest of the conductor: what power on earth had got *Stokowski* into tights? Amid a welter of twangs, all embarked upon a mass rendition of, possibly, a galliard, although it sounded as if the lute section might have been making a stab at a pavane. When it ground to a halt, Melchior stepped out from among the trees in a burst of flashbulbs to address us, bearing aloft, on a crimson velvet cushion with gold fringe that I knew for a fact, because wardrobe told me, came off the set of *Elizabeth and Essex*, the Shakespeare pot that held, and you know I kid you not, vertible soil, rich with association, from the Forest of Arden.

Melchior smiled upon us, I had to put a hand out and steady myself on Nora's arm just the same time she put her hand out for *my* arm. He smiled and then he said: 'Friends,' in his voice like Hershey's Syrup, and although the old enchantment instantly overcame me, I quivered with anxiety: would he now continue, 'Romans, countrymen', so tense with the significance of the moment that he cued himself into the other speech? But he did not get the chance to get it wrong.

'Friends!'

Genghis Khan dragged his eyes off Daisy, took one look at Melchior and leapt up as if shot.

'Cut!'

Melchior clutched the casket and gaped.

'Take five minutes break, you guys,' said Genghis.

The lutenists left off anxiously trying to tune up on the q.t., the photographers stopped snapping. There was a babble of surprise. Peregrine and Irish rocked together, overcome with mirth. The Lady A. exhibited puzzle and affront, but not half so much as her husband did, who dropped his dignity pronto, and snapped at Genghis: 'What is the meaning of . . .'

'Get 'em off!' roared Genghis. Daisy, I saw, was stuffing her hankie in her mouth or else she would have burst out laughing, too.

'What?'

I thought his costume was a masterpiece, myself. It was balletic, really; there was a high, spiky crown of what might have been fishbones. And a long, black wig, down his back. And a fur bolero over his chest, which was bare. And a necklace of what looked like babies' skulls. And snakeskin tights.

How well he filled those tights!

'Get 'em off!'

Because the way that Melchior filled those tights was the snag; Genghis hadn't gone to all this expense so that his wife would be upstaged by her co-star's package, and he explained, in loud and rasping tones, that, before the show went on again, Melchior must retire to his dressing room and don an extra heavy-duty athletic supporter. Or even two.

'Get it?'

Otherwise, one felt, Genghis would tear off the offending parts with his bare teeth. And now all present were too scared to laugh. Even Irish sobered up, although Daisy wasn't the only one red in the face and chewing on a hankie, I can tell you. It took a moment or two for her husband's predicament to sink into the Lady A.'s gentility and then she took a daughter by each hand and swept off with some dignity. I admired her for that. It was suddenly so quiet on the stage you could hear little Saskia's voice trailing behind them: 'Mummy, what had Daddy done? Mummy? Why are we going away? Mummy, why is everybody angry with Daddy?'

First Melchior went bright red. Then he went stark white. His dark eyes glowed like hot coals. He clutched his casket of sacred soil and glared at Genghis, mute with fury. If he'd had any class,

I mean, *real* class, he'd have turned upon his heel and stalked off then and there. But that's unfair. Think what was at stake. The entire production was at stake. His Hollywood future – that is, his chance to take North America back for England, Shakespeare and St George. That is, to make his father's old dream everybody's dream. And his chance to make an awful lot of money, too. Don't let's forget the money.

But, for the moment, it was a Mexican standoff. Genghis glared. Melchior glared. They went on glaring at each other under the fascinated attention of the fairies and the fools and the scriptwriters until Peregrine it was who broke the tension, and he broke it with a trick. Although his belly was still agitating with suppressed merriment, he kept his presence of mind, picked his way over the electric cables, among the lights and cameras, knelt down in front of his brother, then and there, with Genghis and the rest of us looking on.

'I know what's causing the trouble,' said Peregrine.

With one swift pass of his hand he removed, from the problematic portion of Melchior's costume, a scarlet macaw.

He rose up, bowed to every quarter of the compass, every section of the audience, presenting the macaw upon his finger to us all as it flexed its wings and turned its head inquisitively from side to side. Something about its sharp little beady eyes reminded me of Grandma.

'I think you'll find everything perfectly acceptable, now,' said Peregrine to Genghis, who was lost for words.

But the macaw wasn't lost for words. It cocked its head to one side and announced in stentorian tones: 'It ain't no sin!'

It hopped off Peregrine's finger, took to the air and landed on Daisy's shoulder, which gave the poor girl a chance to laugh, which was just as well as she was just about to choke.

'It ain't no sin!' said the macaw again, dancing from foot to foot and winking. 'It ain't no sin!'

And then, thank God, reprieve. First Genghis Khan chuckled reluctantly, then he let rip a coarse guffaw. The cameras clicked, the cameras whirred, the cameras flashed and the show was on the road again. Thank God for that macaw. It saved the situation. It was trained up for a Mae West promotion, apparently. It was an escape.

In the midst of all this, I saw that one of the gorillas from studio security had got hold of Daisy's raincoated shadow, clamped one of its great, hairy paws over her mouth to stop her noise, was escorting her outside in the most unceremonious way, in a fireman's lift, but he also looked quite bored about it, as if he'd done the same to her before. What on earth was going on? But now a heavy silence suddenly fell; all eyes were turned towards Melchior, as he held aloft the Shakespeare pot as if it were the Holy Grail.

'Friends, we are gathered here together in remembrance of a sacred name – the name of Shakespeare.'

Irish, I noticed, was raising a brown paper bag to his lips in a spontaneous toast to Peregrine. The macaw had taken off again and was flapping about somewhere under the roof. Peregrine got hold of the brown paper bag and drank a toast to the macaw.

'I bear here, in this quaintly shaped casket – a casket in the image of, for me, the greatest of all our English heroes – only a little bit of earth. Nothing more. Earth. And yet it is especially precious to me because it is English earth, perhaps some of the most English earth of all, precious above rubies, above the love of women. For it is earth from William Shakespeare's own home town, far away, yes! Sleepy old Stratford-upon-Avon, earth gathered up and borne hither as tenderly as if it were a baby by two lovely young Englishwomen, nymphs, roses, almost as precious to me as my own daughters ... my nieces. Peaseblossom! Mustardseed!'

He called us and we knew what we must do, although he'd betrayed us once again, and this time, in public. Even so, we flitted up to him and knelt one on each side, coiling round his knee, Nora in yellow, I in pink, both of us near tears. Almost as precious as his own daughters, indeed!

'Dora ... Leonora ...'

He got us wrong, of course. He didn't even know us well enough to smell the difference, but he was well away, now it was family time. He waved his arm towards Peregrine, exiled among the writers.

'And my brother, my own brother . . . welcome! Welcome to our great enterprise, in which you've played so noble a part! And welcome, welcome, to all of you come together here, so many, many folk, to engage with us in the great task at hand, to ransack all the treasuries of this great industry of yours to create a glorious, an everlasting monument to the genius of that poet whose name will be reverenced as long as English is spoken, the man who knew the truth about us all and spoke those universal truths in every phrase . . . who left the English language just a little bit more glorious than he found it, and let some of that glory rub off on us old Englishmen too, as they set sail around the globe, bearing with them on that mission the tongue that Shakespeare spoke!'

When he said that, as it came rolling out, you could almost see the tongue, on a red satin cushion, under glass.

Melchior now swung on his heel and made a sort of obeisance; his voice switched to a mellifluous croon.

'Let us hail the vision of this great man . . .'

Genghis Khan, thwacking the crop against his thigh, stood up and took a bow, sneaking a peak at Melchior's crotch to make sure all was still in order.

'This great man, who first came to me in London and said, "Let us give the world the splendour of your art, and, what is more, let us dedicate that splendour to Shakespeare!"'

Everybody clapped, having no option, except Irish, who had got his paper bag back and formed a permanent attachment to it.

'And let us hail the Queen of Fairyland herself – Titania!'

Daisy Duck parked her bum on the arm of her chair, gave the cameras a friendly wave, plus a glimpse of cleavage, and climbed up to the dais next to Melchior. Puck had managed to keep his hands to himself for ten whole minutes, but now he goosed a passing vole, who squealed. The macaw, high on a strut, abruptly extruded a greenish, semi-liquid substance that gathered sufficient impetus as it sped downwards to announce its arrival on terra firma with a lingering SPLAT!

'Now, we poor players, let us all take hands.'

He clasped Daisy Duck's hands very firmly and gave her the

full force of his lovely smile, hot and brown as Bovril, and she fluttered. Tough as old boots, yet she visibly fluttered. There was a universal satisfied stir and contented rustle in the studio. It was as if he'd put them under a spell, that voice, such glamour. Everybody reached out to catch hold of everybody else as if it were New Year's Eve, time to sing 'Auld Lang Syne'. Fairy clutched Amazon, Amazon clutched Athenian, rude mechanical clutched lover, Nora and I clutched one another but not before that Puck copped hold of my spare hand.

> Give me your hands, if we be friends,
> And Robin shall restore amends.

Melchior raised his face to the bright lights on this concluding piece of nonsense, with his lips a little bit ajar in that selfsame knicker-shifting smile that must have been the downfall of my poor mother. Daisy looked at him as if the heavens had opened and she'd glimpsed inside. Smitten. The thunderbolt had struck. Cameras whirred, clicked, flashed. But Puck cried out with rage, dropped my hand like a hot brick and commenced to pummel with his little fists in the disputed region of Melchior's athletic supporter, yelping the while: 'That's my line, you bastard!'

Out of the corner of my eye, I saw Irish lean over and throw up.

Genghis Khan struck down Puck's hands with one cut of his crop and hissed: 'Ever heard of the face on the cutting-room floor?' That shut Puck up. He fell back. Then Melchior raised aloft the casket of earth in the hand that was not holding on to Daisy Duck.

> Every fairy takes his gait,
> And each several chamber bless,
> Through this palace, with sweet peace . . .
> In the blessed name of . . . SHAKESPEARE!

He looked deep into Daisy's eyes and she looked deep back. Then he let go of her, dipped his hand in the pot, scattered the earth from the Forest of Arden around him on the floor in a lovely, stately gesture and raised two fingers in benediction. What a splendid pontiff he would have made, given half the chance. Then the ancient instruments started up again and I saw Daisy furtively wipe away a tear because it had all been so very lovely and, furthermore, while Peregrine assisted Irish from the scene as the best boy tipped sand from a fire-bucket over Irish's deposit, little Miss Sharp Eyes here was privileged to witness a positive disturbance in Melchior Hazard's perhaps not wholly well-functioning jockstrap that boded ill for marital bliss all round.

Ghengis Khan's office was full of orchids, he grew them himself. He liked the carnivores best and often fed them flies while some little actress quaked on the couch on the other side of his desk, where he kept a photograph of Daisy in a silver frame displayed conspicuously to show the poor things to what dizzy heights Genghis Khan could take a girl if she was nice to him. The very sight of Daisy made them drop their drawers. It was all a dream come true for Genghis. Crude power. He was the Master/Madam of a very peculiar brothel, where all the girls for sale were shadows; he bought and sold them, but the cash involved was just as real as the cash he used to pocket long ago, in Brooklyn, when he had all his hair and the Brooklyn wife he'd left for Daisy and had started out in life as a trolley-car conductor. They used to thank him at the garage when he brought his vehicle back at night. I mean to say, he could have sold it for scrap, couldn't he? How could a boy of such vision resist Hollywood? So out he came and made his dreams come true. Literally. That was how he made his living, making dreams come true.

He carried on like a bloody dictator in that studio. The studio covered about the same area as, say, Monaco, and employed about the same population, and had a barber shop of its own, a dentist, a hospital, a canteen, a police department, as well as the actors and the directors, assistant directors, assistants to the assistants, second unit directors, art directors, costume designers, needlewomen, cameramen, assistant cameramen, key grips, best boys, gaffers, carpenters, scene painters, make-up girls, hairdressers, pimps, astrologers, whores, fortune-tellers, abortionists, writers, assistant writers, writers of additional dialogue, and common fellows, and all day long they bustled about the dusty streets of the lot, although at night it was a ghost town, only the nightwatchman, a few dogs, an abandoned newspaper blowing down a cardboard street.

There was a lawn, where you could eat your sandwiches, and a big lilypond with carp in it. Daisy's Persian cat came to the studio with her and used to sit and stare for hours into the lily-pond. Sometimes it would slip its paw up to the elbow in the water, but the fish twitched and swam away, she never caught anything. Perhaps her shadow on the bottom of the pool warned them off.

Daisy loved that cat. She went out with a net one afternoon, after she'd had a couple with Peregrine for old times' sake, caught a carp, tossed it, all alive-oh, to Pussy. 'There!'

She told me: on the wedding night, between the satin sheets, he said, whatever you want, Daisy. Anything. And she said, a million bucks. In cash. He blenched, chewed a cigar ragged, but he was daft with love, he made a few phone calls, kicked ass. She sat up in bed in her negligée. First of all the hotel manager came in, ushering the chairman of the bank, in monkey suit and white gloves, as if it wasn't three o'clock in the morning, and he was followed by a copper with holsters. Enter a little messenger boy in bum-freezer and pillbox, carrying a carpet bag; another little messenger boy, likewise; lastly, a third to match. Concluding the procession, another policeman.

At a sign from the chairman of the bank, the boys all set down their bags on the wall-to-wall and bowed. Their eyes were bug-ging at the sight of Daisy Duck in her nightie, I can tell you, they sneaked peeks from the corners of their eyes until the chairman snapped his fingers and they scampered out. One of the coppers asked for an autograph. Genghis Khan, rendered solemn by the presence of so much money, shook the hand of the chairman.

As soon as they were alone again, Daisy opened up the carpet bags and there it was. Her million. In hundreds, fifties, twenties. Nothing, to her regret, smaller than a ten, so that she was some-what disappointed by the sheer volume of paper that she emptied out on the bed, but it was new, and fresh and crisp as spinach.

If there'd been a burner in the room she might have cooked it up and ate it, but no burner, nor oil nor lemon for a salad, so she *rolled* in it, like a dog in shit. Ripped off her satin nightie to feel the touch of greenbacks on her skin, scooped up handfuls and poured them over herself, shrieking with glee, and kicked her heels up to the ceiling until Genghis, unable to hold back, ripped off his jodhpurs and consummated that morning's marriage *toot sweet*, leaving the greenbacks somewhat stained.

Stained or not, back to the bank they went, next day. Daisy never forgave him for that. She'd wanted to stuff a mattress. She'd never forgiven him and now she was wreaking her revenge.

She'd been an old man's folly, as far as he was concerned. He'd cast off that old, grey-haired, loyal Brooklyn wife for Daisy, the one who'd stuck with him through thick and thin since trolley-car days and was now mad with love, poor thing. She was the phantom caller on Daisy's telephone, it turned out. Yes; the cast-off Brooklyn wife kept calling Daisy up, she wouldn't speak, there would be heavy breathing and a tear-stained silence. She'd called her up in New York, those times; no wonder Perry said, 'Poor cow.' And, Daisy said, she called up all the time in Hollywood, in spite of vile abuse. 'And,' said Daisy, 'she follows me around.' So *that* was the solution to the mystery of Daisy's rain-coated shadow whom I'd seen expelled from the studio, that time! I felt quite sorry for her, but Daisy didn't spare her a second thought. She was the wife in residence, and she was going to make Genghis pay.

In spite of all that, Daisy was neither more nor less pretty, more nor less smart than any other one of the hundred, nay, thousand girls who lay back on the couch and thought of star-dom while he shoved it in. But she was the one who got the wedding-band because she didn't care.

And now, she didn't care who knew she didn't care. Before our father could say, 'Ill met by moonlight', she had him up against a pasteboard tree, in the wood near Athens, under a giant daisy, in the lunch break and all the lights went out, they fused them. She thought that that macaw had got it right: 'It ain't no sin.' She was in love, she was like a force of nature, but Genghis Khan was blind and deaf. Blind, deaf and dumb. He thought that he who paid the piper played the tune. An orchid never bit him back before.

And now began a dreary time. Early to bed, up before dawn and out along the mean streets as the forlorn lights were extinguished one by one to join our fellow-workers on the production line. But we ourselves weren't so much part of the process as pieces of the product. They laid us back in chrome recliners and sprayed us with paint, as if we were a motor chassis. We watched the mirror as if the faces it reflected were those of two other women. Greenish in colour; spangles on the cheekbones. Arms and hands, greenish. The green looked weird on monochrome. We had on artificial fingernails that looked like bark. Genghis Khan was staking his all on Art.

We had been cast adrift from what we knew and how to do it. We felt we had been dislocated. Or, as if we, too, had surrendered to the dream but did not know for sure who dreamed us.

We had a lot of dancing to do. A woman came out from the east, specially. Black hair scraped back, scrawny throat, leotards. None of your one, two, three kicks, for her. Angular movements, she said. She stuck out her bum and did peculiar things with her fingers. No tap-shoes, no character shoes, no point shoes; we danced barefoot. Very arty. She told us, if we smiled, she'd kill us.

I'll say this for Daisy, I didn't recognise her in the dailies. I wouldn't say she looked every inch the fairy queen; she looked as if, given half a chance, she'd drop her frock and twirl her tassels but Irish cut her lines down until she scarcely said a word, just stood in the wood and shimmered, and that big head took a lovely photo, I must say, even if it made cows' eyes at Oberon all the time. The Lady A. kept off the set, she knew which way the wind was blowing. All the same, she toddled over for a photocall occasionally, pictured picking up her daughters from the lot, plastered all over the papers, next day. Nothing a republic loves better than a Lord, unless it is a Lady.

Peregrine hovered round those girls all the time. He was foolish fond. Saskia would curl up on his knee and he'd fetch a little something for her out of her ear or her nostril. A pearl. A flower. The ends of her mouth went down to see the rose, she was a mercenary bitch even in those days. Skin like milk and amber eyes. Peregrine watched her wistfully as she danced off towards Melchior as soon as she saw him coming, leaving behind his own little gift without a second thought, as often as not.

When Genghis Khan saw the rushes of the fairy dance, he put Art on hold. Out went the lady in leotards, in came a little henna'd man who used mascara with discretion. One, two, three, kick! We joined up; we went down on our hunkers and kicked like cossacks; leaned over backwards and plucked daisies with our teeth; somersaulted over one another; the splits. We'd been here before, we could have done it in our sleep. Bucks, wings, struts, stumps, shuffles, coffee-grinders. If Melchior hadn't been so besotted with the wife of Genghis Khan, he wouldn't have let him get away with the production numbers but Genghis Khan thought he was hedging his bets. Kaleidoscope effects; fifty identical twins, twenty-five of each. One, two, three, kick! Then we stood on one leg. He wanted a cascade, a water ballet, he drenched us. Water, water, everywhere! Did he think it was the bloody *Tempest*?

The foxgloves trembled, the King and Queen of the Fairies were up to their usual tricks. And, to complete my pleasure, Irish was waiting in the dressing room eager to berate me. He berated me, then wept. I'd have a pound of schlap on, my wig kept flashing on and off, all I wanted was a good wash, a sit-down, a cup of tea. He clutched my knees, he cried so much he soaked my tights, but I never promised him anything.

I was his flawed chorine. Like a glass he didn't know was cracked until it fell apart when he poured his passion in it. But what's a girl to do? It was a real treat when he read me *Daisy Miller* out loud. But we'd reached the point in our relationship when, in a straight choice between him and Henry James, I'd have taken Henry James any day even if Henry James were dead and not much of a one for the girls when living, either. The more I said, 'It was lovely, Irish, but it's over,' the keener he became. I said, 'I'm very busy with my German lessons, Irish,' and he called me his beloved harlot.

I never went to his place, any more. On Sunday, I slept in at the Forest of Arden, got up late, lay in the blue, unnatural air beside the blue unnatural pool. Nora was never there on weekends any more. She was busy making ravioli. I felt that we were drifting apart.

I wasn't the only lonely one. Daisy's cat slept on the canvas chair marked 'Delia Delaney', it never stirred a muscle, it lay quite flat and sometimes, when Genghis Khan came on to the set, he'd pick up that cat and cuddle it in a way that told me Daisy wasn't available in the cuddling department any more. He'd gaze at her cooing at the King of the Fairies and he'd massage that white cat's back until you thought he'd snap its spine. Don't think Daisy was oblivious; she knew full well he went through hell. That was the way she kept her chaps in line.

By the time we got our make-up off, it would be dark outside and there was a wind, sometimes, that smelled of the desert and the valley would be full of lights like diamanté in a black box, and a soft, deep dew was falling. As we were driven home to our thatched cottage, our steak and baked potato, our turned-down bed and early night, I felt we were marooned in Wonderland and victims of a plot.

I know full well who plotted it. Not Melchior. Not Peregrine. Not even Genghis Khan. My German teacher was keen to ascribe everything to a cash nexus but I didn't need him to tell me what was going on.

The love of Mammon lay behind it all.

We worked like slaves. Take after take after take. The same routine, the same song, the same line – over and over and over. We were both product *and* process, simultaneously, and it very near broke us. And what did all our hard work add up to? Just another Saturday night at the pictures! Your one shilling and ninepenn'orth. Your helping of dark. What an equation. Our sweated labour = your bit of fun.

'Like tarts,' said Nora, with prim distaste.

I thought: as soon as all this is finished, we'll go straight back to Brixton. We'll softly and silently steal away, although we'd had plenty of offers, don't think otherwise. We could have stayed out there, cut ourselves a nice little niche out there, hit the high spots. But I was pining away for home – for the whirr and rattle of the trams, the lights of Electric Avenue glowing like bad fish through a good old London fog, longing for rain and weather and bacon sandwiches, for the healthy chill of 49 Bard Road on a frosty morning, for the smell of home, the damp, the cabbage, the tea, the gin.

'Cockney to the core,' said Perry fondly. I felt I was in exile. I knew just what my German teacher felt. I thought that Nora felt it, too. I thought she, too, was pining away for home. But when I said to her: 'I'm counting the days until the wrap, aren't you?' she said, 'It all depends on Tony.'

I saw which way the wind was blowing; she nourished aspirations towards the shoes and rice, the white lace and the orange blossoms. All of a sudden, even though I'd got thoroughly pissed off with her when she cramped our style in London, I started to miss Grandma, and not the way you miss a toothache when you lose a tooth, either.

Then Perry buggered off. He reached his boredom threshold and was gone. He didn't forget his salary cheque; he left a note on the white piano in his suite: 'Find me poste restante in Hazard, Texas; I've saved enough to buy a ranch.' I looked it up in the gazetteer. It was in the panhandle. When our grandparents played it late last century, it was a one-horse town but, from what the gazetteer had to say, it seemed the horse had died. Bit of a change from Hollywood! That's why he went, of course.

So, no Peregrine no more.

Then something started to go wrong with time. We were all spellbound, now. The shooting schedule started out at eight weeks. Then it stretched to twelve. Then to twenty and then on ad infinitum. The director didn't have his mind on the job, for one thing. He and Titania got on with, ahem, making the beast with two backs whenever the company knocked off for a ham and Swiss on rye with mayo. And nothing would satisfy Mascara, he was an obsessional, he was a perfectionist. And that 'wood near Athens' was a deathtrap. A couple of bunnies were concussed by swinging dewdrops; a gnome missed his footing on a toadstool and fractured a fibula; we backed into one of the spiky conkers by mistake, laddered our tights, punctured our posteriors and Nora's went septic, off work for ten days on her front and *hors de combat* in the Forest of Arden, swearing and cursing and leafing through *Brides* magazine.

The next Sunday morning, Nora on her belly, me on my back enjoying to the full my weekly lie-in, high drama strikes. Daisy herself comes knocking at the door.

'I'm pregnint!'

Was she going to pass it off as Genghis's? Once we'd rubbed the sleep from our eyes and drunk our orange juice, we earnestly advised this course. Daisy accepted juice, herself, but poured into her goblet a slug from the silver flask she always carried with her. She was still in her nightie (café au lait chiffon) and hadn't combed her hair but she'd brought us a breakfast of lox and bagels in spite of her fluster, she was a dear, really. She stopped in the middle of splitting her bagel. Her jaw dropped. What? Put one over on Genghis? What kind of a girl did we think she was?

Such moral horror as suffused her features! You never saw anything like it. We were quite surprised and felt shoddy, by comparison, as if we lived in an ethical twilight, a cockroach world of compromise, lies, emotional sleight of hand. And so we did, I suppose. We called it 'Life'. But Daisy wanted something better. So did Irish, come to think of it. It's the American tragedy in a nutshell. They look around the world and think: 'There must be something better!' But there isn't. Sorry, chum. This is it. What you see is what you get. Only the here and now.

'He really wants children, you know,' Nora suggested delicately.

How did she know this herself? Easy. He'd offered her one. There was a memo from his desk, delivered to the set: Miss Leonora Chance, please call. She thought she ought to go, although she had a twinge of unease on account of Tony, who was jealous as Othello. We weren't wanted on the set that day so I was busy with my studies (W. for Wedekind).

He only made her wait for half an hour, in itself a wonder. He had a sliding time-scale for appointments. Actors cooled their heels from seven hours to five days, depending on their box-office. Agents, a week to three. Writers, six weeks minimum. Irish once waited five months in the outer office.

But Genghis Khan's very own navy-blue-suited secretary sat Nora on a leather sofa, even offered her some coffee before she retired behind her mahogany desk to be evasive on the telephone. Over her head was a big Grünewald crucifixion, the kind where the Christ has gangrene. No matter where you sat in that outer office, the eyes of that agonised Christ would follow you around. Nora took her coffee black and patted her handbag; she hadn't forgotten to bring with her the wee, pearl-handled handgun Tony gave her on her birthday, just in case.

She knew, because Daisy told her so, that all the time she sat and waited, Genghis would keep an eye on her through a special spyhole he'd had drilled in one of those Grünewald eyes.

Then she was buzzed in; she was admitted to the holy of holies, the orchid arbour. He was leaning over a glass case. Although he wore white gloves he did not wear a shirt. He was giving a close inspection to something that looked like a rotting pudenda and didn't answer her cheery, 'What'cher, Mr Khan?' but dropped a scrap of raw meat into the orifice, which gnashed its snappers in appreciation. There was a plate of steak tartare on his desk beside the photograph of Daisy which Nora could not help but note stood upside down. He stripped off his bloody gloves and tossed them in the wastepaper basket. He gave Nora his full attention.

'I'm not going down on my knees to you,' he said. 'Not to an actress. Why, actresses go down on their knees to me!' He gave a caw of mirth. Perhaps he thought this quip would break the ice. Nora, sat on a leather chair with a dental look about it, crossed and recrossed her legs and fingered the outlines of her little gun. 'Out with it,' she said. He was quite taken aback to find the chorus girl so forward, so earthy; 'out with it' is *not* a US idiom. She hastily translated: 'Say what you've got to say and get it over with.'

'My mother's name was Leonora,' he said. 'I've chosen you to bear my child.' He must have been fond of his mother, the sentimental old thing. He pressed a button on his desk and Nora's chair collapsed. She was everso surprised. The back fell down, the seat shot out, it turned into a chaise longue and she went sprawling, legs in the air. While she had been fingering her bag, she must have accidentally slipped the safety catch because the gun went off – her bag was ruined – and blew a hole in the orchidarium. The secretary came beating on the door: 'Everything all right, Mr Khan?'

Nora always had respect for Genghis after that because he took one look at the gun, one look at her, switched on his intercom and told the secretary everything was fine.

'I'd feel everso much more comfortable if you'd put your shirt back on, Mr Khan,' she said, so he did and then something inside him broke, he grovelled, he said his heart was broken and he wanted his revenge on Melchior, etc. etc. etc. Then he said: 'Well, if you won't, how about your sister?' Then he said, could she put in a good word for him with Daisy, anyway?

But Genghis Khan was yesterday's papers as far as Daisy was concerned. She vowed she'd marry Melchior if it was the last thing she did. We tried to stop her but she leapt into her white roadster again as soon as she'd gobbled up her bagel and roared off in the direction of Hacienda Hazard.

'She's everso overwrought,' said Nora. 'Do you think we ought to go, too, Dora, to make sure she's all right?'

I reached to ring a cab.

'Oh, yes,' I said. 'Oh, bloody yes. Try and keep me away!'

By chance, the English Colony had foregathered in its entirety at the Hazard place that sunny forenoon in order to consume the contents of a box of kippers that had arrived, like us, on the Super-Chief, and, brunch done, to play a game of cricket on the extensive lawn so there they all were, in the Sante Fé-style dining hall, picking away at bones and spreading the Cooper's Oxford on their toast, the men with their monocles, the women in gloves, while the Lady A. presided behind a silver teapot.

Enter Daisy.

She overshot the drive and screeched to a halt on the cricket pitch, demolishing a wicket. Then in she burst through the French windows, spilling out of her nightie in all directions, hair like knitting the kittens had got at. Besides, you wouldn't recognise her without her make-up, she was a plain little thing, under all that.

It was the Lady A. that I felt sorry for. I could even find it in my heart, at that moment, to feel sorry for Imogen and Saskia. The girls clung to their mother's skirts (she was wearing a lovely mid-calf pink floral crepe de Chine with fichu plus a wide-brimmed straw with an old rose ribbon), too scared to cry, too overwhelmed by the horror of it, the madwoman in her underwear, the screams, the tears, the recriminations. Meanwhile, the English Colony, ever unflappable, took their final bites of kipper and laid their knives and forks together on their plates.

'Such kippers, Attie! Delish. Quite like home.'

'Lovely party, Attie. Must run!'

'Darling Attie, 'byee. Don't forget, our place next week. Roast beef!'

They made their excuses and left; you'd never have thought Daisy was raving all the while, improvising innumerable variations on the theme of: 'It's your baby, I swear it! Your baby! This baby's got a right to a father!'

Nora and I held hands, at that, and could not bear to look at Melchior. The Lady A., too British or too embarrassed to bring up the rights of her own babies, gave the girls a little hug and said:

'Now, you just run upstairs, and see what Nanny's doing.'

They wore white organdie. Saskia had a pink sash, Imogen a blue one. They wore their hair in braids. At their age, we were keeping our Grandma.

'Be off with you, like good chicks,' said Melchior, undergoing stress.

'Scoot!' said Daisy, with menace.

The Lady A. felt the side of the teapot. Evidently the temperature was no longer satisfactory. She rang a handbell.

'I'm sure we'd all feel better for a cup of tea.'

That stopped Daisy in her tracks. She rolled her eyes.

'I can't *believe* this!'

And sat down suddenly on the chintz settee with a big, hissing sigh, as though expending all the air inside her. She was deflated. The Lady A. held out her arms to my sister and me.

'Nora . . . Dora . . . How lovely to see you!' She smelled of Arpège. And that's another reason why we took the old trout in, because she gave us a hug and kissed us each on the cheek as if we were family. Then she let Daisy Duck take away her husband. She didn't even put up a fight. She smiled bravely and let him go. By the time the shadows lay along the lawn everything was settled. A swift, Mexican divorce for both parties, to be fitted in while the second unit dealt with Hermia, Helena, Lysander and Demetrius, and then Oberon and Titania could make it legal. They call it 'serial monogamy'. Daisy gave us a lift back to the Forest of Arden; she was planning her new wedding already. She wanted us to be bridesmaids but we said, bad taste.

So that was that.

I do believe that Melchior thought he knew what he was doing when he offed with the old, onned with the new in such spectacular fashion; I think he thought that he was marrying, not into Hollywood but Hollywood itself, taking over the entire factory, thus acquiring control of the major public dreaming facility in the whole world. Shakespeare's revenge for the War of Independence. Once Melchior was in charge of this fabulous machine, he would bestride the globe.

And now I come to think of it, his father passed on in America, didn't he? Did that have something to do with his ambition, which now reached its peak? He was drunk with glory. He left *The Dream* largely to its own devices, to Mascara's inventions, to Genghis's interventions. He was certain it could come to no harm, that he could do no wrong.

But some sixth sense told me we'd passed that fine line that divides the socko from the flopperoo some time before; now the production headed faster and faster towards disaster.

But what about Genghis?

'You can deal with Genghis,' I said. 'He wants to make a mother of you, after all.'

'Oh, no, I can't deal with Genghis. Tony would kill me. *You* deal with Genghis. He'll never tell the difference?'

'What about poor old Irish?'

'I thought you weren't seeing Irish any more. Oh, go on, Dora; you can do it. My opinion is, that Genghis Khan will ring us up and propose to whichever one of us answers the telephone in' –

and here she consulted her watch – 'about fifteen minutes' time, as soon as Daisy gets home and tells him he's been relegated to second division.'

And so it turned out. I didn't want to do it but Nora was inexorable. That's how I knew she was in love.

We decided to announce all three engagements – Daisy to Melchior, myself to Genghis, Nora to Tony – at the end-of-shoot party on the 'wood near Athens' set. I sent a telegram to Grandma: 'I'm going to marry the most powerful man in Hollywood when his divorce comes through.' I had brushed up my Shakespeare; I recognised for what it was the game that Nora and I had played out once before as romance. And now we'd perform the 'substitute bride' bit, as in *Measure for Measure* and *All's Well That Ends Well*, as farce. I didn't want to do it. I broke down in the post office when we went to send the telegram. But Nora wouldn't let me off the hook. I'd never known her quite this way before. She said that when the shoot was over, she was going to take instruction. 'They're a very devout family, Dora.'

She sent a telegram to Grandma, too. 'I'm going to marry the most wonderful man in the world as soon as I've converted.'

He telephoned her every night when we came in from work; he chattered away impenetrably in Sicilian and she never understood one word but she would stand there blushing while he was talking to her. She would look pliant and voluptuous. She clutched the receiver as tenderly as if it were his prick but *that* she kept her hands off. The plan was, a white wedding. I was at a loss for words.

The studio publicity went to town on me and Genghis. Hedda Hopper hinted coyly at romance. Rumours were dropped of secret dates and private suppers. All the US asked: 'Will this great man of the cinema propose to little Miss Nobody from Nowhere, England?' Louella Parsons ran a piece about the first Mrs Khan, the poor old Brooklyn wife: 'I knew it would never last with Delia but I thought that he would come back to his senses in the end and come home to me.' Louella ran a piece about me: 'I'm planning on a beige and ecru trousseau.' She ran a picture of me, except that it was Nora's picture, by mistake. *Photoplay* ran a spread. Hedda Hopper scooped; she ran an interview with

Genghis: 'My English rose: this time its for keeps, says Mr Holly-wood.'

Genghis and I were a hot number on paper. In the flesh, no. Now I was a fiancée, he put me on a pedestal. No nooky until the ring was on my finger, he declared, and I wasn't going to argue with that. I'd gone on to automatic, I felt I didn't have a will of my own. I did what Nora wanted because I loved her best.

The telephone began to ring for me, too, every night. It was a phantom caller. Just heavy breathing and sometimes a sob, some-times as if she'd started saying something and then choked it back, not knowing what to say. I had inherited the Brooklyn wife. I saw that raincoat whisking round the lot; I felt unseen eyes upon me.

I waited for a sign from Grandma, a letter, a telegram. Nothing doing. I waited in vain but still I waited because I knew what she'd say. 'Come off it, gel. It just won't do. Come home.' But now I was so mixed up in it all, I couldn't get out by myself. I told my German teacher everything. 'Go ahead and marry him,' he advised me. 'Marry him and ruin them. That's the way to do it. What I say is, fuck the bourgeoisie.' It was a dizzying prospect. Did I have the temperament for a Delilah?

If ever I ran into Irish on the lot, he'd turn away.

And God alone knows where Peregrine had got to.

Daisy's beloved cat now took to sleeping on my chair. That cat knew in its bones how Genghis's wife was a better bet for an ongoing cat-food supply than Melchior's wife. Not that it would have taken a cat of more than average intelligence to foresee the cash *The Dream* would lose.

We wrapped up with the rude mechanicals. They were another catastrophe, more mechanical than rude, worse luck – like robots. Lifeless. There's a kind of reverence the custard-pie brig-ade can't keep out of its voice when it plays Shakespeare and it scuppered the entire proceedings in that department, although Melchior had personally imported the rudest man in England to play Bottom.

Yes! Gorgeous George.

George had gone from strength to strength since Nora and I first caught his act, that time, on Brighton Pier. 'Clown Number

One to the British Empire.' He'd started a riot at the Royal Variety Show when he held up a couple of spuds and said: 'King Edwards.' That was just before the abdication. Peregrine had a theory and convinced his brother of it, as follows: all the comic roles in Shakespeare were originally intended for stand-up comedians. Melchior swallowed it whole. First of all, Melchior wanted George to get his clothes off, somehow, as a little reminder, according to Melchior, of the essential *Englishness* of Shakespeare, but Peregrine had managed to persuade his brother that Bottom was supposed to be a citizen of Athens, Greece, and hence unlikely to sport a map of the British Isles on his pecs, let alone Africa on his abdomen. They let him keep his famous plus-fours, too; at least, those plus-fours were famous in the UK, and or so Melchoir thought, in his folly and delusion, soon to be famous in the USA, to boot.

So there was George, in golfing garb, plus brogues, all pink and purple, he should have been in Technicolor; you burst out laughing just to look but when he opened his mouth, he took the smile right off your face. He was like a fine wine if only in the one respect, he didn't travel. The moment he stepped off his native soil, he stopped being funny. In California, he was not bawdy, he was lewd. Genghis Khan caught the rushes and kicked up hell; not Genghis Khan's idea of a class act, no, indeed! So Bottom's part was cut to pieces, until he had almost as little to do as Daisy and, these days, he wore a baffled look as if, when nobody laughed, he didn't know what to do with himself.

Gorgeous George's stab at global fame was dying on its feet. Melchior, at his wits' end, adopted the following stratagem: fairies, all around, peeking through the leaves to watch, the idea being, if the audience sees the fairies laughing, then it might even bring itself to raise a titter, too. But it was hard going, I can tell you.

'Thisbe,' said Bottom, 'the flower of odious savouries sweet —'

'Savours! Savours!' bellowed Melchoir through his megaphone. He cut a dashing figure in his snakeskin tights; he'd dressed ready for the party afterwards and, in former days, George would have been quick with the repartee, I can tell you, but now poor old George was shillyshallying with nerves. I thought, the poor sod's on the skids, he should never have come to Hollywood.

'Thisbe, the flower of odours savours sweet –'

He must have thought, to hell with it! Because, suddenly, a flicker of authentic George illuminated his now cadaverous features. His eyebrows worked and he gave his bum a wiggle to ram home the idea of 'Bottom'. He sang out his line in grand style and he gave that 'odours' the full force of all his genius for innuendo. I blushed. Perry had another theory: that a truly great comedian could make a laundry list sound filthy. George touched greatness at this moment.

'– odours savours sweet –'

'Cut!' cried Melchior, white with rage.

The wretched business wasn't in the can until past seven but could we then adjourn to hot baths and stiff drinks? Could we, hell. The doors burst open and in came a torchlit procession, those bloody lutenists, again, in costume as ever was; plus the entire English faculty of UCLA in their graduation robes; and a hundred-voice boys' choir drafted in for the occasion, piping up in trebles: 'The Boar's Head in Hand Bear I.'

So they all came in, plus an Elizabethan feast borne by blue-chinned men in shirts slashed to the waist and knee breeches; it turned out Tony's uncle catered it and not quite seasonal, also, overdoing the garlic and marinara sauce. The fairies stumped over en masse to the bar and started on the serious drinking. Nanny came for Saskia and Imogen because the Lady A. thought it would be in the worst possible taste for the girls to attend their father's engagement party and Imogen went quietly but Saskia cried and clung to her father's leg until Daisy lost her temper and snapped: 'Beat it, kid!' At which Saskia's eyes spat fire but what could she do? She was only twelve and had no rights.

Then Irish came in on a bender, white of face and red of eye and upright only with the greatest difficulty, to press into my hands his poisoned gift, the page proofs of *Hollywood Elegies*, inscribed to his 'gilded fly', and signed with his full name, thank God. I sold it at Sotheby's last winter when we were a touch pressed as to how to pay the electricity bill.

'If I'm a fly,' I said to him, 'what does that make you? Fly-paper?'

Then, big-hearted me, I introduced him to the Helena. She'd come out from an East Coast stock company, she was a Bryn Mawr graduate, English major, low mileage, only one careful boyfriend. I wanted nothing but happiness for poor old Irish. I was really very fond of him. But what he wanted for himself was, an infinitely renewable virgin – one he could do every night who'd be untouched again by morning. My German teacher said it was inherently a metaphysical desire and I agree with him. *His* needs were much simpler and we parted friends.

Journalists in hats came in. Harlots, actresses and wives in satin frocks came in. The English Colony in its entirety in gloves and pearls came in. An entire swing band plus leader in d.j. and baton came in, to battle it out musically with the massed pluckers; Genghis confided he'd had it up to *here* with lutes. Tony came in in a nice black suit and black fedora and Nora ran to his side, blushing and giggling. An Italian tenor came in with a mandolin and sang 'Come Back to Sorrento' in high counterpoint to the swing band playing 'Satin Doll' and the consort of lutes still having a valiant go at 'Fine Knacks for Ladies', while Gorgeous George, having stayed himself with a flagon, was trying out a chorus of 'Rose of England' in a defiant and self-conscious manner.

In those days, with Irish's hideous example ever before me, I was quite abstemious but when Genghis Khan took from his jodhpur pocket a little box and showed me the ring inside, I thought: If I don't get drunk tonight, I'll kill myself.

It wasn't a diamond as big as the Ritz, only the size of the Algonquin. It sat on my hand like a knuckleduster as we took the floor to foxtrot amidst an explosion of flashbulbs. My chin skidded the top of his head, he trod on my feet – he wasn't looking where he was going, he was gazing helplessly at Daisy in her Titania gown, wrapped round Melchior like skin round sausage. I try to laugh but it was wry. I felt sad.

Sad. Nothing more than sad. Let's not call it a tragedy; a broken heart is never a tragedy. Only untimely death is a tragedy. And war, which, before we knew it, would be upon us; replace the comic mask with the one whose mouth turns down and close the theatre, because I refuse point-blank to play in tragedy.

So tragedy it wasn't. But I couldn't help thinking of that blond tenor and the last time I'd swapped beds with Nora, which made me sentimental. And I do believe old Genghis thought *his* heart was breaking, he lurched, he stumbled, I led, I steered him, picking my way with care among the towering foxgloves, the swollen daisies, the vicious conkers on the silver gravel floor. Genghis patted my behind but I knew his heart was not in it; he gazed at Daisy and burned with vengeance.

Hope for the best, expect the worst, as Grandma used to say. I hoped that Genghis Khan would think he'd had enough revenge by marrying Daisy's lover's daughter; I did hope so, I was always partial to Daisy. But what I thought he'd really do was, smash them.

High above the heads of the convivial throng I saw the crown of spikes that showed me where my father was. Hither and thither, the perfect host, graciousness personified. I caught a glimpse of Irish as Helena helped him from the scene. Little did he know that she would play herself in the movie based on his final years; I forget who it was played me. Some painted harlot. Poor old Irish didn't have long left. Keeled over at *The Dream* premiere, outside Graumann's Chinese. Dicky ticker. Nora and I had gone home, by then. 'Don't worry,' they said, carting him out of the way of the stars, 'it's only a writer.' Then *Hollywood Elegies* came out, but what's the point of a posthumous Pulitzer? Ross O'Flaherty, RIP.

I saw my German tutor, who'd gate-crashed, looking starved, as usual. He'd got some front-office type by the arm and was haranguing him. Puck passed by and goosed me. The noise, the smoke, the smell of garlic, the blaring lights were beginning to discompose me. Not to mention the liquor. Nora waltzed by with Tony, clinging close; her eyes were closed, a dreamy smile upon her lips. I'm going to throw up, I thought. Influence of Irish. Never thrown up at a party before.

I sat in the cool, white bathroom for a while, listening to the gently plashing gurgling water in the cistern, which soothed me. I looked at myself in the mirror and saw my eyes were bright as if I were on drugs, bright as the diamond for which, to tell the truth, I'd sold myself. My heart went thump, thump, and I felt shuddery. A cluster of retching pixies broke in upon my troubled solitude but I wasn't fit to go back to the party and face Genghis's damp hands, my father's empty triumph, my sister's mindless bliss, Irish's contempt and the cynicism of my German tutor, which he called common sense, and though I knew in my heart he, out of all of them, knew about life, I was only a girl and did not want to believe him. I never listened to the news, in those days.

I *was* feeling sorry for myself, I can tell you, so I picked about a bit in those dense, artificial woods, and the music and the voices filtered, altered, through the weird shadows and everything started to go strange. I knocked my knee on a dewdrop and as I rubbed the bruise, the foliage parted.

I thought I'd gone mad.

I saw my double. I saw myself, me, in my Peaseblossom costume, large as life, like looking in a mirror.

First off, I thought it was Nora, up to something, but it put its finger to its lips, to shush me, and I got a whiff of Mitsouko and then I saw it was a replica. A hand-made, custom-built replica, a wonder of the plastic surgeon's art.

The trouble she'd gone to! She'd had her nose bobbed, her tits pruned, her bum elevated, she'd starved and grieved away her middle-age spread. She'd had her back molars out, giving the illusion of cheekbones. Her face was lifted up so far her ears had ended up on top of her head but, happily, the wig hid them. And after all that she looked very lifelike, I must say, if not, when I looked more closely, not *all* that much like me, more like a blurred photocopy or an artist's impression, and, poor cow, you could still see the bruises under the Max Factor Pan Stik, however thickly she applied it, and the scars round where the ears should be. Ooh, it must have hurt! It was a good job for her we were about the same height, Daisy was a real shortarse.

Before me stood the exxed Mrs Khan, who loved her man so much she was prepared to turn herself into a rough copy of his beloved for his sake.

'How much do you want?' she said. I'd heard that voice so

often, breathing brokenheartedly down the telephone. I was quite moved to hear it speak.

'How much do I want for what?'

'My husband back again.' Her lip quivered, her eyelids fluttered. Fancy taking so much trouble over a man. My sentimental heart went right out to the old bag. Would you believe it, she really loved him.

Then came a great noise, drowning out the party sounds – Genghis, on the megaphone, and he was paging me.

'Dora! DORA!!'

All the lutes began to play at once and, oh, my God! they played the Wedding March. If her face could have crumpled, it would have, but it was too tightly stretched.

'I thought it was an engagement party,' she wailed. 'Not a wedding party!'

'So did I!' I said. I panicked. I didn't think twice, I offed that diamond bruiser as if it were a burning coal. 'Here. Shove it on your finger. *You* go and marry him. Go on. You've done it before, haven't you? But I should get a veil on, sharpish, if I were you.'

I don't think she believed it, at first. She kept on turning the ring round and round in her hands, which were wrinkled and freckled on the backs, they can't do a thing with hands, cosmetically, but there was no time to find her some gloves, let's hope he doesn't look until too late. She stared at me in the strangest way; I couldn't make it out, at first, but, then, she couldn't call her face her own, could she, and after a bit I realised she was giving me a smile.

'DORA!!!'

All around us, crystal dewdrops shook and tinkled, such was the decibellage of his cry. She gave me a quick little peck on the cheek. Then she showed a clean pair of heels, never saw a woman move so fast, not a thank-you or a backward glance – off, before I changed my mind. And that was the nearest I ever got to wedded bliss, thank you very much.

I thought I'd better slip into something inconspicuous, for the nonce, as it wouldn't do to have *three* Chance sisters walking round, under the circumstances, so I was making for the exit when I tripped over Bottom, right over, fell flat on my face.

Bottom was dead to the world, feeling no pain, forgetful at last of the miseries and humiliations of the last few months, and wouldn't be needing his ass's head. I got off his plus-fours, too, and his jacket, and so I inadvertently exposed the British Empire, all that pink on his torso, not to mention the lesser breeds without the law. I didn't want our nation's shame out in the open for all to see so I rolled him under an imitation bush, picked off a handful of imitation leaves and covered him up. It felt like the end of something, when I did that, but there was no time to ponder as to the end of what.

I've done many a quick change, in the wings, in panto, in revue, but never one as quick as this. And so it came to pass that it was as Bottom the Weaver, in plus-fours and an ass's head, that I went to my own wedding. I was beginning to see the funny side. It isn't every day you see yourself get married.

It was a strange night, that night, and stranger still because I always misremember. It never seems the same, twice, each time that I remember it. I distort. Remember, though I was on my feet and compos mentis, I was still half tight, if not more so; everything seemed disembodied, distant, peculiar. The tin roof over our heads seemed to have cracked open and disappeared, somehow, because there was real, black sky above us, although the crescent moon was made of painted plywood and swung backwards and forwards with Puck perched on it, looking perky. The swing band was pizzicatoing away and Puck was vocalising with them, in that high soprano that made you think you'd died and gone to heaven:

'It's only a paper moon, sailing over a cardboard sea.
But it wouldn't be make-believe, if you'd believe in me . . .'

A brisk wind made the stiff twigs rattle yet I doubt that wind came from a machine because it blew all the sweet wet dewiness of the California night through the set.

And I no longer remember that set *as* a set but as a real wood, dangerous, uncomfortable, with real, steel spines on the conkers and thorns on the bushes, but looking as if it were unreal and painted, and the bewildering moonlight spilled like milk in this wood, as if Hollywood were the name of the enchanted forest where you lose yourself and find yourself, again; the wood that changes you; the wood where you go mad; the wood where the shadows live longer than you do.

These days, half a century and more later, I might think I did not live but dreamed that night, if it wasn't for the photos, see? This one of Bottom, being hugged by –

There I go again! Can't keep a story going in a straight line, can I? Drunk in charge of a narrative.

Where was I?

There I was, one of the crowd, among the fairies, goblins, spirits, mice, rabbits, badgers, etc. etc. etc crowding around the brides, who all three seemed somewhat taken aback, even put out, by the spontaneous nature of the unexpected marriage ceremony and were babbling agitatedly to one another whilst minions scurried hither and thither, pushing aside the undergrowth to create more of a chapel-like atmosphere and bringing in stands of calla lilies, babies' breath and satin bows. Some girls from wardrobe sprinted in with wedding veils and orange blossom wreaths so there was a bit of trying on of those while the three grooms consorted together in a male huddle, clearing their throats, pulling on ciggies and looking anxious.

Then came a diversion. A little old lady that I'd never seen before popped up out of nowhere, maybe up through a trap in the floor, as if in a thunderclap. Tony looked quite post-operative with shock. She'd got on a long black overcoat and a big black veil and she flung her arms round Tony's neck and burst into floods of tears and Italian exclamations and so did he. The old lady came out of the clinch long enough to look daggers at Nora and then she and Tony were at it again, so that Nora blushed and cowerèd behind her veil. Then Tony's Mamma – for it was she, freshly arrived from Little Italy on the train – disengaged and commenced haranguing him. Daisy, meanwhile, was taking a surreptitious swig from a silver flask while the substitute Dora had cannily covered herself up with the thickest veil and now perched upon a dewdrop, biding her time.

Then the lutes began to play, of all things, 'Home on the Range'.

Clip-clop, clip-clop, clip-clop.

Picking its way delicately among the detritus on the floor now entered the scene the biggest white horse I ever saw and, on top of it, the biggest cowpoke, in the biggest goddamned white hat and a chequered shirt with a silver star on the lapel. Genghis Khan hugged himself, he was so pleased to see the cowboy, but Melchior looked quite green. Tony's Mamma was now upbraiding him so fiercely he did not even give the cowboy a glance, but everybody else laughed, cheered and clapped so I brayed, too, and stamped my hooves.

Genghis Khan looked proud and shy. This impromptu cowboy wedding was his brilliant idea, it seemed. Clip-clop, went the horse, and stopped. The cowboy twanged out in a broad drawl that halted just this side of self-parody:

'Which of you goshdarned sinners is the best man?'

Puck leapt gracefully off his half-moon, assisted by a wire, and, dangling three feet in the air above us, squeaked: 'I am!'

'Got the goshdarned rings, sonny?'

A monstrous suspicion awoke within me. I knew that voice. I knew that bulk.

Puck displayed a handful of gold.

'Let's get the ball rolling!'

Everything was hurting my eyes, the glitter, the bright, white light, but I knew who it was, all right, on that white horse. It was –

'Let it be known to all present,' sang out the cowboy, 'that by the powers invested in me as sheriff of the county of Hazard, Texas, I now pronounce you men – and wives.'

Tony's Mamma let out a shrill scream of outrage. Too late. Three rings slipped on to three fingers. Three women pushed back three veils. I couldn't help it, I started crying. I made a lovely bride. I looked quite radiant. I wept buckets, inside that ass's head.

Then Tony's Mamma, gibbering with fury, heaved up a vat of marinara sauce and – emptied it all over Nora.

Blood on the bridal veil! All those tomatoes, it looked like a massacre. Mamma fell backwards, clutching her heart. A coronary? Tony cried out and flung himself down beside her. Then – bang! bang! bang! Machine-gun fire? No, only a barrage of champagne corks from the buffet timed to blast off in unison as soon as the knot was tied but we only found *that* out afterwards, it was panic stations, at the time. All present flung themselves down on their bellies. The white horse took fright and reared up. The cowboy's hat fell off. Red hair. I'd known it was Peregrine from the very first moment but Melchior's jaw dropped and Daisy creased up. Then, pandemonium.

The iris closes.

Everything went blank.

I knew I should have gone to comfort Nora but I couldn't take any more, I was punch-drunk. I clawed my way out through the nightmare party into the cool, dark outdoors and blundered straight into, was almost winded by –

'I say, steady on,' she said.

My nostrils filled with the aroma I loved best in all the world, surpassing all others – that consummate blend of gin, cabbage, stale undergarments, mothballs.

'Grandma!'

Flash! A passing paparazzo took a picture of an old lady who looked like St Pancras Station, monumental, grimy, full of Gothic detail, startled in the arms of a half-man, half-donkey.

'Who the fuck are you?' she said.

She seemed to fill up all the space available, so there wasn't any room left in the whole of southern California for insecurity. She had her oilcloth carrier with her, evidently her only luggage. Daisy's white cat, who had been sleeping peacefully on a bank of wild thyme the while, now made its appearance like a cork from a bottle out of that madhouse behind us. It stopped short when it saw Grandma. It rubbed its head against her knee and started to purr. She bent down and picked it up.

'I feel the need of something to cuddle,' she said.

She'd flown, as it turned out, the intrepid old cow. She'd pawned the grandfather clock and flown. Not all the way, of course, only from New York, but it got her here in half the time.

As soon as she'd got our telegrams, she'd gone to Thomas Cook's in Piccadilly. 'Get me to Hollywood *toot sweet*.'

We took the white cat to Brixton with us, in the end. It didn't have any time for Daisy any more. It never showed much sign of either sex while it lived with Daisy but it turned out she never got pregnant because Daisy would lock her in a wardrobe when she came on heat and as soon as that cat arrived at Bard Road, it turned into a breeding machine. The founding mother of the Chance cat dynasty. We had her all through the blitz. Six kittens twice a year, regular, until the cat flu took her off in '51. She was our only souvenir of Hollywood unless you count our silver-fox trenches, about which the less said the better, and a few signatures in a few books.

So we went home with Grandma, sadder and wiser girls. Tony's Mamma prevailed, of course. What? Her son marry a born-again virgin? Not good enough for Little Italy! Nora was so angry she never shed a tear but broke his jaw when he came round to take back the engagement ring and went on packing. Meanwhile, Genghis Khan and the imitation Dora lived happily ever after, once he'd got over the shock, and if you believe that, you'll believe anything, but I do know, for a fact, he never got together with Daisy again and though he tried to ruin her career, she didn't give a damn. It finished Melchior in the movies, though. Kaput. The end.

Furthermore, it turned out, after all that, that Daisy *wasn't* pregnant, just a touch of dysmenorrhoea and a twinge of indigestion. She came on with a vengeance in the middle of the wedding night and by the end of the honeymoon they were fighting like terriers so Daisy went to Mexico again and Melchior came home to London, wifeless, childless, jobless, hopeless, quenched. Then war was declared in the nick of time; he joined up pronto and turned into a war hero. The Fleet Air Arm. No, really. Who'd have thought it?

But Hollywood was a closed book to him, thereafter.

Daisy still sends us a card at Christmas. Not a shred of malice in her. Turn on the telly, you'll see her. She's worn well. She never had the looks to lose and so she never lost them. Still blonde, still with that same rude joke of a mouth. She does the matriarchs in soaps, these days. She gives good décolleté, for an octogenarian.

Still on the go. I was always fond of Daisy.

Four

'ᴇᴛ other pens dwell on guilt and misery.' A., for Austen, Jane. *Mansfield Park*. I do not wish to talk about the war. Suffice to say it was no carnival, not the hostilities. No carnival.

Yes, indeed; I have my memories, but I prefer to keep them to myself, thank you very much. Though there are some things I never can forget. The cock that used to crow, early in the morning, in Bond Street. And I saw a zebra, once, he was galloping down Camden High Street, one night, about midnight, in the blackout – the moon was up, his stripes fluoresced. I was in some garret with a Free Norwegian. And the purple flowers that would pop up on the bomb-sites almost before the ruins stopped smoking, as if to say, life goes on, even if you don't.

We kept a patriotic pig in the back garden, fed him with swill – potato peelings, tea leaves. Grandma loved that pig and wouldn't listen to one word about the slaughterhouse, of course, but it ended up the funeral baked meats after Grandma copped it. She'd have created something shocking if she'd known we'd feasted off her beloved porker, nicely roasted, as soon as we'd cremated her, but what else could we have done for the funeral tea? People had come for miles, we couldn't give them grated cabbage. Old Nanny brought up a bushel of apples for the sauce from the Lady A., who'd retreated to the sticks in a state of disarray. No flowers, by request; we stuck to Grandma's principles on that score, at least.

Cyn and her kids were there but not the cabby, he was in North Africa and there he stayed, poor chap, under the desert in a box. Cyn never got over it, she faded away, after that, until the Asian flu took her off in '49. Ex-tenants by the score – geriatric adagio dancers, antique sopranos. Neighbours. The man who ran the salad stall in Brixton market. Publicans galore. Half the cast of *What? You Will?* came, plus the composer's mother, in her new black coat. I half thought that blond tenor might have heard about it on the grapevine and turned up but no such luck.

We missed Peregrine something shocking but he was off being heroic in the Secret Service. God knows what it was but they gave him a medal for it. God knows *where* he was, either; we put a notice in *The Times* and there was a knock at the door, a jeep, an army driver, a dozen crates of crème de menthe, a barrel of Guinness, so the mourners all went home with grease on their chins and strong drink on their breath and that was how Peregrine paid his respects to Grandma.

Once we'd burned the bones – because that pig met its fate strictly on the q.t., it was a hanging matter, to slaughter your own meat in wartime – Nora and I sat down right here, in the breakfast room, in these very leather armchairs, and listened to the silence in that long, narrow house where we would live alone, in future, and had a good cry, just the two of us, for this was childhood's end with a vengeance and we were truly on our own, now, good and proper.

We hadn't just lost Grandma, either. She was the only witness of the day our mother died when we were born, and she took with her the last living memory of that ghost without a face. All our childhood went with her into oblivion, so we were bereft both of her in person and of a good deal of ourselves, too, and when we remembered how we'd mocked her nakedness in her old age we were ashamed.

Now we were on the high road to our third decade, though, looking back from my present great pinnacle and eminence of years, I can scarcely credit it, that, once upon a time, we thought our lives would end when we reached thirty; at the time it felt like the end of the road, all right, even if there hadn't been a war on, and we were never the same again after the war was over, either.

After the war was over, it was always chilly. Our fingers were pale blue for years. Before the war, we were young, and then we were in sunny California; during the war, adrenalin kept you going and there was always some fella or other around to warm you up. But afterwards, there was a weariness, and the blood was a touch thinner, and people said it was the Age of Austerity - yet I do believe that chilliness we felt was more to do with Grandma being gone than with the economic policies of Stafford Cripps or the cold winters of the late forties and all that.

Without Grandma in it, minding the fires, leaving the lights on for us at nights, up in the morning putting on the kettle, banging the big brass gong to tell us she'd scrambled the dried eggs already, and they were congealing on the plate, the house was nothing but a barn and we rattled around uncomfortably, piles of dirty dishes in the sink, the steps filthy, baked beans fossilising at their leisure in the bottoms of pans on the cold stove, etc. etc. etc.

We let the house go. We'd come back to sleep, that was all. Sometimes we'd burn ourselves a slice of toast. The heart went out of this house when Grandma died. The draughts raced through the hall and the rugs rose up and shimmied, we never changed the sheets so they were grey and stained and full of crumbs. Times were a touch hard for hoofers, too, although we put a brave face on it.

Then began those dreary days of touring shows, smaller and smaller theatres, fewer and fewer punters, the showgirls wearing less and less, the days of our decline. The nadir, a nude show-cum-pantomime in Bolton, *Goldilocks and the Three Bares*. 'Take off your trousers, call it *Goldibollocks*,' said Nora to the a.s.m., but he wouldn't. Those nude shows! Music hall's last gasp. There was a law that said, a girl could show her all provided she didn't move, not twitch a muscle, stir an inch – just stand there, starkers, letting herself be looked at. That's what the halls had sunk to, after the war. No more costumes by Oliver Messel, sets by Cecil Beaton. We always kept our gee-strings and our panties on, mind. Never stripped. We'd still sing, we'd still dance. But we felt our art was swirling down the plughole and those were the days when high culture was booming, our father cutting a swathe with the senior citizen roles in Shakespeare – Timon, Caesar, John of Gaunt – but he still didn't want anything to do with us, as ever was.

It is a characteristic of human beings, one I've often noticed, that if they don't have a family of their own, they will invent one. Now we often found ourselves slipping down to Sussex to visit the Lady A. Lynde Court was just a pile of blackened bricks, and they'd sold up the Eaton Square place when they divorced so after the Lady A. came home from California she turfed the tenant out of the Lynde Court Home Farm and moved in with the Aga and the exposed beams. She always kept a full-length portrait of Melchior in her sitting room. That portrait took up most of one wall and cast gloom in spite of the gilt frame because there he was, as Richard III, Tricky Dicky, all in black with an evil glint in his eye. She fixed up a light over it, which she kept on all the time, and always a little bunch of flowers in a glass jar on a footstool in front of it – wild daffs in March, wallflowers, daisies, according to season, always fresh. Even when the snow lay on the ground, out she'd go, scouring the Downs for celandines, early violets, snowdrops, headscarf and wellington boots, always a little dog yapping behind her.

That bitter winter of '46, me and Nora couldn't stand it, to think of her rooting about among the snowdrifts, so we took her a big bunch of hothouse carnations. Cost more than a supper at the Savoy Grill. Bloody Saskia was there, fresh and frisky. Imogen, too. Doing their stint at the Royal Academy of Dramatic Art, were Saskia and Imogen, and Saskia'd brought her best friend with her, some prinking minx in black velvet slax and ballet slippers. Saskia laughed like anything when she saw those carnations.

'How apt!' she said. '"... which some call nature's bastards." *Winter's Tale*, Act IV, Scene iii.'

Little did she know it was a case of the pot calling the kettle black. Her mother was mortified and tried to cover up.

'My little Saskia's playing Perdita this term. Isn't it lovely?'

But if that was the kind of thing they taught her girls at Ra-di-bloody-da, then Nora and I didn't want to know. Such cheap gibes! We rose above.

The girls might be away at RADA but there was Old Nanny to keep her company and a woman in from the village to do the heavy work and I was always tickled when concerned weekend guests asked her: 'How do you survive out here all on your own, Attie?' You could hardly move for help, you even tripped over a little old man crouched above the herbaceous border on your way to the outside lavvy. But the Lady A. would give a little smile and say, she'd got used to solitude, and make some reference to the garden. She was always out there in a big hat telling the gardener what to do. There were articles in magazines. She was famous for her clematis. In the evenings she'd sit stitching away at her embroidery hoop with Melchior glowering on the wall and listen to records on her gramophone the same way she does now, in the front basement of 49 Bard Road. Then Old Nanny used to come to tuck her up in bed at ten, with Horlicks.

Her girls would go and visit their father, sometimes, and come back with new wristwatches and gold crucifixes once owned by Sarah Bernhardt and The Duse and copies of the *Complete Works* signed by Ellen Terry but never so much as a Christmas card arrived for her from Melchior, as though it had been *her* fault they split up.

As the Lady A. grew older, so she looked more and more British. Her features became more transparent, her expression ever more modestly valiant. She started to wear cardigans. She'd begun to look sad even before the war broke out; sadness became her, like pastel shades. She developed a reputation for sadness in spite of, or perhaps because of, her indomitable smile, real Mrs Miniver smile.

That farmhouse was lovely. Mellow brick, lichened tile, nestling in a Down, the vista rimmed with English Channel. There was a little walled orchard with lambs in it. I always think of that orchard in early spring, primroses among the roots of the apple trees, first buds, blue smoke rising from the chimney and Nor' and me getting out of the village taxi, red morocco heels, mud.

I've never been so cold in all my life as in that farmhouse. Cold and scared. Not even in air-raid shelters. At night, we'd huddle up in our cold bed with our silver-fox trenches spread out on top of the quilts for extra warmth, bruising our toes on the stone hot-water bottles Old Nanny had tucked in for our comfort, watching the moonlight through the lattice, listening to night-birds hoot and shrieks of mice and voles when owls pounced. Things were killing one another all around. We were stiff with cold and frozen with terror. Give me Railton Road at half past Saturday midnight, any time.

To tell the truth, picturesque and evocative as that farmhouse was, we only went down there because we were fond of her.

She'd put us up in the one bed, in always the same white-washed room, Old Nanny used it as a sewing room – iron bed-stead, pitch-pine washstand and a dressmaker's dummy which cast a headless shadow that gave me the willies. I'll draw a veil over the bathroom, with the iron tub that formed an informal vivarium for every spider in Sussex. We never ventured into the darling buds' room but the Lady A.'s was a shrine to Guess Who, all the photographs of him, plus one, just one, of Perry, snapped drawing Saskia out of a top hat. There was a steep staircase of narrow steps of polished oak – the Lady A. wouldn't have carpet-ing, she said she loved the living wood – down which Nora and I would pick and slither, fully aware that Saskia and Imogen, if they were home, were laughing at our shoes.

A big Chinese bowl full of pot-pourri on a worm-eaten oak chest in the hall gave out a sad, pungent smell of old ladies and heartbreak. There were watercolours everywhere perpetrated by Lyndes of long ago in Venice, the Alps, the lakes; faded chintz; old rugs worn to a web. Everywhere a threadbare, expensive shabbiness that had a class to which we knew we never could aspire. Not the Lucky Chances. We were doomed to either flash or squalor.

The food was nothing much. We lived in hopes she'd get the East Sussex black market organised but Old Nanny always asked us to be sure to bring our coupons and served up cottage pie, shepherd's pie, nothing ever looked like whatever it was made of although the plates were Chelsea and the knives and forks were silver, knobbed, blackened, engraved with the Lynde seal, a peli-can pecking at its breast. Rotten food. All the same, we were still nervous as to which ancestral fork to use.

And always bloody freezing, not just in bed. We'd sit at table in our fur coats in spite of the satirical gaze of Saskia and Imogen in their ballerina-length dirndls, turtlenecks and inherited upper-class capacity to withstand extremes of temperature. No love lost, and they could scarcely abide to see we'd got our feet under the table, at last, not now that they'd been abandoned, too. So when the Lady A. said, could we possibly come down for Saskia and Imogen's twenty-first, Nora said satirically: 'Go on!'

'No, truly, my dears,' said the Lady A. 'I want you both to be there.' Then she twinkled, just a little, but it was a rare sight these days and I was glad to see it. 'It'll be a real family affair!'

A nod is as good as a wink. We'd not seen hair nor hide of Perry since VJ Day, except a postcard from Rio de Janeiro showing a macaw, but I knew the Lady A. still kept a soft spot for him after all these years and I'd even hoped that she and Perry might make a go of it, one fine day. I taxed her with it, once, when we were having Lapsang in the orchard. It was May and the apple blossom was out but, all the same, I kept my coat on.

'Don't you ever miss Perry?' I asked her tactfully.

She had the grace to twinkle right up at the very thought of him but she twinkled dismissively.

'One doesn't *marry* a man like that, my dear,' she said. Faded blue eyes, broken veins, a straw hat tied under her chin with a silk paisley scarf. The dowager sheep. But she knew a thing or two about Perry. Here today and gone tomorrow, not so much a man, more of a travelling carnival. I warmed my fingers on her china cup, since I had no option – it didn't have a handle, although it *did* have a big crack down the side – and wondered if my own mother had thought the same thing about Melchior, that he was splendid over the short haul but would never go the distance.

My feeling was, neither of the brothers were built to be good husbands. But I didn't say a word. A lot was left unsaid at the Lady A.'s. I've never known such profound silences as those Lynde silences especially when her daughters were there, silences in which the unspoken hung like fog that got into your lungs and choked you.

'God knows why we keep on going down there, anyway,' said Nora. 'We could stay up here on a Sunday, have a bath, do our hair.'

She hadn't the slightest desire to grace the darling buds' twenty-first, not she. Perry can come to us, she said. She was adamant. 'No! No! And no!' Then our Uncle Perry called us up and said he'd drive us down, we could be back to Brixton that same night.

'But not birthday presents,' said Nora. 'Not for those vipers. I draw the line at birthday presents.'

Because we were going down exclusively for the Lady A.'s sake, weren't we? We took *her* a bottle of Scotch. So there was Peregrine, blowing the horn outside in Bard Road in a bloody great Bentley convertible ready to take us to Lynde Court Home Farm for the worst Sunday lunch of our lives.

'Sorry I'm late,' he said. 'I slipped in a quick visit to a friend in Gunter Grove.' Big wink, the reprobate. But it was only twenty minutes.

Perry was bigger than ever and brown as a berry from the Brazilian sun and you'd never have believed, from the cut of his jib, that he'd turned sixty, nor that his twin brother was just at the time rehearsing *Lear*. Not one grey hair in all that russet mop, nor yet a crow's-foot among the freckles, and as full of bounce and bonhomie as when he first knocked on the front door. Of course, his fortunes had turned, again, since he struck oil.

Yes. Oil. That bit of semi-arid scrub he'd bought out of sentiment with his money from *The Dream*, his ranch in Hazard, Texas. Oil. He was filthy rich again and the back of the Bentley was stacked with cans and packages and bottles, most with labels from Rio, Paris and New York, I was glad to see, because, back here in Brixton, it was still half a rasher of bacon a week, a little pat of butter, that was your lot, that was rationing.

He sat and beeped the horn and there was a general rustle of net curtains all along Bard Road as the old biddies sneaked a peek at our escort.

He gave us the biggest hugs and kisses but he wasn't his usual self, I could tell. It was my turn to sit in front and he was all of a twitter, nervous, joyful, on edge, abstracted, all at once. He jumped red lights; the speedometer touched ninety, once, and when he braked to miss a fox, Nora, in the back with a box of Belgian chox, shot forward, got her nose stuck in a violet cream. Sometimes he broke into snatches of song; sometimes he did not hear a question and needed his arm tugged. After a few miles, Nora and I maintained a sympathetic silence. 'Hope for the best, expect the worst.' I knew in my water there'd be tears before bedtime so I crossed my fingers and so did Nora because we didn't want the old devil's feelings hurt, nor those of the Lady A., either, this day of all days, but I couldn't see how else the day might end.

Of course, we'd always known deep down inside he was their father. We tried to pretend otherwise. I was jealous as hell of it, but there you are. Biology is biology. You can't fool a sperm. I'm not sure that Melchior ever knew. If 'his' daughters were red-heads, then so had his own mother been and, besides, who'd have thought it of the Lady A., Caesar's wife in person? Perhaps those girls themselves smelled a rat and were unhappy; you might put all the bad behaviour down to that, if you felt so inclined, though you wouldn't have felt half so magnanimous if you'd met them.

Streatham, Norbury, Thornton Heath, Croydon. Nora had eaten all her chocolates by Redhill and said she was lonely in the back so she climbed over the seat and inserted herself between us. He'd brought the sunshine with him, we put the hood down and sang: 'Please direct your feet To the sunny sunny sunny side of the street.' He perked up. We were still girls, only just past thirty; we cut a dash, the three of us. Little did we know it was to be our last ride together.

He started to open up a bit by the time we got to Three Bridges and told us about Brazil. That was his new enthusiasm, the jungle and its denizens. He was going to give a lecture at the Royal Society, wasn't he, about the butterflies he'd discovered in the jungle and after he'd given this lecture he was going to go right back and look for more.

'I'm going,' he announced grandly, 'to devote the rest of my life to lepidoptera.'

We raised our brows at one another. Another fad. Like conjuring. Like movies. Like oil. Like espionage. How soon would he reach his boredom threshold in the jungle? We didn't know, we never could have guessed, that he would reach oblivion first.

Saskia, it turned out, was doing the honours in the kitchen. She'd just, that winter, made her first appearance on any stage in one of her father's productions, a witch in *Macbeth*, typecasting, along with her velvet-slacked best friend, but she'd shown more interest in the contents of her cauldron than her name in lights and so it came to pass that her best friend, the RADA Gold Medal winner, was picked out to play as Melchior's Cordelia, while Saskia tinkered with the pans.

She's ended up as television's top cook, of course. Every time I switch on the set there she is, eviscerating something, skinning something else, having a go at some harmless piece of meat with her little chopper.

Old Nanny had been banished from the kitchen and Saskia was catering her own lunch party, trying out a roast duck and green peas, and the Lady A., not of the class or generation that cooked, itself, was nevertheless doing her fumbling, incompetent best to help, because it was the girls' birthday, and Old Nanny was sitting in the orchard in a deck-chair with her feet up and a copy of *Tatler* and *that* was Old Nanny's treat, before she stirred her stumps to serve up. Even Imogen had roused herself and was out in the garden laying the table because they'd decided to eat outside since it was such a lovely day and Imogen was weighing the napkins down with pebbles so they wouldn't blow away. There was a bunch of pinks in a glass jar in the middle of the starched white cloth under an arbour of old-fashioned roses and the lilacs were out, the Lady Attie's famous white lilacs, that featured in *Country Life*, once.

As we drew up, I saw a Roller, parked already, and was overcome with that indigestible mix of emotions I always felt each time that he came near me – joy, terror, heartsick, lovesick. The white lilacs didn't help. That perfume. I felt as if someone had taken hold of my heart and squeezed it.

There was a grey wing over each ear; our father had aged more evidently than his brother, but very graciously. We were all a little frigid with one another, at first, although the Lady A. was twinkling away valiantly, but Perry popped a cork and we drank a toast: 'To the girls!' before we sat down and I joined in, much as I disliked them, and so did Nora, because, however randomly we'd been assembled, we were all family, and they were the only family we had. After the second bottle, things began to thaw, a bit.

Soup. Old Nanny was now pressed back into service and bore

a steaming tureen out of the kitchen, more proud of Saskia's handiwork than she'd ever been of her own, so we had some of that, to start with, a nettle soup Saskia had discovered in an old book, or so she said. An old, Elizabethan soup. Perhaps Shakespeare had eaten just such a soup! When she said that, she gave her 'father' a special smile, she and Imogen worshipped the ground, etc. etc. etc. Shakespeare may well have eaten that filthy soup but I doubt he'd kept it down. I forced in a spoon or two out of politeness and it was very, very bitter, but the men, foolish fond, drank it all and Perry asked for seconds.

Then the duck came in, swimming in blood. I gagged, had a spot more champagne, to fortify myself, picked out, for my share, the merest sliver of blackened skin – that duck was certainly well-cooked on the outside – but the peas, when I helped myself, bounced off the server and Saskia gave me a dirty look, as if she'd known I'd show my true colours at some point during her elegant repast so, to spite her, I scooped the peas up and ate them with my pudding spoon. But the men finished off that duck between them, engaging in a battle as to who could eat most and praise her best although I was racked with hunger and heartburn until it occurred to me: 'Has she done it on purpose?' A poison meat! Her face gave nothing away, calm and oval as a cake of soap.

She'd done her hair up in a huge, soft chignon. If only we'd inherited that red, red hair. We were still brunettes, at that time, but permed by then, of course. Poodle-cuts. She'd got on a twin-set of heather-coloured wool and pearls but Imogen, always the fey one, had 'dressed up to match the Downs around us', she simpered, in an eighteenth-century shepherdess's dress, complete with crook with a blue bow on it. Happily, I saw no sign about her person of her pet white rat, although it said in the William Hickey column she never went anywhere without it.

'Delicious, darling,' said the Lady A. 'Clever Saskia!' But she ate like a bird, herself.

It was a peculiar meal. The ugly food, the flies, and little stinging creatures and ants crawling up your leg – all the discomfort of eating in the garden – and the precarious peace among the Hazard clan all gave the occasion a special flavour, sweet and sour, like Chinese pork. After we'd toyed with a disgusting sylla-bub, came a cake, ordered from Harrods, thank God, with twenty-one candles. They blew, we clapped. Perry brushed his eyes with his hands and I saw that he was on the verge of tears.

I never thought what it might be to be a father until that mo-ment, when I saw Perry almost cry. Yet, truly, I think he loved Nora and myself as much as he loved Saskia and Imogen, if not more. But not, you understand, in the *same way*. We were not flesh of his flesh.

But then, again, a person *isn't* flesh of its father's flesh, is it? One little sperm out of millions swims up the cervix and it is so very, very easy to forget how it has happened. And Melchior, whose flesh we were, or, rather, whose emission sparked off our being, felt for us only occasional pity and now and then a vague affection that seemed to puzzle him as to the cause. But he was head over heels in love with Saskia and Imogen, too, and when they blew out their birthday candles, I saw his eyes were moist, as well.

I wished we'd come by train and got a taxi from the station, as per usual. Then we could have buzzed off, pronto. As it was, we'd have to stay until Perry was good and ready to depart, which might be hours.

Then the Lady A. rapped her glass with her knife and said that Peregrine wanted to give a little speech. He got up on his feet, his face an April study of joy and sadness, as Irish might have put it, and he said:

'My lovely girls, all four of you' – his eyes crinkled round the edges as he raised his glass in our direction, but Saskia looked daggers – 'I can't tell you how much it means to this old sinner to be among you all on the day you two precious copperknobs finally reach your majorities, key of the door, licence to marry . . . but don't rush off and marry too quickly, dearest ones, and leave us all lonely.'

They smirked.

'It was tough, I can tell you, to think of a present fine enough for you two on this day of days. I cast around in my mind for a long time, I furrowed this old brow. Not baubles, or bangles, or beads, but something that would last, something as beautiful as

174

you both that would go on for ever. So . . . here you are, with all my love.'

His eyes were swimming, now, as he took from each jacket pocket a wrapped box just diamond bracelet size. They smirked in pleasurable anticipation.

'Look what's inside, my darlings!'

He watched expectantly as they tore off the wrappings. The boxes were of metal, it turned out, with little holes drilled in the top. Curiouser and curiouser. Imogen got hers open first, peered in, then gave a little scream and dropped it. Saskia looked at hers and said: 'Good God!'

Inside each box was a little nest of leaves and, inside the nest, a caterpillar.

'Named after you,' said Peregrine. 'Saskia Hazard. Imogen Hazard. Two of the most beautiful butterflies in all the rain-forest. You'll go down in all the textbooks. As long as people love butterflies, your names will be on their lips, you'll have a kind of beautiful eternity. They are rare species, just like you both.'

Saskia and Imogen stared blankly at their boxes. No doubt they'd hoped for a little oil well each.

'Is that all?' said Imogen. She poked the caterpillar with her fork. It did not stir. 'I think mine's dead,' she said.

Saskia snapped her box shut and dropped it on the table.

'Thanks a lot,' she said, with heavy irony.

Peregrine's face crumpled. All at once he looked his age. More. He looked a hundred. He looked a hundred and ten. And he deflated. Instantly, within his suit, as if somebody had stuck a pin in him and let the energy out. Perhaps Melchior was fond of him, after all, in his way; anyway, he hurried up to smooth things over. He got up, too, and raised his glass.

'To your birthdays, my darling buds of May!' We all knocked back another glass and then he said: 'I, too, have prepared a very special present for my best beloved daughters . . . a new –'

Such timing. All eyes were upon him.

'– stepmother!'

Then, oh! was I glad I'd come, all right! What a picture! Their jaws flew open, their eyes popped out. Imogen let out a wail. Saskia rose up and seized the cake knife. Her chignon unravelled. Red snakes of hair flew out around her head while hairpins rattled down like hail.

'What's this?'

Melchior stood his ground.

'I'm going to marry my Cordelia,' he said, tenderly. His tongue caressed the 'I' and rolled it round.

'Your Cordelia,' repeated Saskia flatly. Her rage departed her, replaced by amazement. She let the cake knife drop. 'Your Cordelia!'

'Your Cordelia!' echoed Imogen, a beat behind. 'But your Cordelia is – '

'– is my best friend!' wailed Saskia.

And so she was. The RADA Gold Medallist, plucked from obscurity to play against Melchior's Lear and now to marry him, in spite of the horrid shadow that a superstitious person might have seen cast over them by the union of Ranulph Hazard and Estella Ranelagh, which also kicked off with such a May/December union and ended in tears both before, after and during bedtime. At least Melchior hadn't tucked Cordelia into the boot and brought her along to show her off at this psychologically inappropriate moment but he must have realised what a bombshell his news would be. Even the Lady A. looked green around the gills but Perry lightened up wonderfully and clapped his brother on the shoulder.

'No fool like an old fool!' he bellowed.

'Why,' gritted Saskia between her teeth, 'that scheming little bitch, I'll – '

'Oh, Saskia, Saskia,' said the Lady A. 'Don't stand in the way of your father's last chance of happiness – '

Saskia picked up the birthday cake on its plate and pitched it against an apple tree. It shattered. Crumbs and candles scattered everywhere. Then she started to break the pots, throwing the dessert plates on the ground and stamping on them. Imogen, giggling in a febrile manner, laid about her smashing glasses with her ribboned crook, sparing nothing. When he saw his caterpillars reduced to pulp, Perry gave a piteous whimper. The Lady A., apprehending carnage among her heritage tableware, started to wring her hands and ululate while Saskia's wails approached hysteria, whereupon Melchior smartly smacked her cheek, the way they do in the movies.

'Stop that, young lady!'

She shut up at once, put her hand to her cheek, stared at him incredulously with her blue Lynde eyes. Then, tears. He took her in his arms, murmuring, 'Hush, hush, darling.' She shook him off and flounced into the house, slamming the door behind her, followed a minute or two later by Imogen, except that Imogen had to open the door her sister had just slammed before she could slam it herself. The rest of us were left staring at one another across the broken crockery and I never felt more spare in all my life and neither did Nora. We got up in unison.

'I'm going to call a bloody taxi,' I said. 'I've had enough of this.'

'Don't go before you've had coffee,' said the Lady A. heroically but Perry was pushing back his wicker chair so peremptorily it fell over, briefly trapping beneath it a small, yapping dog, probably a Yorkshire terrier.

'I'm off, too,' he announced. 'Back to the jungle. Now. This minute. I'll look forward to the company of crocodiles, after the bosom of my family.'

We found the bottle of Scotch we'd planned to give the Lady A. rolling around forgotten in the back of the car so we drew up on a verge and passed it round. Perry looked like the picture of Dorian Gray, I'm sorry to say, a ghastly sight. The sky closed in, the sun disappeared and all was cold and grey as we went home.

'And yet I love them,' he said. 'God, I love them. That's my punishment, isn't it? My crime is my punishment.'

He wouldn't come in with us. He sat in the car and watched us climb the steps with a face a mile long. We turned and blew him kisses and waved goodbye but he didn't budge. Finally we were so chilled we went inside and closed the door. I had a premonition: 'We won't see him again.' His hair was still bright, foxy red. It was twilight, the lamps just coming on. There he sat, in that grand car that was about to bear him off on his last journey.

We peered out between the curtains and watched him draw away, at last, into the dusk. He went back to his rooms in the Albany and packed a bag. He cancelled his lecture at the Royal Society; he left for Southampton that very night, he was good as his word. After the Lady A.'s accident, we tried the police. We even tried Interpol. They couldn't find him, he was travelling incognito, he'd erased himself.

That was that.

If he babbled of green fields in Cuzco or Iquitos, we never heard.

Our footsteps echoed in the hall of 49 Bard Road with an inconsolable sound. 'Empty,' the echoes said. 'Empty.'

'They should have made a go of it,' Nora said. 'In spite of everything.'

'She told me once, "One doesn't marry a man like that!"'

'I didn't mean him and the Lady A. I meant him and Grandma.'

Nora had the forethought to bring the Scotch in with her and though never my favourite tipple, any port in a storm. We put on the electric fire in the front room and had a couple and got the gramophone going and after we'd rolled the rug back we dug out all the golden oldies, the old favourites, Jessie, Binnie, 'I'll See You Again', even though we never thought we never would see him again, and the scratched and faded ones, songs about the harbour lights and parting, dolefully prophetic, did we but know it, and the 'baby songs' such as 'Is You Is or Is You Ain't,' and finally we found at the bottom of the stack the very first one of all, the one he brought us all those years ago when we first found out what joy it was to sing and dance, 'I Can't Give You Anything but Love.'

We were singing and dancing and loud music playing and both of us a touch tiddly when the phone rang and it was the Lady A.'s Old Nanny and so it came to pass, in the fullness of time, that the Lady A. moved into the front basement minus the use of her legs, because what Nanny had to tell us was, the Lady A. had taken a tumble down those very shiny and uncarpeted stairs we'd warned her about so often, come cracking on her bum to land

178

on the stone flags in the hall and so jarred, snagged or dislocated her spine that she'd never walk again, but we didn't know that, then, only that the Lady A. had gone arse over tip and Old Nanny didn't know which way to turn.

'Have you called the ambulance?'

She'd had the presence of mind to do that, at least.

'What about Saskia and Imogen?'

She burst into such a harangue I couldn't make out one word and had to hold the receiver some distance from my ear, the noise was causing me such distress. But when I finally got the gist, I scarcely could believe it, because it turned out they'd buggered off.

It seemed that Melchior had left them shortly after we did, under a cloud, and the Lady A. had taken to her bed, emotionally prostrate. Old Nanny, doing the washing-up, crouched over a sinkful of dishes, heard raised voices in the room above and then a godalmighty crash, bang, wallop! and she went flying out of the kitchen with the drying-up cloth in her hand to find the Lady A. moaning in her Viyella nightie all of a heap at the stairfoot.

Then the girls came flying down the stairs, both of them clutching kit-bags, carriers, pillowslips, bulging with this and that, and pushed Old Nanny brusquely aside, off into the night they went. They hiked down to the village in their little flatties and knocked up the baker who, out of a brute feudal loyalty to the Lynde clan and their kin, drove them to the station in the bread van, unaware of the terrible accident that had just occurred back at Lynde Court Home Farm.

Did she fall or was she pushed? That was the question. But not a word, not a whisper upon the subject ever wormed its way through the Lady A.'s stiff upper lip. If ever we raised it, even if everso tactfully, she would look teddibly, teddibly British and, quietly but firmly, change the subject. But I *do* know those dreadful girls had just made her sign the Home Farm over to them both, plus all that remained of her last bit of capital, before she took her tumble. We couldn't help but be aware of that because now she hadn't got a penny to bless herself, and nowhere to go, either.

Peregrine was gone. I called my father but it turned out he was overnighting at his fiancée's basement flat in Gunter Grove, so no joy there, either. The Lady A. lay flat on her back in Lewes General Hospital with one tear trickling out of the corner of her left eye, enough to break your heart.

And that was how we came to inherit the Lady A., though she's no trouble, really, even if she used to thump on the ceiling with the head of her silver-knobbed cane: 'Stop that racket immediately!' during the one, two, three, hop! days of the Brixton Academy of Dance.

She used to babysit our little Tiff, too, when she was a toddler. She used to sing her a lullaby, about horses, all the pretty little horses. 'Sing,' I say; more of a tuneless hum, but Tiff went to sleep, anyway. She taught her how to cross-stitch, though I can't say it's a talent Tiff's ever used.

And the unrighteous prospered.

I always thought Saskia's fame was to do, mostly, with the back of her neck. She had a lovely nape, on which that knot of scarlet hair sat like a Rhode Island red on a clutch and her nape was on display in all she did, intimate, exposed and sexy as she bent over the stove to poke around with a spoon suggestively in a pot or stick a prong into a drumstick with quite sadistic glee. I never saw anything so rude as her TV shows, not even Gorgeous George at the Royal Variety Performance.

We watched her jug a hare, once, on television, years ago, when she was just getting into her stride. She cut the thing up with slow, voluptuous strokes. 'Make sure your blade is up to it!' she husked, running her finger up and down the edge, although the spectacle of Saskia with a cleaver couldn't help but remind me and Nora of how she'd run amock with the cake knife on her twenty-first. Next, she lovingly prepared a bath for the hare, she minced up shallots, garlic, onions, added a bouquet garni and a pint of claret and sat the poor dismembered beast in that for a day and a half. Then she condescended to sauté the parts briskly in a hot pan over a high flame until they singed. Then it all went into the oven for the best part of another day. She sealed the lid of the pot with a flour-and-water paste. 'Don't be a naughty thing and peek!' she warned with a teasing wink.

Time to decant at last! The hare had been half-rotted, then cremated, then consumed. If there is a god and she is of the rabbit family, then Saskia will be in deep doodoo on Judgment Day. 'Delicious,' she moaned, dipping her finger in the juice and sucking. She licked her lips, letting her pink tongue-tip linger. 'Mmmm . . .'

As we watched this genuinely disgusting transmission, the ghost of Grandma manifested itself in a sharp blast of cabbage. When we saw what Saskia did to that hare, we knew that we did wrong by eating meat.

Why do we go on doing it, then? I'll tell you straight. We're scared that, if we eat too much salad, one fine day, we'll find we've turned into Grandma.

Saskia jugged a hare for Tristram, once, that cooked his goose. She was living in a bijou houselet in Chelsea, in those days, penning the occasional article for *Harper's Bazaar*. ('Eel . . . oh, curvaceous, curvilinear, cursive denizen of the deep!' and etc. etc. etc.) She must have thought long and hard as to how to revenge herself upon the third Lady Hazard for taking away her father and finally she wrote to little Tristram, then only a lad, at Bedales, hinting at Hazard mysteries to which only she, Saskia, held the key. God knows what she wrote or promised, who can tell; or whether he came ringing her doorbell on his half-term holiday out of prurience or duty, but she had his bondage trousers off before you could say *crème renversée*, although she was old enough to be his mother.

In fact, exactly the same age as his mother and now she felt she'd evened scores and she and My Lady Margarine made friends, again, and once even did a ketchup commercial together but Saskia never forgave a grudge and, when we ran into one another, which we did now and again, at the stocking counter in Peter Jones' store, once, another time waiting for a taxi in Sloane Square, I could tell from the look in her Lynde-blue eye that when she saw me she still thought of only one thing: 'Cascara evacuant'.

She was revenged upon her father's wife, and on her father, too. The twins never forgave him for cutting off their allowances. Old Nanny told us how he'd given the girls this glad news after we left, that afternoon of their twenty-first. Cool as you please, he'd told them he couldn't afford to support two families and now the girls were old enough to earn their keep, he'd see they got nice jobs. As they sat gaping, he assured them they weren't losing a friend but gaining a mother and then it came on to rain so he hopped in his Roller and was off while they were still stunned with shock, before they had a chance to berate him. And that was the root cause, according to Old Nanny, of the dreadful quarrel over funds that transformed the whilom Lady A. into our Wheelchair and left her homeless, penniless, reliant on the left-hand line.

Old Nanny told us everything, of course. She went on telling us everything even after she moved in with Melchior to raise little Tristram and little Gareth. What else could she do, poor old cow, she was stuck. The Lady A. hadn't the cash to keep her, now, and what would *we* have done with an Old Nanny clicking her tongue against her teeth when she saw the gin bottles in the wastepaper basket and the condoms in the toilet?

Though, alas, the little rubber swimmers sadly declined in numbers during the sixties and dropped off altogether in the subsequent decade, which was nothing to do with the Pill, everything to do with lack of opportunity.

Old Nanny often picked up the 137 bus in Camden Town and popped over the river and when she told us the news about Saskia and Tristram, the Lady A. dropped her embroidery frame with a shocked squeak. He was a babe, just seventeen, in those days, while Saskia had pushed forty aside some time before and was now steering towards her climacteric. Yet it wasn't the May and December aspect of their union that affected us so much, we were quite French about that; it was, that we all knew Saskia. Old Nanny had reservations of her own, however.

'Prohibited degrees,' said Old Nanny. She was drinking a cup of tea. I noticed how she always drank her tea from the wrong side of the cup, in our house. Admittedly, Nora was a careless washer-up, especially after sundown, but Old Nanny never went to the lavatory in our house, either, not even when you could tell she was busting for a wee. I wondered, are we letting standards slip?

'Prohibited degrees.'

'Cheer up, Nana. Remember, Melchior's not her –'

But Wheelchair put her finger to her lips because Old Nanny wasn't supposed to know. (Although she *did* know, of course; she it was who personally confirmed our worst suspicions, years ago. But Wheelchair never knew she knew and thought she ought to keep it from the servants.)

'But, then,' said Nora, 'perhaps Perry –'

Why hadn't we thought of it before? The wicked old man! 'Just been visiting a friend in Gunter Grove', indeed! But how had he met My Lady Margarine and why had they done it? Was Peregrine bent on perpetrating the Hazard tradition of disputed paternity even unto the bitter end? But none of us had any means of checking out the theory, since Peregrine was gone, and only Old Nanny on speaking terms with the third Lady H., and she wasn't intimate, so we could only speculate, thus: that Tristram was red as fire, in the mould of Peregrine and of poor, passionate, murdered Estella, while gaunt and hollow-eyed Gareth had raven hair and Bovril eyes – the boys, in fact, the duplicates of Peregrine and Melchior themselves, in person, at least, though not in personality. So who had been the master of ceremonies was anybody's guess.

Not that we'd ever met Gareth. He was a mystery. He converted when he was seventeen, found God the same time Tristram discovered sex, and departed to a seminary shortly after. Never a word from that department, not a letter nor a Christmas card, for the actor and the priest might have a good deal in common but the Jesuit and the chorus girl, outside lewd jest, not.

Perhaps that Saskia put something in young Tristram's food, some love potion she'd got out of the same old book in which she found that emetic Shakespearian nettle soup we'd had on her birthday. Back he went to her, back and back and back. It remained a deadly secret outside the family, of course. He boasted a wide variety of official girlfriends, of whom our little Tiffany had the highest profile, headlines in the *News of the World*, and, do you know, I think he really loved her.

Love. What is love? What do I mean by love? For a while he

wanted her nearby. But it turned out she was not sufficient to break him of the Saskia habit, even if Saskia was sixty if she was a day. His sexuagenarian mistress. Saskia, the sexy sexuagenarian.

'Come off it, Dor', *you* wouldn't have said no to a chap when you were sixty, if you'd had any offers,' reproved Nora. She thought I was jealous.

Perhaps I am.

Saskia.

But Wheelchair grieved about it, too, and all the more because her daughters had now maintained their radical indifference to her for well-nigh forty years and she thought she'd snuff it without another sight of them, so we knew we'd have to take her with us when the invitation to our father's birthday party came at last, even if she wasn't on the official list, and this is just what we are about to do, as soon as we've got ourselves suitably tarted up.

'What shall we wear tonight?' said Nora.

No problem for Wheelchair. She'd got a lovely Norman Hartnell gown left over from the forties we could still fork her into, she ate like a sparrow, she never put on a milligram. White satin bodice, tulle skirt, which we would fluff up so as to conceal her carriage. Pearls. Her daughters robbed her blind, stuffing pillowslips with bibelots, but they'd refrained from snatching the pearls off her neck. We gave her a bath with her favourite Floris's Tuberoses poured in. What a business that bath was! Nora took one arm, I took the other, we lowered her. Nora scrubbed her back with a flannel. Then we wrapped her up in a big, soft towel and Nora did her hair.

'You're very good to me,' said Wheelchiar with a suspicious quiver.

'Pipe down, you old bag,' said Nora. You've got to be firm with her, or else she cries. We dusted her with talc, tucked her in a rug and left her in the kitchen with the fire on and a fresh pot of tea, watching *Brief Encounter* on afternoon television. We had to wait for the water to heat up again until we could have our own baths. I picked up a scent bottle and inhaled nostalgia.

'Tell you what,' I said to Nora. 'You put on some Shalimar, tonight; I'll use Mitsouko.'

'Quite like old times,' she said with a glint.

'Don't let's exaggerate.'

Because here was a couple of scraggy hags about to ease into frocks that first saw light about the year our Tiff was born, for we had bought no evening wear since then, having no need for it in middle age; and it was our little Tiff who'd brought us our lovely scent, for old times' sake, bless her little heart, got it for us from the duty-free when Tristram took her to Tuscany for a week.

That was an ill-fated trip. Although he *must* have loved her, for a little while, at least, because she was the first girl he was ever brave enough to take to visit Saskia.

Saskia's villa was perched on a hill between Florence and Siena, among the fields of Chianti, pine trees up the drive, you know the kind of thing. You may even have seen it featuring in her bloody programme. She wrote it off against her taxes because she'd done a series there, *In Bocca Toscana*. I caught it once, repeated in the afternoons, I was housebound with a stinking cold, there was Saskia, caressing a ham. 'Lucky the porkers of Parma!' she intoned. 'They dine every day on curds and whey, like so many little Miss Muffets, and posthumously achieve porcine apotheosis – prosciutto!'

I questioned Tiff closely when they got back and she rabbited on about ripe figs and fresh basil for a while before she admitted she'd been incapacited with the runs for the greater part of their stay, confined to bed in the spacious room with the tiled floor and view of vineyards, her only entertainment a stack of Saskia's videos, which she'd been forced to watch endlessly, not being of a reading temperament, but which had given her so much confidence, although she'd never even boiled an egg before, that she proposed fixing for us, then and there, a spaghetti *carbonara*, only we said, no way.

These gastric disorders sounded to me as though Saskia had slipped a little something extra into the *trippa fiorentina*, but, all the same, Saskia had been sufficiently polite to this unexpected wee scrap as to arouse my suspicions, because she was a snob and a half, ordinarily. But Tiffany suspected nothing and was over the moon. 'His family has started to accept me! See how his aunt has taken me to her bosom!'

Bosom of flint. Tiff didn't know, how could she, that a history existed already between Tristram and that woman and I must admit she was good-looking, still, had always been good-looking, with that pale skin and red hair, even if she always had to paint in her eyebrows and eyelashes. Half the drama went out of her appearance once she'd had a good wash. But little Tiff looked best of all with no make-up on, with her hair just hanging down her back and –

– and there I go, again, thinking of little Tiff when it behooves the Chance girls to put on their brightest smiles, check out their wardrobes for their smartest gowns, and celebrate their father's centenary.

I thought, there must be something upstairs we can wear because we've never thrown a stitch away but stowed the old schmutter in Grandma's room, the big first-floor front with the bay window, the best room in the house, although neither of us had the heart to take it over and move in after she went, so all her old stuff was still there, too.

It was perishing cold in Grandma's bedroom and gloaming, only the one forty-watt bulb, but I didn't want to open the curtains, as if the light might scare away the smell of mothballs, boiled cabbage and gin hanging in the air, by which we liked to think she made her posthumous presence felt. Her photos were still lined up on the mantelpiece. Peregrine in pride of place, in the middle, in his conjuring suit, with a dove perched on every plane surface, like a statue in a public square, and a smile you could warm your hands on, even though it was a photograph and he was dead. Lots of pix of us, stark naked in babyhood in the backyard with, if you looked carefully, a neighbour at once outraged and prurient peering through the fence. As baby sparrows in our very first panto, when we were half-pints. In black tights and blonde bobbed wigs from *What! You will!* Even a still of Peaseblossom and Mustardseed, all moonlit in the wood, and a lovely snap from the Forest of Arden, partying it around the pool with Peregrine. In sailors' hats, as forces' sweethearts. Always the two of us, together, forever young on Grandma's mantelpiece.

She never liked that portrait Cecil Beaton did for *Vogue*, she always kept it in the dressing-table drawer. He'd done us up as painted dolls, rouged spots on our cheeks and terrible aritificial grins, sitting on the floor in frills with our legs at angles, as if they were made of wood. Rich men's playthings. Very subtle. His Nanny used to hold the flash, you know.

Our Cyn was on the mantelpiece, on her wedding day; Our Cyn with one, two, three, in arms and various stages of toddlerhood; I was glad Grandma went before the Asian flu took Cynthia in '49, she never wanted to outlive any of us.

And there was her enormous bed she never shared, to my knowledge, all the time we knew her except, towards the end, with the occasional cat. Her bed, stripped, the naked pillows huddled like a corpse. We felt we ought to hush and tiptoe.

As we opened up the wardrobe, we saw ourselves swimming in the mirrored door as if in a pool of dust and, for a split second, in soft focus, we truly looked like girls, again. And going through those cast-offs was a trip down Memory Lane and a half, I can tell you. First, there was the lingerie – silk, satin, lace, eau de nil, blush rose, flesh, black and red ribbons, straight up and down things from the twenties, slithering things from the thirties, curvy things from the forties, waspies, merry widows, uplift bras. At the very bottom of the pile, I seized on something navy blue – the bloomers from our dancing class! From Miss Worthington's dancing class! To think that Grandma had kept our old bloomers!

Then there were the frocks. Some things we'd put away in plastic bags: bias-cut silk jersey, beaded sheaths that weighed a ton. Others we'd covered up with sheets, the big net skirts, the taffeta crinolines, halter necks, strapless, backless, etc. etc. etc., all heaped high on Grandma's bed.

'Half a century of evening wear,' said Nora. 'A history of the world in party frocks.'

'We ought to donate it to the V and A,' I said.

'Why should somebody pay good money to look at my old clothes?'

'They used to pay to see you without them.'

'They ought put *us* into a museum.'

'We ought to turn this house into a museum.'

'Museum of dust.'

Nora rummaged among the rags and gave a soft little chuckle. She held up a foamy white georgette number with crystal beads.

'The Super-Chief!' she said. 'Remember?'

'"She wore something sheer and white and deceptively virginal, that emitted a hard glitter when she moved, a subtle, ambiguous cobweb softness veined with a secret of ice. 'Got a light?' Half trusting, half insolent, a hoarse voice, older than that pale face with its purple heart of lipstick, flourishing its rasp of gutter like a flag, with pride."' I for Irish, Ross 'Irish' O'Flaherty. *Hollywood Elegies.* The very frock! He never knew I'd borrowed it from Daisy.

'Why don't you sell it to that library in Texas? I read in the paper they bought a crate of his empties.'

But I'd spotted an ambivalent memento of hers, to tease her with.

'Here, Nora . . . I never knew you kept this.'

'Gimme!'

She snatched it out of my hands, the veil they'd brought out of wardrobe on *The Dream* set for her to marry Tony in.

'The bastard,' she said. 'I hope he's six feet deep in concrete.'

She stuffed the veil out of sight under her air-raid warden's siren suit and something chiffon slithered to the floor.

'Dora? Remember this?'

She held it up. Floral print, big splashy roses, rhodies, peonies, muted tones, dusky pinks, soft mauves, lavender. I pressed it to my face, it was as soft as dust. First kiss, first love, eyes as blue as sugar paper and skin like cream.

'I pray you, love, remember.'

He never came back from the Burma Road. Some comic told me, backstage, *Nude Frolics* '52, in Sheffield.

'Here, Dora, nothing to cry about.'

'Do *you* remember his name?'

She asked me, whose name, with her eyebrows.

'You gave me a present the day we were seventeen, remember?

Today's our anniversary, fifty-eight years ago today. It was my first time, remember?'

She tried and tried but she could only remember her own first time and the goose and the miscarriage and then the corners of her mouth turned down.

'Sometimes,' she said, 'I feel a little lonely in the world. Don't you ever feel a little lonely, too, Dora? No father, no mother, no chick nor darling child. Don't you even want something to cuddle?'

No darling child. Which was the nub of it, as far as she was concerned, as well I knew, but no use crying over spilled milk, although that be not the appropriate metaphor in this instance. Too late to do anything about it, now.

'I must admit, sometimes, it gets everso lonely, especially when you're stuck up in your room tapping away at that bloody word processor lost in the past while I'm shut up in the basement with old age.'

'Don't talk like that about poor Wheelchair.'

'I don't mean Wheelchair and well you know it. I mean *our* old age, the fourth guest at the table.'

'Look on the bright side,' I counselled her. 'I've got you and you've got me and we've both got Wheelchair and you could call her our geriatric little girl, seeing as we bathe her, feed her, change her nappies, even. Our father might have reneged on the job but we *did* have a right old sugar daddy in our Uncle Perry and well you know it. We never knew our mother but Grandma filled the gap and you can say that again.'

The bulb flickered on, off, on again as if to signify Grandma's assent.

'All the same,' she said, 'I wish . . .'

She crumpled up that old chiffon and cradled it to her bosom.

'If little Tiff had come to us,' she said, rocking the chiffon baby in her arms, 'I'd –'

I knuckled out my swimming eyes. No more tears, today.

Then a funny thing happened. Something leapt off the shelf where the hats were. No, not leapt; 'propelled itself', is better because it came whizzing out like a flying saucer, slicing across the room as if about to knock our heads off, so we ducked. It knocked against the opposite wall, bounced down to the ground, fluttered and was still.

It was her hat, her little toque, with the spotted veil, that had spun out like a discus. And as we nervously inspected it, there came an avalanche of gloves – all her gloves, all slithery leather thumbs and fingers, whirling around as if inhabited by hands, pelting us, assualting us, smacking our faces, so that we clutched hands for protection and retreated like scared kids as more and more of Grandma's bits and pieces – oilcloth carriers, corsets, bloomers like sails, stockings hissing like snakes – cascaded out of the wardrobe on top of us. We backed off until our calves hit the side of the bed with a shock of cold metal and then the wardrobe door closed of its own accord upon its own emptiness with a ghastly creak, leaving us looking at our scared faces looking back out of the dust.

'Grandma's trying to tell us something,' said Nora in an awed voice.

Creak, creak went the door.

'She's telling us Memory Lane is a dead end,' I said. I could hear her voice clear as a bell: 'Come off it, girls! Pluck the day! You ain't dead, yet! You've got a party to go to! Expect the worst, hope for the best!'

We threw caution to the winds and raided the jam jar where we keep the seventy-plus emergency fund, that is, cash for wreaths for sudden funerals and taxis to hospices, etc. etc. etc. The shops were still open, we threw on our silver-fox trenches, we dashed off to the market. Down Electric Avenue, past the vegetable stalls. 'Here, gel, fancy a widow's comfort?' he says, thrusting forth an aubergine. 'Is that the best you can do?' I riposted.

All of a sudden, I was feeling chipper. Then I spotted them. 'Here, Nor', here come the Animal Rights.' We drew ourselves up to our full height; we've learned to be defensive about our trenches.

'It'd look better on a fox, auntie,' said the young man, knees poking through his trousers, shaven nape, why does he make us run the gauntlet every time?

'It wouldn't look better on *this* fox,' said Nora, on her high horse. 'Which was humanely trapped in the Arctic Circle by the age-old methods of an ecologically sound Inuit hunter circa 1935, young man, before either you or your blessed mother, even, was yet pissing on the floor, which trapper has probably succumbed to alcohol and despair due to having his traditional source of livelihood taken away from him and, anyway, these foxes would be long dead, by now, besides, and rotted, if we weren't wearing their lovingly preserved pelts.'

'I'm glad you're feeling guilty, girls,' said the young man.

He slipped us the usual tract. 'I like to sink my teeth into a nice juicy sausage, too!' Nora confided lasciviously. He covered up his privates *toot sweet.*

'I sometimes think Grandma was born before her time,' I said to Nora.

'At least he doesn't picket flower stalls,' she said.

You can buy anything you want in Brixton market. We got stockings with little silver stars all over, 'more stars than there are in Heaven', recollected Nora. I shoved over a twenty for the stockings and spotted Old Bill on the back. That gave me a start, to see how Shakespeare, to whom our family owed so much, had turned into actual currency, not just on any old bank note but on a high denomination one, to boot. Though not as high as Florence Nightingale, which gives me satisfaction as a woman.

Lovely, shiny stockings and a couple of little short tight skirts in shiny silver stuff to match, that clung on like surgical bandage, and showed off our legs. Legs, the last thing to go. We were modelling stockings as late as the late sixties, I'd have you know; Bear Brand. They had to cut us off mid-thigh, of course, so the wrinkles wouldn't show. For women of our age, our legs still aren't half bad. Nora toyed with a spaghetti-string boob tube in lynx-print Lycra; I thought, maybe something with feathers . . . Kids gathered round, tittering; the man at the red mullet stall shook his head, sadly. They thought the Chance sisters had gone over the top, at last. There was a sale of gold stilettos, so we treated ourselves to those. We came back with an armful of junk, earrings, beads, everything you can think of, cheap and cheerful, we haven't laughed so much in years, and the water was hot enough for us to share a bath, by then. After that, we slipped on our towelling robes, we creamed off our morning faces, we started off from scratch.

Foundation. Dark in the hollows of the cheeks and at the temples, blended into a lighter tone everywhere else. Rouge, except they call it 'blusher', nowadays. Two kinds of blusher, one to highlight the Hazard bones, another to give us rosy cheeks. Nora likes to put the faintest dab on the end of her nose, why I can't fathom, old habits die hard. Three kinds of eyeshadow – dark blue, light blue blended together on the eyelids with the little finger, then a frosting overall of silver. Then we put on our two coats of mascara. Today, for lipstick, Rubies in the Snow by Revlon.

It took an age but we did it; we painted the faces that we always used to have on to the faces we have now. From a distance of thirty feet with the light behind us, we looked, at first glance, just like the girl who danced with the Prince of Wales when nightingales sang in Berkeley Square on a foggy day in London Town. The deceptions of memory. That girl was smooth as an egg and the lipstick never ran down little cracks and fissures round her mouth because, in those days, there were none.

'It's every woman's tragedy,' said Nora, as we contemplated our painted masterpieces, 'that, after a certain age, she looks like a female impersonator.'

Mind you, we've known some lovely female impersonators, in our time.

'What's every man's tragedy, then?' I wanted to know.

'That *he* doesn't, Oscar,' she said. She still has the capacity to surprise me. Fancy her knowing about Oscar Wilde. I did her nails, she did mine. After some debate – should we match them to our lips? – we fixed on silver, to match them to our legs. She did my hair, I did hers. Silver, too, worse luck. We disappeared behind a cloud of scent and re-emerged, transformed, looking just like what, for all those years, the bloody Hazards always thought we were, painted harlots, and over the hill, at that.

'Oh, I say!' Wheelchair murmured, tapping her lips with a tissue to set the Lancome Bois de Rose. 'Don't you think you've gone a little far?'

In her white ballgown and pearls, she looked quite lovely, not so much Miss Haversham, more the Ghost of Christmas past.

'Got to keep up with the times, darling,' said Nora.

'Not me,' said Wheelchair. 'I live mostly in the past, these days. I find it's better.'

Her eyes swivelled reverently round to that portrait of Melchior she'd insisted on bringing with her when she came, although we'd had to cut it down to fit it in and she no longer kept flowers in front of it because we refused point-blank to fetch her any and she couldn't go out and get them herself.

So she was still eating her heart out for Melchior, after all these years, was she? Don't think she was a hypocrite, to have loved him all those abused, neglected decades, when she hadn't been averse to a fling in her youth herself and brought home a brace of bonny babes whose biological origins owed more to A. N. Other's DNA. If you think she was a hypocrite, then you know sod all about women. No. She loved old Melchior, all right, and, poor cow, she still loved her wicked daughters, too, for there they were, on her bedside table, beside the phials of pills and the half-bottle of Malvern water, in a rosewood frame, the darling buds of bloody May as ever was, looking as if butter wouldn't melt in their mouths.

Rain came and settled at the window. April showers. The twenty-third of April. Yes! The destination of Melchior had been prepared for him since birth; he was doomed to wear the pasteboard crown. Hadn't he first seen light of day on Shakespeare's birthday?

So had we two, of course. But all the little children in Bard Road were singing a hymn to Charlie Chaplin the day that we were born and Grandma took us to the window to look at the shirts and bloomers dancing on the washing-lines all over Lambeth. That made a difference, you know. We were doomed to sing and dance.

Then we did Wheelchair's nails, just a manicure and buff, she's never said but I know she thinks varnish is vulgar. We gave her a squirt of Arpège. The phone never rang. Each time I looked at it, it didn't ring. And Brenda never came round again, either.

Five

E crossed over the river to the other side. The river lies between Brixton and glamour like a sword. I wonder why they call it Old *Father* Thames.

In Regent's Park, the bushes crouched like bears and the stands of daffs and tulips wore a pale and ghostly look as they swayed in our birthday wind, which was getting fresh, again, moist after the rain, and warm-ish. In the street outside the Hazard home, what a bustle! A retinue of vans, blaring lights on stands, power cables to trip you up and a muster of personnel – bald men in specs and parkas conversing in huddles, girls in jeans hither and thithering with clipboards, plus fans, the idle and the curious, rubbernecking in quantity.

The Hazard residence was very handsome. Once or twice, we'd sauntered past it casually, just to have a little look . . . love locked out, ducky. Stuccoed, pillared and porticoed, with a bay thrust out front and a flight of stone steps to the door up which we'd often dreamed one day we might ascend and now would do so to the manner born, although we'd have to commission some staunch retainer to deal with Wheelchair.

But Wheelchair balked at the sight of the TV crews. There she was, in the back of the cab – we'd booked a hack, we'd never have got her into a minicab – she wept and wailed. What? Trans-mitted all over the country on the nine o'clock news carted about like laundry? What a public humiliation! Behold, the sad decline of the most beautiful woman of her time! She set up a lament but, luckily, Nora had slipped a big white chiffon square into her gold-mesh evening bag, in case the poor old thing's shoulders got chilly towards the end of the evening, so she dropped it over

Wheelchair's head. Instant hush. I hailed a passing minion, who was all done up in hose and doublet.

'Just carry this lady up the stairs, will you, and we'll follow with the appliance.'

'Pleasure,' he said, smiling and coaxing Wheelchair the way they do the very old, the same way they do kiddies. She was so light he hoisted her up easily in his arms in her white gown and her veil and she looked like a nun, or a ghost, or a very ancient bride until, out from under that veil, she gave him a flash of her Lynde-blue eyes and he blushed, he straightened his back, he bore her off with surprise and pride amidst a whirr of TV cameras, a staccato barrage of flashbulbs and a mutter: 'Who's that? Who's she?' because, when her eyes flashed, her beautiful old bones stuck out, suddenly, she turned back into the Lady A. of long ago and they all gaped.

Nora struggled with the wheelchair, trying to fold it up, while I paid off the cabby.

All round us, scenes of the kind poor Irish loved to hate were taking place. Swish cars drew up to disgorge tuxedos and long frocks from interiors that lit up at the moment of exit so each couple made a brief but striking cameo appearance. The crowd went wild. Though all the guests so far looked old crocks like us I'm bound to say there was not one body I recalled from days gone by, no doubt because they were all legitimate.

And then I felt a tugging at my sleeve, some old cove in rags, begging. As soon as I set eyes on him, he struck a chord, although I couldn't place him, not at first.

At my age, memory becomes exquisitely selective. Yes; I re-member, with a hallucinatory sensitivity, sense impressions. A hand on my breast, even if I cannot recall precisely whose hand. The taste of a bacon sandwich back in the days when bacon in the pan buzzed like a bee in a lavender bush. The sensation of sunlight on the tender nape the day we'd had our hair cut for the first time. But it takes an effort to dredge up anything else, I can tell you. I couldn't for the life of me remember the brand name of Irish's favourite tipple, when I tried, the other day, even though he chucked a bottle of it at me when we parted in lieu of farewell. A full bottle, to boot. It smashed against the wall and trickled down. 'Oh, look,' I said, 'it's left a map of Ireland.' He couldn't see the joke. 'He must have loved you very much, to toss a whole bottle,' said Nora, when I told her.

But what was the brand? If you get little details like that right, people will believe anything.

Old Bushmills? Perhaps it was Old Bushmills. Poor old Irish. Gone to the great distillery in the sky these many years.

I've got a perfectly serviceable memory in some respects but not in others and there I was, racking my brains, when he rasped out: 'Spare us half a bar for a cup of tea, lady.'

He stretched out his hand and I glimpsed, between the edges of his unspeakable shirt, off which the buttons had all fallen, below the stained lapels of his ex-army greatcoat, the outlines of Europe and Africa. The penny dropped. Before me stood all that was left of Gorgeous George.

Lo, how the mighty are fallen. Though I saw which way things were going back then, in *The Dream*. It was a wonder he'd hung on for another half-century. When I came to think about it, he must have been as old as Melchior, himself; as old as Perry, if Perry'd lived.

I found I had reminded myself of untimely death and the festive mood that I was striving bravely to achieve evaporated.

But why, in that case, had we put on our gladrags and come out into the night when our hearts were freshly broken? Good question. For our old man's sake, I suppose. To celebrate the author of our being, even if he had relegated us to the 'remaindered' pile.

I may never have known my father in the sense of an intimate acquaintance, but I knew who he was. I was a wise child, wasn't I?

I was stuck staring at Gorgeous George but he didn't recognise me.

'Give us a bob, then,' he said, having relinquished some hope but not all. His voice had been destroyed by time and liquor. The harsh light of the yellow streetlamps took all the pink out of his continents. I'd got a twenty in my hand, ready to pay the cabby. Shakespeare, on the note, said: 'Have a heart.'

'Take that,' I said and pressed his literary culture into the hand of he who once personated Bottom the Weaver. 'Take it for the sake of *The Dream*. You can have it on the one condition, that you spend it all on drink.'

He grabbed hold of the currency, all right, but gave me an old-fashioned look.

'Surely you'd never think that of an old soldier,' he reproached.

'On your way,' I said. 'Don't you know it's Shakespeare's birthday? Cry God for England, Harry and St George. Go off and drink a health to bastards.'

He looked askance at that, as if he misunderstood my turn of phrase, but he wasn't about to make an issue of it, not when the price of an insult was a cool twenty quid, so he toddled off, clutching his loot, scarcely able to believe his luck, no doubt.

'You shouldn't have encouraged him,' reproved the taxi-driver.

'I used to know him, once upon a time,' I said and settled up, slipping him another Shakespeare to compensate for my generosity to the undeserving poor. I can take a hint.

'Come *on*,' said Nora, dancing on the spot.

Up the steps we marched in unison, exhibiting our antique but not quite catastrophic legs with wild abandon; with one accord, we stripped off our silver-fox trenches and trailed them behind us, and all the flashes went off at once. I felt quite revived.

Fame and beauty milled in the entrance hall below as little ladies in period cleavage took the coats and wraps. Lutenists in costume, always a feature of our father's parties, massed on the upstairs landing and ancient music floated from above. There was, bliss! another staircase that went up in florid curves, like Mae West.

'Where's Wheelchair? What did that chap do with her?'

'Search me.'

We gave up on Wheelchair, surrendered our furs and, hand in hand, did another Hollywood ascension up the staircase although I suffered the customary nasty shock when I spotted us both in the big gilt mirror at the top – two funny old girls, paint an inch thick, clothes sixty years too young, stars on their stockings and little wee skirts skimming their buttocks. Parodies. Nora caught sight of us at the same time as I did and she stopped short, too.

'Oooer, Dor,' she said. 'We've gone and overdone it.'

We couldn't help it, we had to laugh at the spectacle we'd made of ourselves and, fortified by sisterly affection, strutted our stuff boldly into the ballroom. We could still show them a thing or two, even if they couldn't stand the sight.

That house boasted a ballroom and that ballroom was a sight to see. The bay stuck out right over the park and there were long windows at the other end. Red marble columns with gold tops held up the ceiling, which was plastered with acanthus wreaths, pineapples, harps, palm fronds, bunches of grapes and lurking cherubs. There was a ten-gallon wedding cake in the shape of a chandelier hanging by a chain, winking, blinking and sending out rainbows and it was lit with real candles. There were real candles everywhere else, too, in sconces, in branches, in single spies, in battalions, filling the air with the smell of hot wax, warming us all up, flattering complexions which were, one and all, aged, except for those of the waiters, all in doublet and hose, who circulated amongst the throng with fizzing flutes of bubbly on silver salvers, reflected upside down like a conjuring trick in the parquet underfoot.

And my heart stood still, I was seventeen, again, I was a virgin powdering my nose with beating heart, for there was lilac, lilac, everywhere. In bowls, in jars, in cornucopias. White lilac, the evening's floral theme. I was all misty because of the smell of lilac as we processed in the long line towards where our father was receiving, in an alcove, seated on a sort of throne.

He wasn't wearing either monkey suit or tails, unlike most of his guests, but had on a rather majestic and heavily embroidered purple caftan. I thought, colostomy; but that caftan made a lovely contrast with his longish, pewter-coloured hair, still thick and heavy. There were rings on his fingers, like a king, or pope, and a big gold medallion round his neck. He looked regal, but festive. My heart gave a thump and the beat started to speed up.

We waited patiently in line to wish him 'Happy birthday', standing between a theatrical knight and a TV presenter who babbled inanities at one another across us, which pissed us off, but we decided to tolerate the invisibility of old ladies – note that, even dressed up like fourpenny ham-bones, our age and gender still rendered us invisible – because it was a special occasion, although as a general rule, we debate invisibility hotly. I snatched at the champagne a couple of times as it waltzed past, I was bloody nervous, I can tell you.

I looked round for Wheelchair but I couldn't see her anywhere and would have started to worry about her if I hadn't started to worry about myself, specifically, to worry about my bladder capacity because the theatrical knight kissed Melchior's hand once, then twice, then yet again for the cameras because first something went wrong, then something else and life was like a loop of tape repeating itself and I wished I hadn't had that second glass of bubbly when I remembered how I'd pissed myself from nerves the first time I met him. But Nora remained calm, although the lutenists were playing tunes to break your heart, 'Semper Dowland, semper dolens', 'Lachrymae'.

The third Lady Hazard, wearing a Vivienne Westwood somewhat too witty for her years, stood watchful guard beside her husband, her hand, weighed down by diamonds, protectively upon his shoulder but her eyes roving all round the thronged room, where the odours of expensive scent and aftershave vied with the lilac and the candle-wax and the smell of delicious cooking began to waft upstairs, too. A doublet and hose tottered past beneath a groaning tray of chicken-legs; I was starving, we'd skipped lunch, but we couldn't kneel down and ask our father's blessing flourishing a drumstick, could we? My Lady Margarine wore a smile so fixed it strained the stitches of her nip and tuck but you could tell she wasn't happy.

Of course! She was looking out for Tristram.

Of whom no sign.

I wondered if the mysterious Father Gareth Hazard SJ were going to turn up and, if so, if he would do so in his canonicals. I suffered from a powerful curiosity about Father Gareth; I'd never set eyes on him and would have given a lot to do so in my capacity as unofficial chronicler of the Hazard family because, given the history of fathers in our family, it seemed only right and proper we should have finally turned up a celibate one – a non-combatant, as it were.

The cameramen were everywhere, like flies. You never knew when you'd find one poking his proboscis in your drink. I gleaned from a waiter the info that the entire party, from first hello to last hiccup, was being taped for posterity; our father was bent on making an exhibition of himself until the bitter end.

'Peaseblossom!' he exclaimed. 'And Mustardseed!'

He put an arm round each of us while My Lady Margarine smiled on remorselessly, she didn't pause to change her smile between clients and her thoughts were unquestionably elsewhere or she'd have asked us who the fuck we were, we miniskirted senior citizens on our teetering heels. She no longer knew us from Adam although we remembered *her*, all right, on Sundays at the Lynde Court Home Farm in a patchwork dirndl giggling sycophantically at some barbed jibe of Saskia's. But Melchior gave us each as big a hug as he could manage, sitting down. Then he closed his eyes and inhaled deeply.

'Now, my darlings, you must refresh my memory . . . which of you is it who uses Shalimar and which Mitsouko?'

That smile! And, dammit, we fell in love with him, again, just as we'd done that August bank holiday all those years ago, when he first broke our hearts when he was scared and young and foolish. We saw that he was none of these things, now. We fell head over heels. We didn't need any words. Words would have been no good. His smile. Nora was chucking down buckets and he stretched out his old, veined, freckled hand and touched her cheek hesitantly, tremulously, so as to break your heart.

'You shouldn't cry,' he said. 'Not at our birthday party.'

That did it. Now I was at it too.

'Dad,' said Nora, and I said, 'Dad.' He gave us another hug. 'My lovely girls.' I don't know what changed him. Perhaps . . . perhaps, when he saw poor little Tiff distracted on the game show, he thought of Pretty Kitty for the first time in decades. Perhaps. He kept his profile at an angle so the cameras wouldn't shoot his double chin, he couldn't help it, it was in his blood. Just because he repented in public with half England watching didn't mean it wasn't genuine. He gave us another hug, and another, making up for all the hugs we never got. One fine night filled with white lilac when I was seventeen, he'd asked me to dance and now, by rights, he ought to close the circle, take the floor with Nora, but that TV presenter behind us was pushing and shoving to make his presence felt so we said: 'See you later, Dad,' and pushed off.

We got ourselves another drink and hid behind a pillar to compose ourselves. We were grinning away like Cheshire cats, we couldn't help it. Not that he'd said anything. Not that anything had changed. But we'd had a bit of love.

The chicken passed by, she lifted a thigh off. 'I could eat a horse.' She bit into the flesh. 'Delish.' She was recovering her equanimity. A spike of herb trapped between her front teeth; she hooked it out with her fingernail and looked at it.

'Rosemary,' she said. '*At Table in Tuscany*, BBC 1, Friday evenings, eight thirty. That Saskia's doing the catering.'

She dropped the thigh half-eaten in an ashtray.

'Your mascara's run something awful,' I said. I was dying for a pee, too, so we went off to the ladies' toilet and there we found the Lady A., turned back into Wheelchair as if by some bad spell and tucked away behind the bidet, still veiled, quivering, with Old Nanny done up to look like Juliet's Nurse soothing her with gentle murmurs. They'd stationed Old Nanny in the toilet, evidently, so that she could deal with drunks.

'I couldn't face him,' said the Lady A. 'Not after what I did to him. I loved him but I betrayed him.'

'You need a stiffener,' said Nora. Old Nanny pursed her lips at first but she knocked a quick one back herself once Nora got the gin out of her gilt-mesh bag and we got Wheelchair into the ballroom at last, between us, although she quivered well-nigh to the point of shaking to pieces whenever the crowds parted and she caught sight of Melchior, so we parked her behind a Canova nude, where she had another snifter and settled down to see what on earth would happen next.

What happened next was, Daisy Duck.

There was a fanfare of baroque trumpets. No kidding. I hadn't heard a baroque trumpet in the flesh since the wrap party for *The Dream*. There was a general hushing and muttering and the crowd pressed back but the Lady A. became unwontedly animated and craned forward, would have had her veil off for a better view but I stayed her hand – I had an inkling the time wasn't right, yet, for her to show herself. She grumbled and mumbled but covered up again and settled down to watch the royal entrance happily enough, even if as through a mist.

And royal entrance it was. Tootle, tootle, tootle, too! went the trumpets. Then the lutenists, unaccustomed to the tuning and with a good many bum notes, had a go at 'Hello Dolly' and in she came, to a round of cheers. People stood on chairs. She looked a million dollars, I must admit, even if in well-used notes. Tiny as ever, five foot nothing in her heels, but a stunning advertisement for hormone replacement therapy, I must say, not a line on that skin but, then, sharkskin doesn't wrinkle, does it, don't be a bitch, Dora. She was brown and glossy, like a Sunday roast, plump brown shoulders, bright brown hair with a few grey strands – she was smart enough not to try to look as though she were thirty-five, she'd settle happily for forty. Teeth like a Bechstein grand, I blinked in the glare of her smile. In the slinky wake of her white satin sheath staggered a tiny figure almost invisible under the weight of her bouquet, a hundred red roses. I thought it must be Daisy's gigolo, he came in like a tacked-on afterthought, but he wasn't *my* idea of a gigolo – tiny little man, ill-fitting peroxide hair, one of those grey silk Italian suits that glow in the dark, face like an old child. I hoped for her sake he'd got hidden talents.

Good old Daisy. I could tell at a glance she was tight as a tick.

She got to the middle of the floor and then she stopped. She raised her arms above her head in an extrovert gesture and turned her nonstop, whiter-than-white smile to all four corners before she blasted Melchior with it. 'Hello Dolly' stopped at last, thank God. Roars of applause.

Melchior managed to stagger to his feet, wobbled off the podium and hugged her, making it up in public with her after all those years just as he'd done with us but they spent more time negotiating their profiles to advantage than we had done and Daisy won because, even if half seas over, she was compos mentis.

Because it grieves me but I must admit it – I fear our father's softening of the heart was not unconnected to the softening of his brain. Old nanny told us he'd never been the same since, one day, he was in the Tube on the way to the Garrick Club and some old codger grasped him by the hand and cried out, so all the carriage heard: 'Good God, weren't you Melchior Hazard, once?' He started to mope, after that, to suffer from uncertainty, refused to go out, even hid away that precious old cardboard crown of his and swore he was too old to wear it any more. He was getting a touch dottled. But there you are; no silver lining without a cloud.

Dear old Daisy. She caught sight of us during the camera call, abandoned him in mid-embrace. The media people hallooed after her: what's she doing, kissing those two bedizened bag ladies? We'd been younger than her, once upon a time, but she was wearing well, and worth a bob or two, of course.

The gigolo trailed unhappily a few steps, then unhappily back, carting his roses, at a loss, until Melchior was kind, beckoned him over, relieved him of the roses and, in a spontaneous improvisation, gave them to My Lady Margarine, who looked shocked, and thrust them at that TV presenter, who was still hanging around, who got rid of them to some deliquescent thesp in a Jean-Paul Gaulthier cat suit, and then that bunch of roses started to play pass-the-parcel all round the ballroom until a serving wench retrieved it and took it to the Ladies', where Old Nanny, ever resourceful, stuck it down a toilet bowl for the duration of the party, since there was no other receptacle ample enough to receive it.

Daisy shrieked with joy when she caught sight of Wheelchair in her shroud but no time to catch up because the press now left us in a body and cantered to the door as Margarine pointed like a terrier and began to shake and whimper: here came the prodigal son at last!

How could anyone have thought that Tristram might find it in his heart to skip his father's centenary, even if that very day he'd lost his lover and his child? Wasn't it heart-warming? Heart-warming, my foot. The only decent thing young Tristram could have done was hara-kiri, in my opinion. But the show must go on, must it not?

Tristram looked wrecked. In a d.j., all right, but greenish in the face, as if he'd been throwing up all day, and very tottery on his feet, held up by an aunt on either side. We hadn't spoken to the darling buds since the fateful twenty-first birthday party, only the occasional sighting in a department store. The Lady A. moaned and clutched the arms of her chair. 'Calm down!' we hissed. She sucked in a mouthful of her veil and gagged herself. Daisy produced a silver hip flask from her handbag and offered her a pull; chewing chiffon, the Lady A. shook her head. I was glad to see that time had healed the wounds between these two.

But time does not necessarily heal everything. I felt that old, familiar shudder of distress when I saw Saskia, with her hair redder than ever, done up in a French pleat, looking quite lissom in a putty-coloured sliver of something by Jean Muir. As for Imogen, she'd gone right over the top. She'd got a fishbowl on her head with a fish in it. I kid you not. A live fish. The flashes popped and flared like Guy Fawkes' Night and Imogen turned this way and that, nodding, bowing and smiling and acknowledging the attention, the goldfish slopping around at considerable danger to itself. I furiously pondered the significance of the fish, then it clicked: *Goldie the Goldfish* – her kiddies' programme. She had come to the party as a commercial for herself. She had on a bronze shift sequined in scales and she greeted her father in a manner appropriate to her heroine, she opened and shut her mouth a lot, and it was just as well she'd come along in costume and mimed her birthday greeting to him as a goldfish because it lightened up the mood.

As it was, after the girls – 'girls', I call them; they wouldn't see sixty, again; show us your bus pass, ladies – gave the old man their birthday kisses, one on each cheek, he wept, again, and they retreated, leaving Tristram behind. That was the moment the paparazzi had been waiting for, when he tumbled forward on his knees, his face in Melchior's lap. His shoulders shook. Over the plangent lutes, I heard the sound of sobbing. The cameramen surged round to get a closer view.

His mother crouched down and cuddled him, Melchior cradled his head. Old Melchior did something pathetic, he tried to wave the cameras away, tried to get them to leave them alone so they could endure the moment without the world, his wife and dog looking on, but it was too late in their lives for that. Smile in public, cry in public, live in public, die in public. There was a raw emotion on their faces that you don't see on actors'. Tonight, they were in the newsreel. The worst thing, to see your children suffer.

But when I remembered Brenda's face, that morning, I knew there was an even worse thing and then I cheerfully could have slaughtered Tristram Hazard.

Still the bloody show went on.

Saskia, who was well in control of the situation being, unique amongst mammals, a cold-blooded cow, telegraphed a signal with her eyebrows and the baroque trumpets rang out again. A host of little boys from the Italia Conte School in mini-ruffs and slashed knickers ran round snuffing out the scones with their fingers, releasing dozens of puffs of acrid smoke.

In came the cake.

I should have realised that Saskia would bake the cake. It was her masterpiece. It was enormous. It was a model of the Globe Theatre, I tell no lie. It was spherical, in tiers, roofed with chocolate frosting ridged to simulate tiles. It was big enough to ring a hundred candles all around the roof and they were blazing away as a dozen little pageboys bore in this edifice at shoulder-height, on a sort of litter, amidst roars of applause in which Daisy enthusiastically joined, after parking her bag and hip flask with the gigolo, but the Lady A. was sobbing very quietly and discreetly to herself under her veil and *we* didn't feel like applauding ourselves, not at all, at all.

A pageboy handed Saskia a sword, the kind they fence with. Nora and I sharply ingested breath, recalling another birthday, another cake, a sudden act of shocking violence – but, in what was obviously a well-rehearsed routine, she offered it by the hilt to Melchior, who, well done, old stager! gently thrust Tristram to one side with his foot and rose tottering to his feet.

The only light, that fluttering of birthday candles on the cake, casting weird shadows, making the old man look haggard.

There was a hush; there was a drumroll.

My Lady Margarine, who was distractedly patting Tristram's hand, belatedly remembered her cue.

'A happy hundredth birthday, darling!' You could tell, from the power of her smile, *that* cake wasn't made with butter. Another fine trouper.

Our father lifted up the sword. I felt for him, you could see it was an effort. He lifted up the sword and –

– and –

I would like to be able to say that at this thrilling point, drumroll, celebration, flames, sudden hush, the big cake blew up or cracked open and out popped –

– but, if I did, I would be lying.

What happened was this: drumroll, flames, hush, uplifted cake knife but, before it could descend, came a tremendous knocking at the front door. TREMENDOUS. Such a knocking that the birthday candles dipped and swayed and dropped wax on the chocolate tiles; the boughs of lilac tossed, scattering nodes of bloom; the very parquet underneath us seemed to tremble, about to rise up.

A thrill ran through the room. Something unscripted is about to happen.

They let the wind in when they opened the door. The same amazing wind that whipped up the leaves and Dora Chance's weary corpuscles this morning came roaring and galloping up the stairs into the ballroom, blowing up skirts, so women squealed, buffeting the candle-flames almost to extinction then whipping them back to life, again, whirling the Lady A.'s veil this way and that way, threatening to blow it away altogether, but she trapped it in her mouth. Laughter like sweet thunder blew on the wind in front of him and every head turned to see whom it might be, arriving late, in such a genial tempest.

Who else could it have been?

Remember the old song he used to sing with Irish, 'In Dublin town lived Michael Finnegan . . .' and the corpse jumps up at the wake, a resurrection. And the last line went like this:

'Thunder and lightning!' sang our Peregrine. 'Did yez think I was dead?'

The size of a warehouse, bigger, the size of a tower block, in what looked like the very same scratched, weathered flying jacket he'd worn when we first laid eyes on him when we were still pissing on the floor, splitting a grin, hair as red as paprika – not one speck of grey, evidently untouched one jot by age.

He could have telephoned from the airport, couldn't he, to say he would be here. No doubt they even have telephones in Brazil, in this day and age. But if he'd called ahead, it would have spoiled our wonderment. It was just like Peregrine, to upstage his own brother.

Then, again, it was our Uncle Perry's hundredth birthday, too.

I knew in my water today would be the kind of day things happen.

In on the wind that came with Perry blew dozens and dozens of butterflies, red ones, yellow ones, brown and amber ones, some most mysteriously violet and black, tiny little green ones, huge flapping marbled blue and khaki ones, swirling around the room, settling on women's bare shoulders, men's bald spots. Nora and I got a couple each in our hair.

Melchior dropped the sword and sat down again, abruptly, white as a sheet, and the cameras held their fire, for once, as if Peregrine had not only upstaged his brother but also plausibility. The uncut cake on its dozen legs hovered in front of Melchior uncertain what to do and there was a buzz of questions because of course nobody was left who knew who Perry was, but she and me and him and them, and perhaps Melchior even thought he'd seen a ghost.

But such a material ghost. Ever heavy-footed. The chandelier shook, the lilac shed. The cake veered off to one side at Peregrine's approach. He was wreathed in butterflies. Very, very gently, he detached a splendid, crimson one with an ethereal wingspan about six inches, offered the pulsing handful to Melchior.

'All our daughters,' he said. 'I've named a butterfly for each one. And I've named *this* one after you, you miserable old sod.'

The unmistakable language of male affection. Was it: absence made the heart grow fonder? Or shall we put it down to ambivalence, perhaps? But I was glad to see them fond. Melchior looked at the butterflies, so lovely, so improbable, and then he looked up at his brother, and then he smiled. And then the butterfly curator from the zoo came in with a big net, caught up all the beauties and took them somewhere warm and snug for Peregrine had their welfare at heart. All was uproar and commotion but we pressed forward for our kisses.

'Floradora! You haven't changed one bit!'

I was about to say him nay, draw his attention to the crow's-feet, the grey hairs and turkey wobblers but I saw by the look in his eye that he meant what he said, that he really, truly loved us and so he saw no difference; he saw the girls we always would be under the scrawny, wizened carapace that time had forced on us for, although promiscuous, he was also faithful, and, where he loved, he never altered, nor saw any alteration. And then I wondered, was I built the same way, too? Did I see the soul of the one I loved when I saw Perry, not his body? And was his fleshly envelope, perhaps, in reality in much the same sorry shape as those of his nieces outside the magic circle of my desire?

But when I registered I'd used those words, 'my desire', I stopped thinking in that direction *toot sweet*. I'd properly shocked myself and I had to knock off another glass of champagne to cool myself while Nora came in for her share of hugs and kisses and then Daisy Duck, and all the rest, because not since the Change had yours truly felt such a sudden rush of blood in that department, down there.

Saskia was standoffish and turned the cold shoulder. Imogen tried to slip away but was impeded by her headgear so he grabbed hold of her and gave her such a hug the goldfish slopped out of the bowl and she went down on her knees in a puddle to pick it up again, it was slippery as soap and gave them a fine chase all over the dancefloor while the camera crews and the photographers and the reporters didn't know where to turn next, so much grief, joy, resentment and pursuit was going on, while the multitude babbled and got in the way until suddenly Peregrine caught sight of a certain heavily veiled figure tucked away behind a pillar and stopped short with the gasping goldfish in his hand.

'It isn't . . .' he said.

'Put it back in!' urged Imogen, kneeling at his feet. Perry absently dropped the fish back in the bowl and a hush spread in ever-increasing circles over the crowd until there was perfect silence. All eyes were focused on the invisible Lady A. Her fingers clenched and unclenched on the arms of the wheelchair. She pushed herself backwards, as if she were trying to roll offstage back into the wings, where nobody could see her, but she banged against the wall because there was nowhere to go except here.

Melchior, sensing something was up, craned forward, leaning heavily on Margarine, so he got a good view when Perry plucked off the veil. Then came a bewildered pause. Melchior sank back on his throne, again, with a puzzled look, quite grey with exhaustion, although things were only just livening up. I don't think he'd got the foggiest who the lady in the wheelchair was. You could hear Margarine going: 'Who's that? Who's that?' But Saskia and Imogen backed off aghast, as well they might.

Perry said softly, 'Hi, there, bright eyes.'

The Lady A. said, 'Why! It's Peregrine!' and twinkled.

He wheeled her round to face the crowd.

'Ladies and gentlemen,' he said, 'the Lady Atalanta Hazard. The most beautiful woman of her time.'

Suddenly she looked her old self again, but, due to her white curls, even more like a sheep, to my way of thinking, but it would seem that sheep are irresistible; everybody gasped. Perry led the applause that followed. She scrabbled at her veil, as if half-inclined to cover up again, but I could tell she was pleased. Melchior gave a jump.

'Attie!'

So now all three Lady Hazards were together in one room and I wondered if our mother's ghost was somewhere here, too, floating in the smoky air above the cake, which was waving about, a bit, because its arms were getting tired.

'I've brought you something special, in my trunk,' said Peregrine to Melchior. 'Give us a little light on the subject, if you please.' The little pages dashed up and down relighting everything until the room was brilliant.

Perry must have tipped the baroque trumpets because they let loose another fanfare as half a dozen stocky wee brown men in penis sheaths and feathers, friends of Perry's from Brazil, evidently, heaved in a cabin trunk covered with labels of hotels that had long since ceased trading, shipping lines long since defunct, railways long since torn up. They hauled it into the middle of the ballroom, set it down on the parquet. Peregrine spat on his hands and rubbed, strode boldly forth and first of all I thought: He's going to do a conjuring trick, because he put on his conjuring manner that I hadn't seen for years: 'Ladies and gentlemen, I have nothing up my sleeve.' He was a sprightly walker. A hundred? Never!

'He's made a pact,' said Nora in a whisper.

He addressed Melchior. He gave as low a bow as his paunch permitted.

'Melchior, my dear brother,' he said, 'I give you . . . the future of the Hazard family.'

He lifted up the lid of the trunk.

'If,' he added, 'she'll have you.'

We had an intuition who it was.

Out of that trunk stepped our little Tiff, as fresh as paint, not a tad the worse for wear except her eyes were no longer those of a dove, stabbed or whole, and she looked sound in mind and body almost to a fault. She'd changed her clothes; she'd got on a pair of overalls and those big boots, Doc Marten's, but she looked lovelier than ever, enough to make you blink. Our Tiff as ever was, our heart's delight.

We were all tears and laughter. We skidded across that skating rink of a floor on our ridiculous heels and held her as if we'd never let her go while the baroque trumpets went on and on until I thought: perhaps we've died and gone to heaven. But the first paroxysm subsided and there we still were.

I'll say this for Tristram's reflexes, he was down on his knees in front of her in a flash, laughing and crying at the same time or doing a fair simulacrum thereof.

'I love you, Tiffany' he said. 'Forgive me.'

She stared down at him as if sunk deep in thought, which I was glad to see in itself – she'd never been one for reflection, before. She wiped her nose with the back of her hand, she'd picked up a dreadful cold, somewhere, though not at the bottom of the river, as it turned out.

'Fat chance,' she announced at last.

Tristram was stunned. He sat back on his heels.

'But, Tiffany, I'll marry you!'

'Not on your life, you bastard,' she said, right out in front of all those people. God, I was proud of her at that moment! 'Not after what you did to me in public. I wouldn't marry you if you were the last man in the world. Marry your auntie, instead.'

A palpable hit. Saskia turned white and dropped her glass. Poor old Melchior was at sea, couldn't make head nor tail of *this* bit of cut and thrust, of course, but he was pierced to the heart by the riveting sight of his son's rejection.

'Oh, my dear,' he murmured in that thick, rich, vintage port voice. 'Take pity on him; have pity on your own unborn child.'

I felt quite sorry for Melchior, having his grandchild given and taken away before it was so much as born. He looked so pitiful, and, after all, it *was* his birthday, that Tiff might have wavered but Tristram spoiled it all. He waxed histrionic.

'My baby! Think of my baby!' He tore his hair, he gnashed his teeth.

'Pull yourself together and be a man, or try to,' said Tiffany sharply. 'You've not got what it takes to be a father. There's more to fathering than fucking, you know.'

We each squeezed the hand we held, she squeezed back. I thought, we'll teach the baby tap and ballet, when the time comes. Then came another banging on the door.

'That'll be my mum and dad,' she announced confidently. All the help was in the ballroom, now, transfixed by all this real-life drama, nobody to let in the new arrivals, but a splintering crash indicated that the locked front door posed no problems to a ranked light-heavyweight. Tiff let off her parting shot.

'Not that your old man and mother aren't perfectly welcome to take a peek at the baby when it's born but don't you come sniffing around until you've dried off behind the ears, Tristram.'

He was too stunned to get up off his knees as Bren and Leroy stepped round him to embrace their daughter in a fusillade of flashes. The lutes started up again, Lord Somebody or Other's Puff, I think Perry slipped them a couple of quid. Quite like old times, lights, music, action. There was a patter of applause as Tiff and Bren and Leroy departed for their cab and were followed by no photographers after Leroy sent one of them downstairs on his ear.

Perry said he found our little Tiff by chance, wandering in the street the previous night, on his way from the airport; his taxi nearly ran her over.

'So I took her back with me to the Travellers' Club –'

'Oh, Peregrine!' I cried, struck by an awful thought. 'You never!'

'I most certainly did not,' he huffed. 'What a suggestion! There was a damsel in distress, if ever I saw one.'

Tristram was crying on Saskia's shoulder. I could tell by the look in his mother's eye she'd no love lost for Saskia, either, even if they *had* been best friends at Ro-de-o-do back in the year dot. And here was bloody Saskia now, elbowing her out of her big scene with her own son. Margarine blazed away with thwarted mother love and snatched up a lump of cake, that had sunk down to the ground out of sheer weariness, pulled off a candle that had burned down to a stump, and pressed the cake into her son's hand.

'Eat something, my dear,' she said. 'Just a mouthful, to give you strength.'

There was a piercing screech and crumbs everywhere because Saskia dashed the cake from Tristram's lips and collapsed in a fit in the arms of her sister, who promptly commenced her celebrated goldfish imitation again, her lips opened, her lips closed, oh! oh! oh! but no sound came out. Perry, ever quick off the mark, seized Imogen's goldfish bowl and dashed the water over Saskia, shocking her out of her fit and into you never saw such a shimmy as she shook that goldfish out of her vee-neck.

Yes, she confessed; she *had* slipped something into the cake she'd baked with her own hands for her father's birthday, though whether it would have made him rather ill or very ill or finished him off altogether I never found out because now such a hulla-baloo broke out, lights, cameras, the wailing of that poor old man, the recriminations of his wife, the exclamations of his son, and everbody else putting their vocal tuppence ha'p'orth in as well. Even Perry looked grave and as if he were to blame, stricken with compunction, possibly for the first time in a century. He and the Lady A. drew close together, the guilty parties, when Saskia wailed to Melchior:

'You never loved us!'

It was high time that Saskia got wise. Remember Gorgeous George on Brighton Pier long ago, and the punch line of his joke? I couldn't resist, I came out with it:

'Don't worry, darlin', '*e*'s not your father!'

What if Horatio had whispered that to Hamlet in Act I, Scene i? And think what a difference it might have made to Cordelia. On the other hand, those last comedies would darken considerably in tone, don't you think, if Marina and, especially, Perdita weren't really the daughters of . . .

Comedy is tragedy that happens to *other* people.

Brighton Pier broke up with mirth when Gorgeous George said, ''*e*'s not your father'; when I said the same thing in the Hazard residence, you could have heard a pin drop. Then I wished I'd held my peace and let the world wag on its old, unconscious way, for after that split second of silent, suspended time while they all took it in, if all had been hullabaloo before now it was pandemonium as Saskia sprang at Peregrine and pummelled him with her fists while the Lady A., quick as her wheels allowed, interposed her body, crying out piteously, while Imogen, now aquarium-less, thank God, trotted after the Lady A. begging for full details of the entire scenario and giggling in a hysterically retarded manner but Nora and Daisy Duck, having evidently copiously refreshed themselves from Daisy's hip flask, were clinging to one another for dear life and, I'm sorry to say, laughing fit to bust a gut.

Melchior flashed a 'how could you' œillade at the Lady A., who reared up in her chair – 'bright eyes', indeed! more like Medusa. She got it all off her chest in one go. What a performance. Those who could secure one perched on the little gilt chairs that stood around, the rest roosted on the floor at risk to gowns and trousers and all turned into the perfect audience, quiet as mice, rustling at tense moments, indrawing breath at startling disclosures and sometimes rippling with discreet mirth, while the waiters lolled against the walls, more disengaged, professionals themselves, keeping a critical eye upon the show rather than being carried away by it.

'And wasn't it the Hazard blood?' she cried, full-throated, clarion-like. We'd never heard her sound like that before. 'The Hazard blood! The precious, unique Hazard blood that blinds parents to their children and turns daughter against mother!'

Melchior coughed, spluttered and writhed upon his throne; she'd been bottling up his embarrassment for years and now, pop! bubble, bubble, bubble, or more like hubble, bubble, toil and trouble, out it came all over the floor. Perry got Saskia in a half-nelson and she hushed up, staring at the Lady A. with saucer eyes; she'd never thought her mother had so much passion in her, and neither had I.

'You left me at home hugging the empty womb you couldn't fill, Melchior!'

Spasm of shock.

'You couldn't fill *my* womb, Melchior, although you'd been so profligate of your seed before me, seduced and abandoned an innocent girl, left her to die, alone, and then, to compound the betrayal, you abandoned her daughters –'

– she gestured towards us and Nora swiftly assumed a po-face as a fresh gasp ran through the crowd and all eyes turned towards us, as with the crowd at Wimbledon. I wondered, ought we to take a bow?

'– oh, yes! the daughters you never acknowledged, as though you thought the Hazard blood lost all its virtue once it was mixed with that of a chambermaid –'

He made a furious gesture of denial. She snapped:

'Oh, yes you did!'

Touch of the pantomime; would be riposte: 'Oh, no I didn't!' No such luck. She was unstoppable.

'It was your blood, the Hazard blood, that went to make the "darling buds of May", the girls you loved so dearly even when they robbed their mother of her home and money –'

Gasps; muffled exclamations; all eyes now swivelled towards Saskia and Imogen, who flinched and quailed.

'Your blood, the Hazard blood, runs in their veins but the "darling buds" never sprang from the *seed* of Melchior Hazard!'

'Ooh!' and 'Aah!' said everybody. Myself, I'd been wondering how the Lady A. would verbalise the technical aspect of her adultery, given the refinement of her vocabulary. Having made the distinction between 'blood' and the actual procreative juice, what would she call the latter? 'Jism'? 'Come'? (Or do you spell it 'cum', I'm never sure.) Sperm and semen seemed altogether too technical for her rhetorical mode. I was glad she'd settled on the tasteful compromise of 'seed', although it occurred to me, not for the first time, that a serious language problem existed between the two branches of the Hazard family.

Don't misunderstand me. We've got very fond of her. She's always been welcome to the basement front, we'd never deny her a crust and I know she can't help it – I truly think she'd change if only she could. But, always, the high tone, even today, when she was letting rip and all those decades of understatement were going up in smoke. The nub of what she was saying now was, she'd had a tumble with her brother-in-law, once upon a time, and, as a result, there were two more girls in the world. Sorry, pardon, Melchior. But she couldn't just *say* that, could she? She had to make a meal of it. Some of the things she said were news to me, of course, and made a lot of things make sense, but she was going on about it all as if it were a matter of life and death. And how could we Chances believe that? We knew that nothing is a matter of life and death except life and death.

'Not your seed, Melchior, but those girls were cast in your mould, all the same! They robbed me and turned me out of my own home and spurned the love I felt for them just as you did yourself, Melchior!'

She burst into tears. There was a flutter of sympathetic handkerchiefs. Peregrine's cheeks were streaming, too, and the darling buds clung on to one another, pictures of shame and grief. When the Lady A. had composed herself, she mopped her face with Nora's crumpled veil, blew her nose on it and continued, as if refreshed:

'You left me lonely, Melchior, while you pursued that restless, thirsty quest for fame, while you engaged in that titanic contest with your dead father –'

Titanic conquest? First I've heard of it, I sniffed. But how could

I have heard of it, on reflection? Our father and I had never been on what you could call speaking terms.

'–I was left lonely, with my empty womb. And then –'

But she couldn't finish the sentence, perfect lady that she was. She raised her eyes imploringly to Peregrine and in one bound he was beside her, his arms around her shoulders and her daughters, weeping, scampered over, too, and crouched at her feet in attitudes of contrition. Peregrine looked Melchior right between the eyes.

'They're mine, Melchior, little monsters that they are. Forgive me, Melchior. Forgive us all.'

There was a patter of applause that petered out as soon as people realised that everything was real. Frail, lovely Lady A., her forces spent, exhaustedly accepted a pull at Daisy's flask while the videotape recorded every move for posterity. Daisy was impressed and wondered aloud who held the mini-series rights.

Meanwhile, Saskia and Imogen each seized hold of a piece of the Lady A.'s skirt, kissed it and begged her to forgive and forget, etc. etc. etc. Poor old Perry was left right out in the cold during the ensuing emotional reconciliation and I drew away a little, sunk in my own thoughts, as follows: how a mother is always a mother, since a mother is a biological fact, whilst a father is a movable feast. But Melchior, head buried in his hands, looked the picture of misery and Margarine beat the air with her hands, at a loss as to what to do to cheer him up.

Daisy and Nora had got their heads together. Then Daisy nudged her gigolo back to life – he looked as if he'd gone off into a trance, temporarily. There was some discussion with the lutes and then they struck up all together as such a voice! the voice of an angel soared up and tickled the chandelier – a boy soprano, such purity, such vigour. A voice I'd heard before, in Hollywood but this time it was not raised to warn us against spotted snakes.

'Oh,' he sang, 'my beloved father . . .'

No gigolo accompanied Daisy but he who'd once stood best man to her and Melchior. Bewigged, befuddled, still his vocal cords could move a heart of stone. She'd met him again when he presented her with her 'lifetime contribution on the cinema' Academy Award. He was filthy rich, and gaga, and when she told

him to, he sang. 'My very best marriage,' she said. From Daisy
Duck to Daisy Puck.

'I love thee, yes, I love thee . . .'

Nora signed me with her eyes. It was time for me and she to
go public about our paternity. Our skirts had ridden right up our
crotches, we pulled them down, we patted our hair, our heels
went click, click, click on the carpet, that sexy sound, but we
looked like wizened children got up in our mum's clothes for a
dare and our hearts were brimming over. We pressed our cheeks
against his hands. This was too much for Melchior. He melted
for all to see.

'Oh, my beloved father —'

The crystals rang with the last notes of Puck's glorious aria.
Not a dry eye in the house as Melchior raised his head and gave
his girls a watery, tremulous smile.

'I am the one deserves to weep,' he said, and kissed us.

I could have sworn that then the curtain came down, the lights
went up and there was a standing ovation but, as Nora pointed
out later, there was no curtain, the lights were on already, and it
would have been discourteous of that audience to applaud. So I
imagined all that. But, anyway, after this inexpressibly moving
reconciliation, came a short intermission. Everybody got up and
stretched and vivaciously discussed the action so far while the
waiters cleared the cake away. Nobody blew out the candles on
this birthday, they went out of their own accord, but all our
wishes had come true and we just sat there, beaming.

When the lutes settled down again after their excursion into
Puccini, it was nostalgia-time. I pricked up my ears; forgotten
melodies drifting up from Memory Lane . . . selections from —
what else — *What? You Will!?!* We hummed along and when they
came to 'Oh, Mistress Mine', they did it as a foxtrot and Nora
gave Melchior a nudge.

'Here, old man,' she said, 'What about a dance? Give us the
pleasure.'

She gave him a hand, got him on to the dancefloor. On the
night of my seventeenth birthday long ago he danced with me.
Tonight, on our father's grand centenary, he took the floor with
the other half of the apple and the band played music from the

days when men wore hats. Not a dry eye in the house. Again. He was a touch unsteady on his pins, inclined to wobble, but she knew how to lead, and they were wreathed in smiles of foolish fondness for that which had been lost was found and so on.

But Perry was in a right old state, left out of each and every reunion. He materialised beside me, disconsolate. 'They still don't want to know me,' he said. 'And I can't blame them. God, Dora, I've been a cad.'

I was feeling quite sentimental, watching Dad and Nora.

'You were always good to us, darling,' I reminded him. 'Nora always thought you should have married Grandma.'

'What?!?'

'Made a real family for us.'

He chewed on that in stunned silence until he guffawed.

Once Nora had set the ball rolling, other couples took the floor. Margarine led out Tristram, who was still shaky on his feet but starting to get a bit of colour back. Daisy scooped up her Puck and took him through the motions, for which I was thankful, as he seemed quite out of it unless he was singing. The Lady A. was too preoccupied with her daughters and they with her to pay the dancing much attention but soon everybody else was doing it and Perry stuck out a paw:

'How about it, Dora?'

'I don't fancy a foxtrot, Perry,' I said. 'But I wouldn't say no to a –'

It slipped out before I thought twice. I'm not proud of it, I'm not ashamed of it although I thought, there'll be hell to pay with Nora tomorrow morning; even though he *was* my uncle on my father's side; and don't think I didn't know he got some salve to his battered old male ego out of it, apart from anything else, but I didn't do it just to cheer him up, oh, no. Nor, I swear, was I trying to get even with Saskia. No. It was the tune, the moonlight and the scent of lilac that did it. I hadn't felt like this for twenty years. Nobody noticed when we slipped away because they were all dancing.

The day's exciting wind, having done its bit to liven up the evening, had died down to a little whisper from the direction of the park, full of damp earth and springtime, that blew the white linen curtains ballooning backwards into the front bedroom. It was quite chilly, I shivered. Peregrine went to close the window, then stopped. 'Hark at the lions!' In the distance, in the zoo, over the waving treetops, the lions were roaring their hearts out.

It was a stark white room with operating-theatre walls and a white leather disc on the end of a metal spike for an armchair, bare boards, and an enigmatic bed like something therapeutic with a steel frame. Margarine got some earringed, crewcut decorator in to do it. There were a few spare coats from the party spread on the bed, they spoiled the whole effect – you couldn't afford to have a slipper out of place. I'd clipped the piece about that room out of World of Interiors to go into my Hazard dossier and, oddly enough, although it was a masterpiece of pared-down understatement, the room still had just the same self-conscious look as that other long-combusted bedroom at Lynde Court had done – it was a room designed to be looked at, like Melchior's whole life had been, but now all the dirty secrets hidden in the cupboards had come out at last, had come to fuck in his bed, in fact. We didn't even bother to shove off the coats.

Even in old age, it was easy to see why Peregrine had always had such success with women.

'How long has it been, Dora?'

'Too long, me old cock!' I responded heartily, though, rack my brains as I might, I couldn't for the life of me remember sleeping with him before and I shocked myself, to have forgotten that – if I had forgotten, that is, and if he wasn't making a general rather than a particular enquiry, but it wasn't the time nor place to ask him to elucidate, was it? All the same, to have forgotten so much else, so many other names, yes, all water under the bridge – but to have forgotten whether ever I slept with my beloved Perry ... and then I thought, perhaps he can't remember, either. But, even so.

But don't think I thought these thoughts in a reasoned sequence and a coherent manner. Far from it.

You never forget the first time. I'll never forget the last time, either.

At least, I'm pretty sure this is going to be the last time, but you never know what may turn up.

He cracked his old back and soughed and wheezed. 'Whoa there, old sport! You don't want to peg it on your birthday!'

'Don't care if I do,' he says, red in the face, all of a sweat. 'Not bad for a centenarian, eh?'

I put my arms around him, although they didn't meet, and said: 'I love you more than ever I loved any young kid, short pants, mother doesn't know he's out.'

Not bad for a centenarian.

Not bad at all.

Not bad.

Not –

Nora told me afterwards how the agitations of the steel bed began to make the chandelier downstairs directly beneath it, shiver, so that the music of the lutes, now plucking away at a selection of show tunes for the delight of the dancing guests, was almost imperceptibly augmented by the tinkle, tinkle, tinkle of all the little lustres as the tiers of glass began to sway from side to side, slopping hot wax on the dancers below, first slowly, then with a more and more determined rhythm until they shook like Josephine Baker's bottom –

'What a clatter!' said Nora. 'Like cymbals, darling. Don't you think I didn't guess what you were up to?'

There was just one ecstatic moment, she opined, when she thought the grand bouncing on the bed upstairs – remember, Perry was a *big* man – would bring down that chandelier and all its candles, smash, bang, clatter, and the swagged ceiling, too; bring the house down, fuck the house down, come ('cum'?) all over the posh frocks and the monkey jackets and the poisoned cake and the lovers, mothers, sisters, shatter the lenses that turned our lives into peepshows, scatter little candle-flames like an epiphany on every head, cover over all the family, the friends, the camera crews, with plaster dust and come and fire.

But such was not to be. There are limits to the power of laughter and though I may hint at them from time to time, I do not propose to step over them.

Perry and I had no idea what was going on below, of course.

Not bad for a centenarian at all, at all.

But do not think I went to bed with the ribald ancient who'd arrived with my darling godchild in a box an hour before. Oh, no. I lay in the arms of that russet-mopped young flyer in the weathered leather jacket who'd knocked at the door of 49 Bard Road, and saved us all from gloom the day the war to end all wars ended, just twenty years before the next one started. And wars are facts we cannot fuck away, Perry; nor laugh away, either.

Do you hear me, Perry?

No.

He was himself, when young; and also, while we were making love, he turned into, of all people, that blue-eyed boy who'd never known my proper name. Then who else but Irish passed briefly through the bed; fancy meeting you. There was a whiff of Trumper's Essence of Lime but not Perry, this time, instead, that Free Pole the night I caught a flea in the Ritz. And then a visit from Mr Piano Man, only he'd used a powerful mouthwash, thank goodness. Don't think I'd gone wandering off down Memory Lane in the midst of it all; but Peregrine wasn't only the one dear man, tonight, but a kaleidoscope of faces, gestures, caresses. He was not the love of my life but all the loves of my life at once, the curtain call of my career as lover.

And who was I?

I saw myself reflected in those bracken-coloured eyes of his. I was a lanky girl with a green bow in her mouse-brown hair, blinking away the first, worst disappointment of her life in the sun on Brighton Prom.

When I was just thirteen years old, Perry! You dirty beast!

Evidently, back downstairs in the ballroom, the chandelier, after a last, terrifyingly violent paroxysm, commenced to decelerate until one final chink and tinkle and then it was as morose and static as it ever was, the candles settled down again and everybody had another glass of bubbly.

'And what were *you* doing, Nora?'

'Sitting on our dad's knee, like a good daughter ought to on her old man's birthday, Dora.'

What would have happened if we *had* brought the house down? Wrecked the whole lot, roof blown off, floor caved in, all the people blown out of the blown-out windows . . . sent it all sky high, destroyed all the terms of every contract, set all the old books on fire, wiped the slate clean. As if, when the young king meets up again with Jack Falstaff in *Henry IV, Part Two*, he doesn't send him packing but digs him in the ribs, says: 'Have I got a job for you!'

While we were doing it, everything seemed possible, I must say. But that is the illusion of the act. Now I remember how everything seemed possible when I was doing it, but as soon as I stopped, not, as if fucking itself were the origin of illusion.

'Life's a carnival,' he said. He was an illusionist, remember.

'The carnival's got to stop, some time, Perry,' I said. 'You listen to the news, that'll take the smile off your face.'

'News? What news?'

I saw he was incorrigible but I gave him a big kiss all the same. When he got his breath back, he wiped us both off with a silk scarf he reached for and picked up where it had fallen on the floor, Gucci or Pucci or something like that. It was Saskia's, must have dropped out of her pocket. I discovered I was lying on her mink. She hadn't trusted her fur coat to the promiscuous crush of the downstairs's cloakroom, had she, she must have thought the help might nick it, but look at the horrid stains it had acquired upstairs! When I saw what I had done to Saskia's coat, my cup of happiness ran over.

Then I was seized with panic, and a crippling doubt.

''ere, Perry . . . you're not, by any chance, my father, are you?'

He was quite taken aback, for a moment. Then he laughed until he choked so I had to beat him on the back. He laughed and shook his head and laughed and coughed and sputtered.

'Dora, Dora, I've got *some* standards! I never set eyes on either you or your Grandma until the Armistice, I promise!'

'I thought I'd ask,' I said, 'seeing as how you're everybody else's.'

He reached out for his trousers.

'I'm not your father, Dora. I spent seventy-odd years regretting it, my precious, but mighty glad I am of it, this minute.' Always the *mot juste*, our Perry. He stood up. He commenced to dress.

'But . . . has it ever occurred to you that your mother might not be your mother?'

I was putting on my tights. There was a ladder running from a star. I stood stock-still with one leg stuck up in the air.

'What?'

'Did you ever see your mother's grave, Dora?'

'What are you trying to get at, Perry?'

'I'm not sure,' he said slowly. 'I've got no concrete evidence. But sometimes I used to wonder about your Grandma.'

'Grandma?'

'Her last fling,' suggested Perry. 'Pinning old Melchior down on the mattress and –'

'You've got a very filthy mind, I must say, Perry.' I tucked my tits away neatly into my lynx-print top. 'Possible but not probable. Grandma was fifty if she was a day when we came along and she'd have been proud as a peacock, she'd never have made up some cock and bull story about a chambermaid to explain us away, why should she?'

'Just a thought,' he said. 'She never talked about your mother. I asked her, a couple of times, but she clammed up. She liked to keep her secrets. I asked her, once, where she came from herself and she said, "Out of a bottle, like a bloody genie, dearie."'

'Come off it, Perry. "Father" is a hypothesis but "mother" is a fact. Grandma never buried her, she didn't believe in people's bodies lying around cluttering up the place once the owners were through with them. She had our mum cremated and put the ashes in the garden. We put Grandma's there, too. It's everso good for the roses.'

'Mother is as mother does,' said Perry. 'She loved you just as much as if –'

'Don't start me off, again. Talk about April showers.' I dabbed my eyes carefully on account of the three shades of eyeshadow. He put his flying jacket on. We looked each other up and down. We couldn't stop smiling. I'd known in my bones today would be a red-letter day.

'Come on back downstairs,' he said. 'I've got a little present for you and Nora. Would I forget your birthdays?'

'Just a sec –'

For then I knew what I must do.

Not that I believe in telepathy but Perry caught on at once and we turned that room over together. Not that there was much to turn, since it was so minimal, but then we found that Margarine tucked away all the evidence of Melchior in a slip of a room next door, with a little narrow bed, a brown fug of theatrical prints and a faint aroma hinting at incontinence. The *Interiors* photographer never got wind of its existence.

When I saw that picture on the wall, first off, I thought it was the man himself, because it was of an old man in purple who looked just like. But then I saw how thick and brown the varnish was, how grandiose and nineteenth-century the brushwork. And *this* man wore a crown. It was older by far than Melchior and there was the legend on the frame: 'Ranulph Hazard, "Never, never, never, never, never . . ."'

Here was the source of all that regal, tragic fancy dress – the purple robe, the rings, the pendant. On his hundredth birthday, a man may indulge in any whim he chooses; Melchior had donned the costume of his father. The slandered, the abused, the cuckolded Ranulph. Ranulph, wife-murderer, friend-murderer, self-murderer, 'a little more than kin and less than kind'. You can say that again. The son put on the lost father's clothes and when I saw what he had done I could have cried because I'd never taken into consideration that he'd got problems of his own where family was concerned. His childhood, which stopped short at ten years old, never to go again, like grandfather's clock (only not like *our* grandfather's clock, which is still in very fair fettle, thank you very much). No love, no nothing. And, tonight of all nights, he'd chosen to become his own father, hadn't he, as if the child had not been the father of the man, in his case, but, during his whole long life, the man had waited to become the father of himself.

When, later on, we finally got ourselves home after the wonderful events of the night, I confided some of these thoughts to Nora. She knitted her brows.

'If the child is father of the man,' she asked, 'then who is the mother of the woman?'

Speaking of which, has it ever occurred to you to spare a passing thought as to the character of the deceased *Mrs* Lear? Didn't it ever occur to you that Cordelia might have taken after her mother while the other girls . . .

Melchior had dressed up as his father but had left off that crown. Peregrine climbed up on a stool and rooted round on the highest shelves of Melchior's closet and first he found a box of stiff collars, and then a box of spats, and then a box that once contained a topper. And there it was, inside. Melchior must have come home and hidden it away with all his other posthumous clothing the day the man on the Underground thought he was dead.

It was battered and tattered and the gilt was peeling off but Perry made a few magic passes over it and it came up lovely.

'I made him jump for it, once,' he said. 'You can give it to him for nothing, today.'

Downstairs it was only family. Not one media person left, nor guests, just dirty glasses fallen on their sides, crumpled serviettes, chicken-bones, wilting lilac, candles keeling over. The lutenists were gone, the waiters gone, the serving wenches and the pages were gone, Perry's Brazilian friends adjourned to their rooms in the Travellers' Club, but Old Nanny had emerged from the ladies' toilet to take her rightful place amongst us and they were all sitting round convivially picking away at a big platter of left-over chicken. When I saw the chicken, I felt peckish, but there was a little ceremony I must perform before I could eat it.

I picked a cushion off one of the gilt chairs and shook it. Broken glass fell out. They were all ignoring us with elaborate politeness, except for Nora, who winked, so nobody was looking when I plumped up that cushion and set that old crown nicely out upon it. Where were the baroque trumpeters now that I needed a fanfare? But when I said:

'Father, look what I've found!'

and processed towards him bearing aloft my cushion, Perry began to imitate a drumroll to perfection: 'Rub-a-dub-a-dub-a-dub.' Nora, sitting on his knee, looked sentimental. Daisy smacked away the wandering hand her aged husband had, from force of habit, placed in her bosom and adopted a reverential air. Everybody sat with drumsticks suspended halfway to their mouths as Perry brought the imaginary drumroll to a magnificent conclusion and said, in a round, rich, mahogany-coloured voice well-suited to the occasion:

'Prince of players! Reclaim your crown!'

I stood up on tiptoe. I placed the crown on his long, grey hair. Sometimes you know it's sentimental and sometimes you just don't care. I was a touch long in the tooth for Cordelia but there you are.

'My princesses,' he said. 'My two dancing princesses.' No, he did. Really! If only our mother could have been there to see. But – which mother? Pretty Kitty? Grandma? That's a problem. I don't know what Pretty Kitty might have said, but Grandma would have managed something acid. The Lady A. looked pleased. My Lady Margarine looked pissed off. The darling buds looked chastened.

Yet Nora and I were well content. We'd finally wormed our way into the heart of the family we'd always wanted to be part of. They'd asked us on the stage and let us join in, legit. at last. There was a house we all had in common and it was called, the past, even though we'd lived in different rooms. Then Perry, wearing his conjuring smile, said:

'Look in my pocket, Nora.'

Her lipstick was all over the place because she'd been at the chicken, her hair was coming down, she looked ribald. I daresay I did, too.

'In your pocket, eh?' she said, richly. She had a feel. Then her face changed. I'd never seen her look like that before, not in all the years we've been together. She looked as if she were about to fall in love, was teetering on the brink – but more so. As if about to fall in love terminally, once and for all, as if she'd met the perfect stranger.

'Oh, Perry!' She expelled a sigh and pulled it out.

Brown as a quail, round as an egg, sleepy as a pear. I'll never know how he got it in his pocket.

'Look in the other one, Dora.'

One each. They were twins, of course, three months old, by the look of them.

'*Oooh*, Perry!' said Nora. 'Just what I always wanted.'

'Gareth's' said Peregrine to Melchior. So it turned out the

Hazard dynasty wasn't at its last gasp at all but was bursting out in every direction and, to add to the hypothetical, disputed, absent father that was such a feature of our history, now you could add a holy father, too. Put it down to liberation theology.

Margarine grabbed hold of Perry: have you seen him? How is he? Who is the mother? Where is she?

But who she was or where they both were do not belong to the world of comedy. Perry told us, of course, because we were family, but I don't propose to tell *you*, not now, when the barren heath was bloomed, the fire that was almost out sprung back to life and Nora a mother at last at seventy-five years old and all laughter, forgiveness, generosity, reconciliation.

Yes.

Hard to swallow, huh?

Well, you might have known what you were about to let yourself in for when you let Dora Chance in her ratty old fur and poster paint, her orange (Persian Melon) toenails sticking out of her snakeskin peep-toes, reeking of liquor, accost you in the Coach and Horses and let her tell you a tale.

I've got a tale and a half to tell, all right!

But, truthfully, these glorious pauses do, sometimes, occur in the discordant but complementary narratives of our lives and if you choose to stop the story there, at such a pause, and refuse to take it any further, then you can call it a happy ending.

There was a full moon out over Regent's Park when we piled into Saskia's van, that she'd brought the food in; the inside still smelled of rosemary. Such was the power of Peregrine's personality that nobody, not even Margarine, the official grandmother, nor better yet, Old Nanny, dreamed for one moment of contesting Nora's possession of the newest Hazard twins who, as she found out when she changed their nappies, she let out a squawk – were boy and girl, a new thing in our family.

Not only that. Margarine went personally up to the attic to fetch us a double pram, the one that Tristram and Gareth had when they were babies, so our babies would ride home like royalty, and we planned to stop off at the all-night Boots in Piccadilly for formula and bottles.

Perry took Tristram to one side and asked him, did he want to go back to South America with him to help look for Gareth. Tristram took a big gulp and said, 'Yes.' So that's what's going to become of Tristram. Perhaps he will come back fit to be a father and take up his responsibilities; and perhaps not. Margarine and Melchior looked scared and proud; they loved him. I am not sure if this is a happy ending. I cross my fingers.

The chauffeur came and Daisy and he between them carried Puck down to Daisy's limo, he was well away, borne up and elsewhere on the lovely wind of his own voice.

> While teeing off a game of golf
> I may make a play for the caddy –

Off he went downstairs; when I went to open the window to let the fug out, they were loading him into the car and he was still singing:

'. . . but my heart belongs to daddy.'

'Oh, very apt,' said Nora, but I thought it was bad taste.

The Lady A. nodded off in her wheelchair while we were fixing up the pram business because she was getting very frail, poor old thing, and the evening had tired her out, no wonder, so Perry carried her up to the spare room in his arms, a very touching sight to see. Saskia said, did we need a lift and I was sufficiently overcome by the prevailing spirit of goodwill that I said, take us as far as the Elephant, we'll walk from there, because it's a lovely night and we could do with a walk, clear our heads.

Margarine was going round snuffing out the candles when we bade them our farewells and she kissed the babies and made as if about to kiss us, too, but thought better of it and backed off. The jury is still out on the question of her boys' paternity. But in my heart I think, not. Not her and Perry. No way. He must have known someone else in Gunter Grove. Melchoir with his crown still on, though much askew by now, came to the window to wave and then we got into the back of the van along with several plastic vats of salad which Saskia had forgotten to serve up, so much had been going on.

Tristram was staying in his own old room for the night, to his mother's soft, glowing satisfaction, and Saskia had sufficient savvy to know when not to press him but I could tell by the look in her eyes that if we all stopped short at this point it wouldn't be a happy ending for her, no, sir! She hadn't finished with the boy, by any means, so I thought, the sooner he gets off to Amazonia, the better.

Yet, no matter how fragile or brief it might be, there was a truce that night between the Chance girls and the Hazard sisters. We never said one word about the past, the taunts, the farmhouse, the chicanery, the staircase. Imogen sat in the front, next to Saskia, with the fishbowl on her knee. She looked content enough but she was always a strange one. Now and then she did those goldfish movements with her mouth.

'What are you saying?' Saskia asked her.

'Goldie say: "Goodnight! God bless!"' she said. I felt nauseous. Truce! I reminded myself. Truce!

Nora pushed the pram. I carried the Boots' bag. Gawd, it was heavy. A heart-shaped glow appeared to surround our Nora in the night but you mustn't go away thinking I wasn't pleased about our babies, too.

But coming so late in our lives and so unexpectedly . . .

'What shall we do about the cats, Nora?'

'I thought we might clear out Grandma's old room for a nursery,' said Nora, ignoring my question. 'Get rid of all that junk. Get a bloke in to paint it all white, with maybe a Beatrix Potter frieze. What do you think?'

'We won't be able to go out in the evenings, Nora.'

'*You* can go out, dear,' she said magnanimously. 'I'll be perfectly content to stay at home with these little cherubs.'

She must have thought she heard a coo, because she bent down over the pram to peer under the hoods.

'Babies!' she said, and cackled with glee.

'No fun, going out without you,' I said.

'Come off it, Dora. Grow up.'

'It's all very well for you, Nora. You always wanted kids. Now you've got them.'

She cackled again.

'We're both of us mothers and both of us fathers,' she said. 'They'll be wise children, all right.'

She peered in at the babies, again; they slept on undisturbed. No sound but the whirring of the rubber wheels and a cat, somewhere, giving a mating call. I told Nora what was on my mind.

'Here, Nora . . .'

She cocked her head.

'Nora . . . don't you think our father looked two-dimensional, tonight?'

She gave me a look that said, tell me more.

'Too kind, too handsome, too repentant. After all those years without a word. Remember that terrible bank holiday when he pretended to our faces that he thought we were Perry's? And tonight, he had an imitation look, even when he was crying, especially when he was crying, like one of those great, big, papier-mâché heads they have in the Notting Hill parade, larger than life, but not lifelike.'

Nora sunk in thought for a hundred yards.

'D'you know, I sometimes wonder if we haven't been making him up all along,' she said. 'If he isn't just a collection of our hopes and dreams and wishful thinking in the afternoons. Something to set our lives by, like the old clock in the hall, which is real enough, in itself, but which we've got to wind up to make it go.'

'Oh, very profound. Very deep.'

'Think about it,' she said. 'We can tell these little darlings here whatever we like about their mum and dad if Perry doesn't find them but whatever we tell them, they'll make up their own romance out of it.'

But thinking of the twins put me in mind of something more pressing than family romances.

'Here, Nora . . . if we've got those twins to look out for, we can't afford to die for a least another twenty years.'

'Thank goodness we're a long-lived family.' She'd thought of that herself.

We went past the Oval; we were doomed to a century. Just when I'd been thinking it was high time for the final curtain. Which only goes to show, you never know in the morning what the night will bring and I'd had a little bonus of my own, hadn't I, but Nora never pried because twins we may be but we respect each other's secrets. So we turned into Bard Road, at last, when there came a wee stirring from the depths of the pram.

'What's up, small fry?'

They mewed and rustled.

'I say, Dora, let's give them a song. After all we're song-and-dance girls, aren't we?'

'We're dancing princesses,' said Nora. 'What an old fraud he is!'

'You wouldn't want him any different.'

'I used to want him dead.'

We put our handbags in the pram, for safety's sake. Then and there, we couldn't wait, we broke into harmony, we serenaded the new arrivals:

> 'We can't give you anything but love, babies,
> That's the only thing we've plenty of, babies –'

The window on the second-floor front window of 41 Bard Road, went up, a head came out. Dreadlocks. That Rastafarian.

'You two, again,' he said.

'Have a heart!' we said. 'We've got something to celebrate, tonight!'

'Well, you just watch it, in case a squad car comes by,' he said. 'Drunk in charge of a baby carriage, at your age.'

We'd got so many songs to sing to our babies, all our old songs, that we didn't pay him any attention. 'Gee, we'd like to see you looking swell, babies!' and the Hazard theme song, 'Is You Is or Is You Ain't.' Then there were songs from the show that nobody else remembers. '2b or not 2b', 'Hey nonny bloody no', 'Mistress Mine', and Broadway tunes, and paper moons, and lilacs in the spring, again. We went on dancing and singing. 'Diamond bracelets Woolworths doesn't sell.' Besides, it was our birthday, wasn't it, we'd got to sing them the silly old song about Charlie Chaplin and his comedy boots all the little kids were singing and dancing in the street the day we were born. There was dancing and singing all along Bard

231

Road that day and we'll go on singing and dancing until we drop in our tracks, won't we, kids.

What a joy it is to dance and sing!

Dramatis Personae (in order of appearance)

Dora Chance
Nora Chance
} identical twins, illegitimate daughters of Melchior Hazard but officially known as the daughters of Peregrine Hazard

Tiffany — their goddaughter

(Sir) Melchior Hazard
Peregrine Hazard
} fraternal twins, sons of the marriage of Estella and Ranulph Hazard q.v.

Lady Atalanta Hazard, née Lynde — first wife of Melchior Hazard, mother of Saskia and Imogen

Delia Delaney, née Daisy Duck — second wife of Melchior Hazard, previously second wife of 'Genghis Khan' q.v.

Saskia Hazard
Imogen Hazard
} identical twins, legally daughters of Melchior Hazard, biologically daughters of Peregrine Hazard

Tristram Hazard
Gareth Hazard
} fraternal twins, sons of Melchior Hazard's third marriage

'My Lady Margarine' — third wife of Melchior Hazard, mother of Tristram and Gareth

'Grandma' Chance — guardian of Nora and Dora Chance

Estella 'A Star Danced' Hazard — mother of Melchior and Peregrine Hazard

'Lewis Carroll' — a photographer of children

Ranulph Hazard — husband of Estella Hazard

Cassius Booth — boyfriend of Estella Hazard

'Pretty Kitty' — a foundling, mother of Nora and Dora Chance

'Our Cyn'	a foundling, mother of Mavis, grandmother of Brenda, great-grandmother of Tiffany
Miss Worthington	a dance teacher
Mrs Worthington	her mother, an accompanist
Gorgeous George	comedian and patriot
'Pantomime Goose'	Nora Chance's first boyfriend
Principal boy	wife of Pantomime Goose
Blond tenor with unmemorable name	Dora Chance's first boyfriend
'Mr Piano Man'	musician, composer, boyfriend of Dora Chance
'Genghis Khan'	a film producer
His first wife	a jealous woman
Tony	an Italian American, fiancé of Nora Chance
Ross 'Irish' O'Flaherty	American writer, boyfriend of Dora Chance
Unnamed radical German exile in Hollywood	boyfriend of Dora Chance
'Puck'	male soprano, third husband of Delia Delaney
Brenda	granddaughter of 'Our Cyn,' mother of Tiffany
Leroy	her husband

In no particular order of appearance: rough children, cats, chorus girls, chorus boys, nudes, spear-carriers, comics, fans, Free French, Free Poles, Free Norwegians, soldiers, sailors, airmen of all nations, media personalities, television crews, market traders, pupils of the Italia Conte School, Amazonian tribesmen, photographers, film buffs, the public, extras.